# GRIMMY™: THE POSTMAN ALWAYS SCREAMS TWICE!

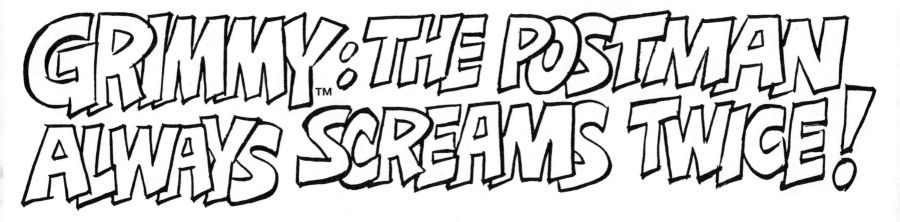

# GRIMMY™: THE POSTMAN ALWAYS SCREAMS TWICE!

## by Mike Peters

TOR®

A TOM DOHERTY ASSOCIATES BOOK
NEW YORK

This is a work of fiction.
All the characters and events portrayed in this book are either fictitious or are used fictitiously.

GRIMMY: THE POSTMAN ALWAYS SCREAMS TWICE



A Tor Book
Published by Tom Doherty Associates, Inc.
175 Fifth Avenue
New York, NY 10010

Tor Books on the World Wide Web:
http://www.tor.com

Tor® is a registered trademark of Tom Doherty Associates, Inc.

Library of Congress Cataloging-in-Publication Data
Peters, Mike.
[Mother Goose & Grimm. Selections]
Grimmy : the postman always screams twice / Mike Peters.
p. cm.
ISBN 0-312-86103-6
I. Title.
PN6728.M67P477 1996
741.5'973—dc20 95-30044
CIP

First Edition: February 1996

Printed in the United States of America

0 9 8 7 6 5 4 3 2 1

We dedicate this book with love and sorrow to the members of the band,
"For Squirrels." To our special friend Bill White and to Jack Vigliatura
and Tim Bender—we will miss your joy and your music.

"For what is seen is temporary, but what is unseen is eternal."—II Corin. v. 16

To the surviving Squirrels, Jack Griedo and Travis Tooke—rock on.

Love,
Mike, Marian, Marci, Ben, Molly and especially Tracy

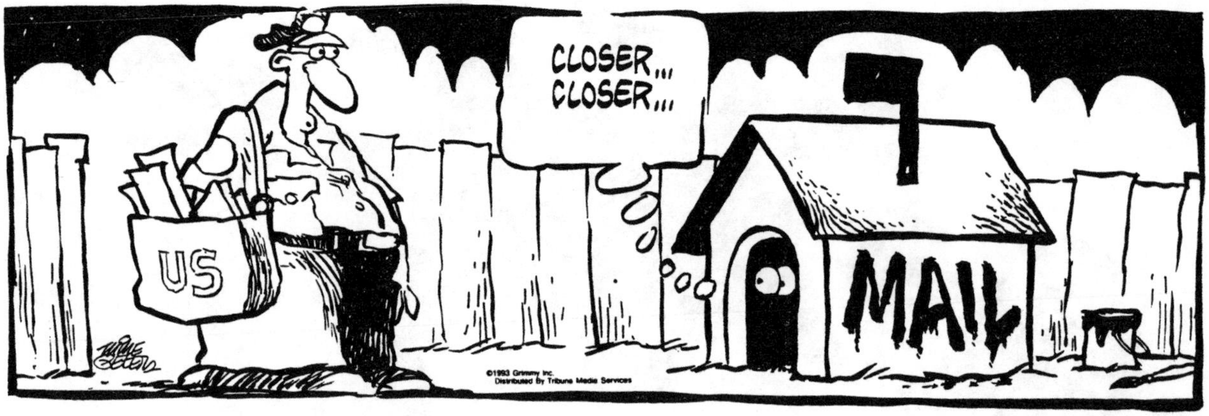
CLOSER... CLOSER...
US
MAIL
©1993 Grimmy Inc.
Distributed By Tribune Media Services

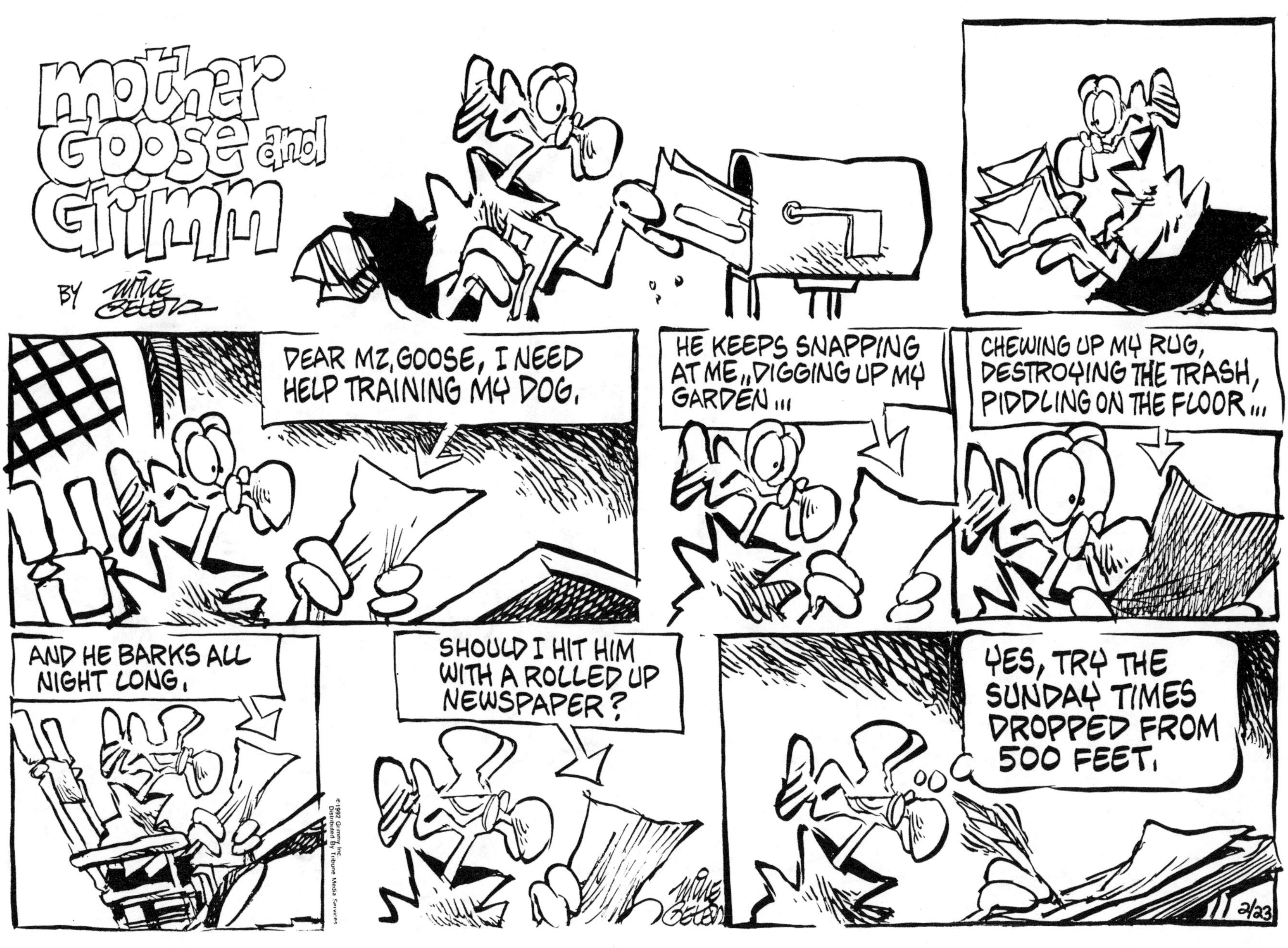
Mother Goose and Grimm
BY Mike Peters
DEAR MZ, GOOSE, I NEED HELP TRAINING MY DOG.
HE KEEPS SNAPPING AT ME,, DIGGING UP MY GARDEN...
CHEWING UP MY RUG, DESTROYING THE TRASH, PIDDLING ON THE FLOOR...
AND HE BARKS ALL NIGHT LONG.
©1992 Grimmy Inc. Distributed By Tribune Media Services
SHOULD I HIT HIM WITH A ROLLED UP NEWSPAPER?
YES, TRY THE SUNDAY TIMES DROPPED FROM 500 FEET.
2/23

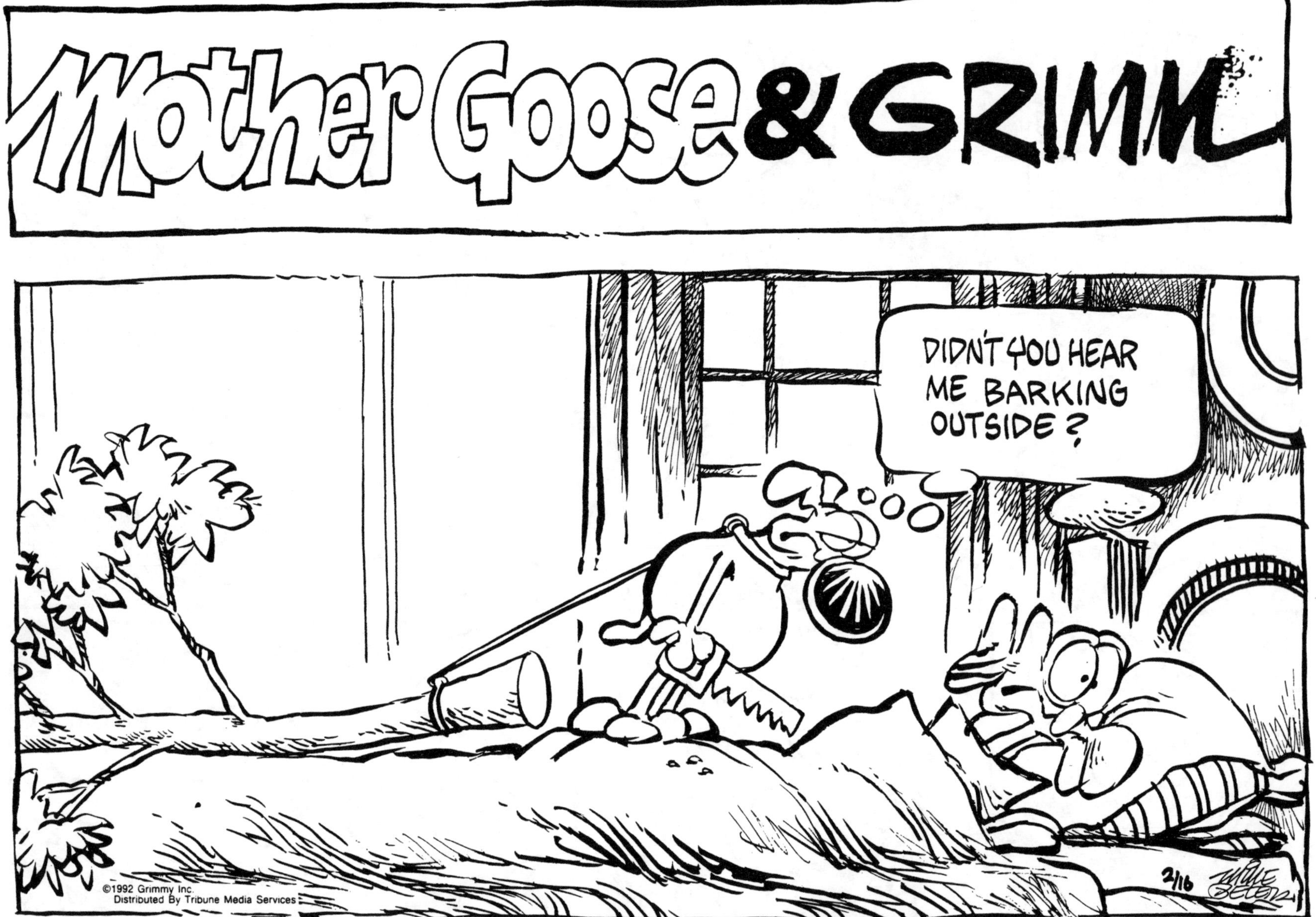
Mother Goose & GRIMM
DIDN'T YOU HEAR ME BARKING OUTSIDE?
2/16

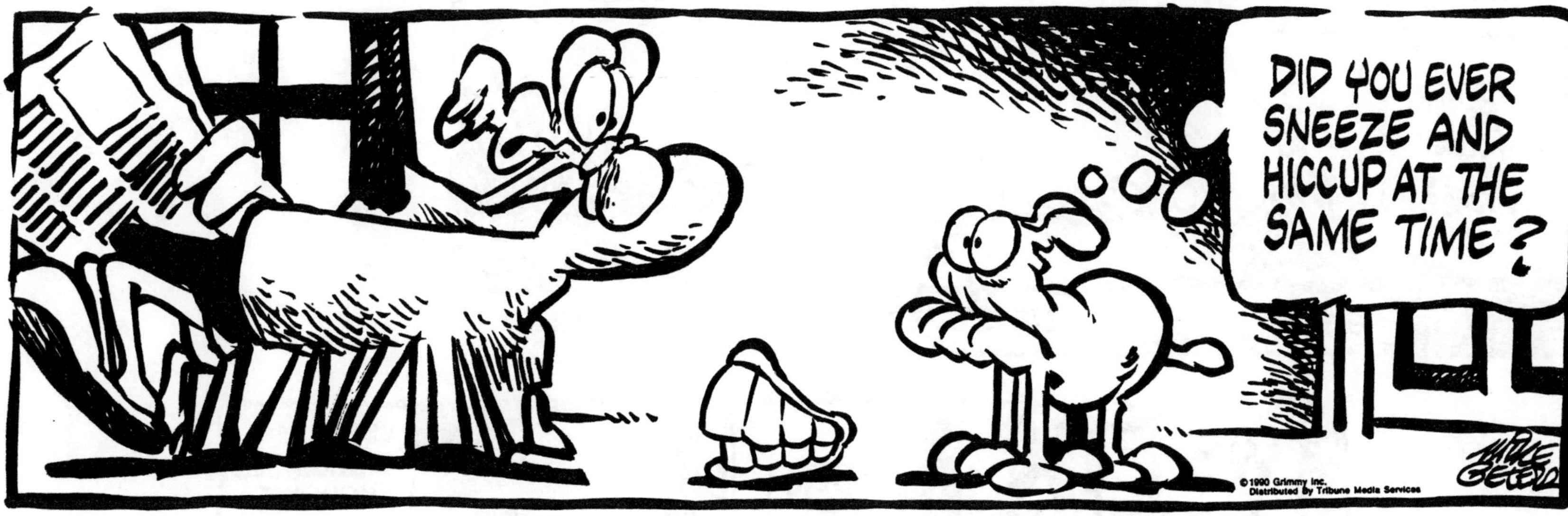
DID YOU EVER SNEEZE AND HICCUP AT THE SAME TIME?
© 1990 Grimmy Inc. Distributed By Tribune Media Services

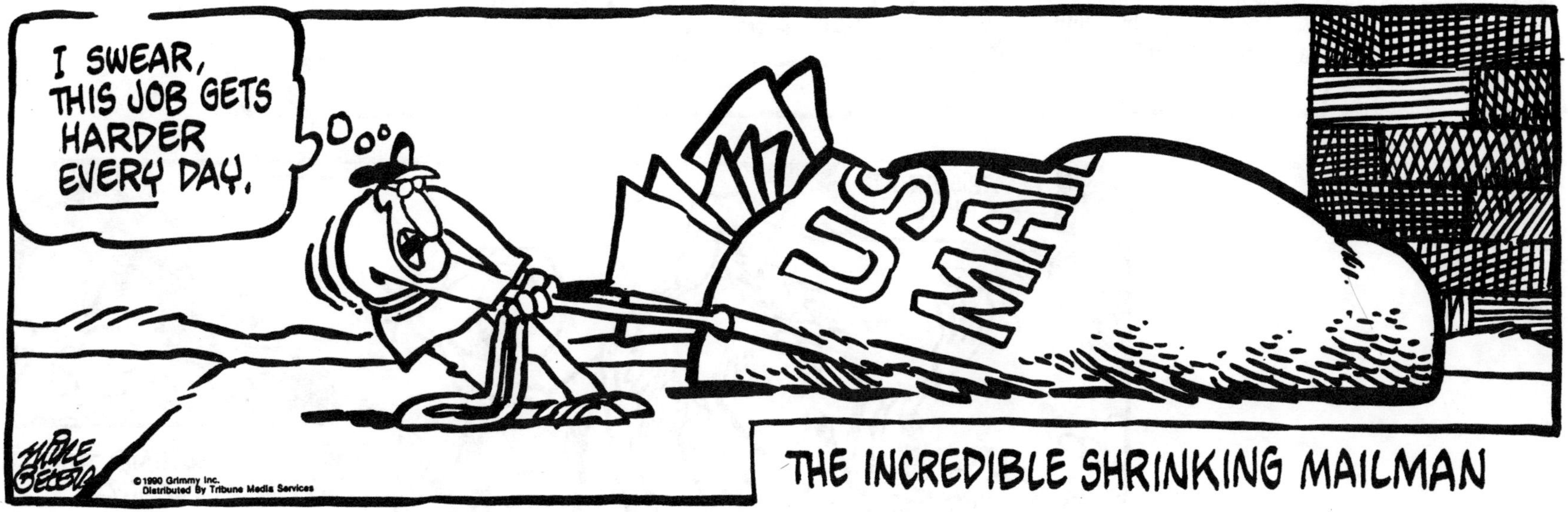
I SWEAR, THIS JOB GETS HARDER EVERY DAY.
US MAIL
© 1990 Grimmy Inc. Distributed By Tribune Media Services

THE INCREDIBLE SHRINKING MAILMAN

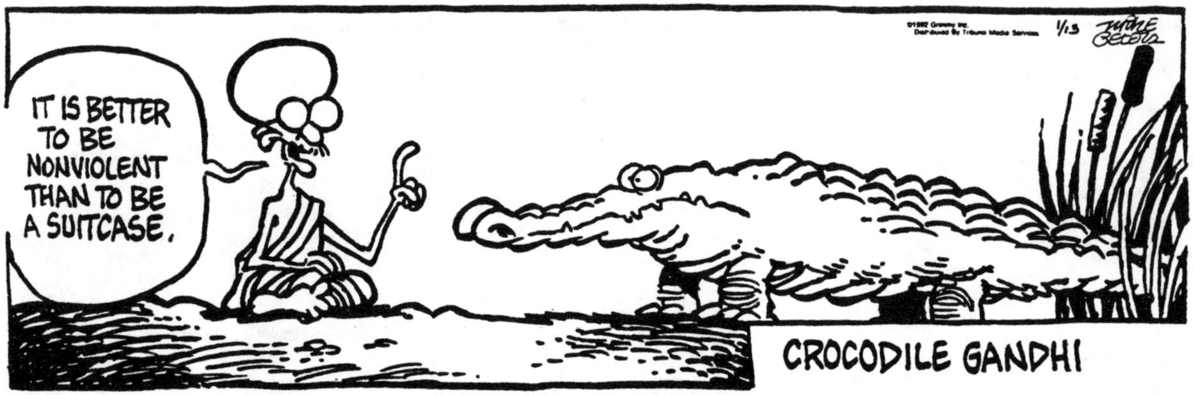
IT IS BETTER TO BE NONVIOLENT THAN TO BE A SUITCASE.

CROCODILE GANDHI

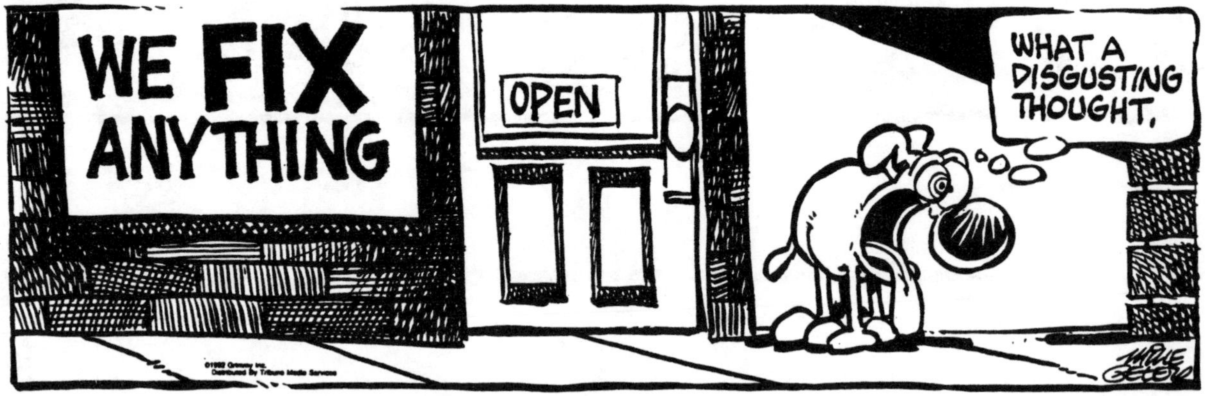
WE FIX ANYTHING
OPEN
WHAT A DISGUSTING THOUGHT.

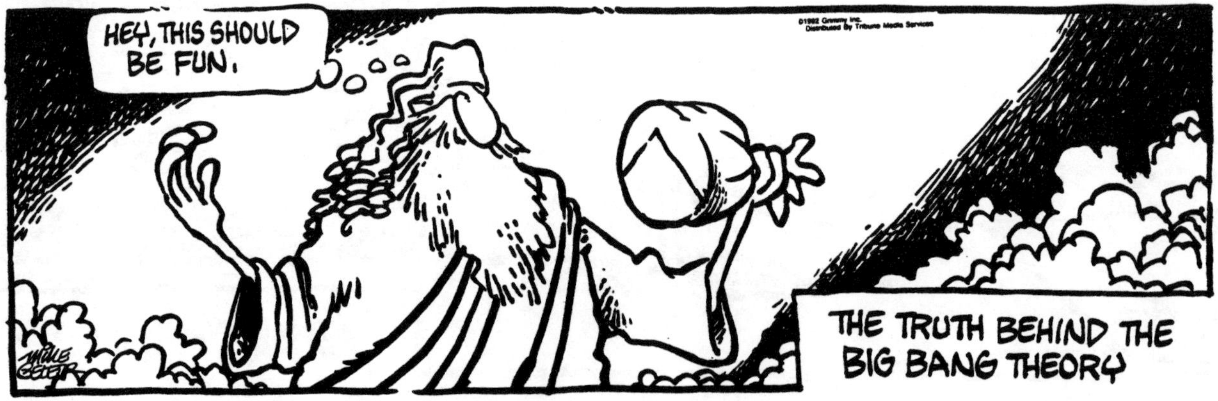
HEY, THIS SHOULD BE FUN.

THE TRUTH BEHIND THE BIG BANG THEORY

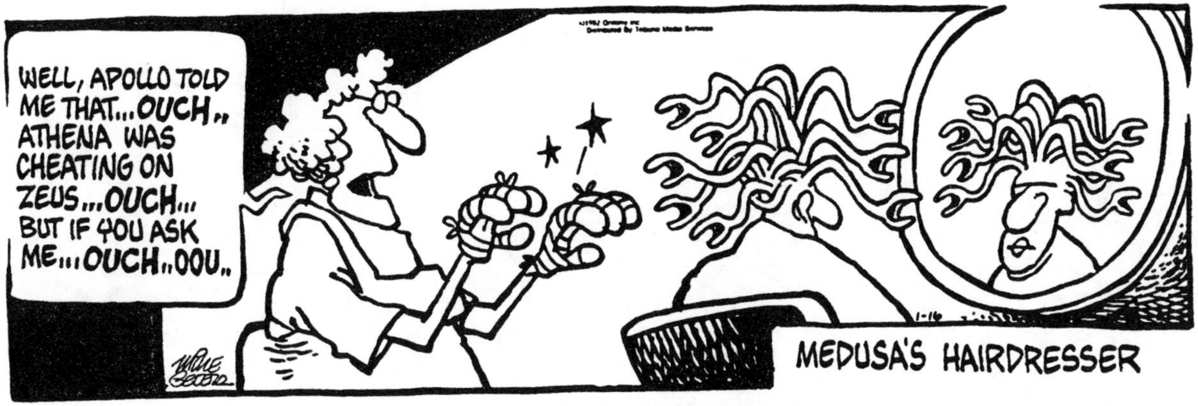
WELL, APOLLO TOLD ME THAT...OUCH.. ATHENA WAS CHEATING ON ZEUS...OUCH... BUT IF YOU ASK ME...OUCH..OOU..
1-16
MEDUSA'S HAIRDRESSER

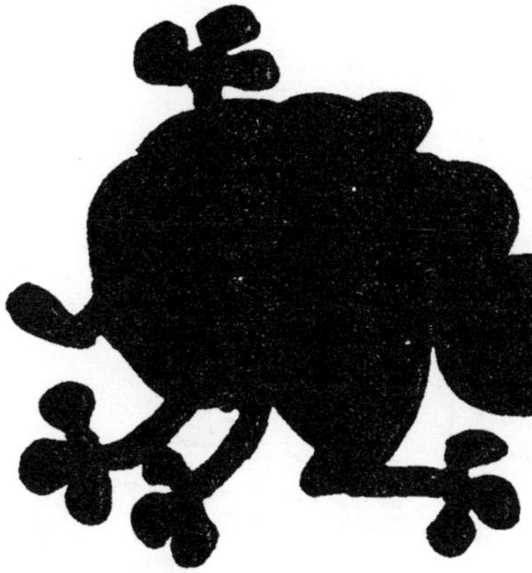

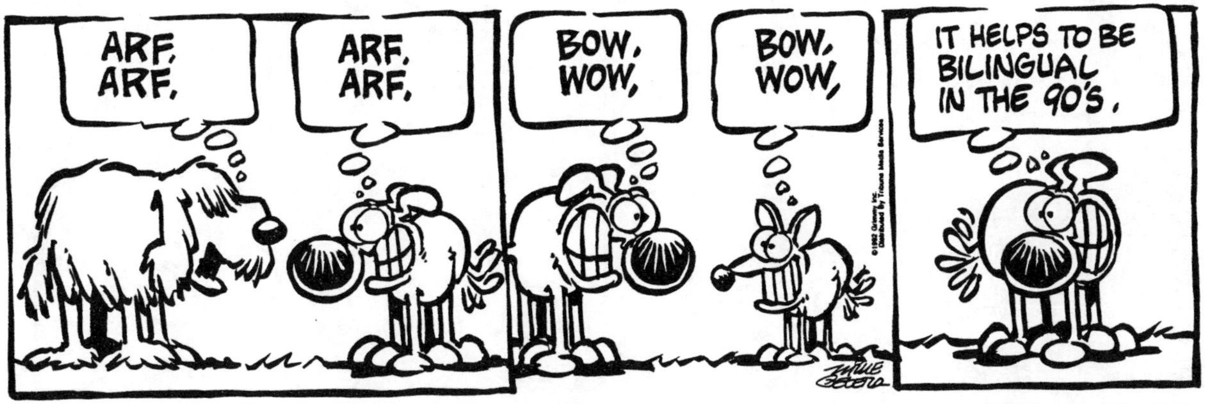
ARF, ARF,
ARF, ARF,
BOW, WOW,
BOW, WOW,
IT HELPS TO BE BILINGUAL IN THE 90'S.

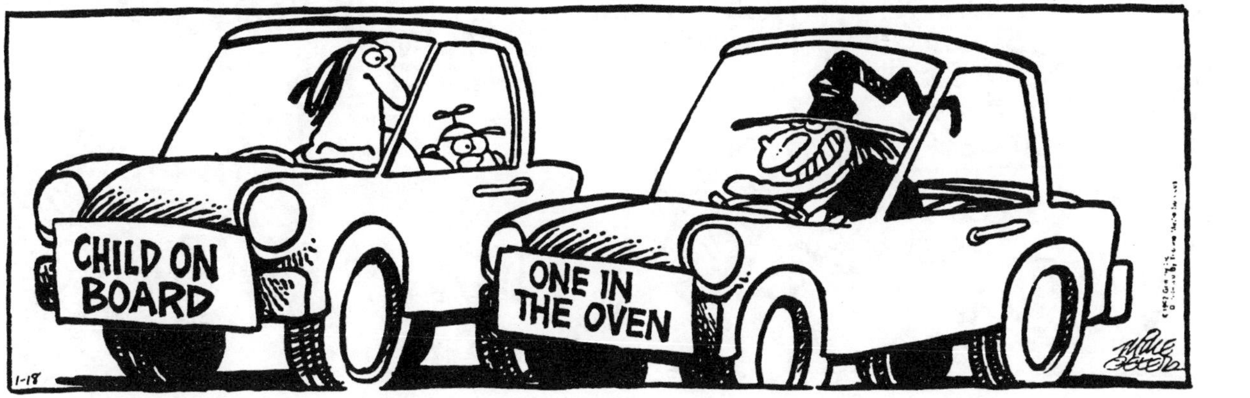
CHILD ON BOARD
ONE IN THE OVEN
1-18

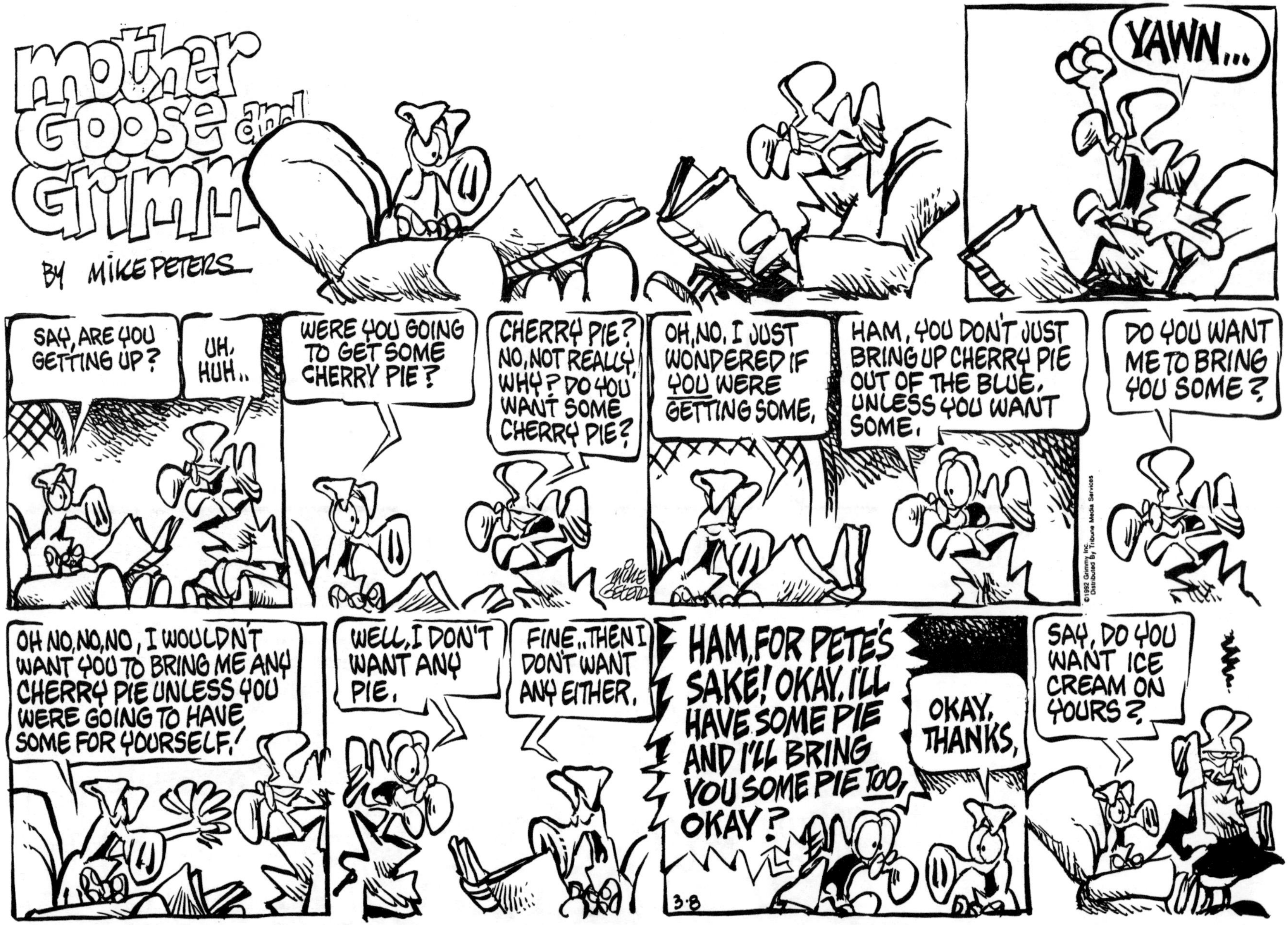
mother Goose and Grimm
BY MIKE PETERS
YAWN...
SAY, ARE YOU GETTING UP?
UH, HUH..
WERE YOU GOING TO GET SOME CHERRY PIE?
CHERRY PIE? NO, NOT REALLY. WHY? DO YOU WANT SOME CHERRY PIE?
OH, NO. I JUST WONDERED IF YOU WERE GETTING SOME.
HAM, YOU DON'T JUST BRING UP CHERRY PIE OUT OF THE BLUE, UNLESS YOU WANT SOME.
DO YOU WANT ME TO BRING YOU SOME?
OH NO, NO, NO, I WOULDN'T WANT YOU TO BRING ME ANY CHERRY PIE UNLESS YOU WERE GOING TO HAVE SOME FOR YOURSELF!
WELL, I DON'T WANT ANY PIE.
FINE.. THEN I DON'T WANT ANY EITHER.
HAM, FOR PETE'S SAKE! OKAY, I'LL HAVE SOME PIE AND I'LL BRING YOU SOME PIE TOO, OKAY?
OKAY, THANKS.
SAY, DO YOU WANT ICE CREAM ON YOURS?
©1992 Grimmy Inc.
Distributed By Tribune Media Services
3-8

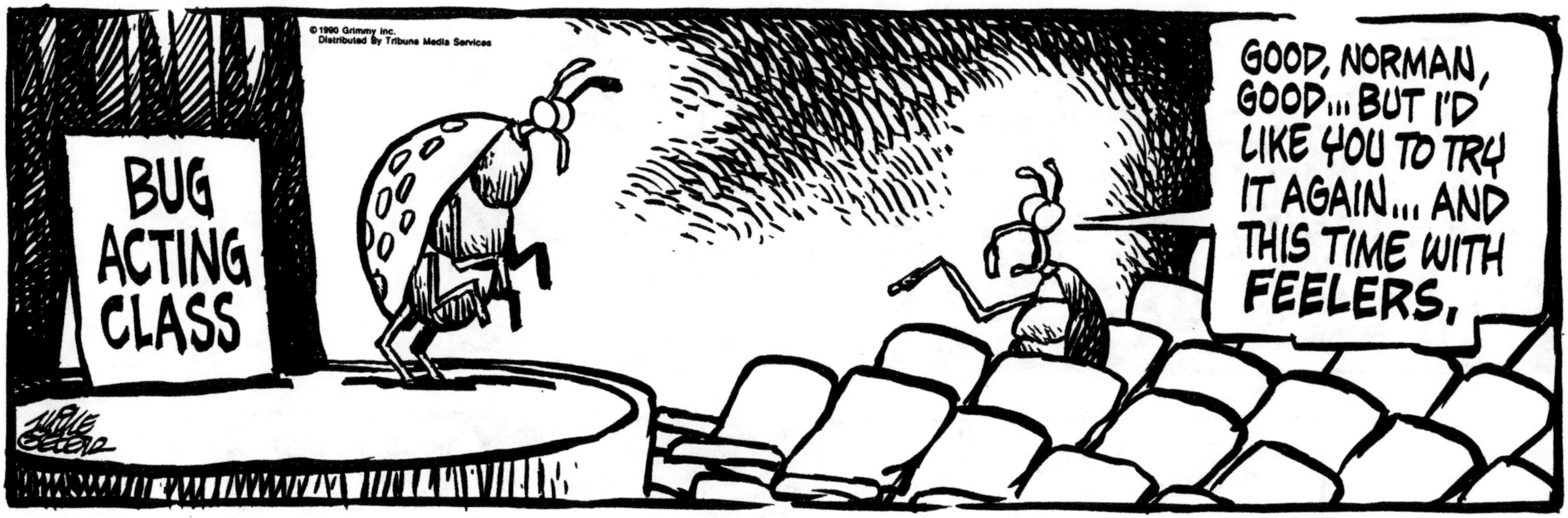
© 1990 Grimmy Inc.
Distributed By Tribune Media Services
BUG ACTING CLASS
GOOD, NORMAN, GOOD... BUT I'D LIKE YOU TO TRY IT AGAIN... AND THIS TIME WITH FEELERS.

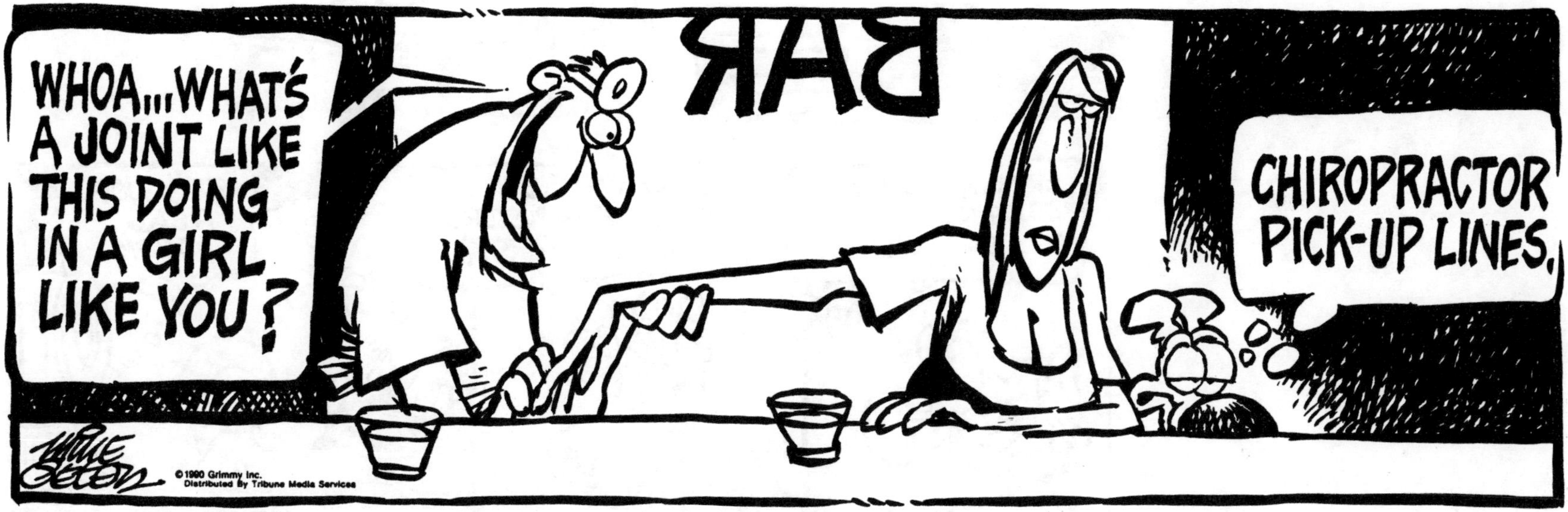
WHOA...WHAT'S A JOINT LIKE THIS DOING IN A GIRL LIKE YOU?
BAR
CHIROPRACTOR PICK-UP LINES.
© 1990 Grimmy Inc.
Distributed By Tribune Media Services

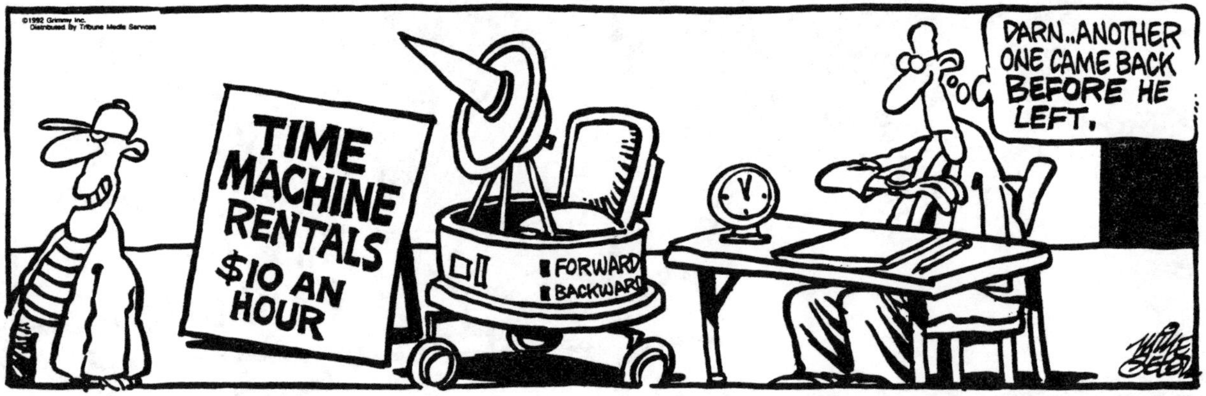
©1992 Grimmy Inc.
Distributed By Tribune Media Services
TIME MACHINE RENTALS $10 AN HOUR
FORWARD
BACKWARD
DARN..ANOTHER ONE CAME BACK **BEFORE** HE LEFT.

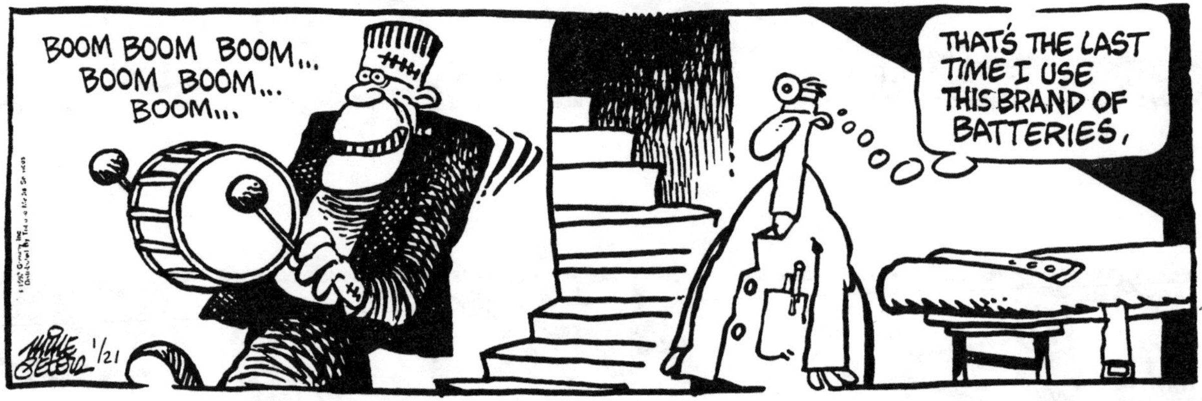
BOOM BOOM BOOM... BOOM BOOM... BOOM...
THAT'S THE LAST TIME I USE THIS BRAND OF BATTERIES.
1/21

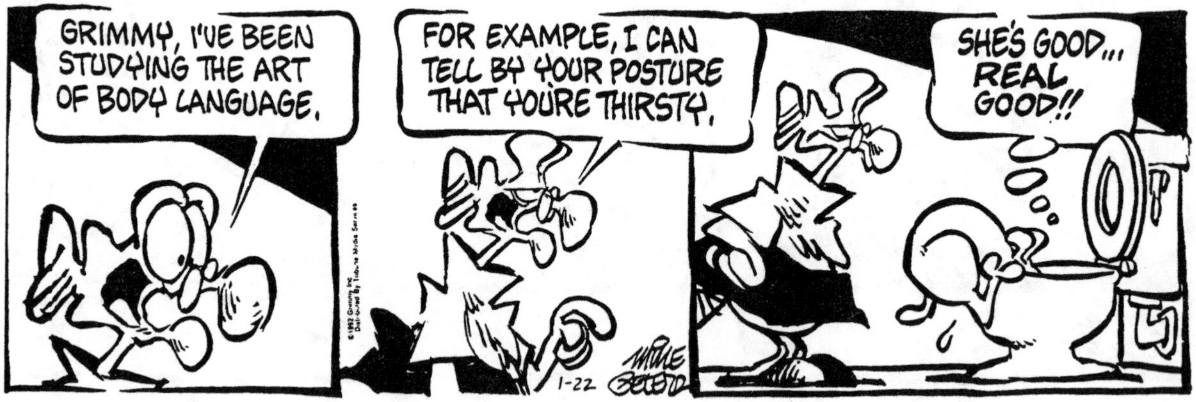
GRIMMY, I'VE BEEN STUDYING THE ART OF BODY LANGUAGE.
FOR EXAMPLE, I CAN TELL BY YOUR POSTURE THAT YOU'RE THIRSTY.
1-22
SHE'S GOOD... **REAL GOOD!!**

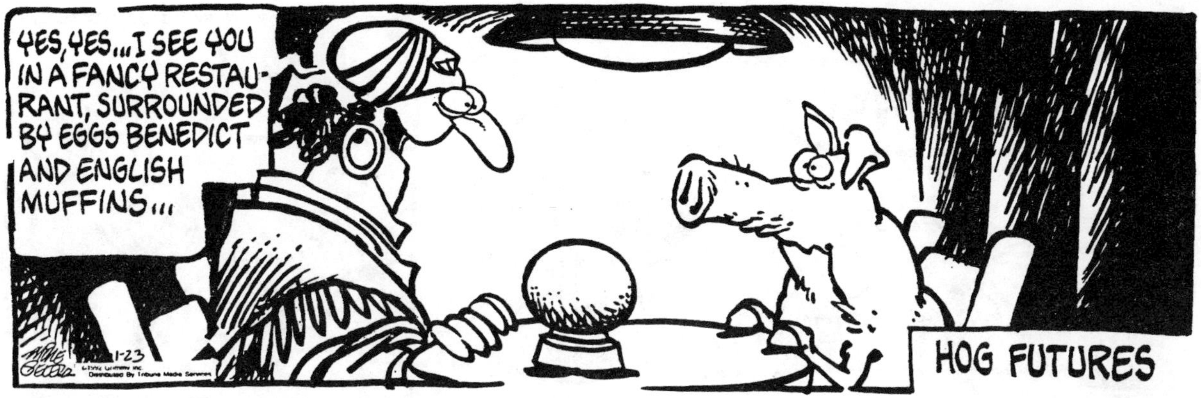
YES, YES... I SEE YOU IN A FANCY RESTAURANT, SURROUNDED BY EGGS BENEDICT AND ENGLISH MUFFINS...
1-23
HOG FUTURES

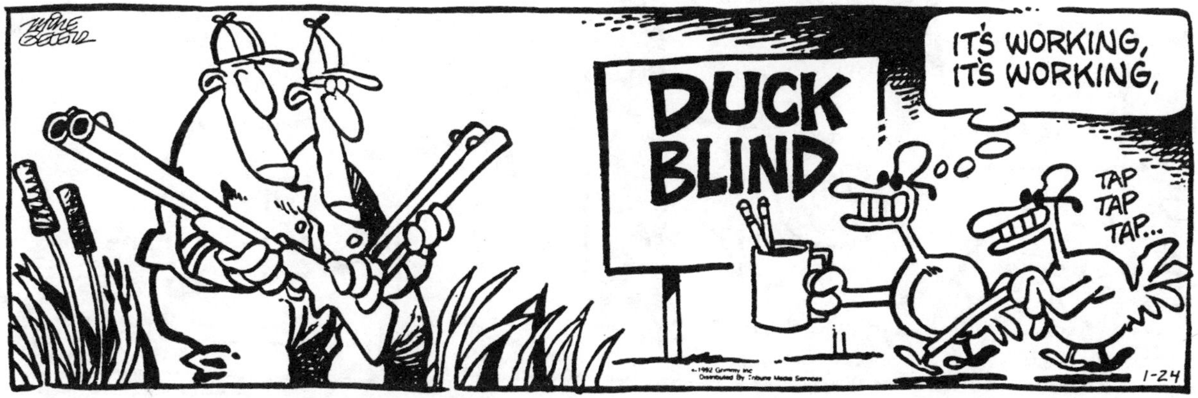
IT'S WORKING, IT'S WORKING,
DUCK BLIND
TAP TAP TAP...
1-24

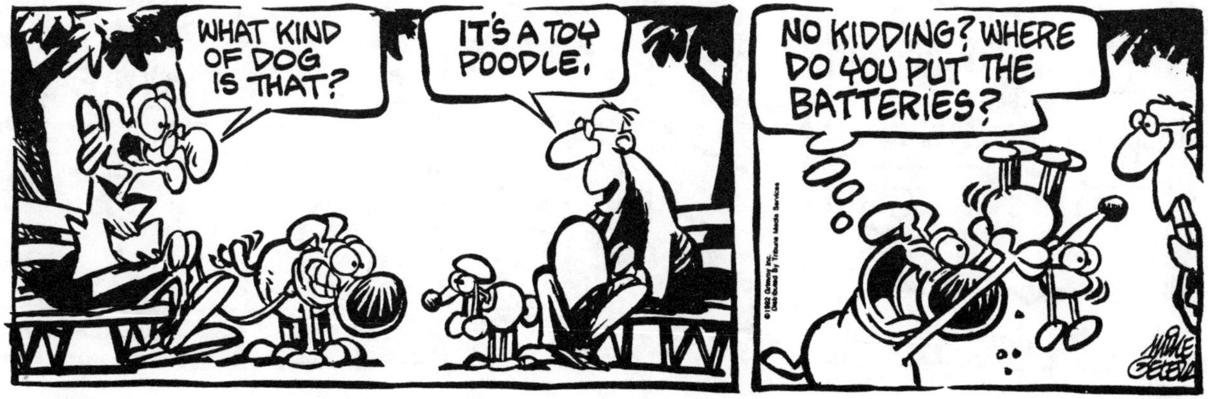
WHAT KIND OF DOG IS THAT?
IT'S A TOY POODLE.
NO KIDDING? WHERE DO YOU PUT THE BATTERIES?

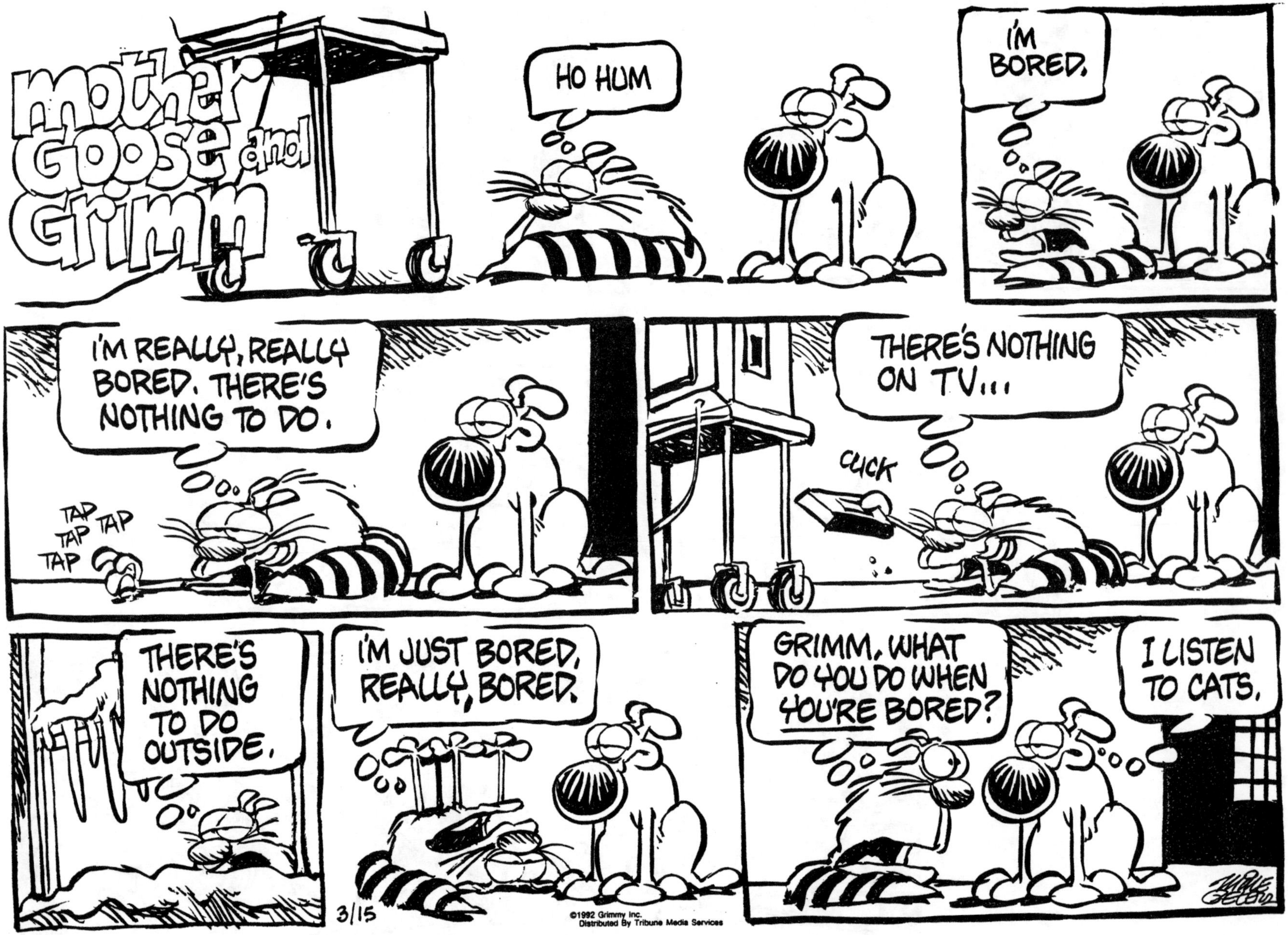

Mother Goose and Grimm
HO HUM
I'M BORED.
I'M REALLY, REALLY BORED. THERE'S NOTHING TO DO.
TAP TAP TAP TAP
THERE'S NOTHING ON TV...
CLICK
THERE'S NOTHING TO DO OUTSIDE.
I'M JUST BORED, REALLY, BORED.
GRIMM, WHAT DO YOU DO WHEN YOU'RE BORED?
I LISTEN TO CATS.
3/15
©1992 Grimmy Inc.
Distributed By Tribune Media Services

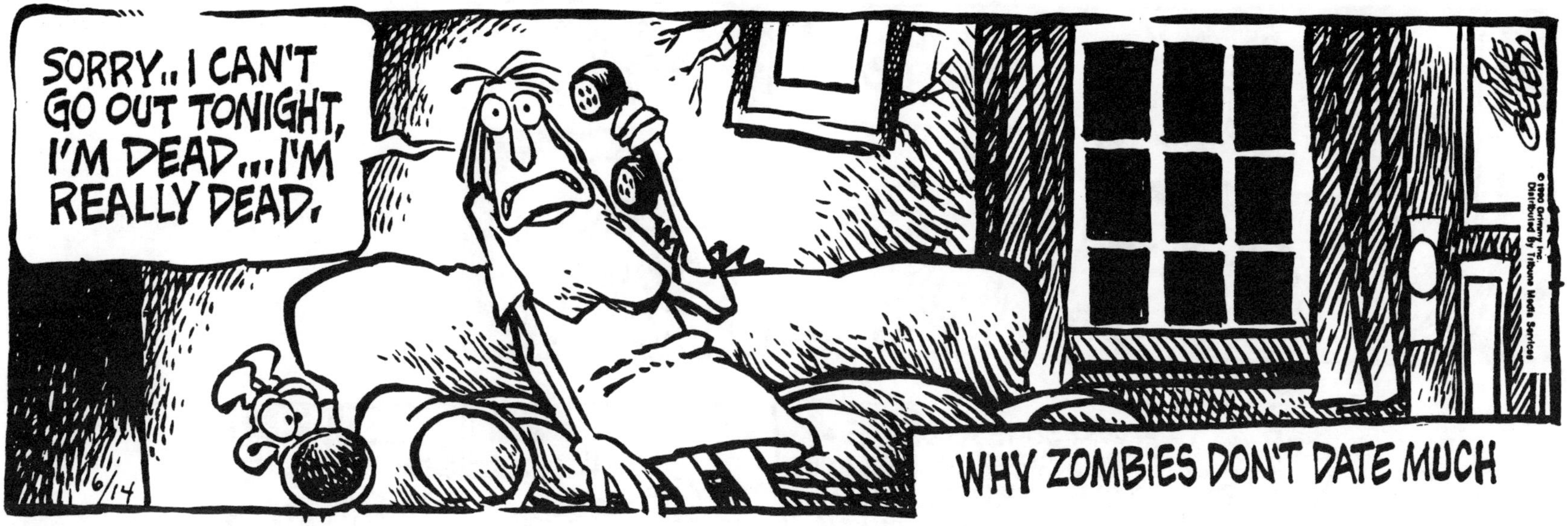
SORRY.. I CAN'T GO OUT TONIGHT, I'M DEAD...I'M REALLY DEAD.
6/14
© 1990 Grimmy Inc. Distributed by Tribune Media Services
WHY ZOMBIES DON'T DATE MUCH

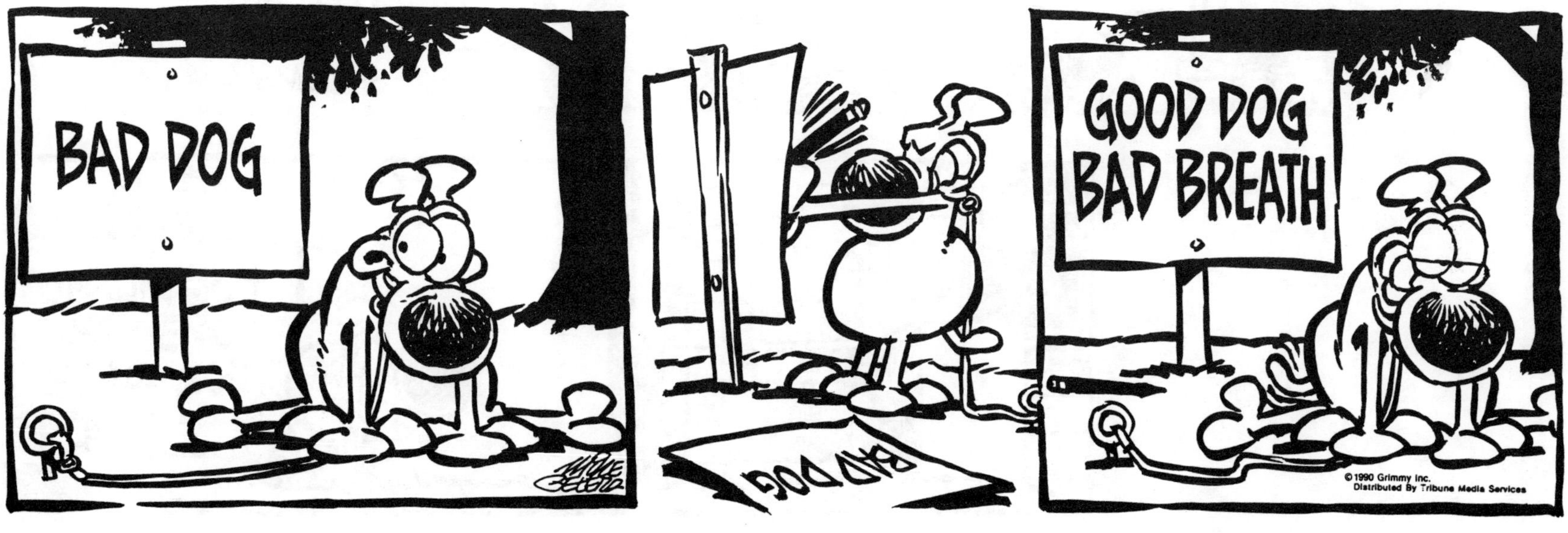
BAD DOG
BAD DOG
GOOD DOG BAD BREATH
© 1990 Grimmy Inc. Distributed By Tribune Media Services

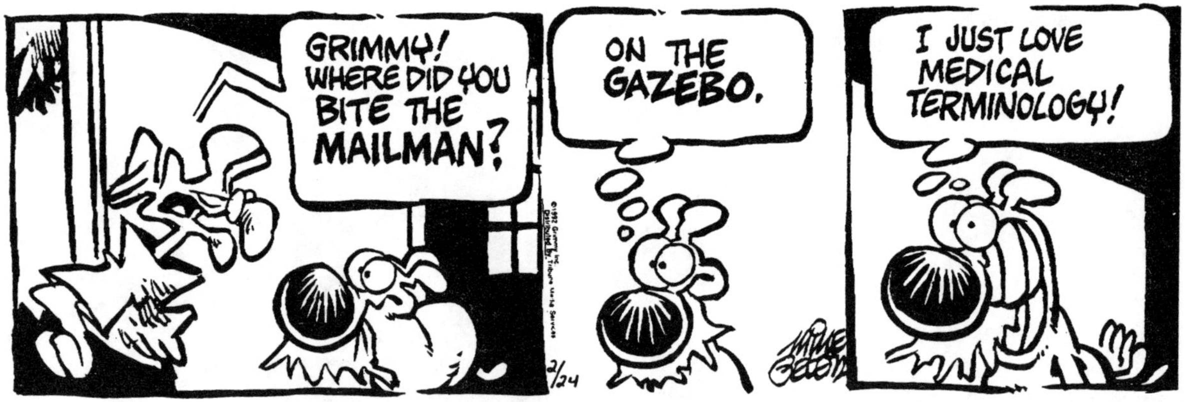
GRIMMY! WHERE DID YOU BITE THE MAILMAN?
ON THE GAZEBO.
I JUST LOVE MEDICAL TERMINOLOGY!
2/24

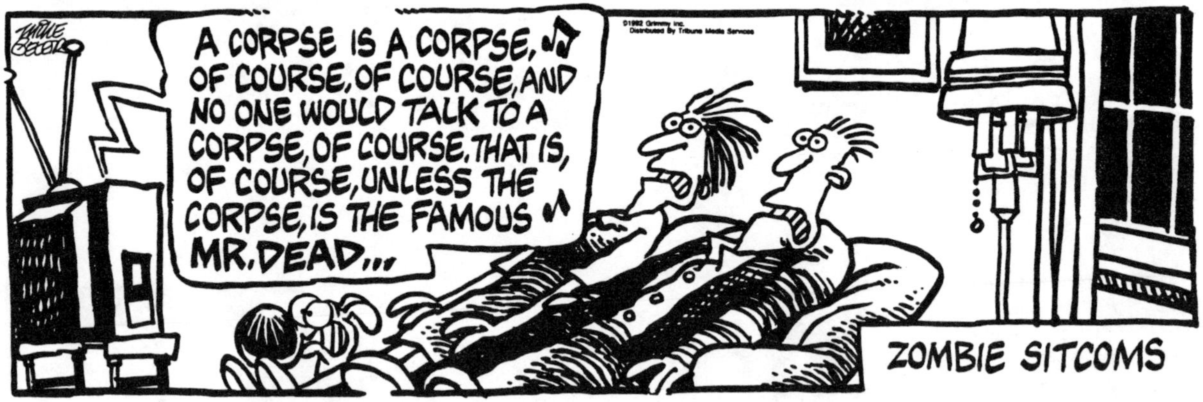
A CORPSE IS A CORPSE, OF COURSE, OF COURSE, AND NO ONE WOULD TALK TO A CORPSE, OF COURSE. THAT IS, OF COURSE, UNLESS THE CORPSE, IS THE FAMOUS MR. DEAD...
©1992 Grimmy Inc. Distributed By Tribune Media Services
ZOMBIE SITCOMS

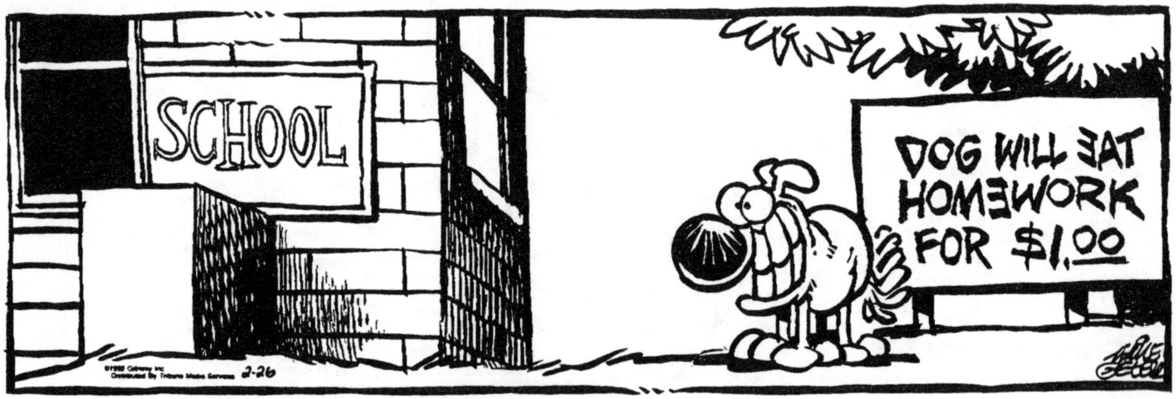
SCHOOL
DOG WILL EAT HOMEWORK FOR $1.00
2-26

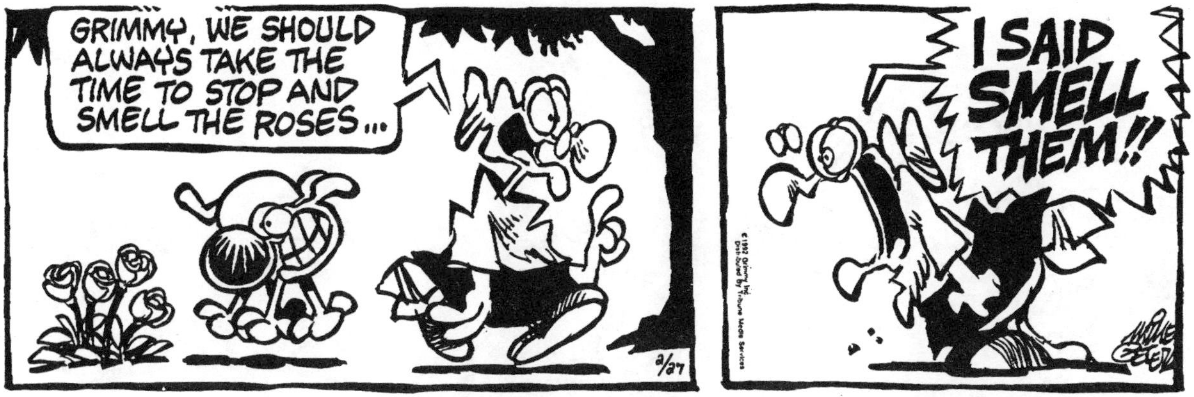
GRIMMY, WE SHOULD ALWAYS TAKE THE TIME TO STOP AND SMELL THE ROSES...
I SAID SMELL THEM!!

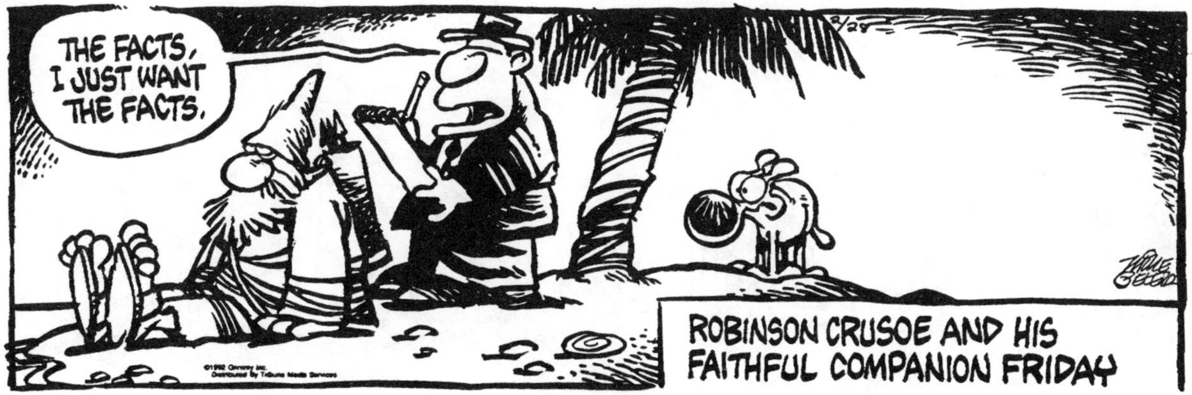
THE FACTS, I JUST WANT THE FACTS.
ROBINSON CRUSOE AND HIS FAITHFUL COMPANION FRIDAY

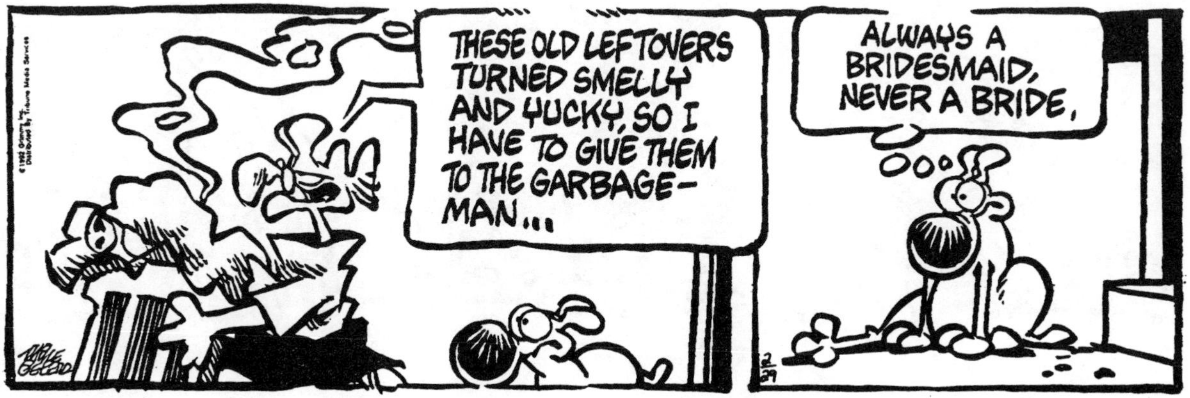
THESE OLD LEFTOVERS TURNED SMELLY AND YUCKY, SO I HAVE TO GIVE THEM TO THE GARBAGE-MAN...
ALWAYS A BRIDESMAID, NEVER A BRIDE.

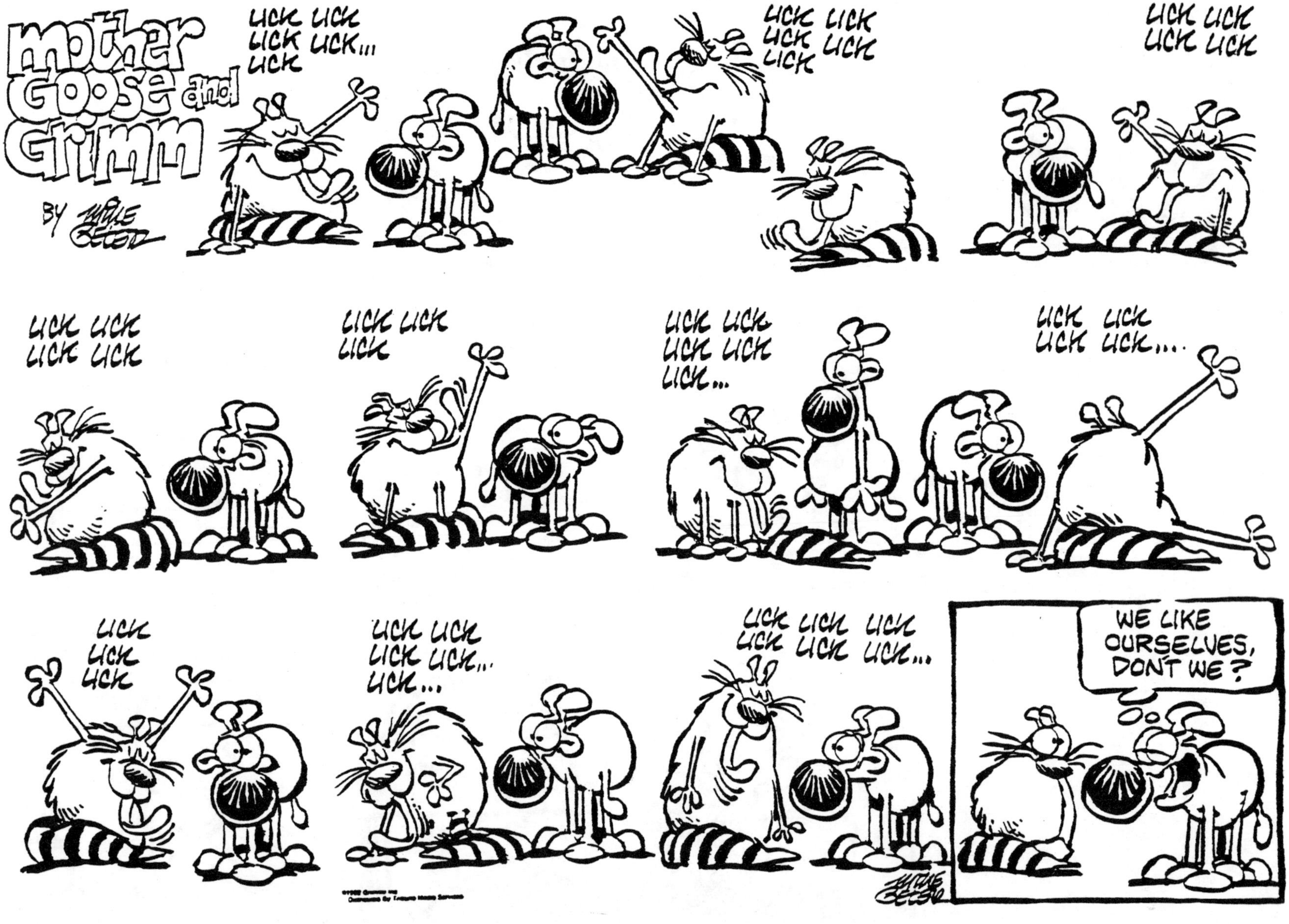
mother Goose and Grimm
BY MIKE PETERS
LICK LICK
LICK LICK...
LICK
LICK LICK
LICK LICK
LICK
LICK LICK
LICK LICK
LICK LICK
LICK LICK
LICK LICK
LICK
LICK LICK
LICK LICK
LICK...
LICK LICK
LICK LICK...
LICK
LICK
LICK
LICK LICK
LICK LICK...
LICK...
LICK LICK LICK
LICK LICK LICK...
WE LIKE OURSELVES, DON'T WE?
MIKE PETERS

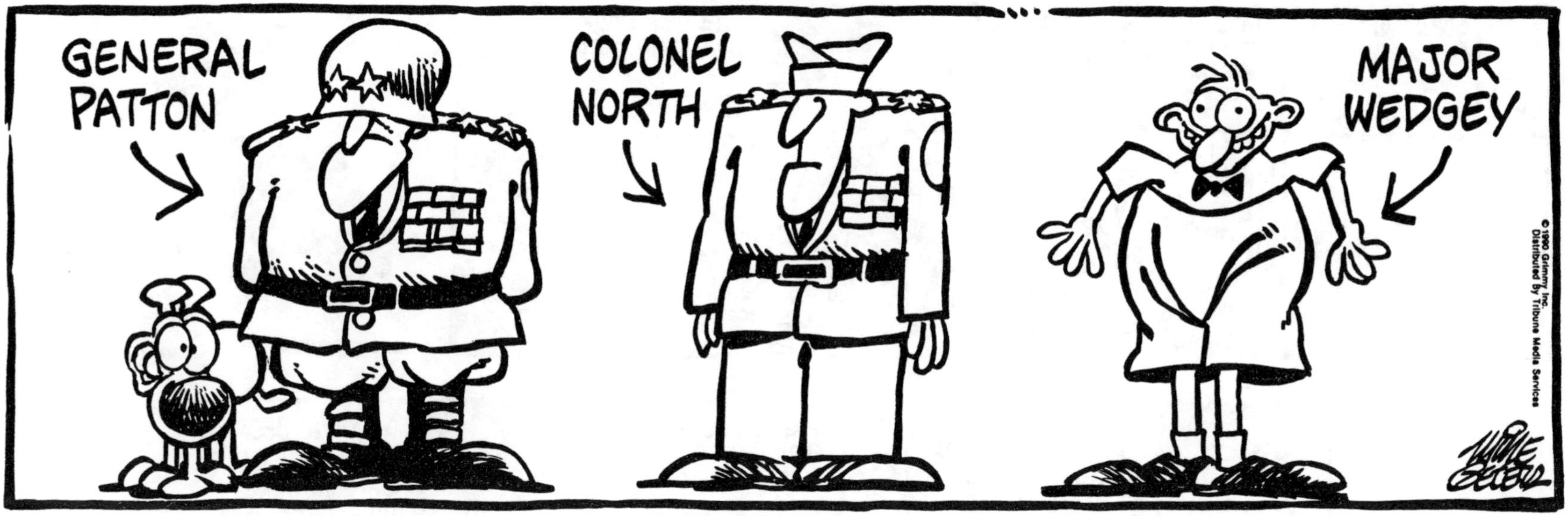
GENERAL PATTON
COLONEL NORTH
MAJOR WEDGEY
© 1990 Grimmy, Inc.
Distributed by Tribune Media Services

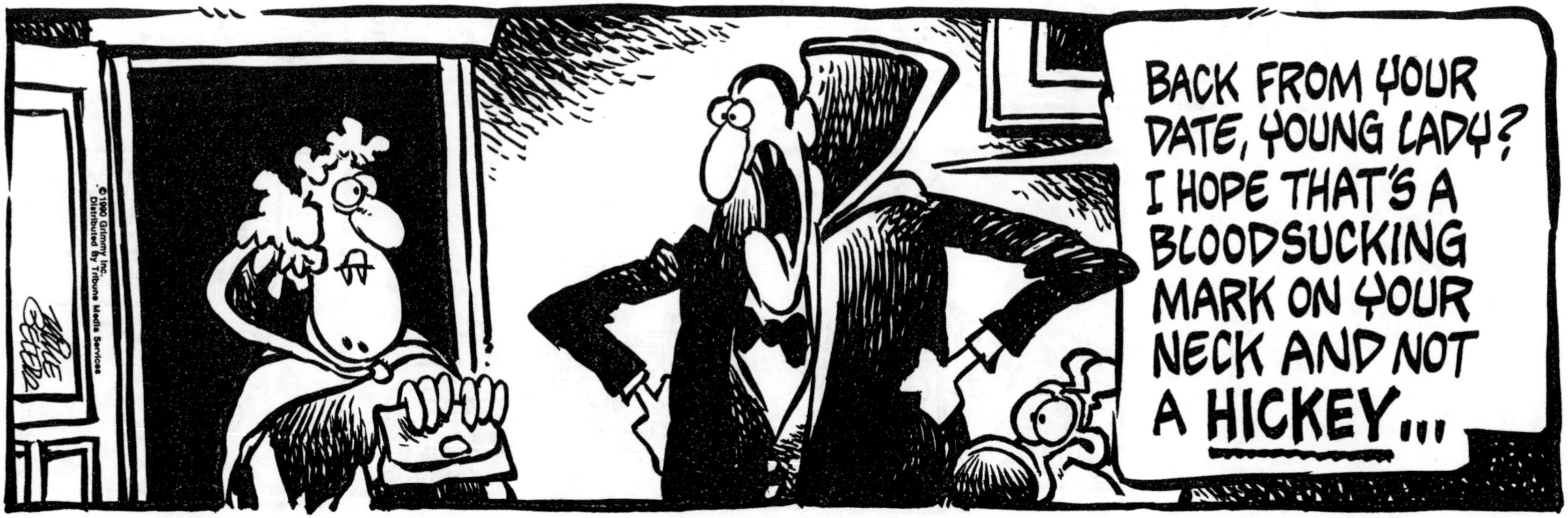
© 1990 Grimmy, Inc.
Distributed by Tribune Media Services
BACK FROM YOUR DATE, YOUNG LADY? I HOPE THAT'S A BLOODSUCKING MARK ON YOUR NECK AND NOT A HICKEY...

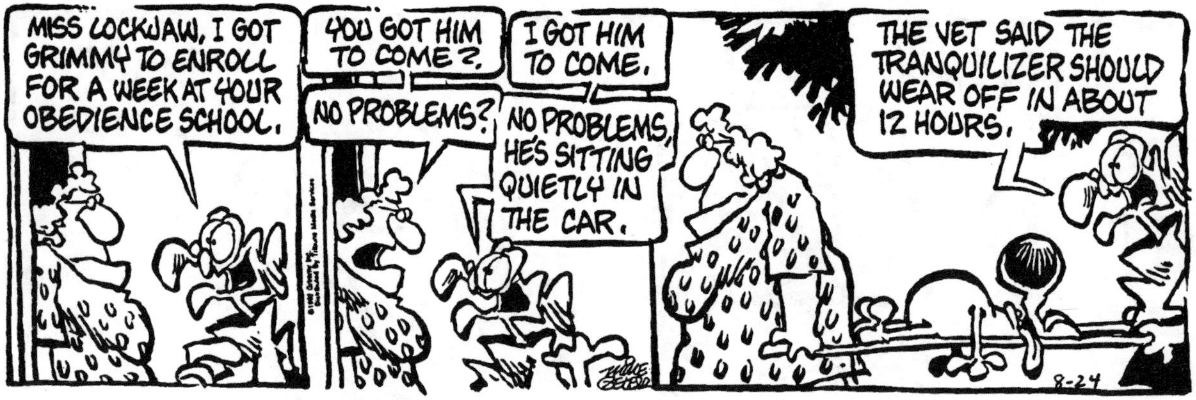


MISS LOCKJAW, I GOT GRIMMY TO ENROLL FOR A WEEK AT YOUR OBEDIENCE SCHOOL.
YOU GOT HIM TO COME?
I GOT HIM TO COME.
NO PROBLEMS?
NO PROBLEMS, HE'S SITTING QUIETLY IN THE CAR.
THE VET SAID THE TRANQUILIZER SHOULD WEAR OFF IN ABOUT 12 HOURS.
8-24


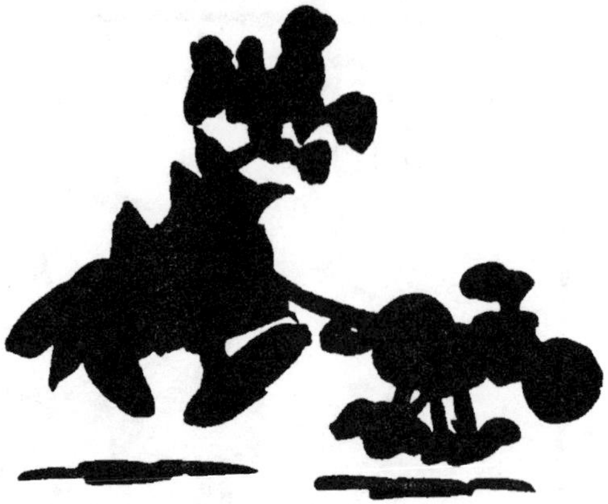

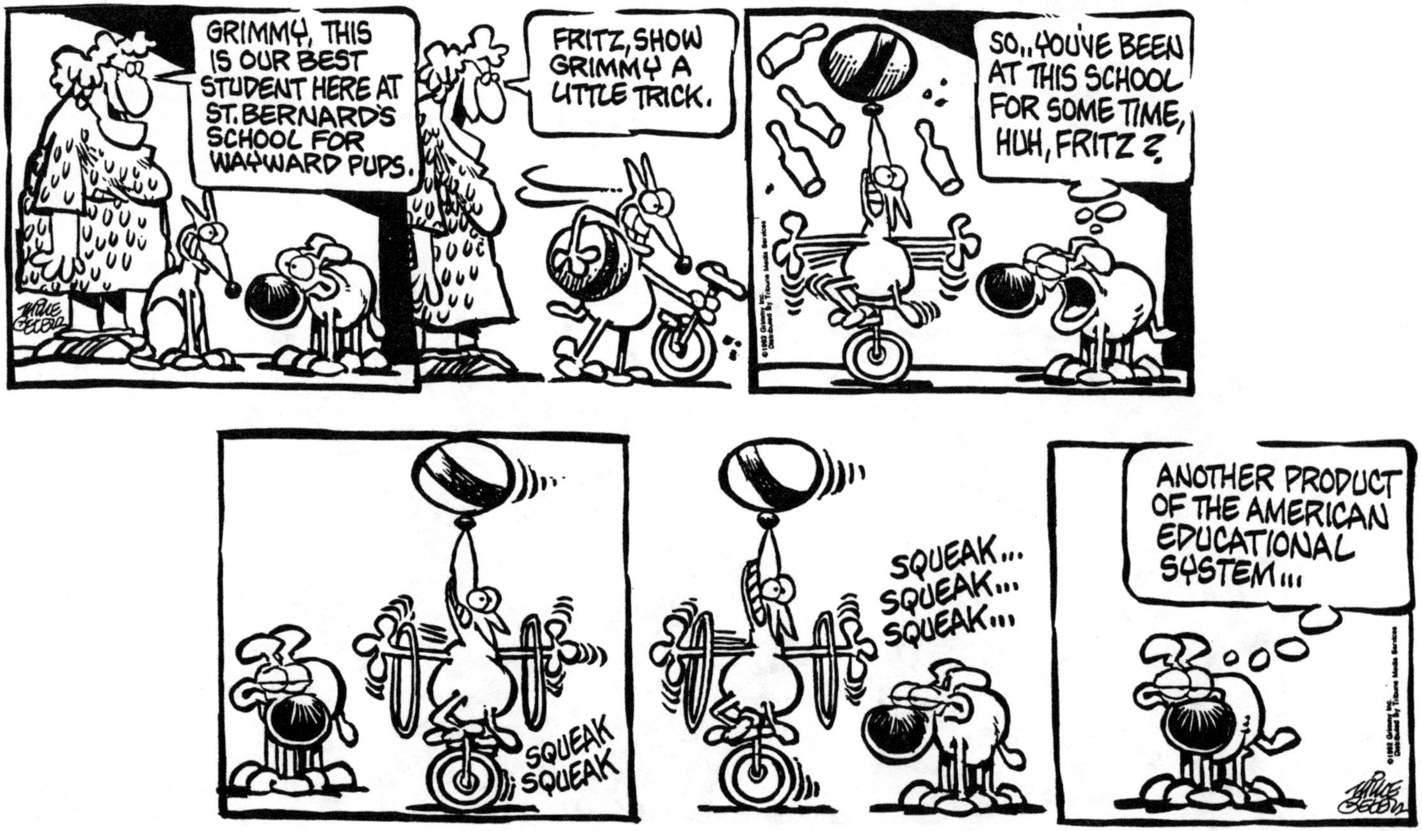


GRIMMY, THIS IS OUR BEST STUDENT HERE AT ST. BERNARD'S SCHOOL FOR WAYWARD PUPS.
FRITZ, SHOW GRIMMY A LITTLE TRICK.
SO,, YOU'VE BEEN AT THIS SCHOOL FOR SOME TIME, HUH, FRITZ?
SQUEAK SQUEAK
SQUEAK... SQUEAK... SQUEAK...
ANOTHER PRODUCT OF THE AMERICAN EDUCATIONAL SYSTEM...

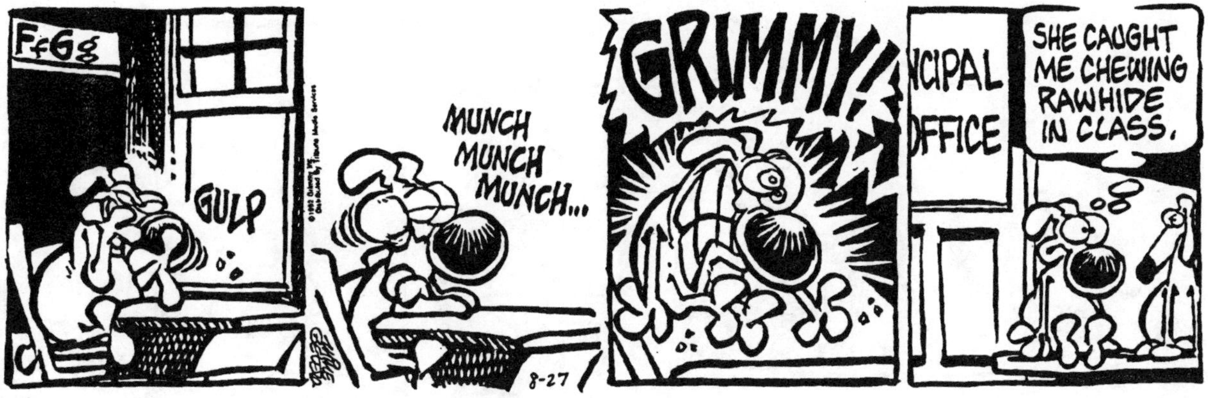
GULP
MUNCH MUNCH MUNCH...
8-27
GRIMMY!
NCIPAL OFFICE
SHE CAUGHT ME CHEWING RAWHIDE IN CLASS.

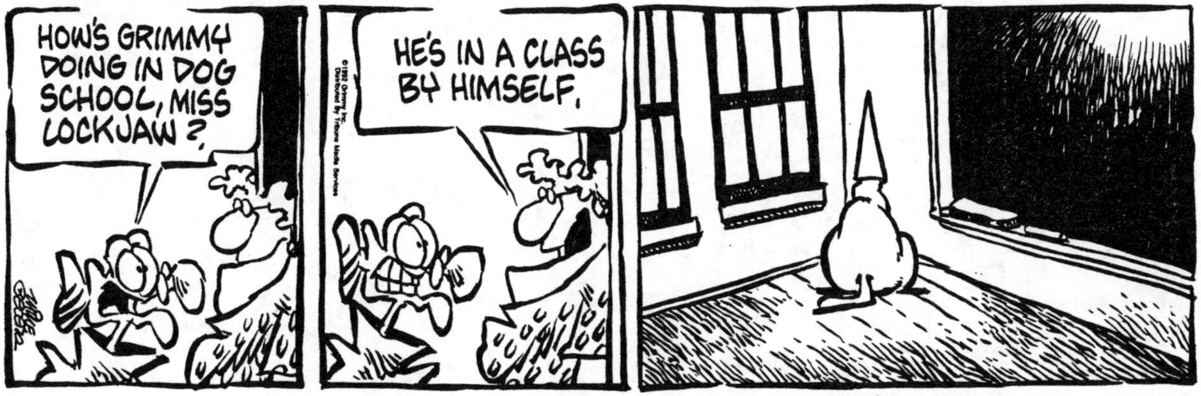
HOW'S GRIMMY DOING IN DOG SCHOOL, MISS LOCKJAW?
HE'S IN A CLASS BY HIMSELF.

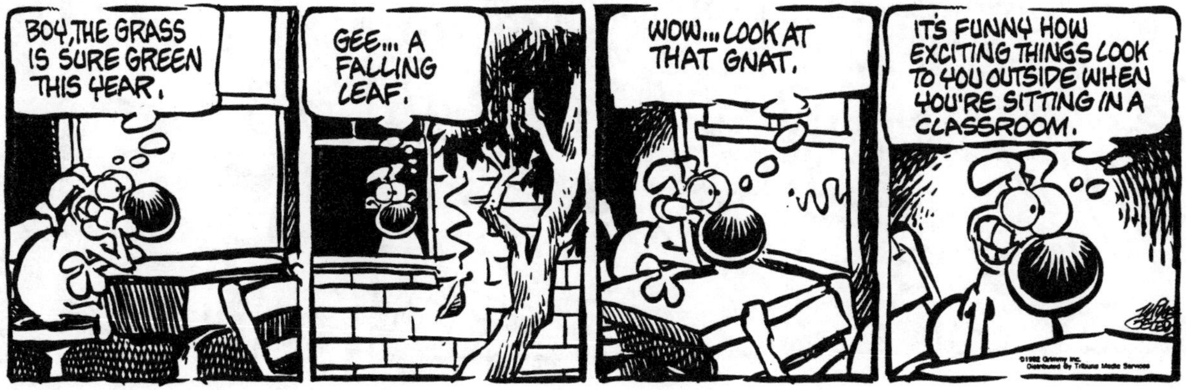
BOY, THE GRASS IS SURE GREEN THIS YEAR.
GEE... A FALLING LEAF.
WOW... LOOK AT THAT GNAT.
IT'S FUNNY HOW EXCITING THINGS LOOK TO YOU OUTSIDE WHEN YOU'RE SITTING IN A CLASSROOM.

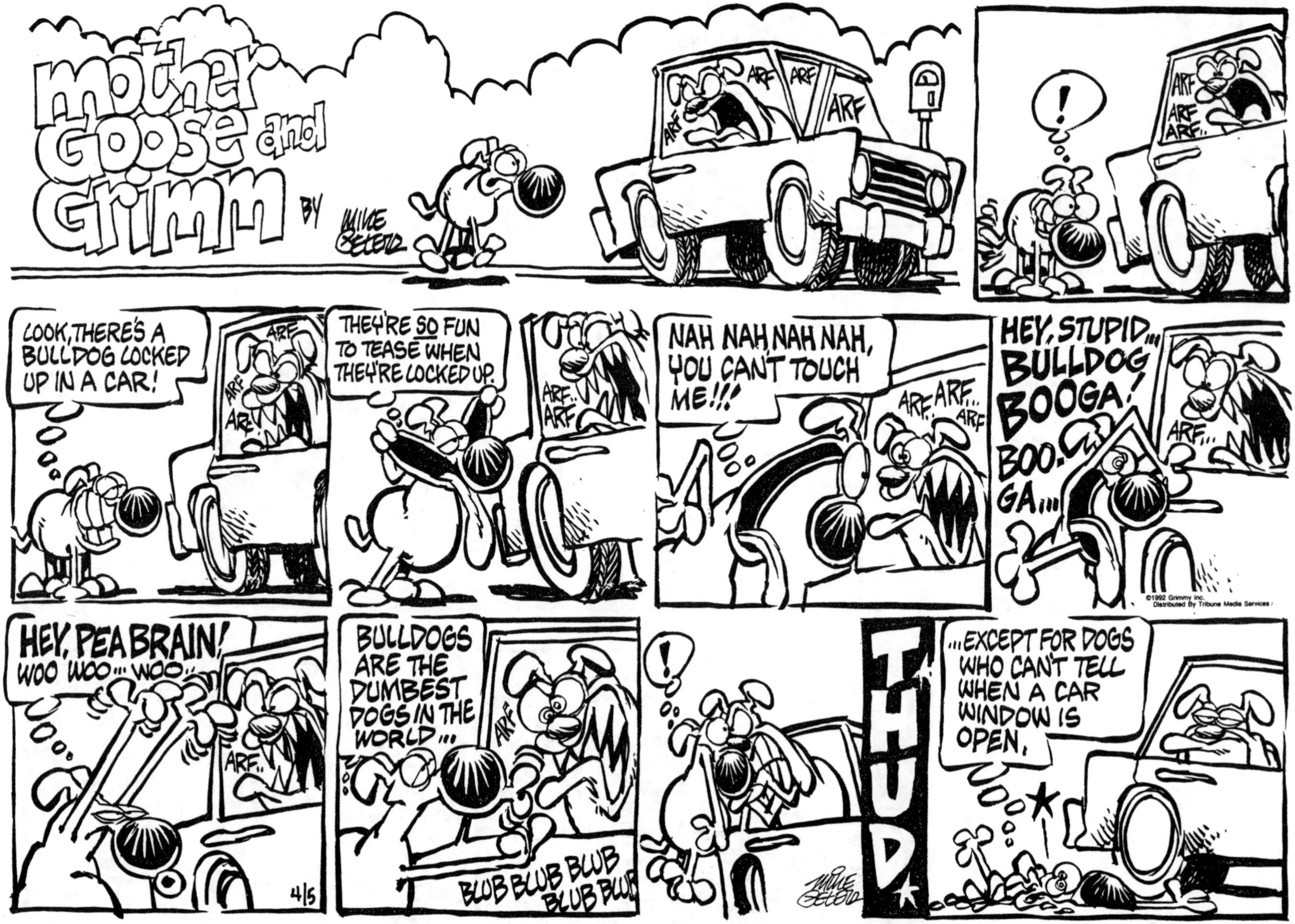
mother Goose and Grimm
BY MIKE PETERS
ARF ARF ARF ARF
!
ARF ARF ARF..
LOOK, THERE'S A BULLDOG LOCKED UP IN A CAR!
ARF ARF ARF
THEY'RE SO FUN TO TEASE WHEN THEY'RE LOCKED UP.
ARF.. ARF
NAH NAH NAH NAH, YOU CAN'T TOUCH ME!!!
ARF.. ARF... ARF
HEY, STUPID... BULLDOG BOOGA! BOO.. GA...
ARF...
©1992 Grimmy Inc. Distributed By Tribune Media Services
HEY, PEA BRAIN! WOO WOO... WOO..
ARF..
4/5
BULLDOGS ARE THE DUMBEST DOGS IN THE WORLD...
ARF
BLUB BLUB BLUB BLUB BLUB
!
MIKE PETERS
THUD
...EXCEPT FOR DOGS WHO CAN'T TELL WHEN A CAR WINDOW IS OPEN.

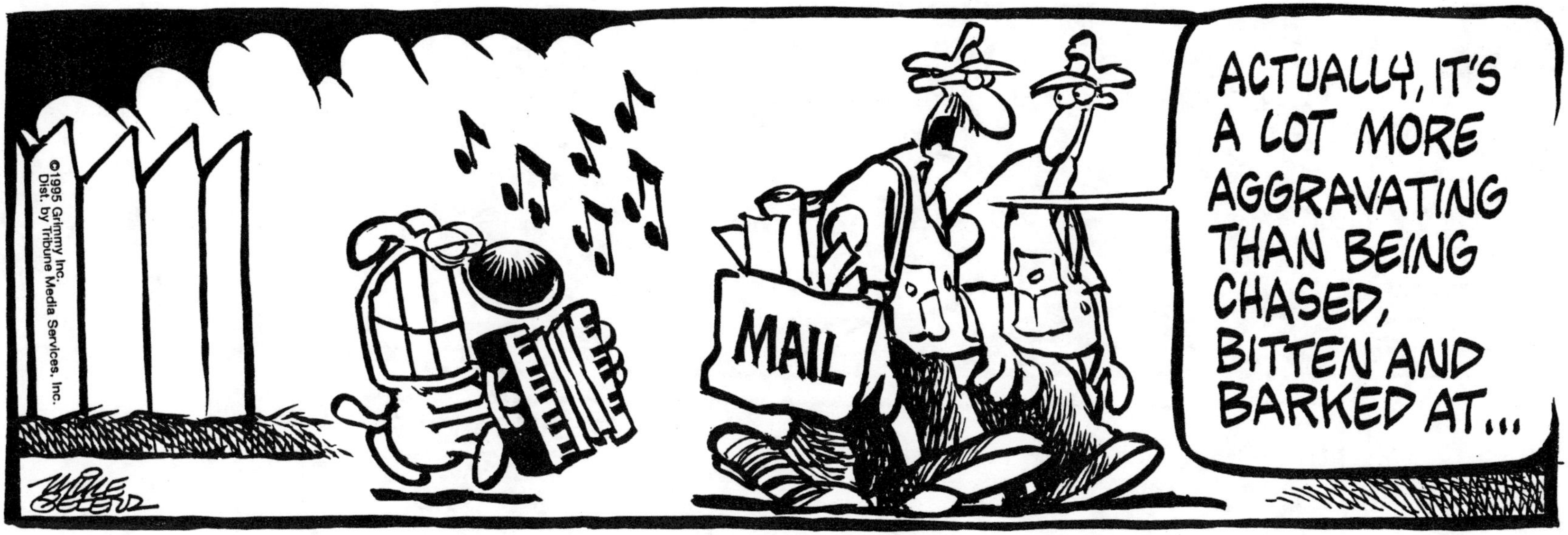

©1995 Grimmy Inc.
Dist. by Tribune Media Services, Inc.
MAIL
ACTUALLY, IT'S A LOT MORE AGGRAVATING THAN BEING CHASED, BITTEN AND BARKED AT...


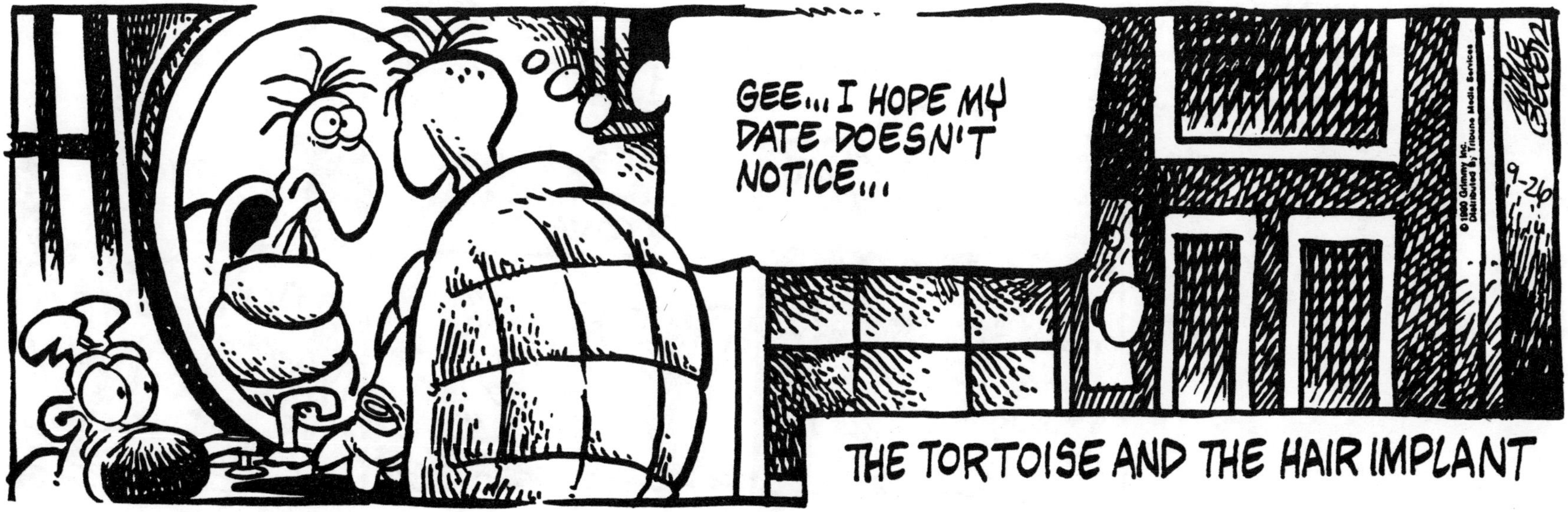

GEE... I HOPE MY DATE DOESN'T NOTICE...
©1990 Grimmy Inc.
Distributed by Tribune Media Services
9-26


THE TORTOISE AND THE HAIR IMPLANT

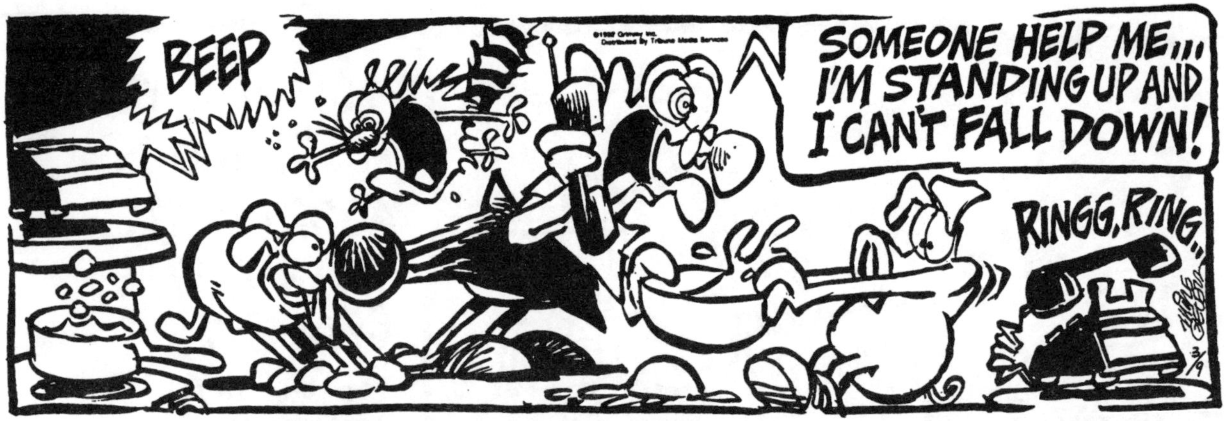
BEEP
SOMEONE HELP ME... I'M STANDING UP AND I CAN'T FALL DOWN!
RINGG, RING...

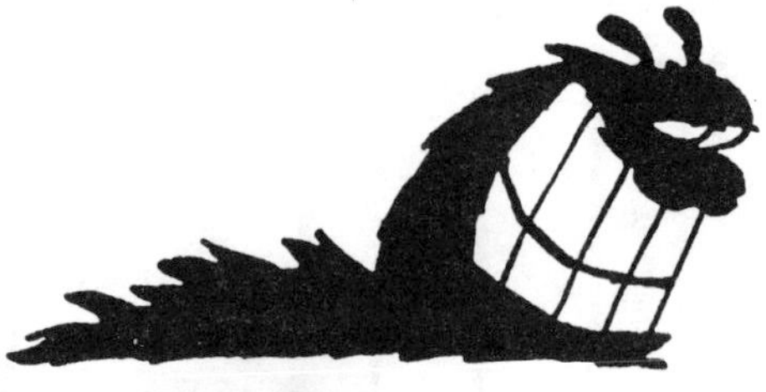

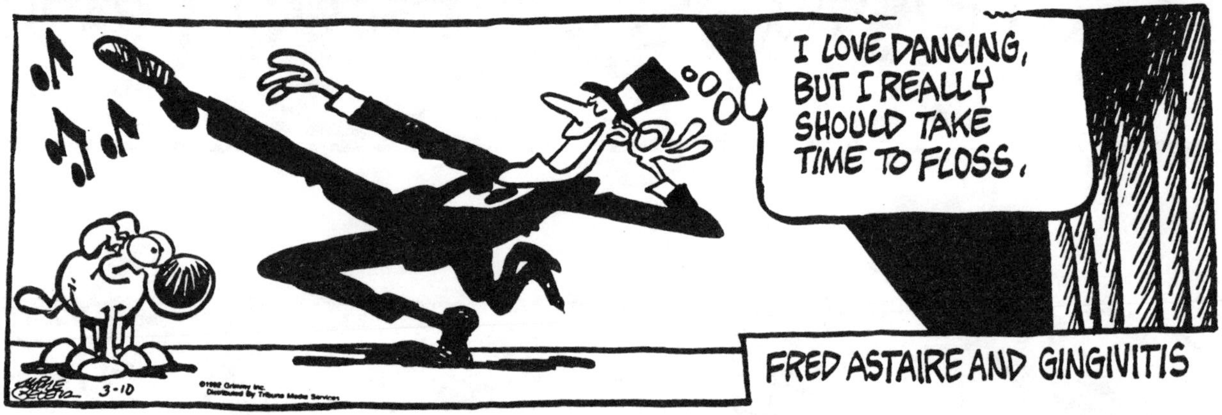
I LOVE DANCING, BUT I REALLY SHOULD TAKE TIME TO FLOSS.
FRED ASTAIRE AND GINGIVITIS
3-10

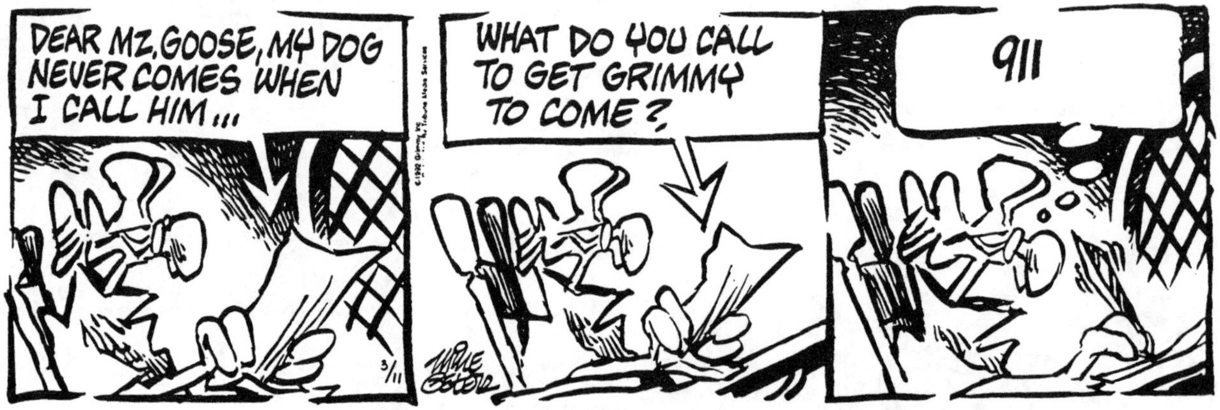
DEAR MZ. GOOSE, MY DOG NEVER COMES WHEN I CALL HIM...
WHAT DO YOU CALL TO GET GRIMMY TO COME?
911
3/11

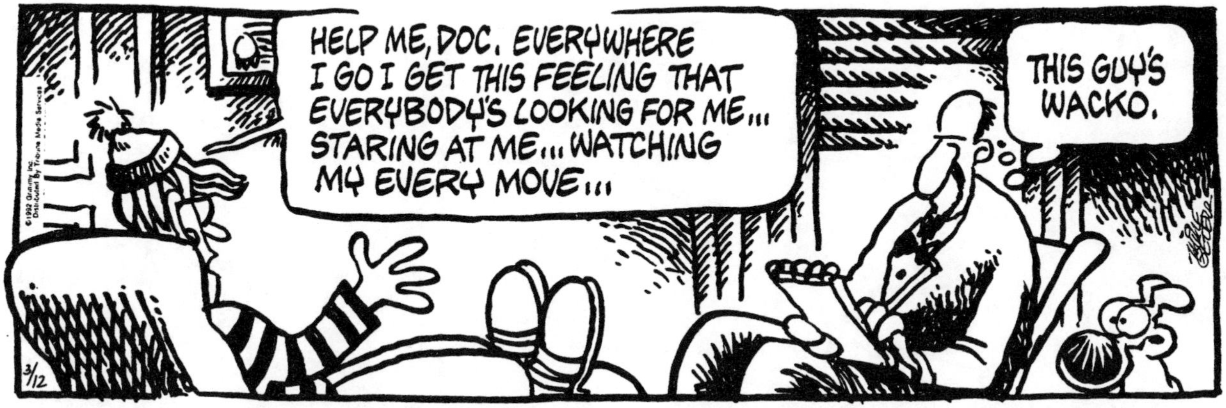
HELP ME, DOC. EVERYWHERE I GO I GET THIS FEELING THAT EVERYBODY'S LOOKING FOR ME... STARING AT ME... WATCHING MY EVERY MOVE...
THIS GUY'S WACKO.
3/12

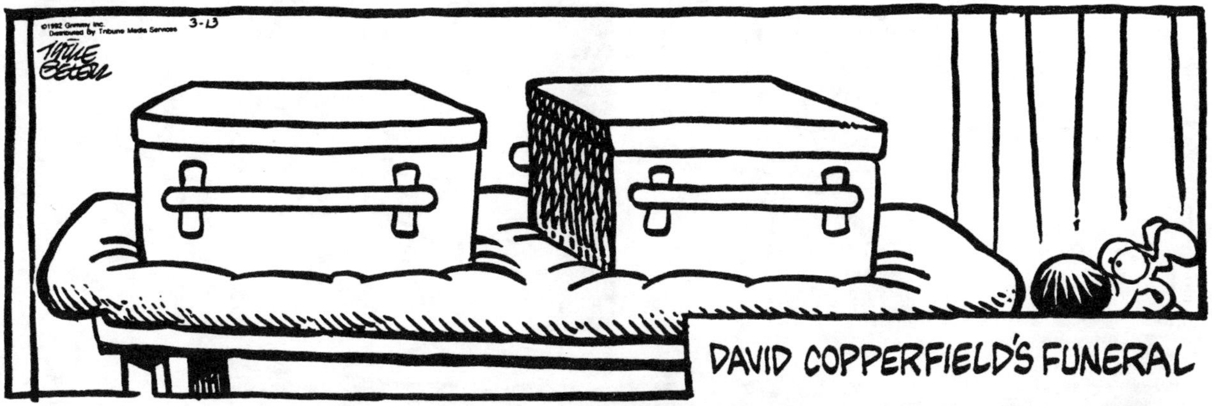
3-13
DAVID COPPERFIELD'S FUNERAL

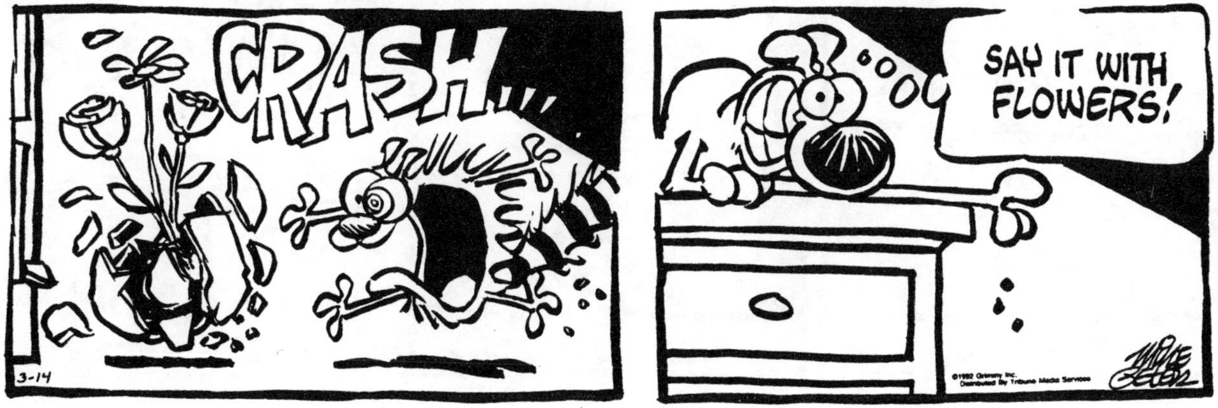
CRASH...
SAY IT WITH FLOWERS!
3-14

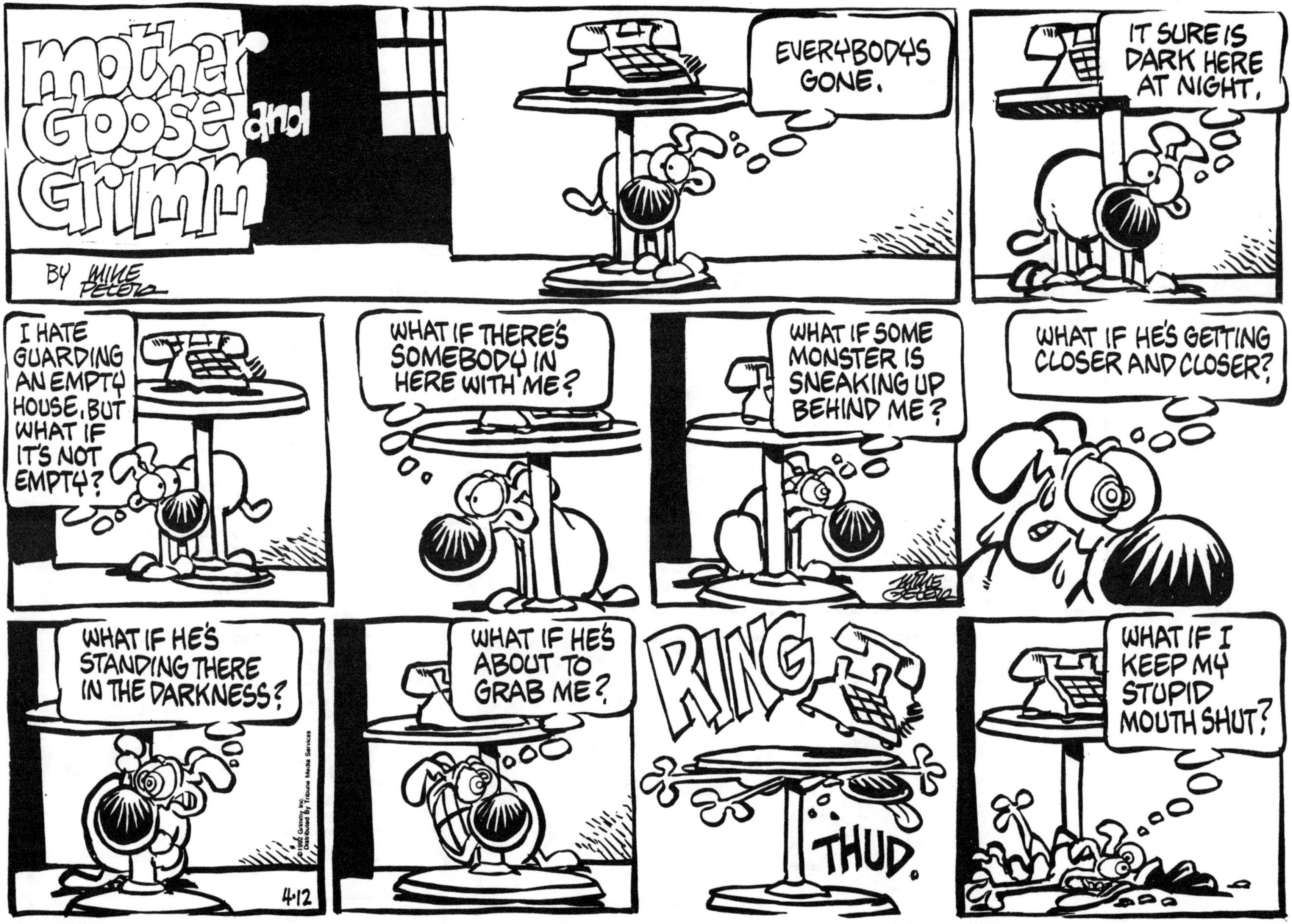
mother Goose and Grimm
BY MIKE PETERS
EVERYBODYS GONE.
IT SURE IS DARK HERE AT NIGHT.
I HATE GUARDING AN EMPTY HOUSE, BUT WHAT IF IT'S NOT EMPTY?
WHAT IF THERE'S SOMEBODY IN HERE WITH ME?
WHAT IF SOME MONSTER IS SNEAKING UP BEHIND ME?
WHAT IF HE'S GETTING CLOSER AND CLOSER?
WHAT IF HE'S STANDING THERE IN THE DARKNESS?
©1992 Grimmy, Inc. Distributed By Tribune Media Services
4·12
WHAT IF HE'S ABOUT TO GRAB ME?
RING
THUD.
WHAT IF I KEEP MY STUPID MOUTH SHUT?

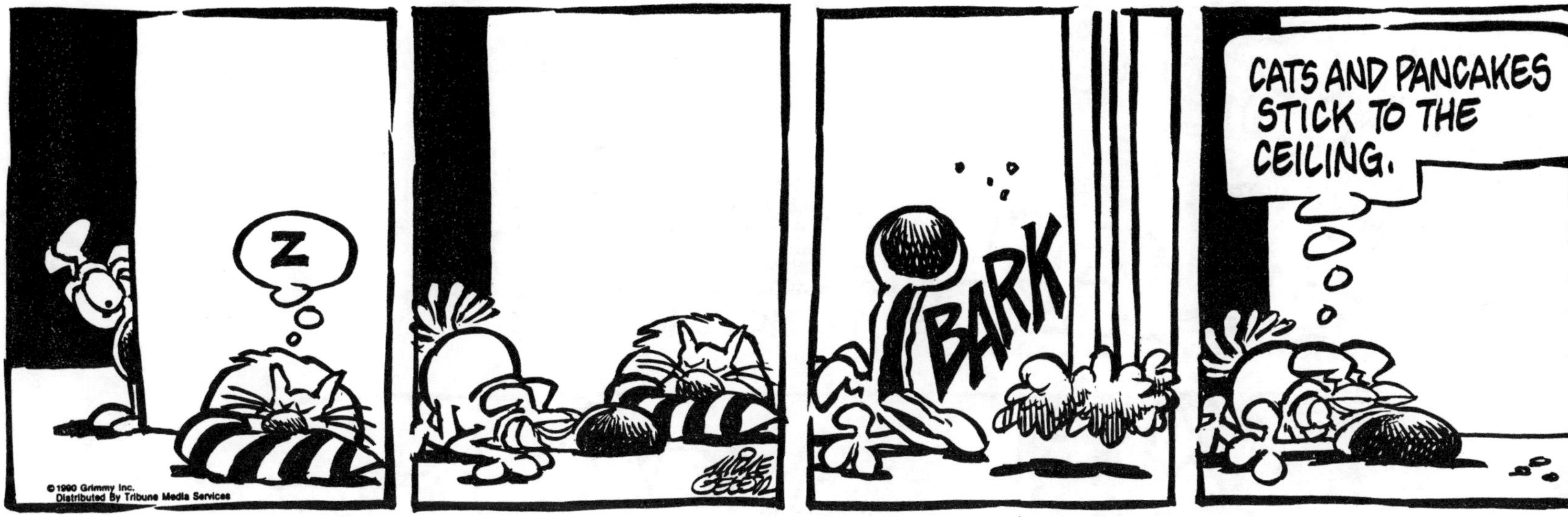

Z
BARK
CATS AND PANCAKES STICK TO THE CEILING.
© 1990 Grimmy Inc.
Distributed By Tribune Media Services


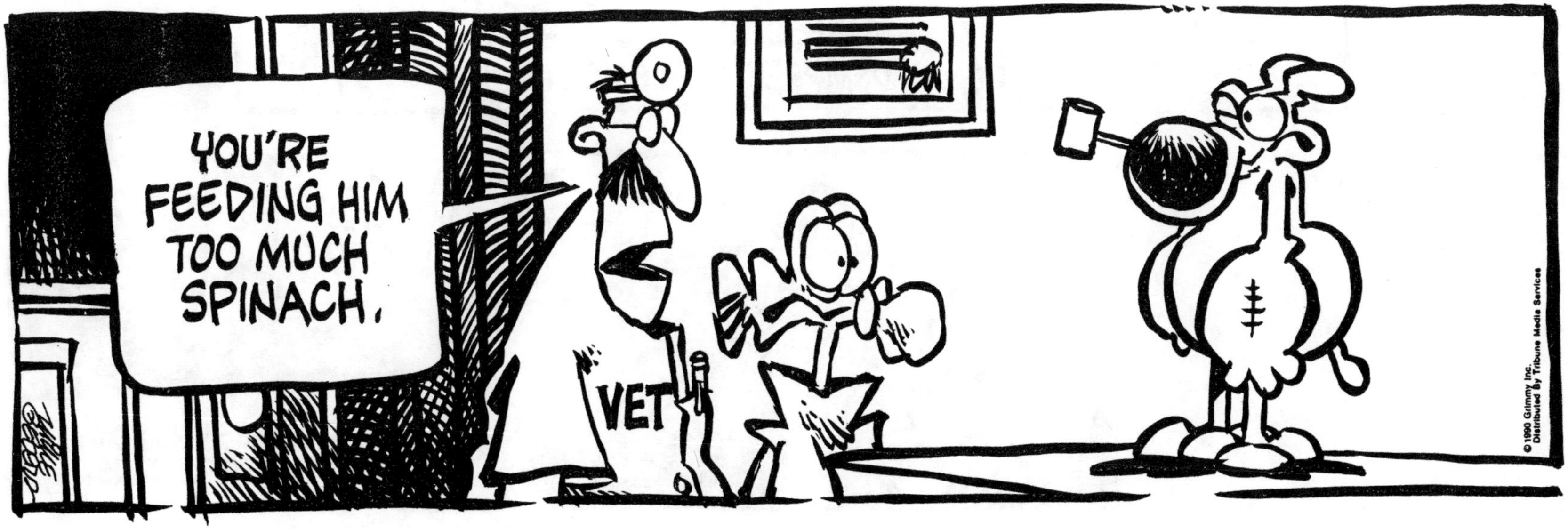

YOU'RE FEEDING HIM TOO MUCH SPINACH.
VET
© 1990 Grimmy Inc.
Distributed By Tribune Media Services

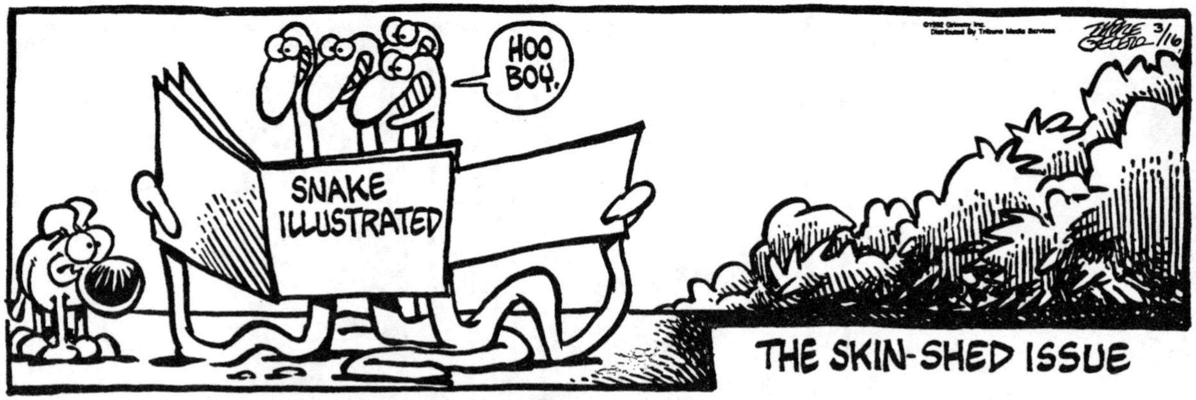
3/16
HOO BOY.
SNAKE ILLUSTRATED
THE SKIN-SHED ISSUE

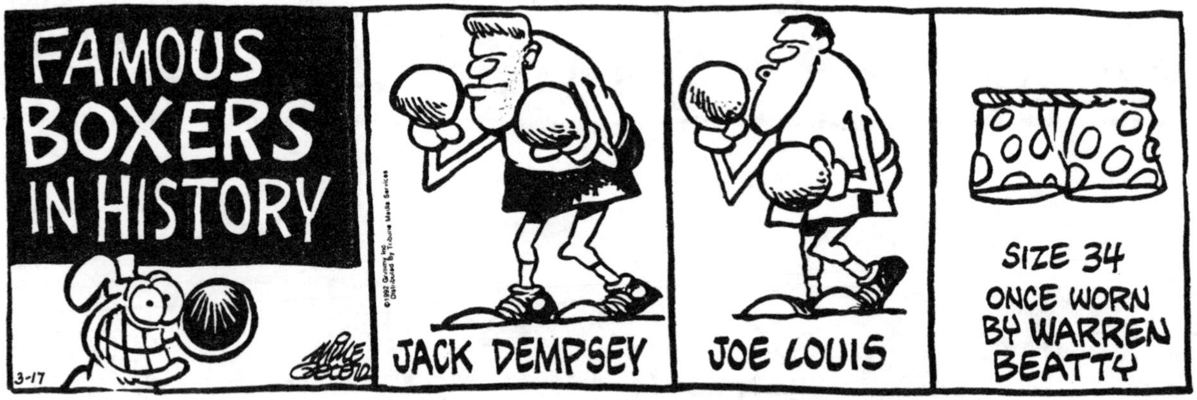
FAMOUS BOXERS IN HISTORY
3-17
JACK DEMPSEY
JOE LOUIS
SIZE 34
ONCE WORN BY WARREN BEATTY

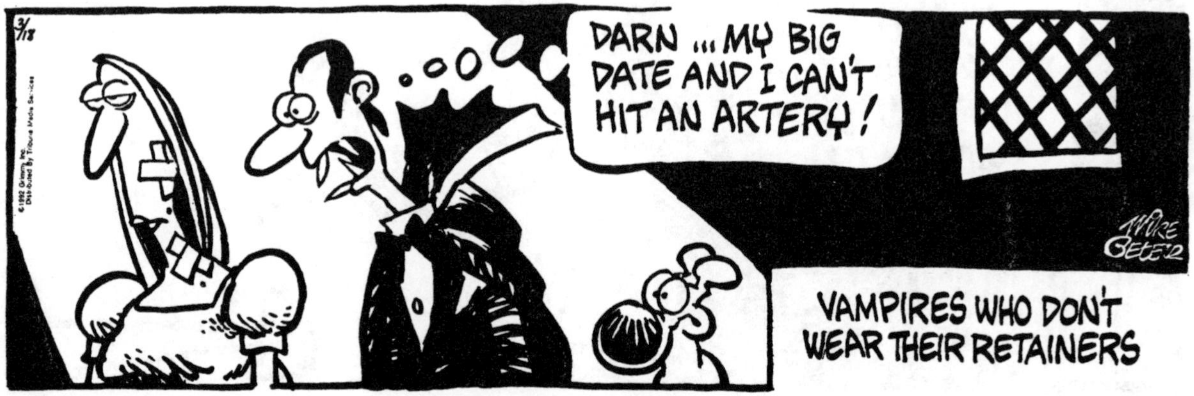
3/18
DARN ... MY BIG DATE AND I CAN'T HIT AN ARTERY!
VAMPIRES WHO DON'T WEAR THEIR RETAINERS

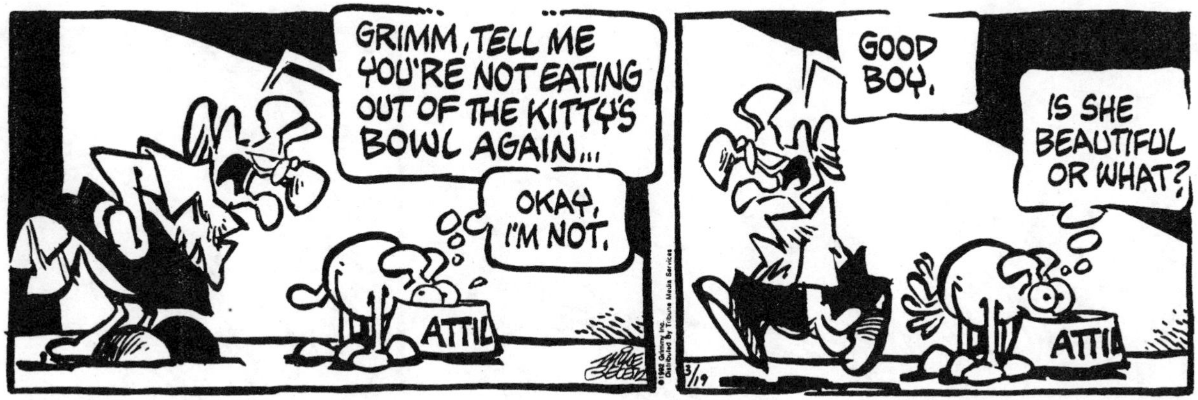
GRIMM, TELL ME YOU'RE NOT EATING OUT OF THE KITTY'S BOWL AGAIN...
OKAY, I'M NOT.
ATTIL
GOOD BOY.
IS SHE BEAUTIFUL OR WHAT?
ATTIL
3/19

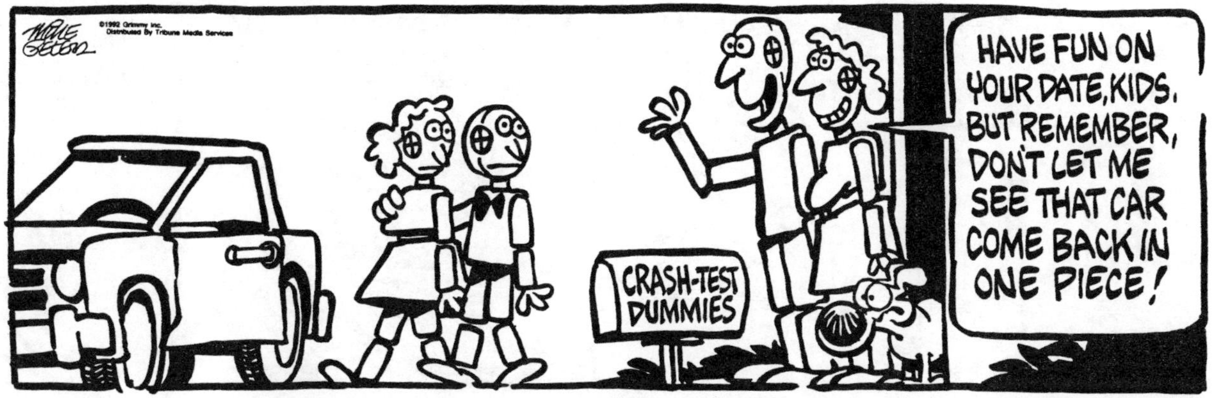
©1992 Grimmy Inc. Distributed By Tribune Media Services
HAVE FUN ON YOUR DATE, KIDS. BUT REMEMBER, DON'T LET ME SEE THAT CAR COME BACK IN ONE PIECE!
CRASH-TEST DUMMIES

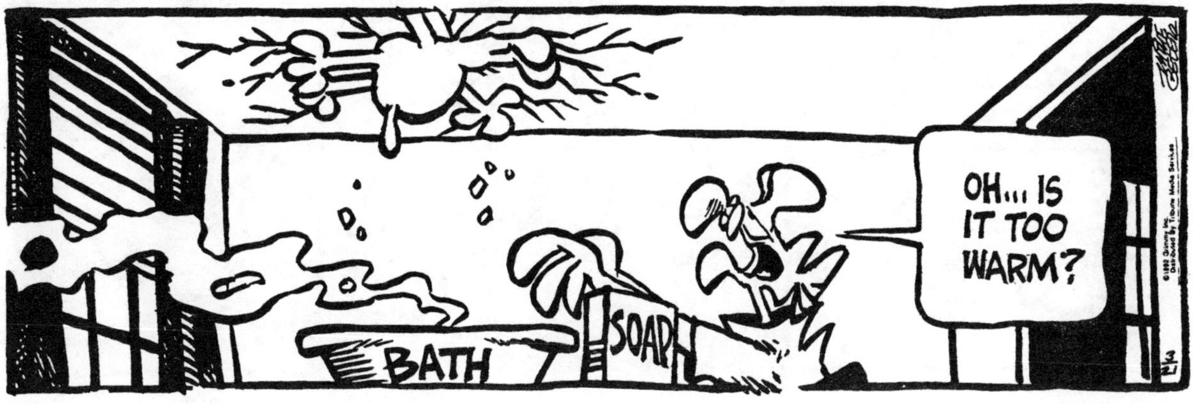
OH... IS IT TOO WARM?
BATH
SOAP

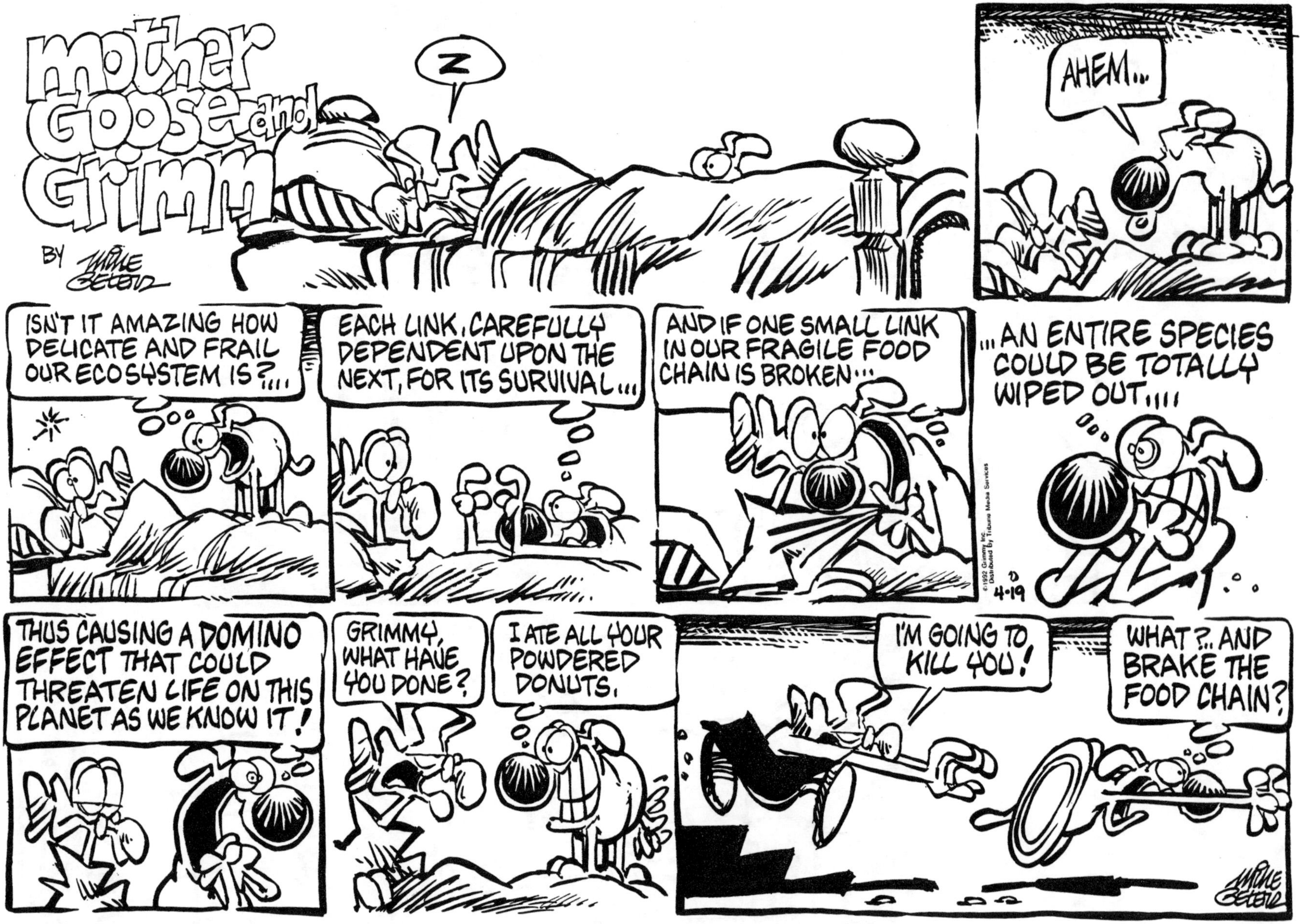
Mother Goose and Grimm
BY Mike Peters
Z
AHEM...
ISN'T IT AMAZING HOW DELICATE AND FRAIL OUR ECOSYSTEM IS?....
EACH LINK, CAREFULLY DEPENDENT UPON THE NEXT, FOR ITS SURVIVAL...
AND IF ONE SMALL LINK IN OUR FRAGILE FOOD CHAIN IS BROKEN...
...AN ENTIRE SPECIES COULD BE TOTALLY WIPED OUT.....
©1992 Grimmy Inc. Distributed by Tribune Media Services
4-19
THUS CAUSING A DOMINO EFFECT THAT COULD THREATEN LIFE ON THIS PLANET AS WE KNOW IT!
GRIMMY, WHAT HAVE YOU DONE?
I ATE ALL YOUR POWDERED DONUTS.
I'M GOING TO KILL YOU!
WHAT?... AND BRAKE THE FOOD CHAIN?
Mike Peters

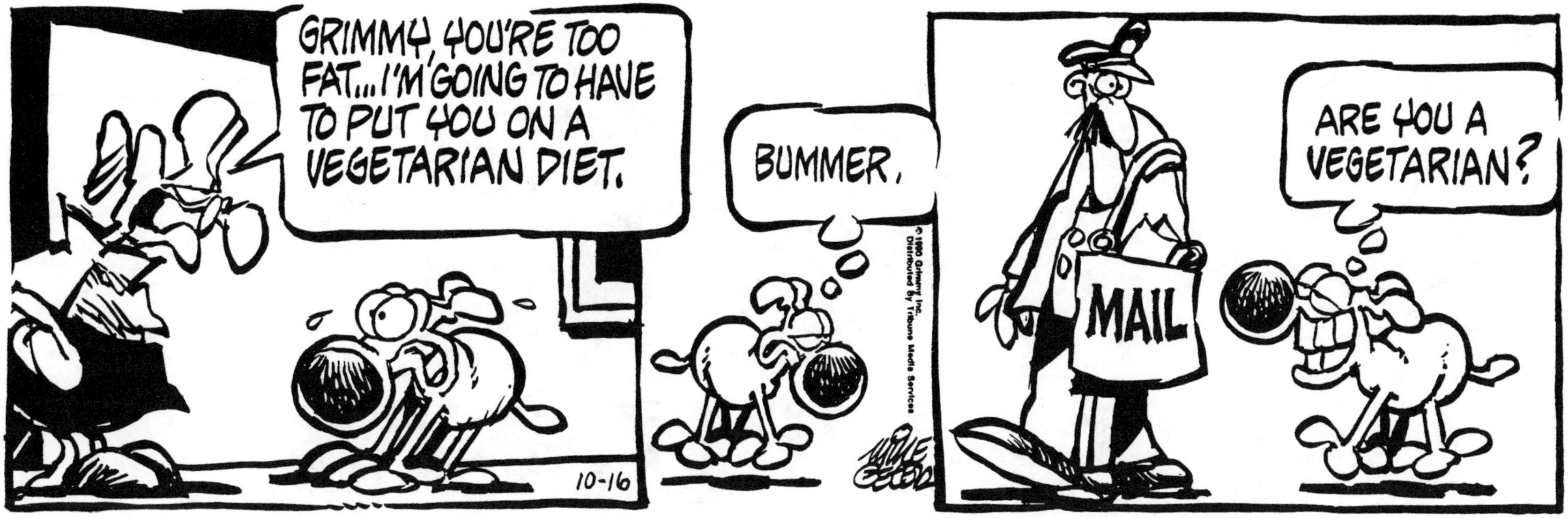
GRIMMY, YOU'RE TOO FAT... I'M GOING TO HAVE TO PUT YOU ON A VEGETARIAN DIET.
10-16
BUMMER.
© 1990 Grimmy Inc. Distributed By Tribune Media Services
MAIL
ARE YOU A VEGETARIAN?

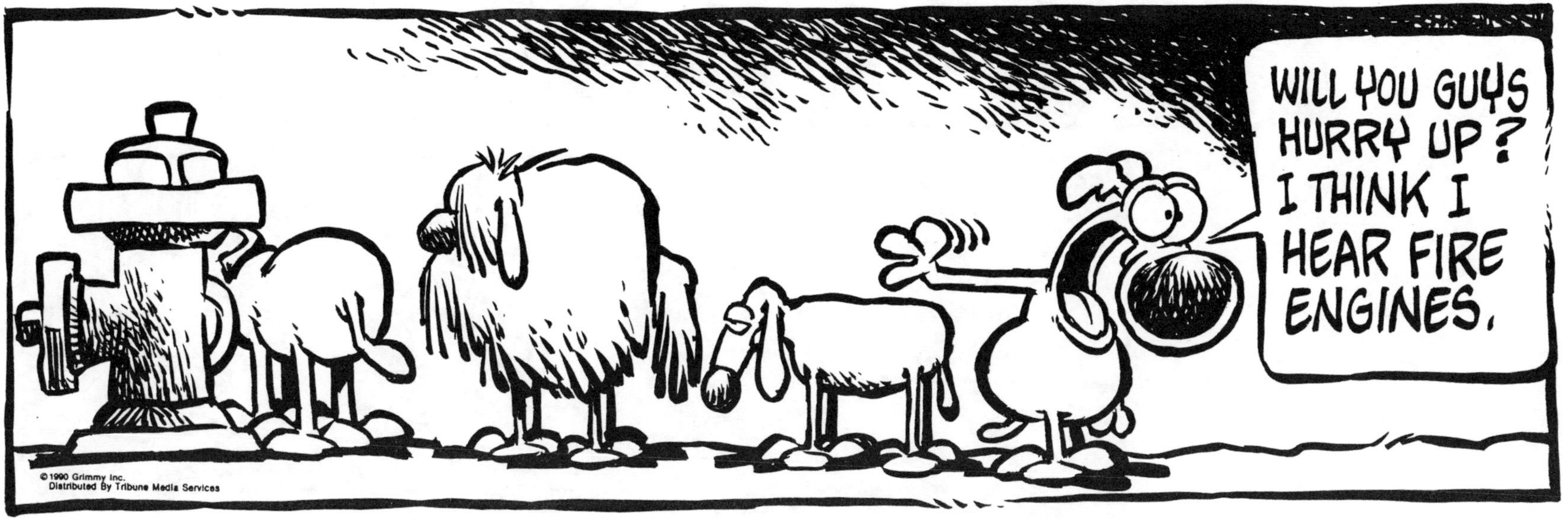
WILL YOU GUYS HURRY UP? I THINK I HEAR FIRE ENGINES.
© 1990 Grimmy Inc. Distributed By Tribune Media Services

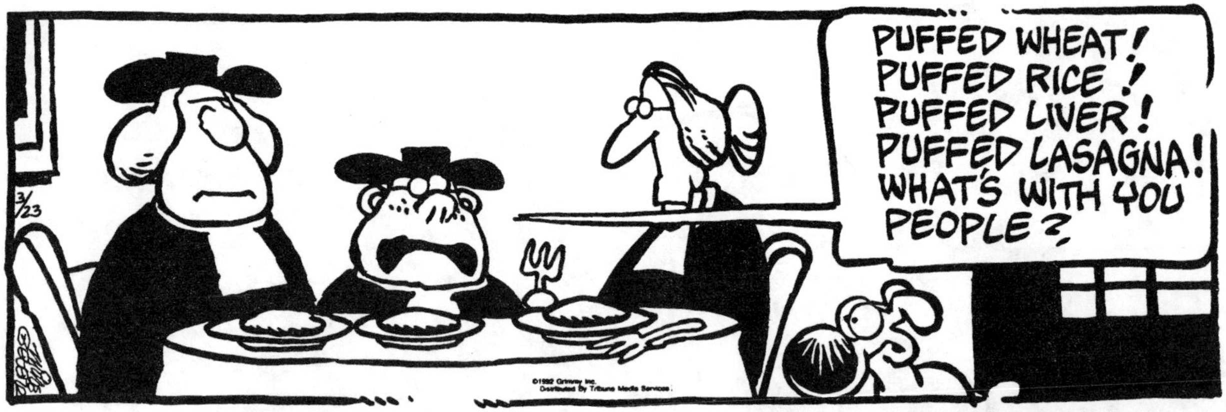

3/23
PUFFED WHEAT! PUFFED RICE! PUFFED LIVER! PUFFED LASAGNA! WHAT'S WITH YOU PEOPLE?


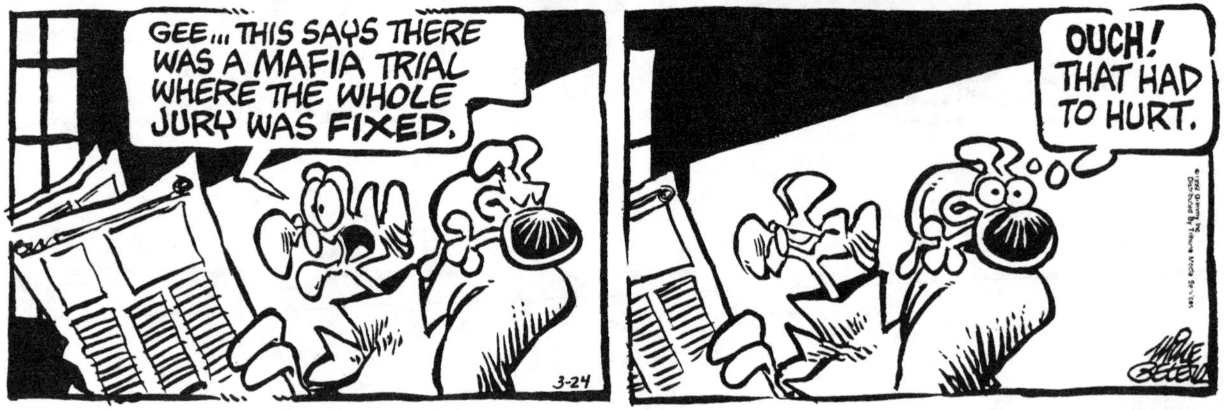

GEE... THIS SAYS THERE WAS A MAFIA TRIAL WHERE THE WHOLE JURY WAS FIXED.
3-24
OUCH! THAT HAD TO HURT.


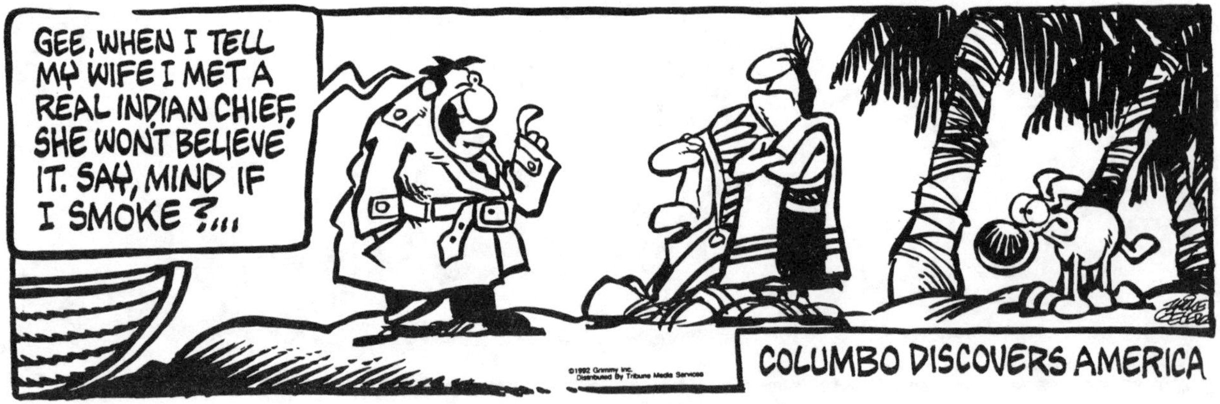

GEE, WHEN I TELL MY WIFE I MET A REAL INDIAN CHIEF, SHE WON'T BELIEVE IT. SAY, MIND IF I SMOKE?...
COLUMBO DISCOVERS AMERICA

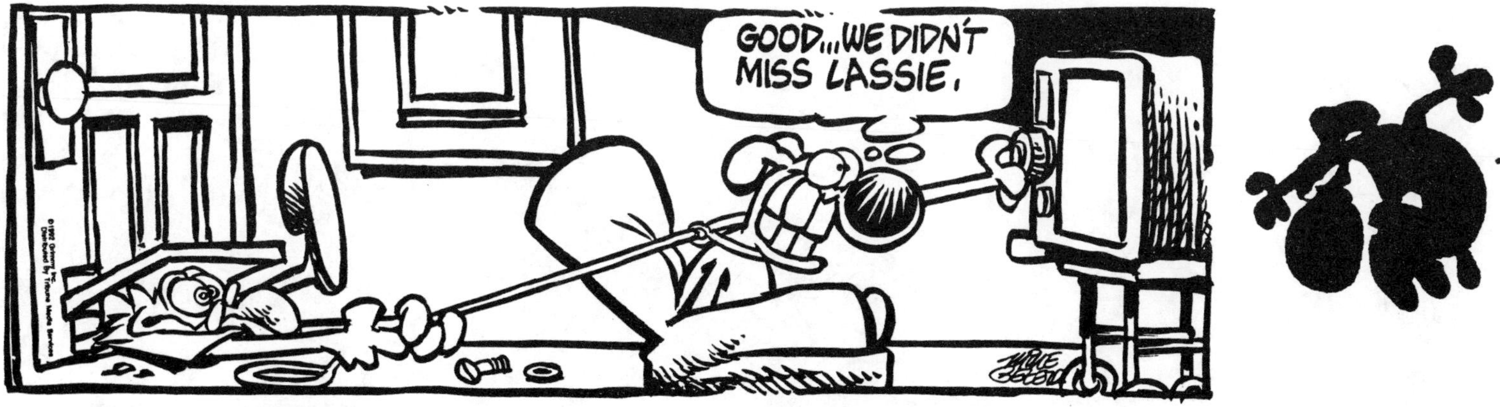
GOOD...WE DIDN'T MISS LASSIE.

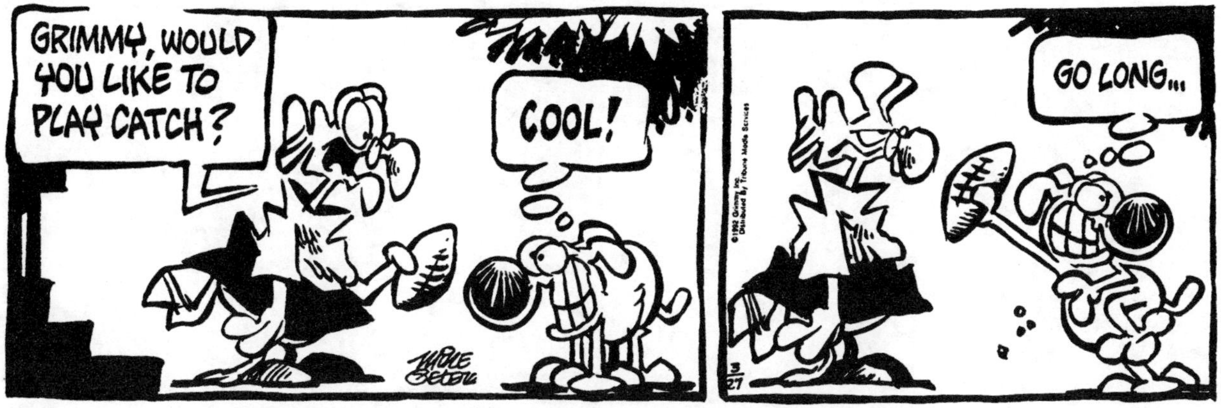
GRIMMY, WOULD YOU LIKE TO PLAY CATCH?
COOL!
GO LONG...

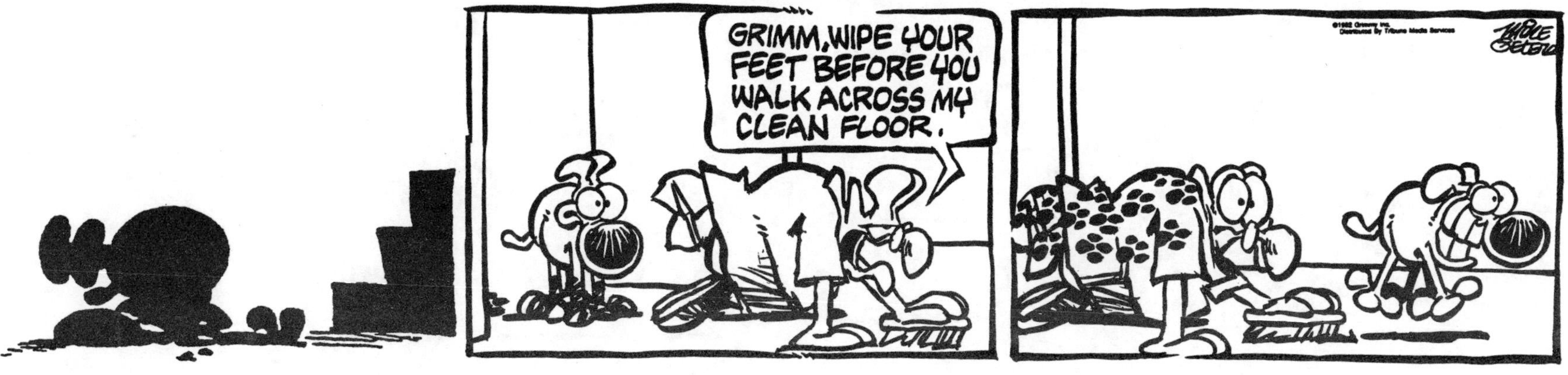
GRIMM, WIPE YOUR FEET BEFORE YOU WALK ACROSS MY CLEAN FLOOR.

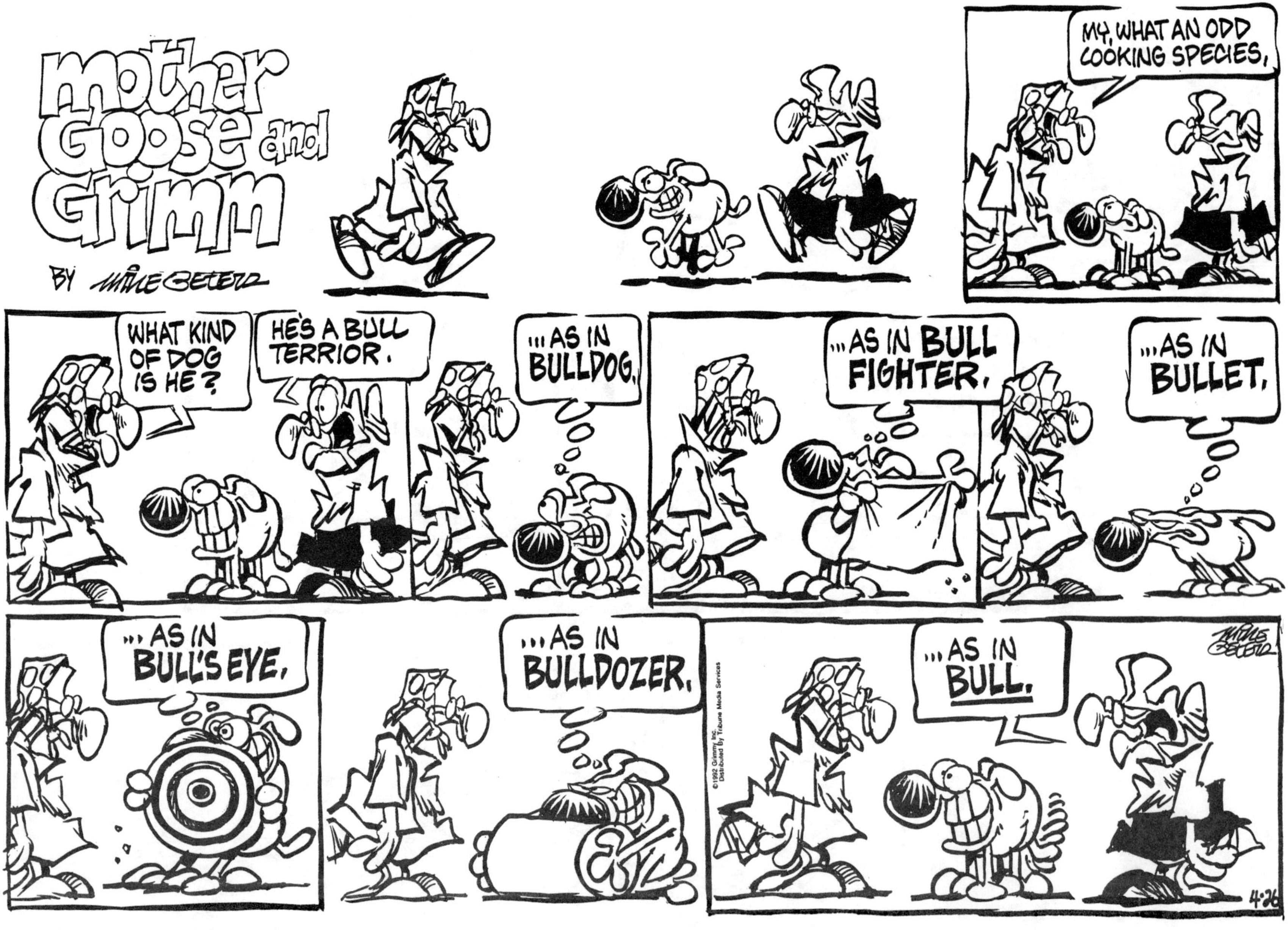
mother Goose and Grimm
BY Mike Peters
MY, WHAT AN ODD LOOKING SPECIES,
WHAT KIND OF DOG IS HE?
HE'S A BULL TERRIOR.
...AS IN BULLDOG,
...AS IN BULL FIGHTER,
...AS IN BULLET,
...AS IN BULL'S EYE,
...AS IN BULLDOZER,
© 1992 Grimmy Inc. Distributed By Tribune Media Services
...AS IN BULL,
Mike Peters
4-26

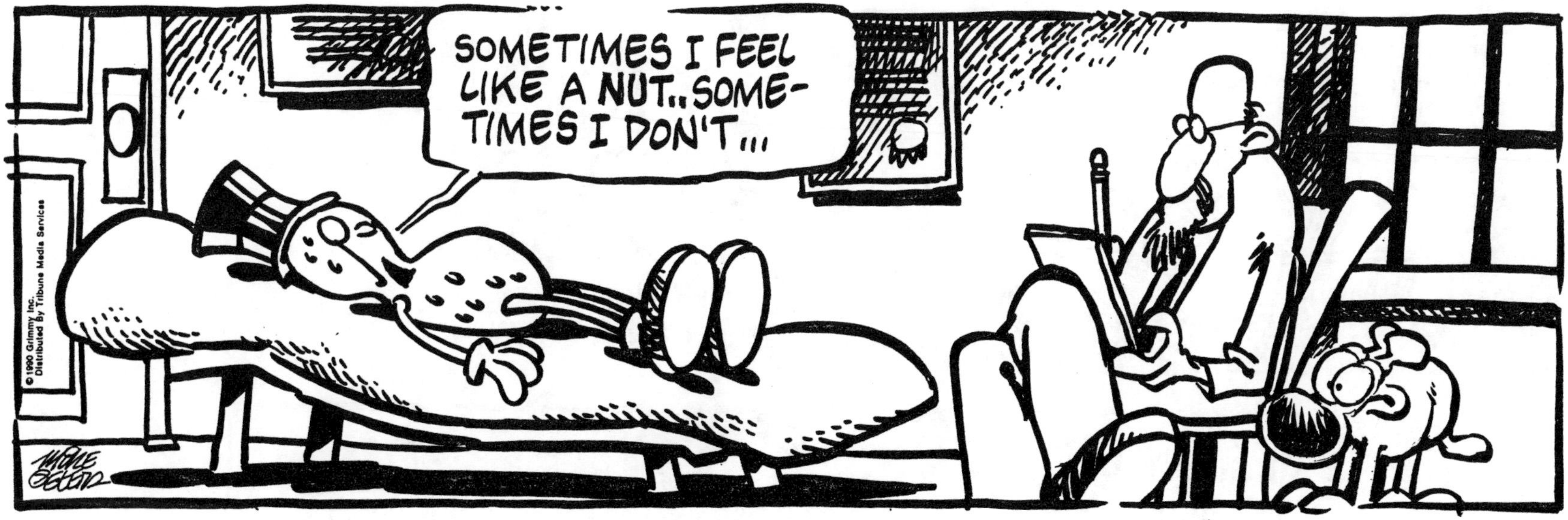
SOMETIMES I FEEL LIKE A NUT.. SOMETIMES I DON'T...
© 1990 Grimmy Inc. Distributed By Tribune Media Services

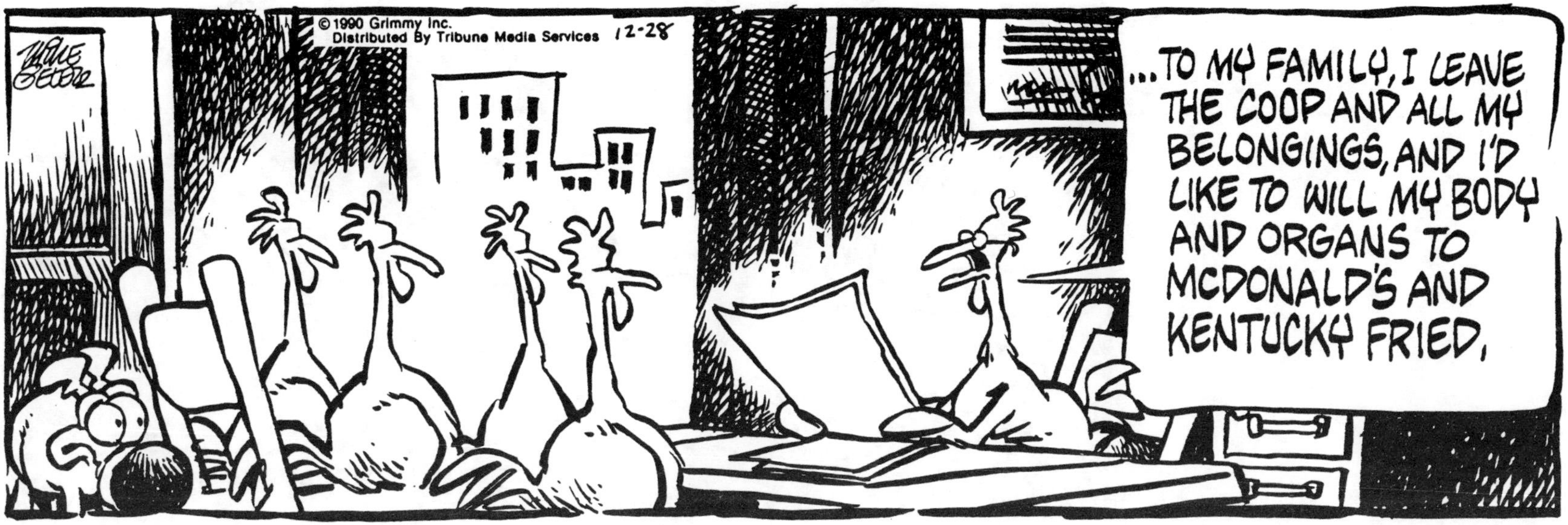
© 1990 Grimmy Inc. Distributed By Tribune Media Services 12-28
...TO MY FAMILY, I LEAVE THE COOP AND ALL MY BELONGINGS, AND I'D LIKE TO WILL MY BODY AND ORGANS TO MCDONALD'S AND KENTUCKY FRIED.

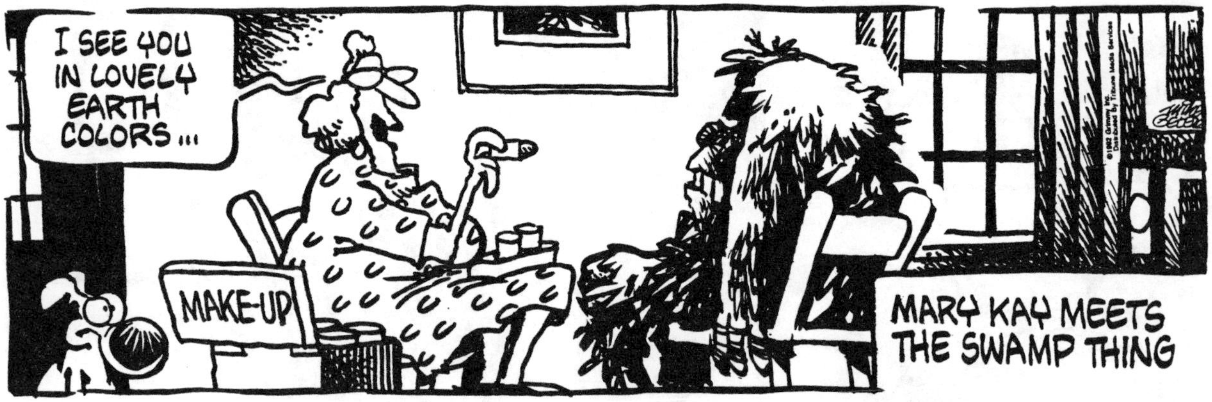
I SEE YOU IN LOVELY EARTH COLORS ...
MAKE-UP
MARY KAY MEETS THE SWAMP THING

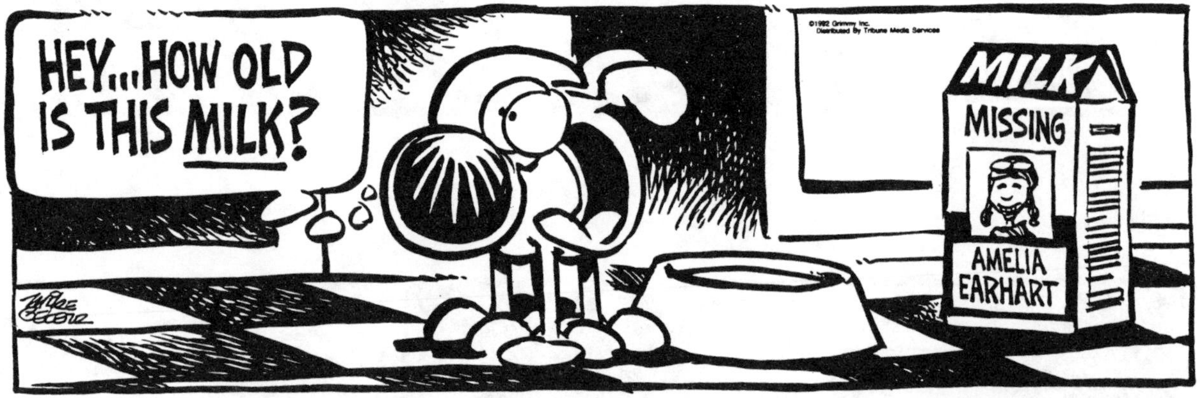
HEY...HOW OLD IS THIS MILK?
©1992 Grimmy Inc. Distributed By Tribune Media Services
MILK
MISSING
AMELIA EARHART

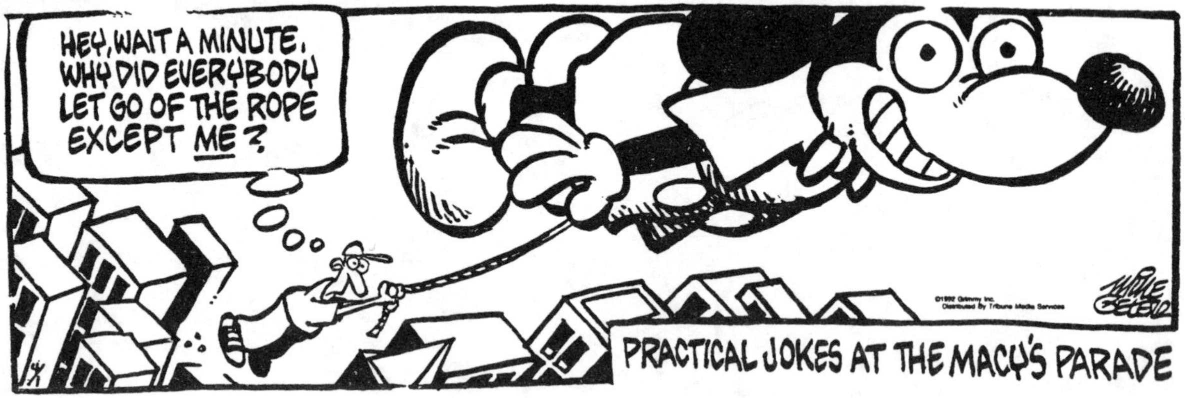
HEY, WAIT A MINUTE, WHY DID EVERYBODY LET GO OF THE ROPE EXCEPT ME?
©1992 Grimmy Inc. Distributed By Tribune Media Services
PRACTICAL JOKES AT THE MACY'S PARADE

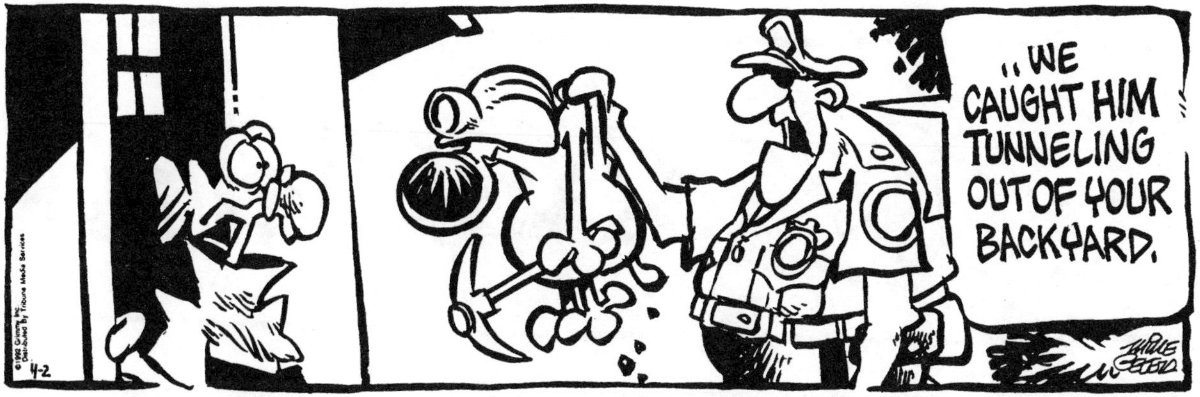
..WE CAUGHT HIM TUNNELING OUT OF YOUR BACKYARD.
©1982 Grimmy Inc. Distributed By Tribune Media Services
4-2

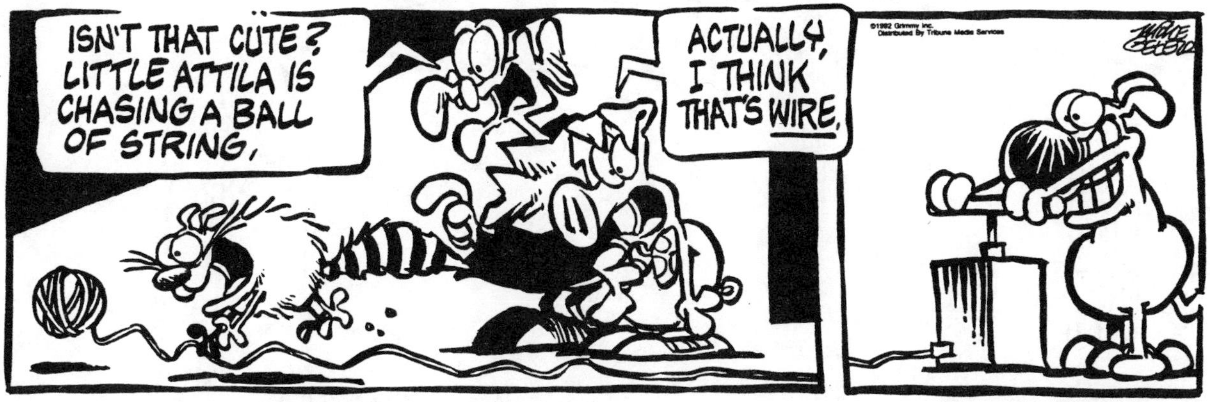
ISN'T THAT CUTE? LITTLE ATTILA IS CHASING A BALL OF STRING.
ACTUALLY, I THINK THAT'S WIRE.
©1982 Grimmy Inc. Distributed By Tribune Media Services

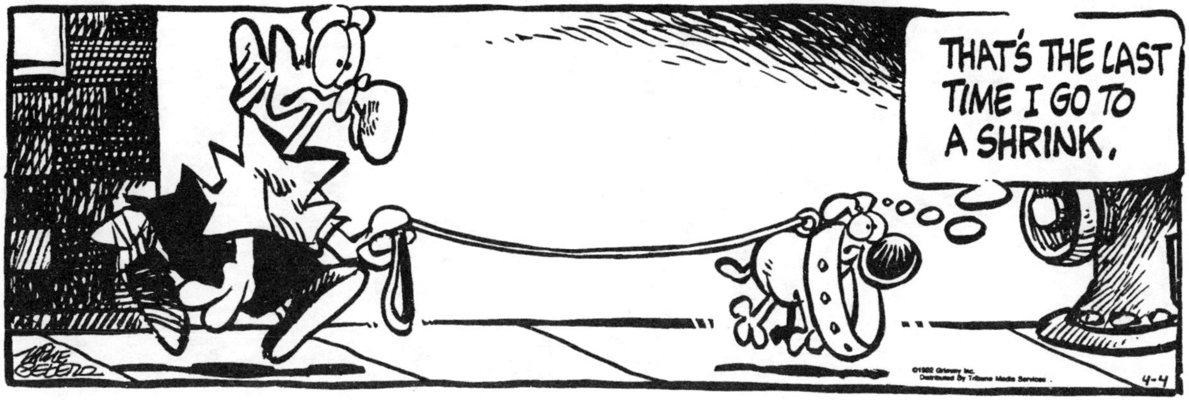
THAT'S THE LAST TIME I GO TO A SHRINK.
©1982 Grimmy Inc. Distributed By Tribune Media Services
4-4

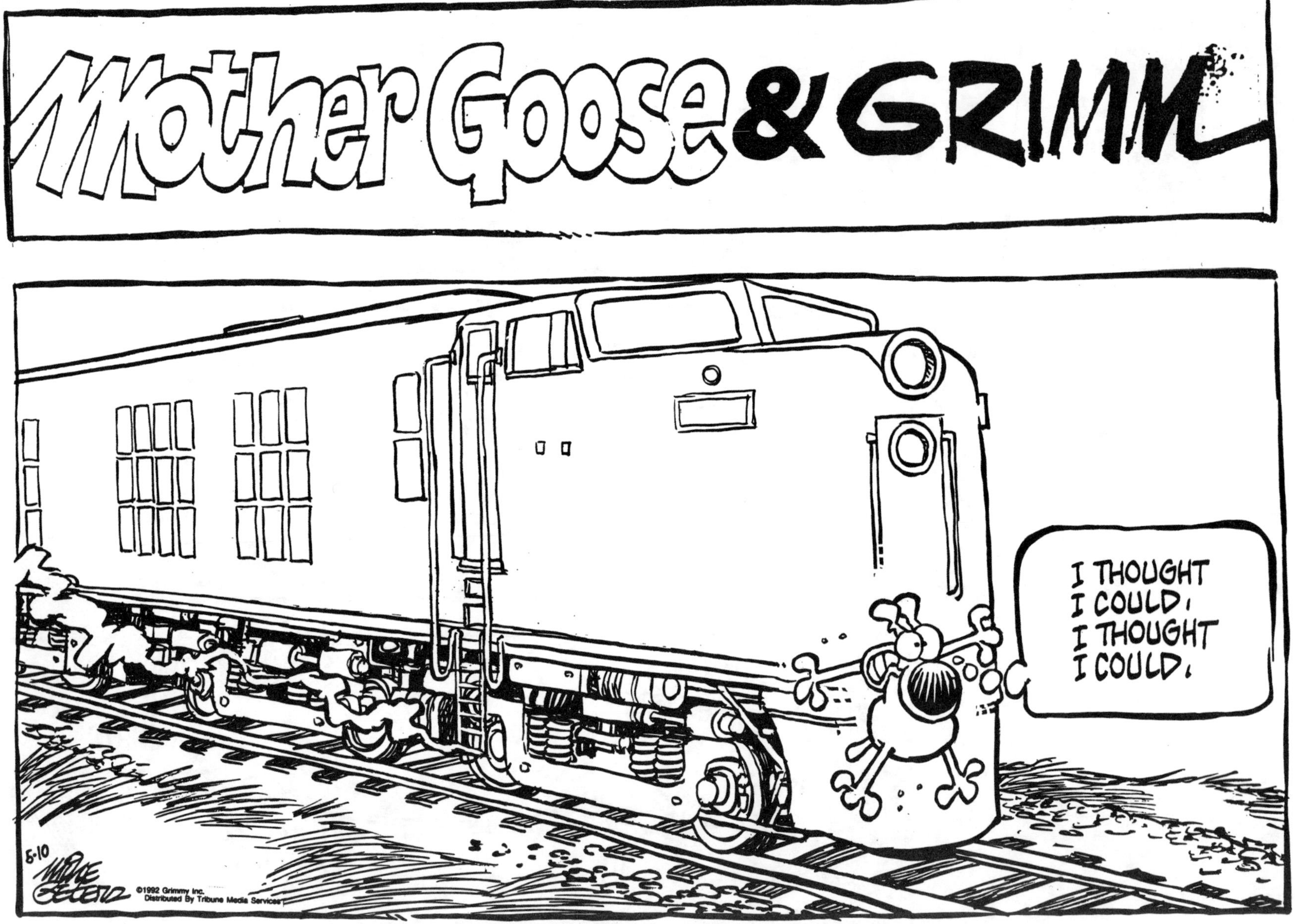
Mother Goose & GRIMM
I THOUGHT I COULD, I THOUGHT I COULD.
5-10
©1992 Grimmy Inc.
Distributed By Tribune Media Services

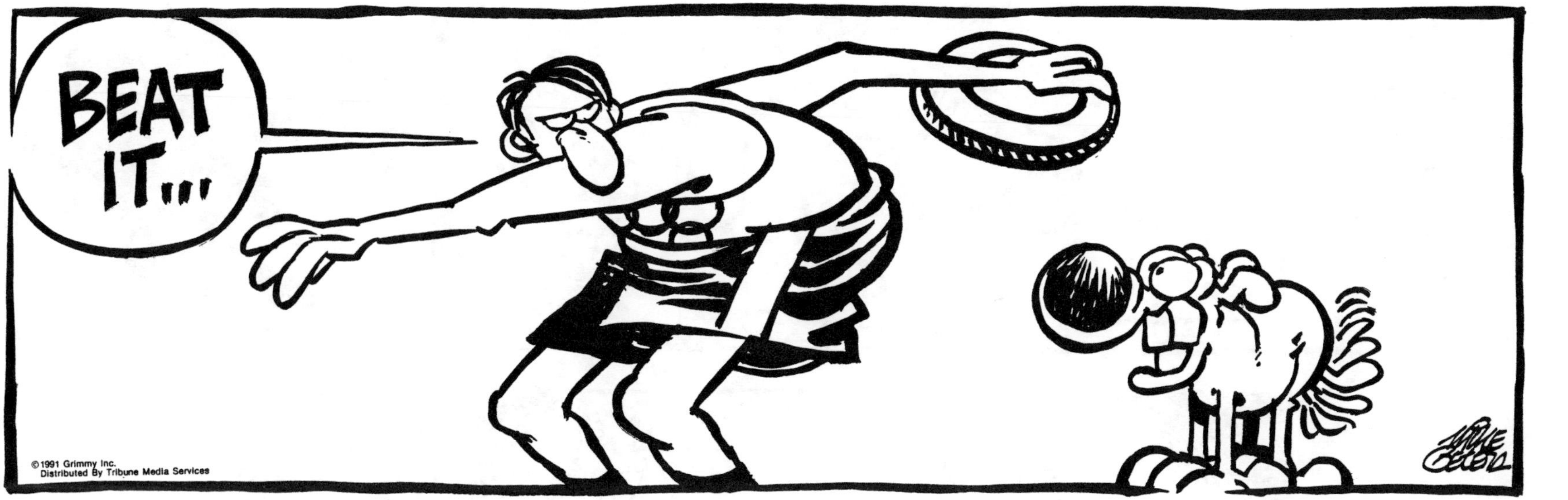
BEAT IT...



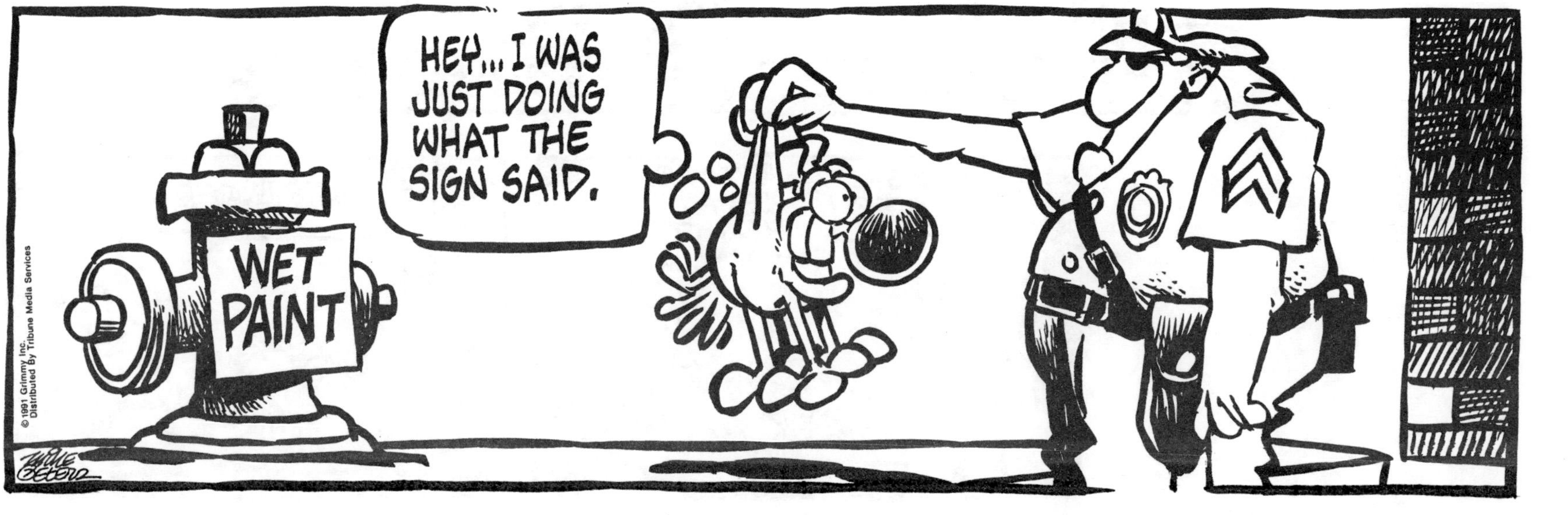
WET PAINT
HEY... I WAS JUST DOING WHAT THE SIGN SAID.

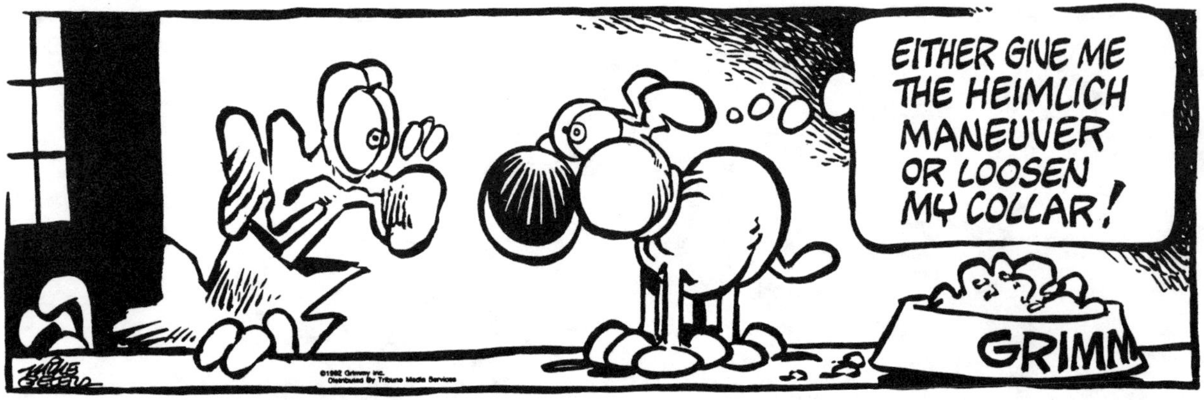
EITHER GIVE ME THE HEIMLICH MANEUVER OR LOOSEN MY COLLAR!
GRIMM

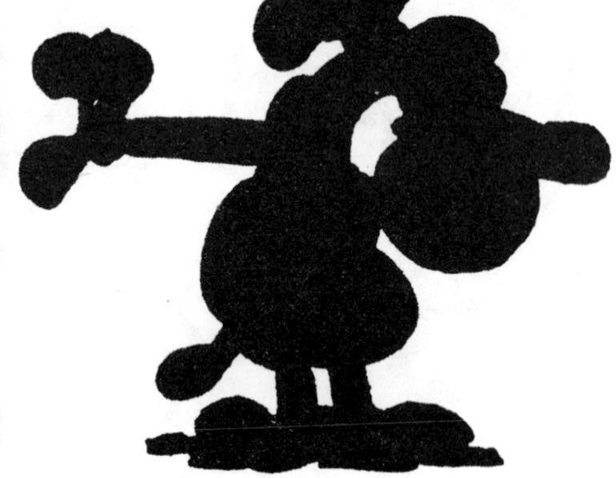

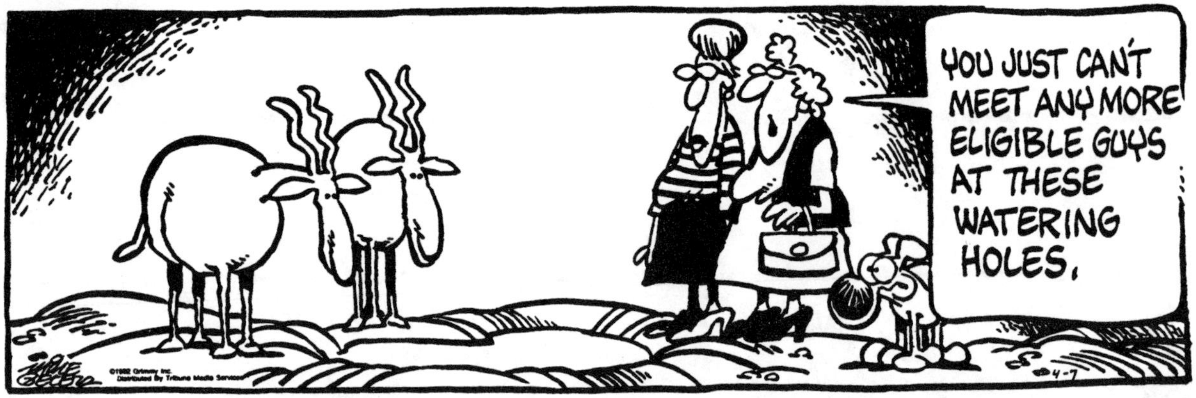
YOU JUST CAN'T MEET ANY MORE ELIGIBLE GUYS AT THESE WATERING HOLES.

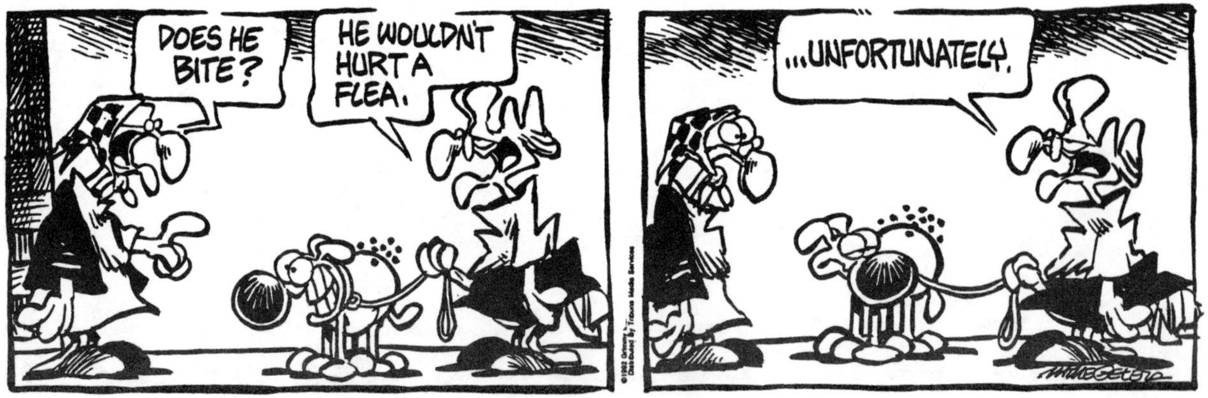
DOES HE BITE?
HE WOULDN'T HURT A FLEA.
...UNFORTUNATELY.

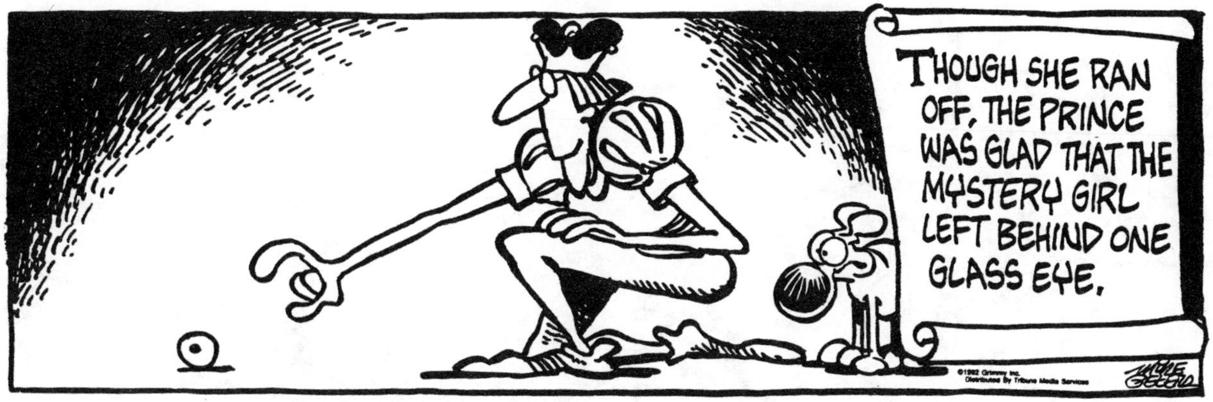
THOUGH SHE RAN OFF, THE PRINCE WAS GLAD THAT THE MYSTERY GIRL LEFT BEHIND ONE GLASS EYE.
©1992 Grimmy Inc. Distributed By Tribune Media Services

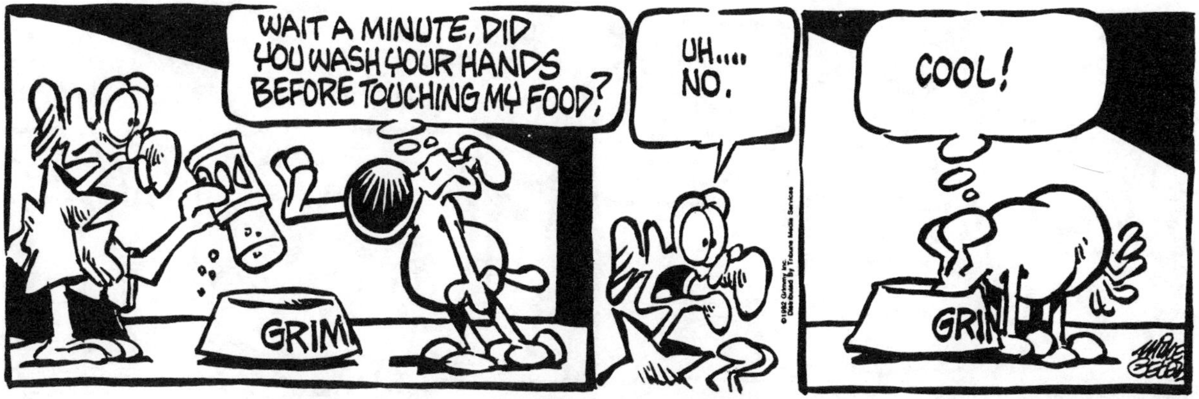
WAIT A MINUTE, DID YOU WASH YOUR HANDS BEFORE TOUCHING MY FOOD?
GRIM
UH.... NO.
©1992 Grimmy Inc. Distributed By Tribune Media Services
COOL!
GRIM

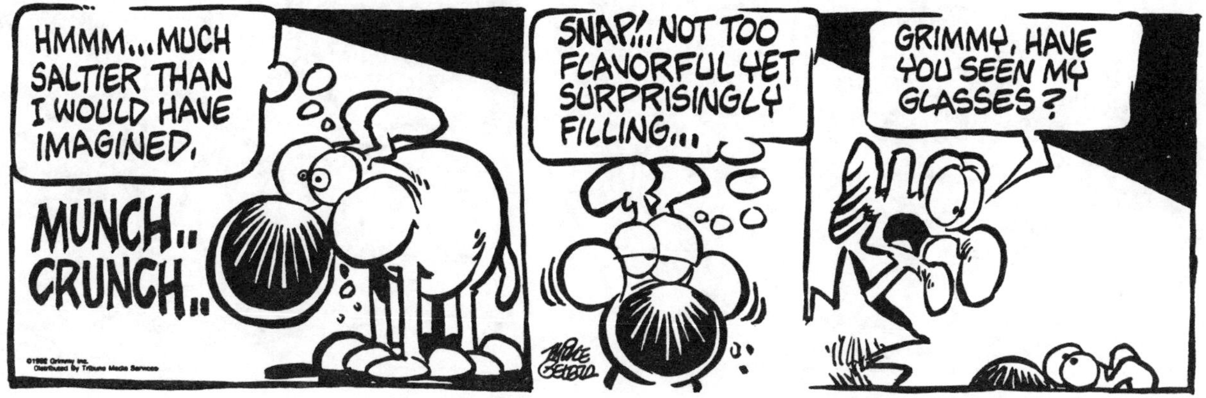
HMMM...MUCH SALTIER THAN I WOULD HAVE IMAGINED.
MUNCH.. CRUNCH..
©1992 Grimmy Inc. Distributed By Tribune Media Services
SNAP!..NOT TOO FLAVORFUL YET SURPRISINGLY FILLING...
GRIMMY, HAVE YOU SEEN MY GLASSES?

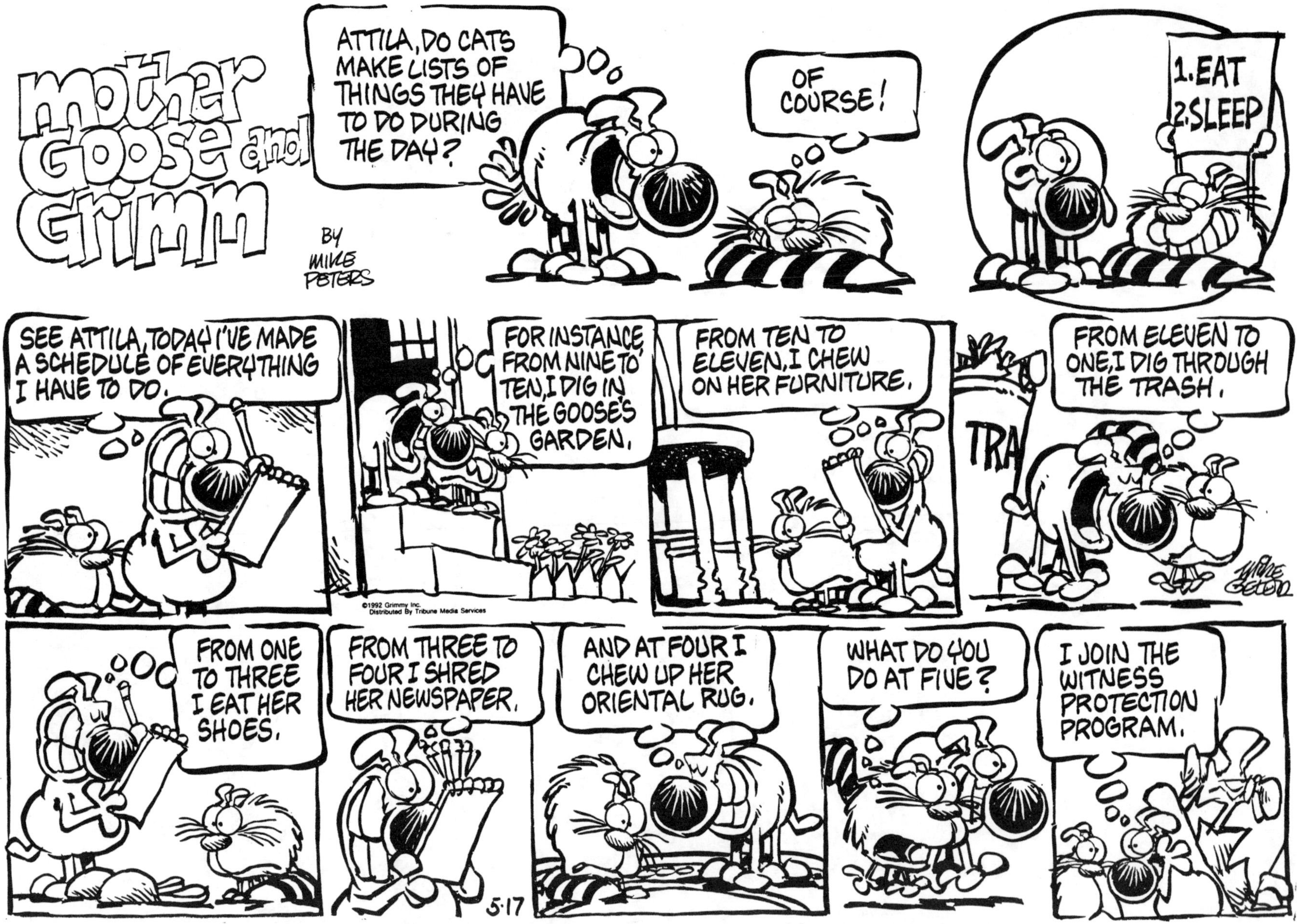
Mother Goose and Grimm
BY MIKE PETERS
ATTILA, DO CATS MAKE LISTS OF THINGS THEY HAVE TO DO DURING THE DAY?
OF COURSE!
1. EAT
2. SLEEP
SEE ATTILA, TODAY I'VE MADE A SCHEDULE OF EVERYTHING I HAVE TO DO.
FOR INSTANCE, FROM NINE TO TEN, I DIG IN THE GOOSE'S GARDEN.
FROM TEN TO ELEVEN, I CHEW ON HER FURNITURE.
FROM ELEVEN TO ONE, I DIG THROUGH THE TRASH.
TRA
FROM ONE TO THREE I EAT HER SHOES.
FROM THREE TO FOUR I SHRED HER NEWSPAPER.
AND AT FOUR I CHEW UP HER ORIENTAL RUG.
WHAT DO YOU DO AT FIVE?
I JOIN THE WITNESS PROTECTION PROGRAM.
5·17

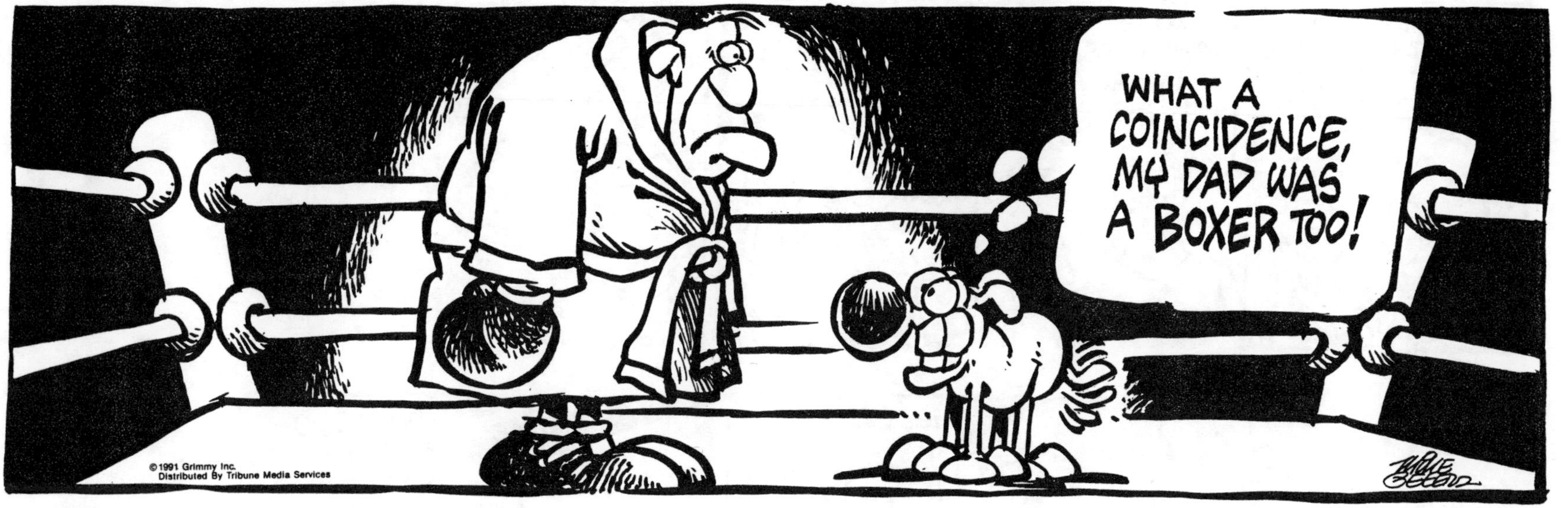
WHAT A COINCIDENCE, MY DAD WAS A BOXER TOO!
© 1991 Grimmy Inc. Distributed By Tribune Media Services

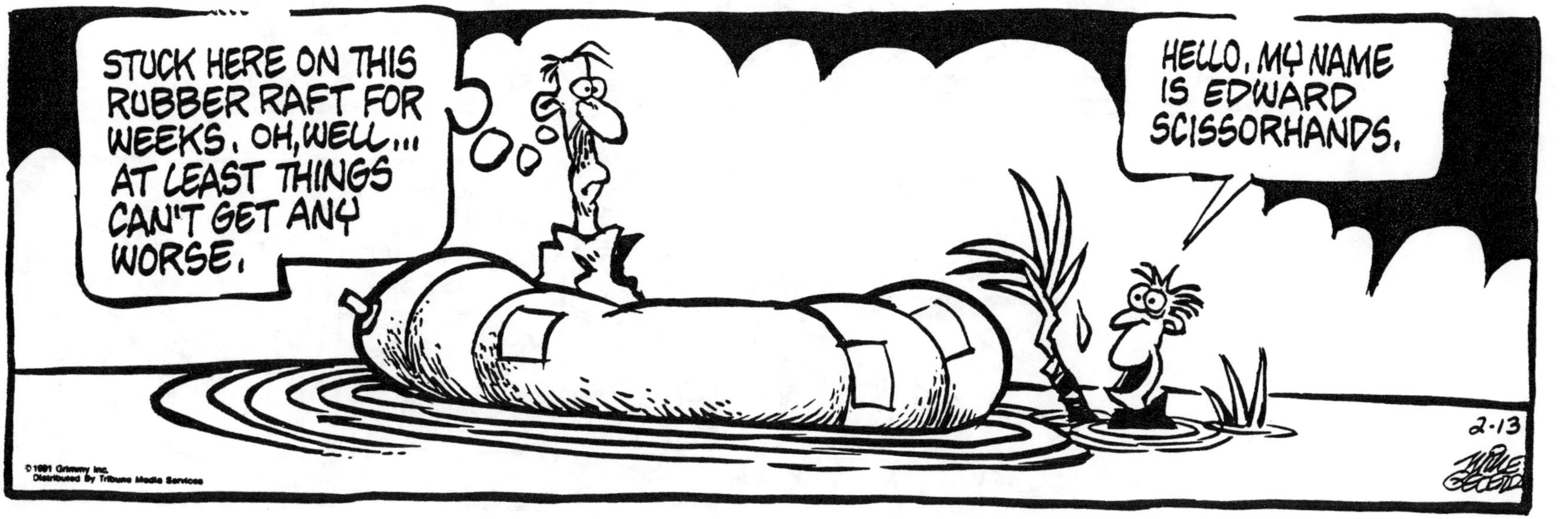
STUCK HERE ON THIS RUBBER RAFT FOR WEEKS. OH, WELL... AT LEAST THINGS CAN'T GET ANY WORSE.
HELLO, MY NAME IS EDWARD SCISSORHANDS.
2-13
© 1991 Grimmy Inc. Distributed By Tribune Media Services

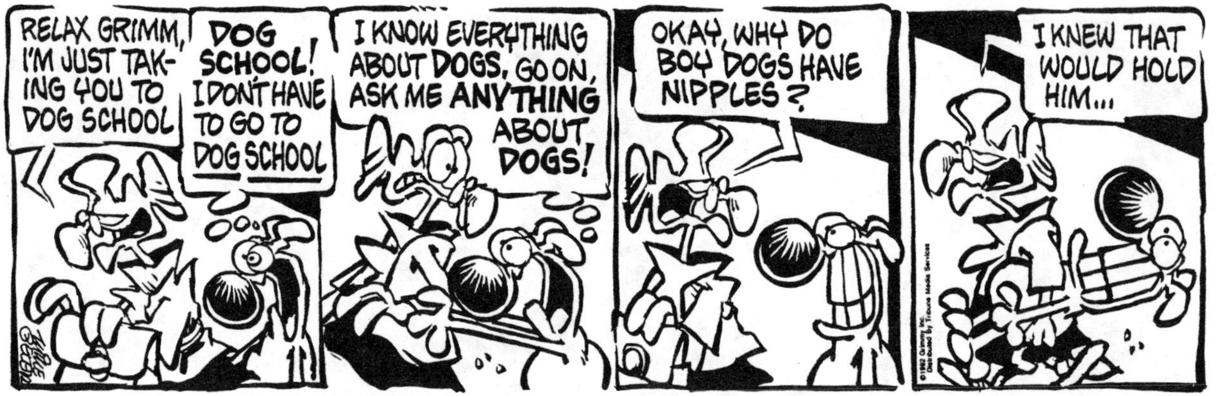
RELAX GRIMM, I'M JUST TAKING YOU TO DOG SCHOOL
DOG SCHOOL! I DON'T HAVE TO GO TO DOG SCHOOL
I KNOW EVERYTHING ABOUT DOGS, GO ON, ASK ME ANYTHING ABOUT DOGS!
OKAY, WHY DO BOY DOGS HAVE NIPPLES?
I KNEW THAT WOULD HOLD HIM...

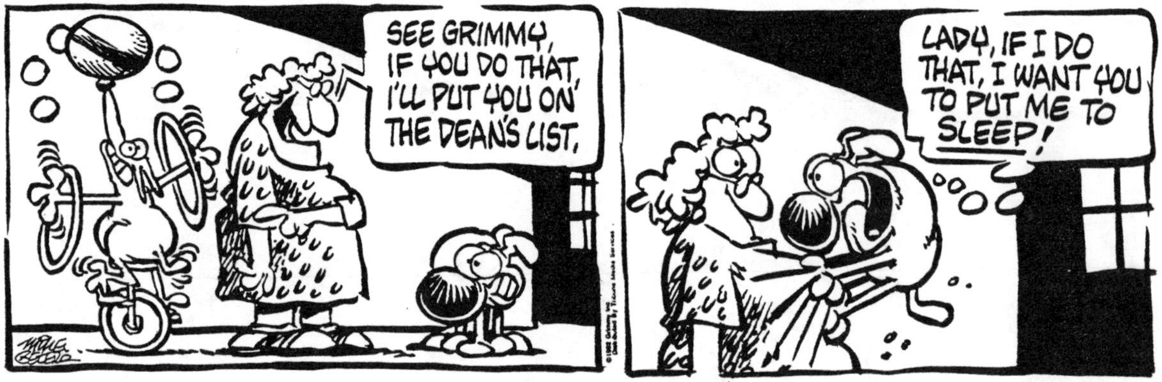
SEE GRIMMY, IF YOU DO THAT, I'LL PUT YOU ON THE DEAN'S LIST.
LADY, IF I DO THAT, I WANT YOU TO PUT ME TO SLEEP!

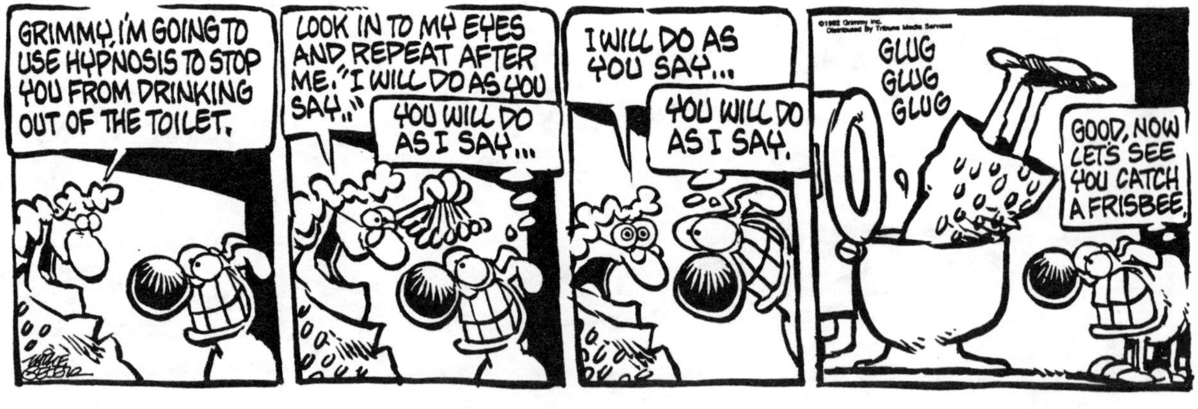
GRIMMY, I'M GOING TO USE HYPNOSIS TO STOP YOU FROM DRINKING OUT OF THE TOILET.
LOOK IN TO MY EYES AND REPEAT AFTER ME. "I WILL DO AS YOU SAY."
YOU WILL DO AS I SAY...
I WILL DO AS YOU SAY...
YOU WILL DO AS I SAY.
GLUG GLUG GLUG
GOOD, NOW LET'S SEE YOU CATCH A FRISBEE.

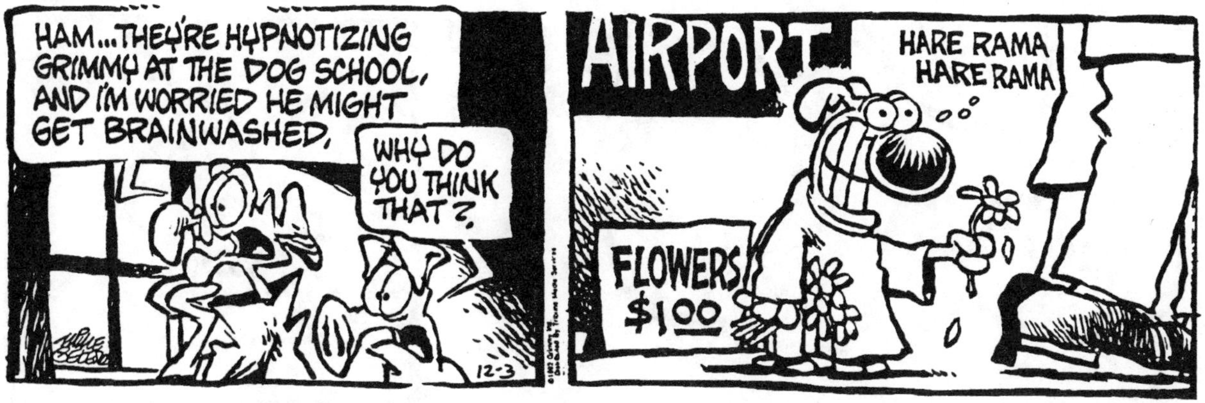
HAM...THEY'RE HYPNOTIZING GRIMMY AT THE DOG SCHOOL, AND I'M WORRIED HE MIGHT GET BRAINWASHED.
WHY DO YOU THINK THAT?
12-3
AIRPORT
HARE RAMA HARE RAMA
FLOWERS $1.00

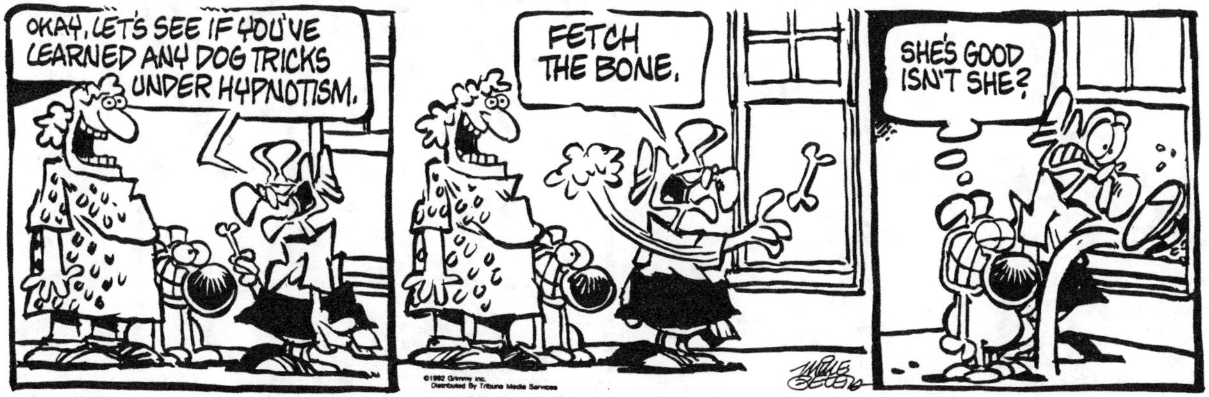
OKAY, LET'S SEE IF YOU'VE LEARNED ANY DOG TRICKS UNDER HYPNOTISM.
FETCH THE BONE.
©1992 Grimmy Inc. Distributed By Tribune Media Services
SHE'S GOOD ISN'T SHE?

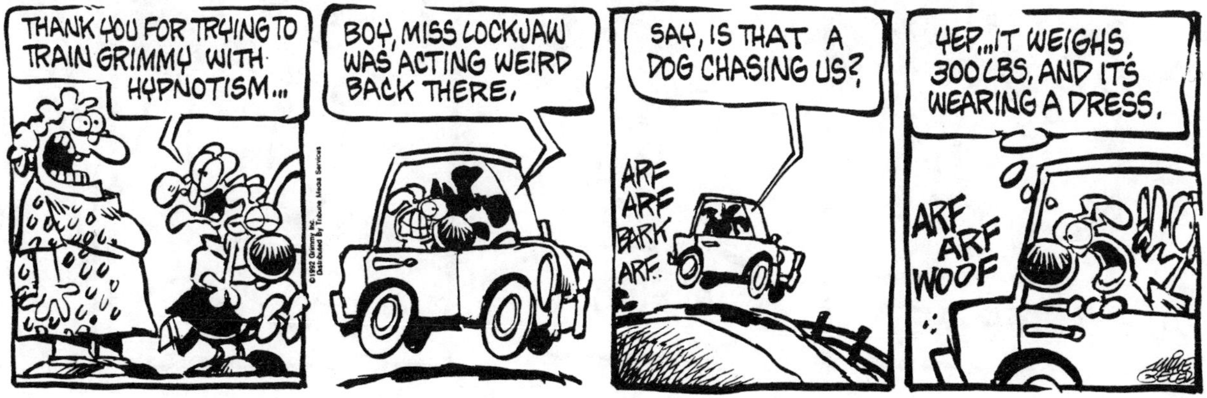
THANK YOU FOR TRYING TO TRAIN GRIMMY WITH HYPNOTISM...
BOY, MISS LOCKJAW WAS ACTING WEIRD BACK THERE.
SAY, IS THAT A DOG CHASING US?
ARF ARF BARK ARF.
YEP...IT WEIGHS 300 LBS. AND IT'S WEARING A DRESS.
ARF ARF WOOF

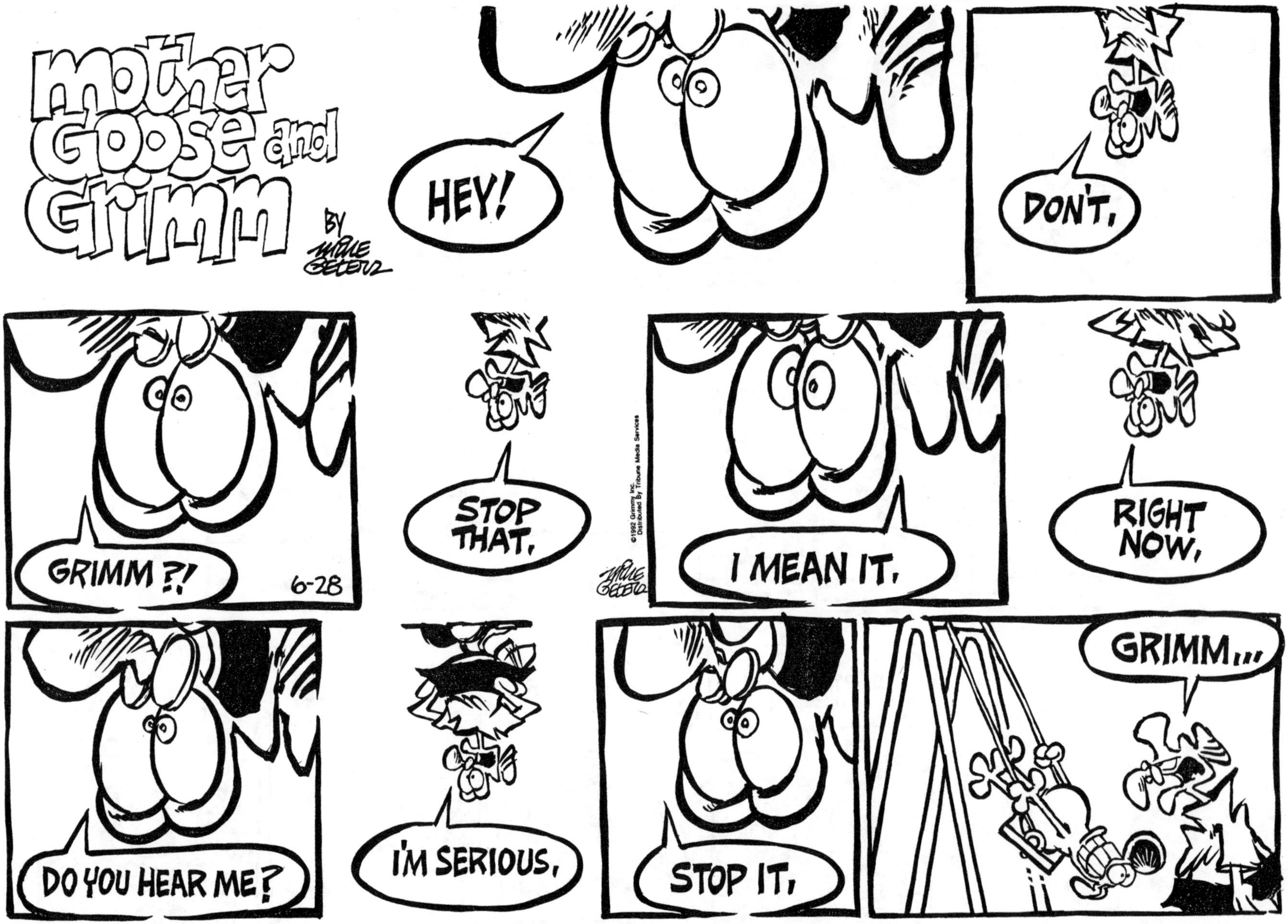
mother Goose and Grimm
BY MIKE PETERS
HEY!
DON'T.
GRIMM ?!
6-28
STOP THAT.
©1992 Grimmy Inc.
Distributed By Tribune Media Services
I MEAN IT.
RIGHT NOW.
DO YOU HEAR ME?
I'M SERIOUS.
STOP IT.
GRIMM...

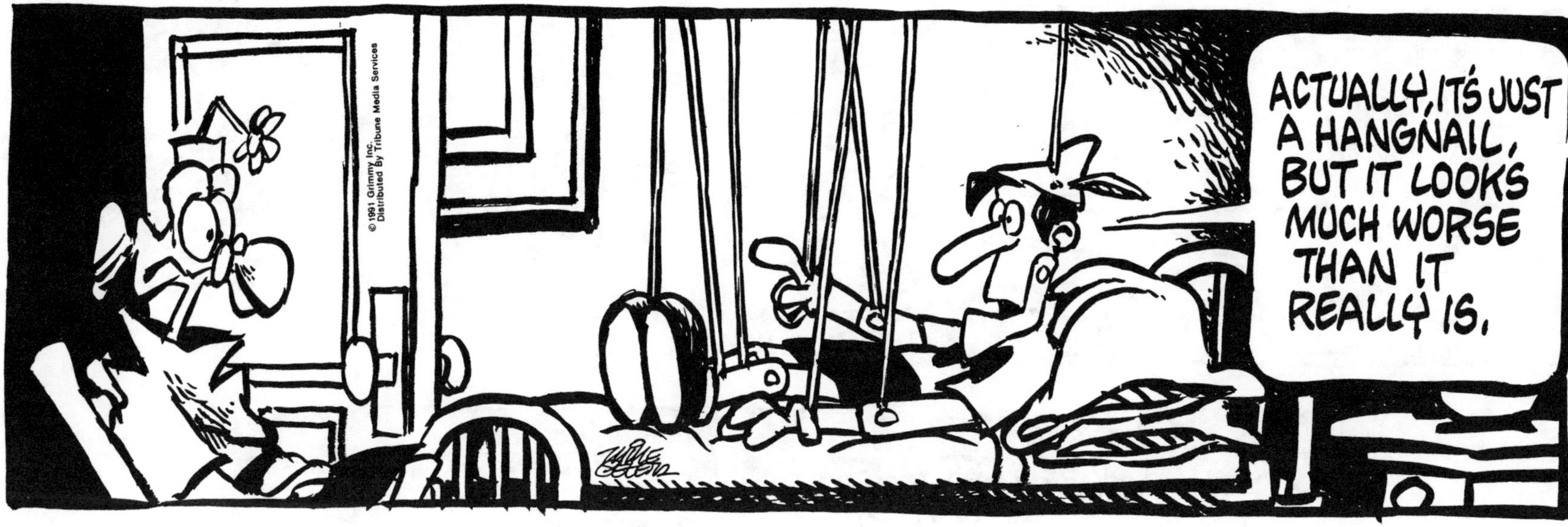
© 1991 Grimmy Inc.
Distributed By Tribune Media Services
ACTUALLY, IT'S JUST A HANGNAIL, BUT IT LOOKS MUCH WORSE THAN IT REALLY IS.

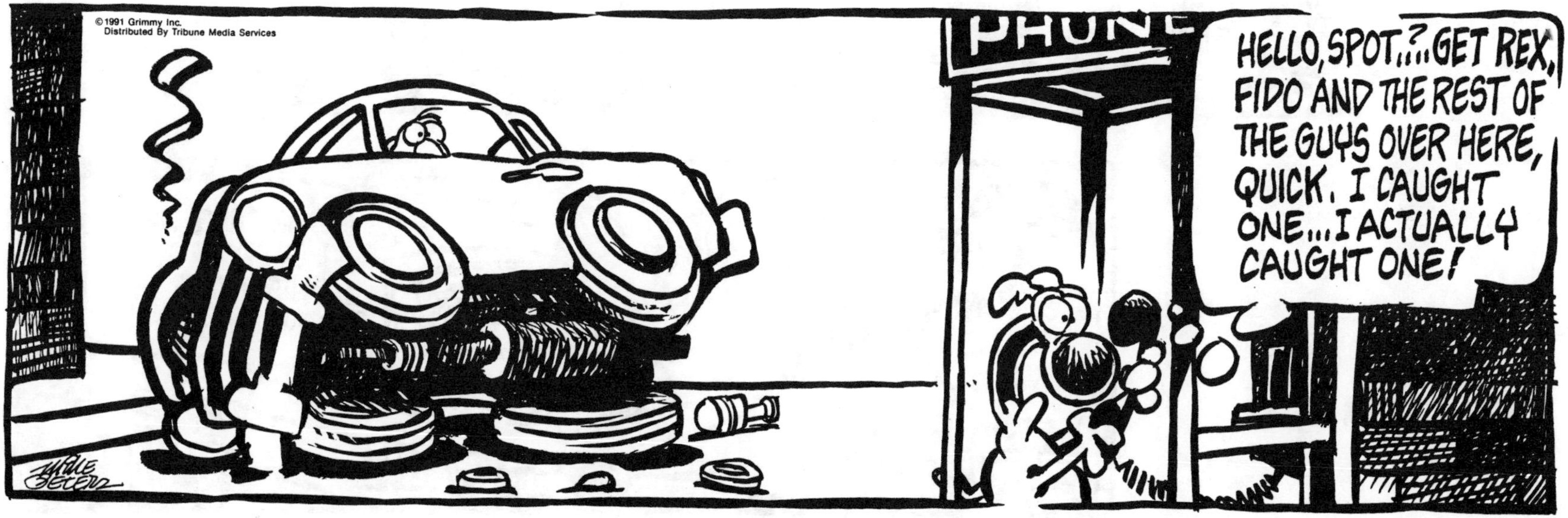
© 1991 Grimmy Inc.
Distributed By Tribune Media Services
PHONE
HELLO, SPOT..?..GET REX, FIDO AND THE REST OF THE GUYS OVER HERE, QUICK. I CAUGHT ONE...I ACTUALLY CAUGHT ONE!

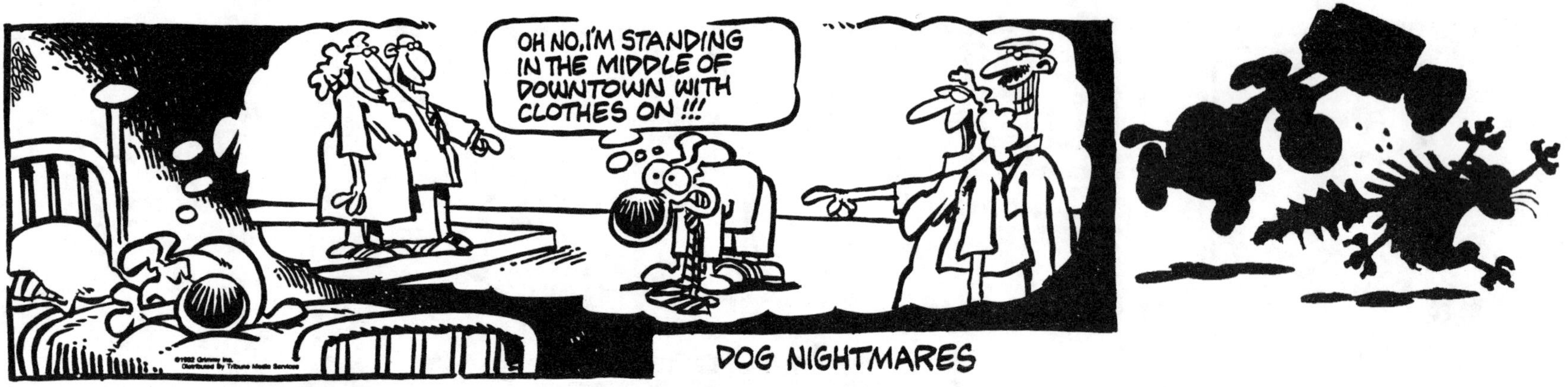
OH NO, I'M STANDING IN THE MIDDLE OF DOWNTOWN WITH CLOTHES ON !!!
DOG NIGHTMARES

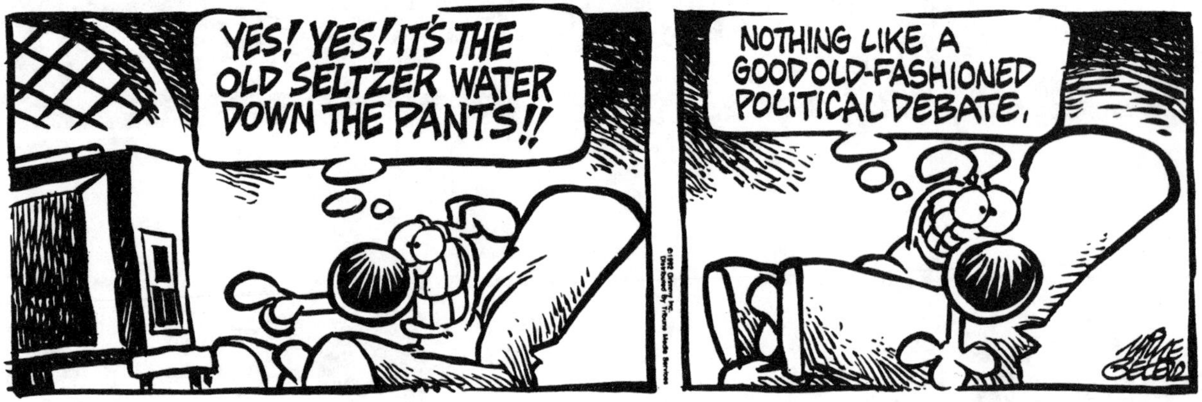
YES! YES! IT'S THE OLD SELTZER WATER DOWN THE PANTS !!
NOTHING LIKE A GOOD OLD-FASHIONED POLITICAL DEBATE.

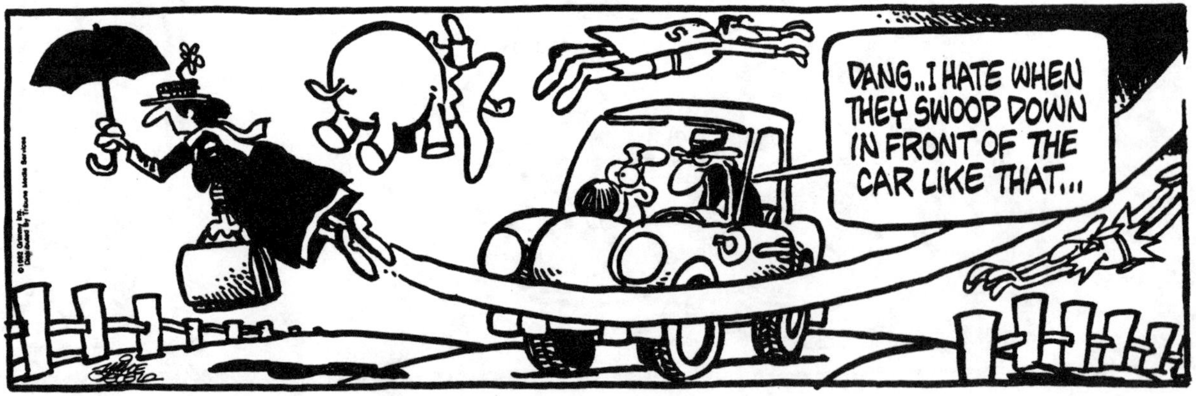
DANG.. I HATE WHEN THEY SWOOP DOWN IN FRONT OF THE CAR LIKE THAT...

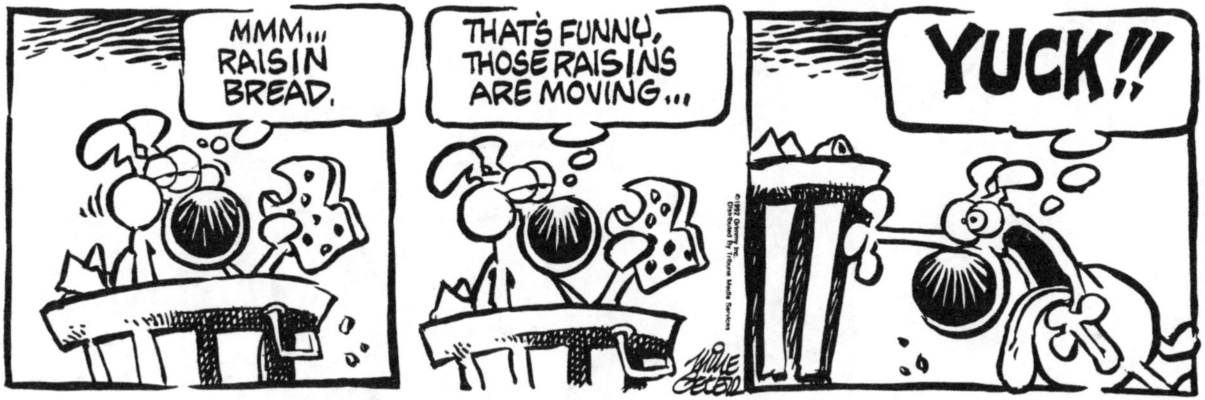
MMM... RAISIN BREAD.
THAT'S FUNNY, THOSE RAISINS ARE MOVING...
YUCK!!

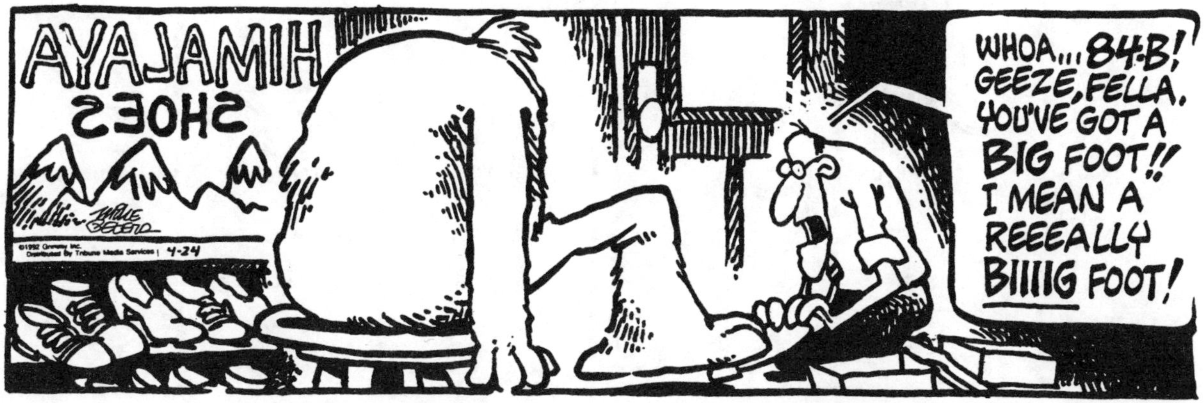
WHOA... 84-B! GEEZE, FELLA, YOU'VE GOT A BIG FOOT!! I MEAN A REEEALLY BIIIIG FOOT!
4-24

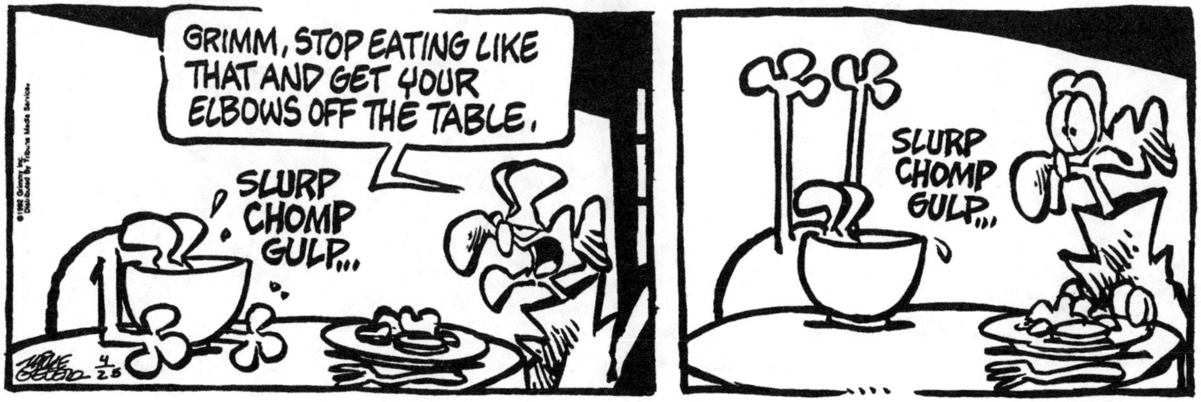
GRIMM, STOP EATING LIKE THAT AND GET YOUR ELBOWS OFF THE TABLE.
SLURP CHOMP GULP...
4/25
SLURP CHOMP GULP...

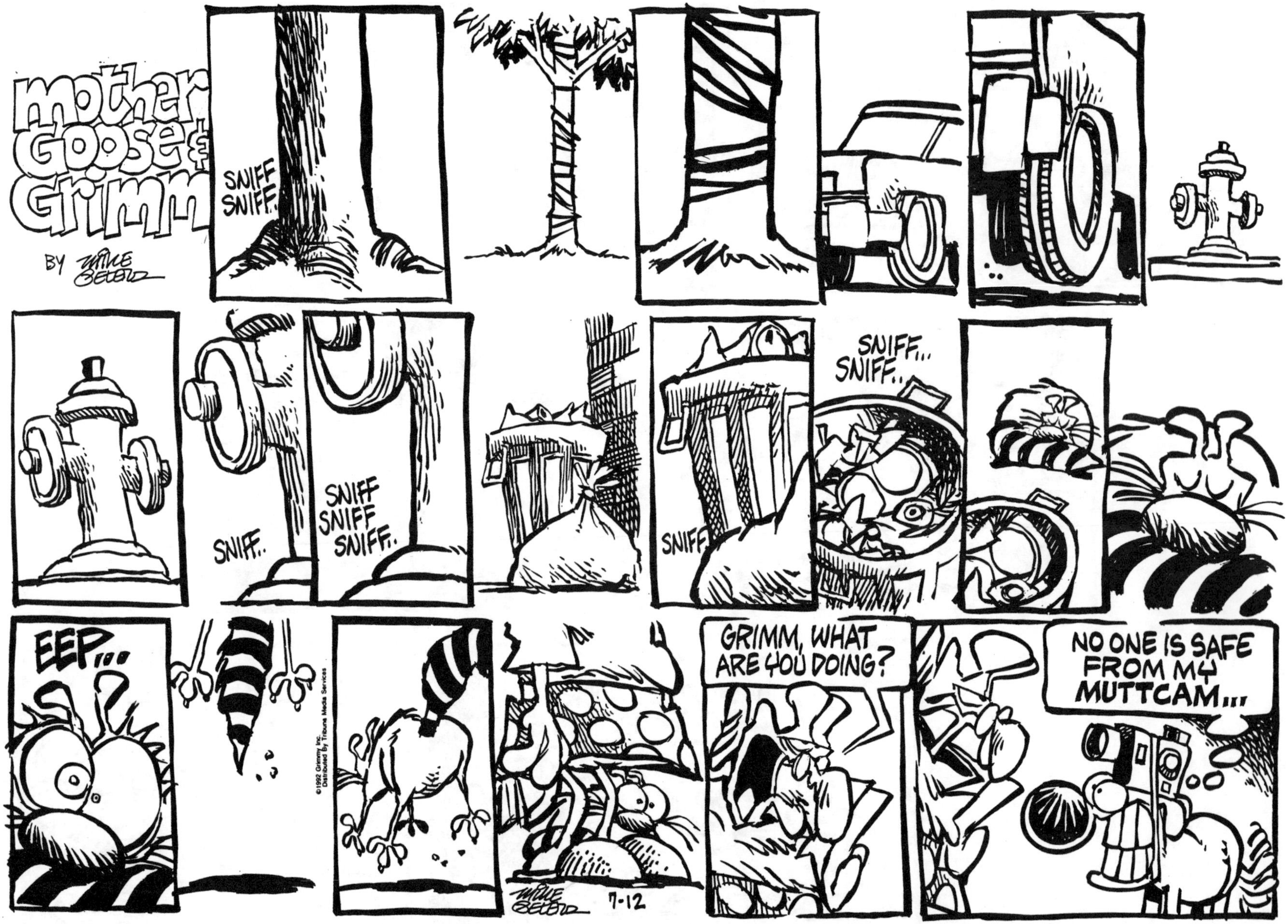
mother Goose & Grimm
BY MIKE PETERS
SNIFF SNIFF
SNIFF..
SNIFF SNIFF SNIFF..
SNIFF
SNIFF... SNIFF..
EEP...
©1992 Grimmy Inc.
Distributed By Tribune Media Services
7-12
GRIMM, WHAT ARE YOU DOING?
NO ONE IS SAFE FROM MY MUTTCAM...

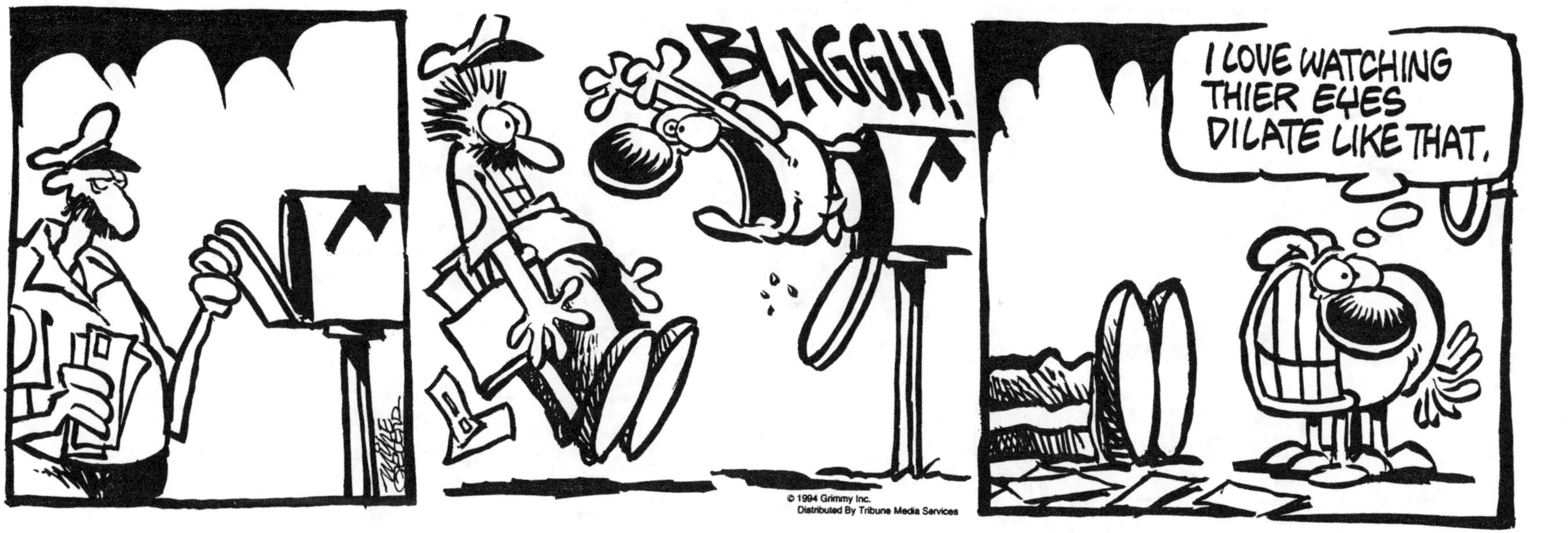
BLAGGH!
I LOVE WATCHING THIER EYES DILATE LIKE THAT.
© 1994 Grimmy Inc.
Distributed By Tribune Media Services

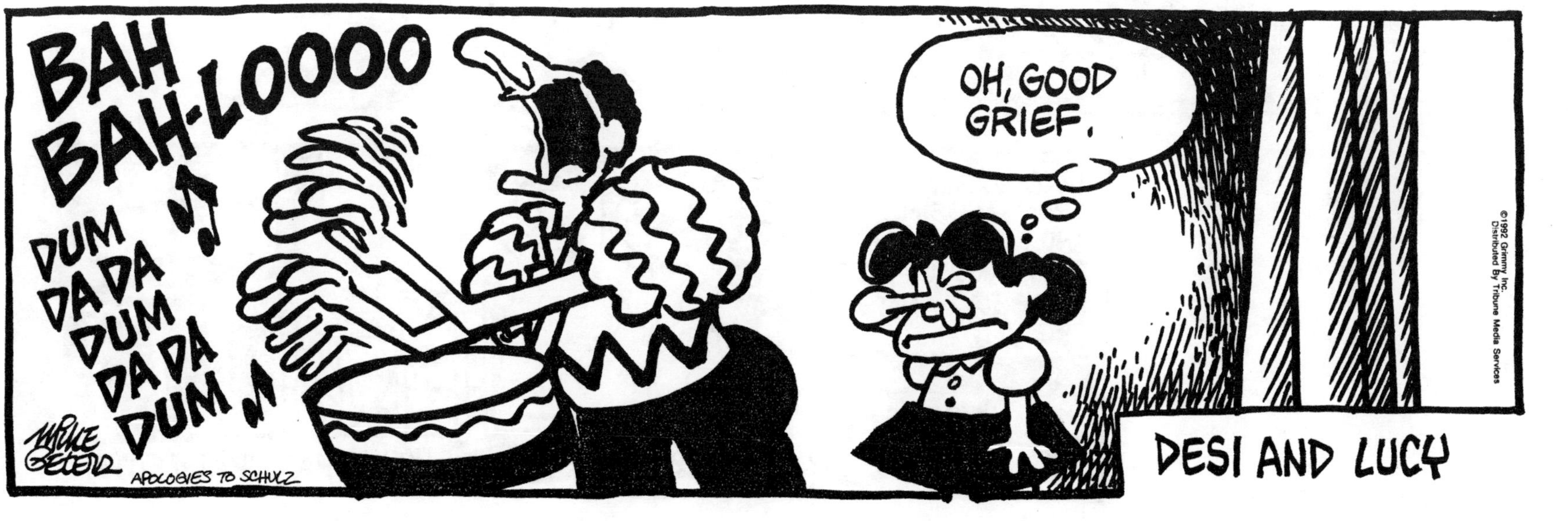
BAH BAH-LOOOO
DUM DA DA DUM DA DA DUM
OH, GOOD GRIEF.
APOLOGIES TO SCHULZ
©1992 Grimmy Inc.
Distributed By Tribune Media Services
DESI AND LUCY

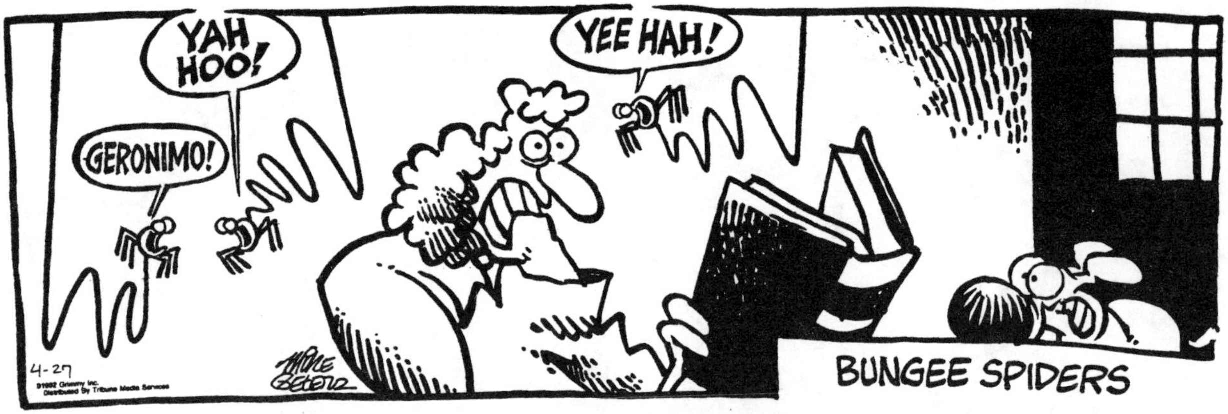
GERONIMO!
YAH HOO!
YEE HAH!
4-27
©1992 Grimmy Inc. Distributed By Tribune Media Services
BUNGEE SPIDERS

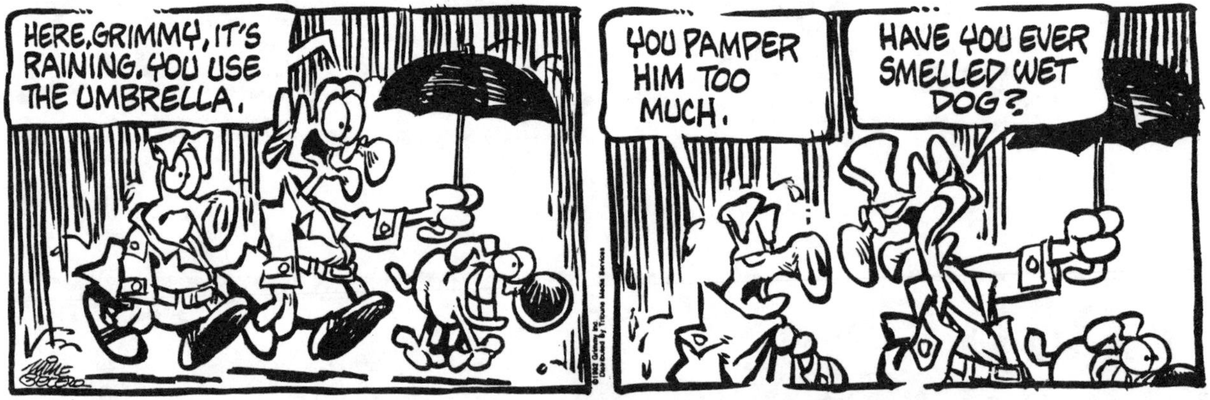
HERE, GRIMMY, IT'S RAINING. YOU USE THE UMBRELLA.
YOU PAMPER HIM TOO MUCH.
HAVE YOU EVER SMELLED WET DOG?
©1992 Grimmy Inc. Distributed By Tribune Media Services

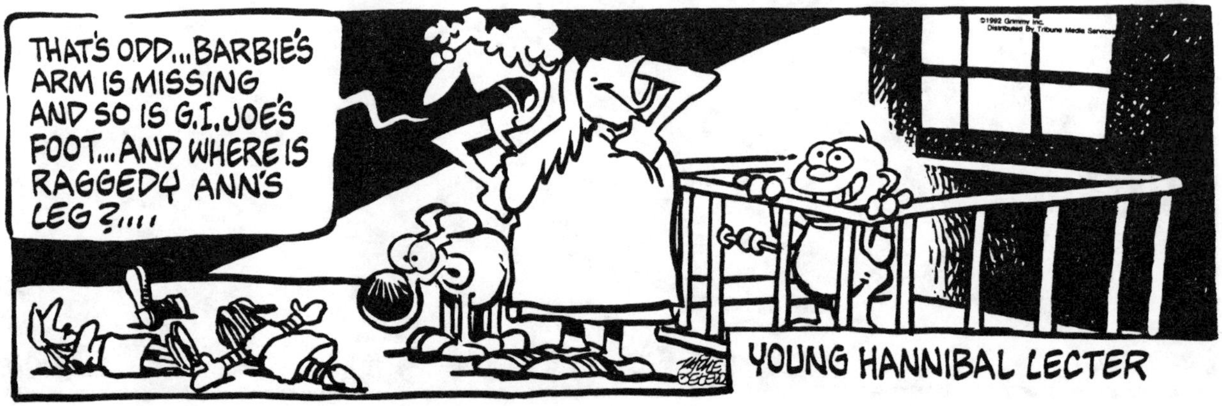
THAT'S ODD... BARBIE'S ARM IS MISSING AND SO IS G.I. JOE'S FOOT... AND WHERE IS RAGGEDY ANN'S LEG?....
©1992 Grimmy Inc. Distributed By Tribune Media Services
YOUNG HANNIBAL LECTER

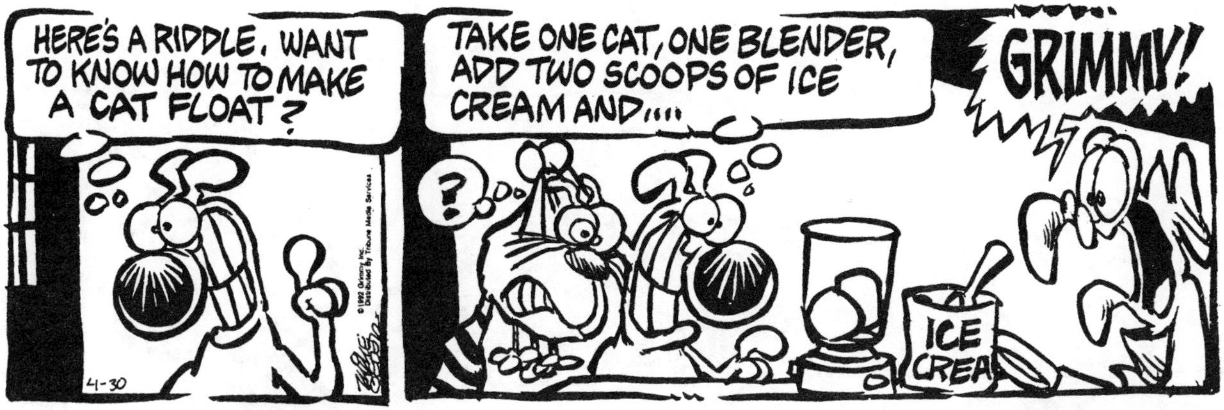
HERE'S A RIDDLE. WANT TO KNOW HOW TO MAKE A CAT FLOAT?
4-30
©1992 Grimmy Inc. Distributed By Tribune Media Services
TAKE ONE CAT, ONE BLENDER, ADD TWO SCOOPS OF ICE CREAM AND....
GRIMMY!
ICE CREA

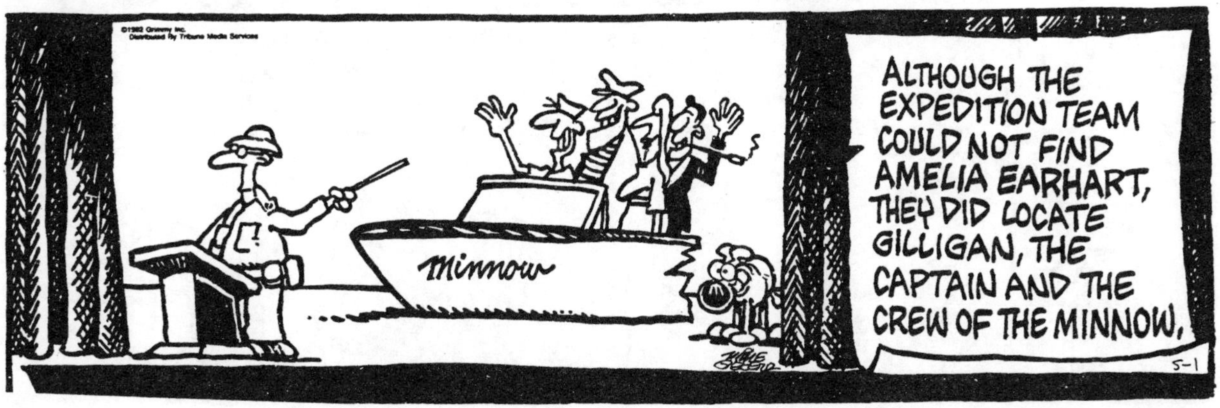
©1992 Grimmy Inc. Distributed By Tribune Media Services
MINNOW
ALTHOUGH THE EXPEDITION TEAM COULD NOT FIND AMELIA EARHART, THEY DID LOCATE GILLIGAN, THE CAPTAIN AND THE CREW OF THE MINNOW.
5-1

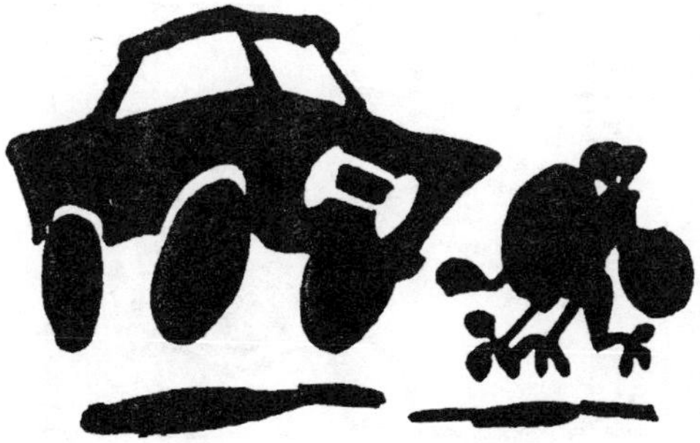

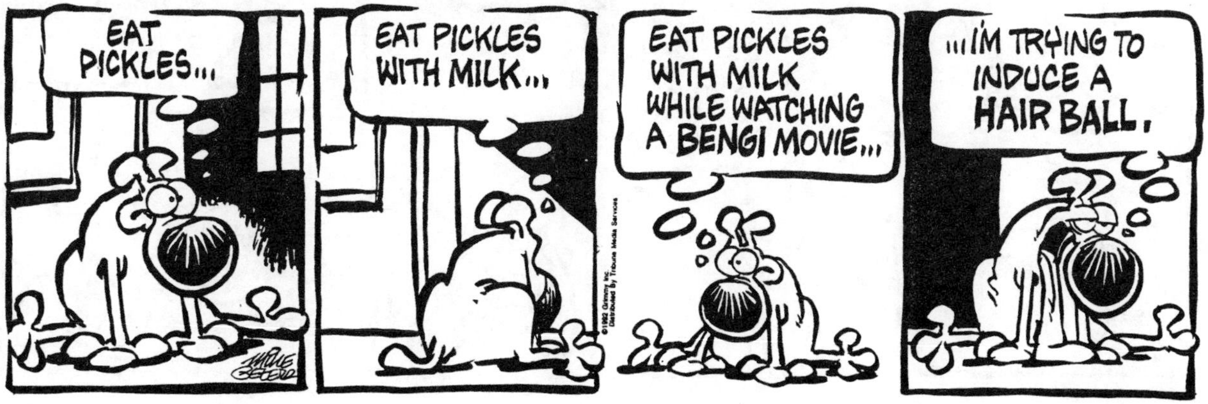
EAT PICKLES...
EAT PICKLES WITH MILK...
EAT PICKLES WITH MILK WHILE WATCHING A BENGI MOVIE...
©1992 Grimmy Inc. Distributed By Tribune Media Services
...I'M TRYING TO INDUCE A HAIR BALL.

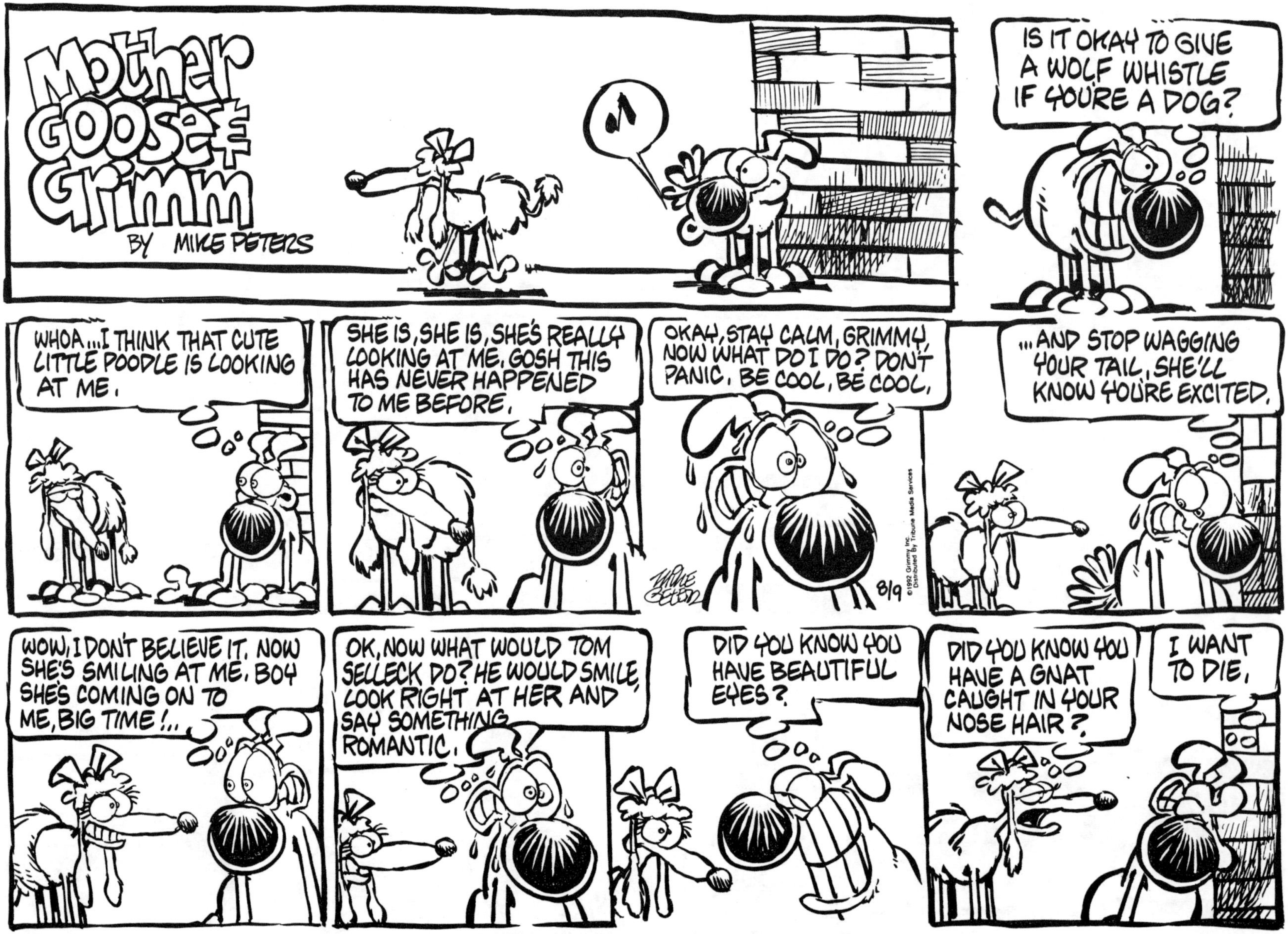
Mother Goose & Grimm
BY MIKE PETERS
IS IT OKAY TO GIVE A WOLF WHISTLE IF YOU'RE A DOG?
WHOA...I THINK THAT CUTE LITTLE POODLE IS LOOKING AT ME.
SHE IS, SHE IS, SHE'S REALLY LOOKING AT ME. GOSH THIS HAS NEVER HAPPENED TO ME BEFORE.
OKAY, STAY CALM, GRIMMY, NOW WHAT DO I DO? DON'T PANIC. BE COOL, BE COOL.
©1992 Grimmy Inc. Distributed By Tribune Media Services
8/9
...AND STOP WAGGING YOUR TAIL, SHE'LL KNOW YOU'RE EXCITED.
WOW, I DON'T BELIEVE IT. NOW SHE'S SMILING AT ME. BOY SHE'S COMING ON TO ME, BIG TIME!...
OK, NOW WHAT WOULD TOM SELLECK DO? HE WOULD SMILE, LOOK RIGHT AT HER AND SAY SOMETHING ROMANTIC.
DID YOU KNOW YOU HAVE BEAUTIFUL EYES?
DID YOU KNOW YOU HAVE A GNAT CAUGHT IN YOUR NOSE HAIR?
I WANT TO DIE.

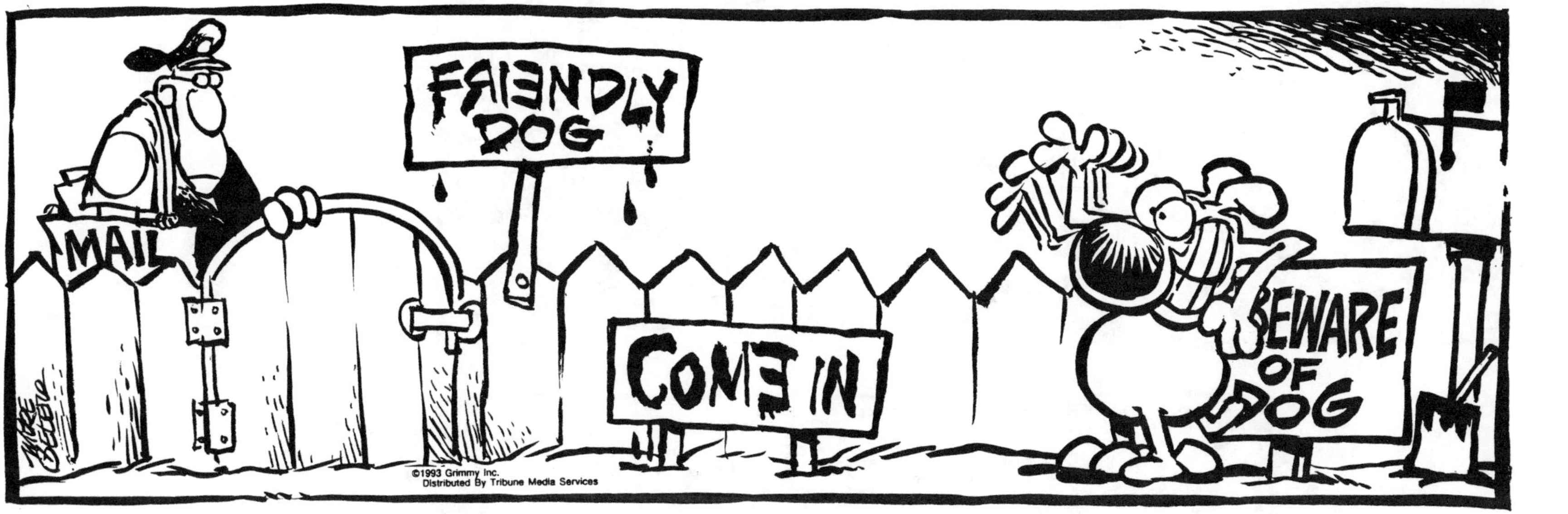
MAIL
FRIENDLY DOG
COME IN
BEWARE OF DOG
©1993 Grimmy Inc.
Distributed By Tribune Media Services

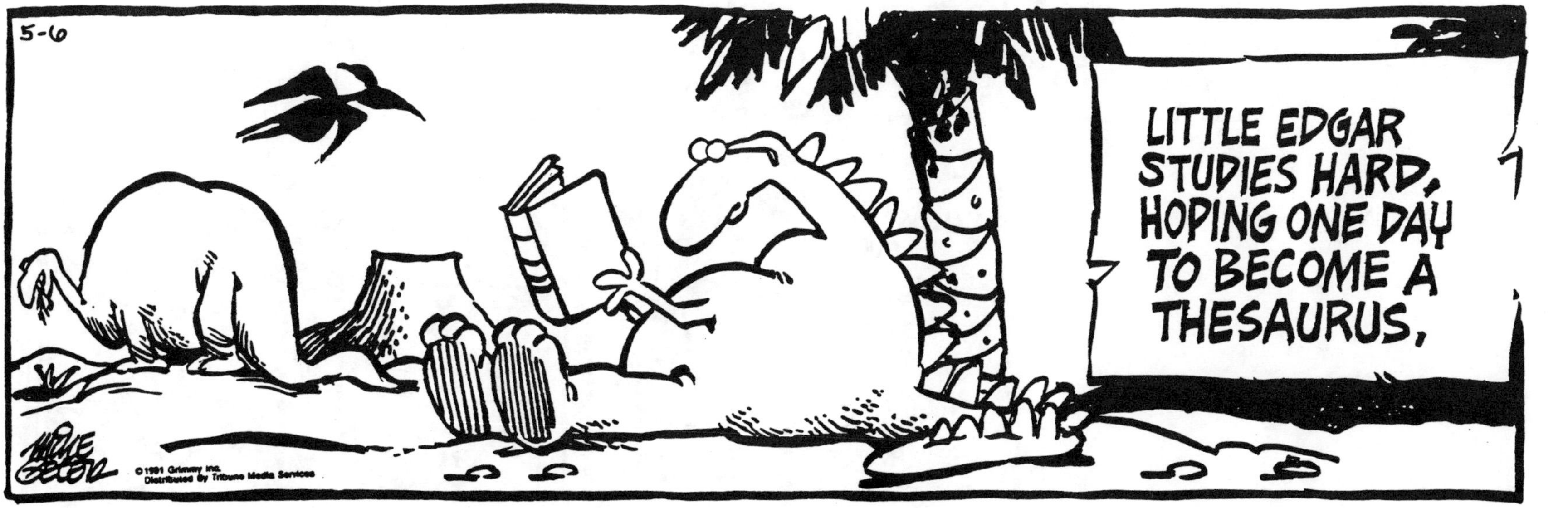
5-6
LITTLE EDGAR STUDIES HARD, HOPING ONE DAY TO BECOME A THESAURUS.
©1991 Grimmy Inc.
Distributed By Tribune Media Services

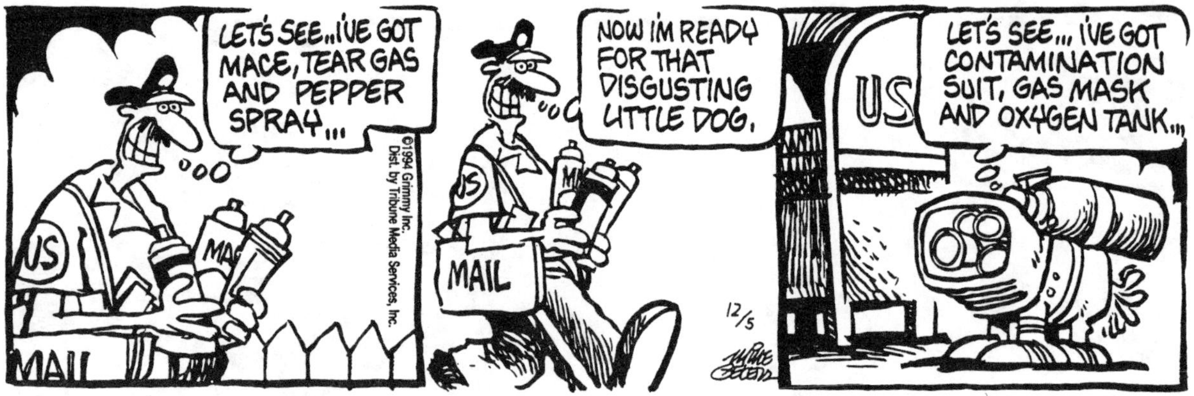
LET'S SEE...I'VE GOT MACE, TEAR GAS AND PEPPER SPRAY...
MAIL
©1994 Grimmy Inc. Dist. by Tribune Media Services, Inc.
NOW I'M READY FOR THAT DISGUSTING LITTLE DOG.
MAIL
12/5
US
LET'S SEE... I'VE GOT CONTAMINATION SUIT, GAS MASK AND OXYGEN TANK...

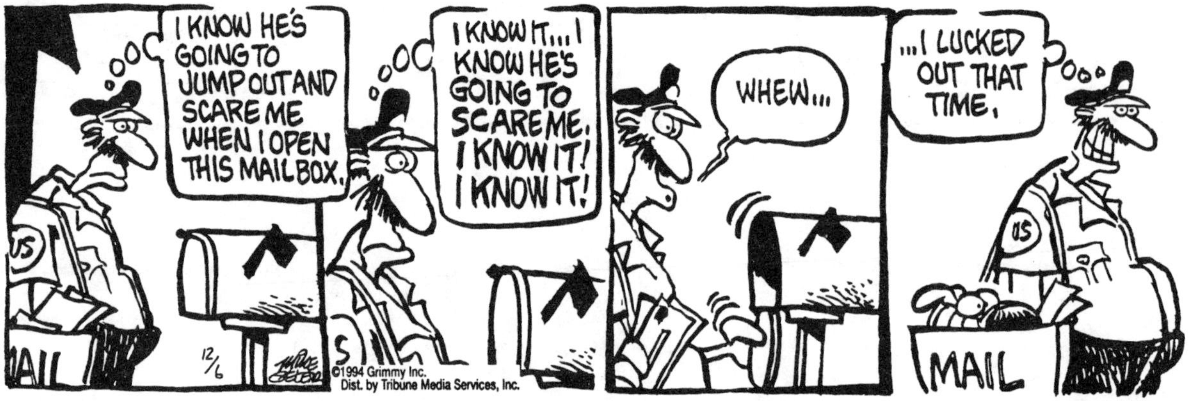
I KNOW HE'S GOING TO JUMP OUT AND SCARE ME WHEN I OPEN THIS MAILBOX.
12/6
I KNOW IT... I KNOW HE'S GOING TO SCARE ME. I KNOW IT! I KNOW IT!
©1994 Grimmy Inc. Dist. by Tribune Media Services, Inc.
WHEW...
...I LUCKED OUT THAT TIME.
MAIL

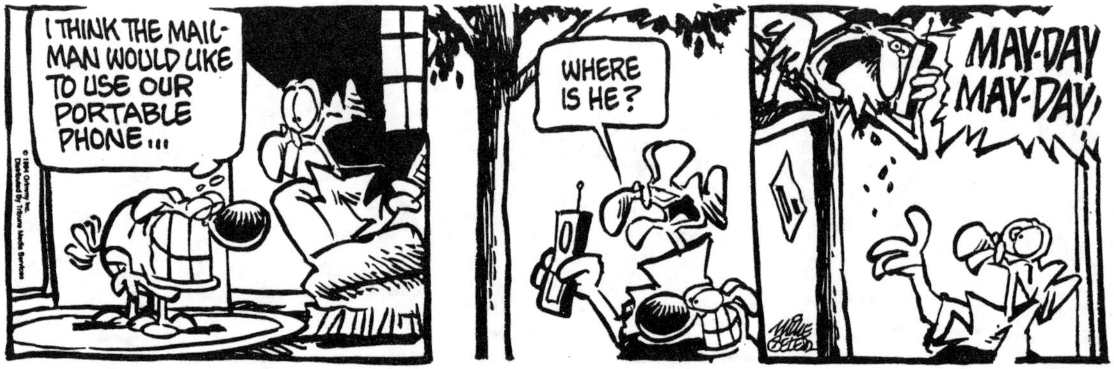
I THINK THE MAILMAN WOULD LIKE TO USE OUR PORTABLE PHONE...
WHERE IS HE?
MAY-DAY MAY-DAY!

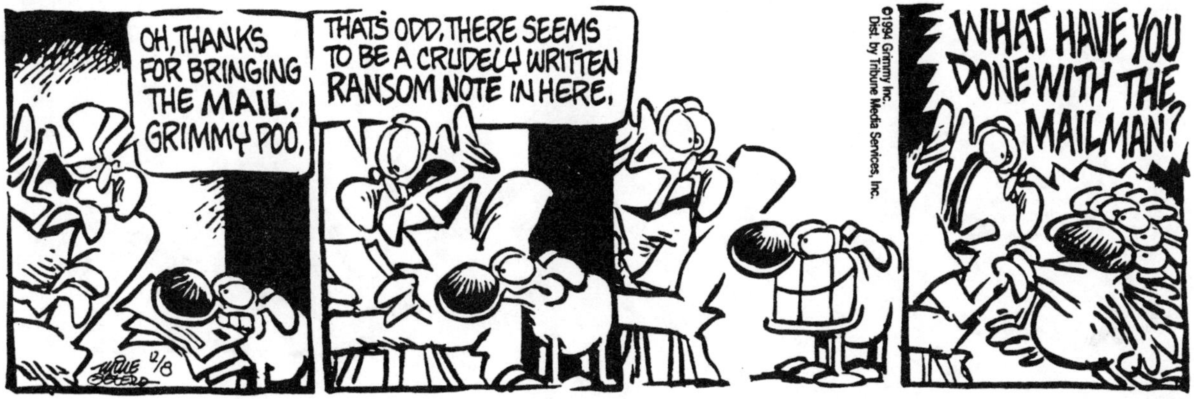
OH, THANKS FOR BRINGING THE MAIL, GRIMMY POO,
THATS ODD, THERE SEEMS TO BE A CRUDELY WRITTEN RANSOM NOTE IN HERE,
©1994 Grimmy Inc. Dist. by Tribune Media Services, Inc.
WHAT HAVE YOU DONE WITH THE MAILMAN?

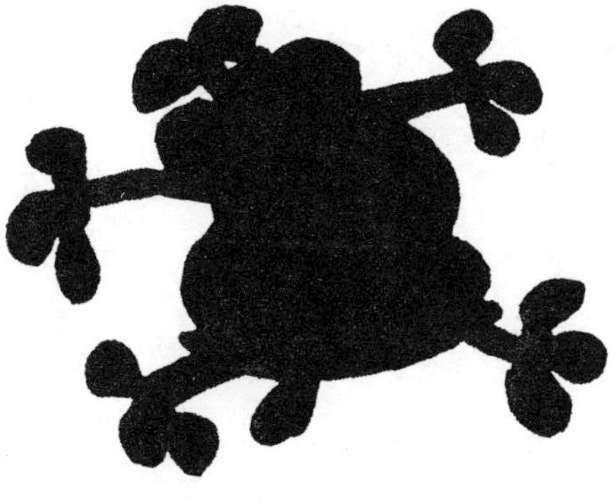

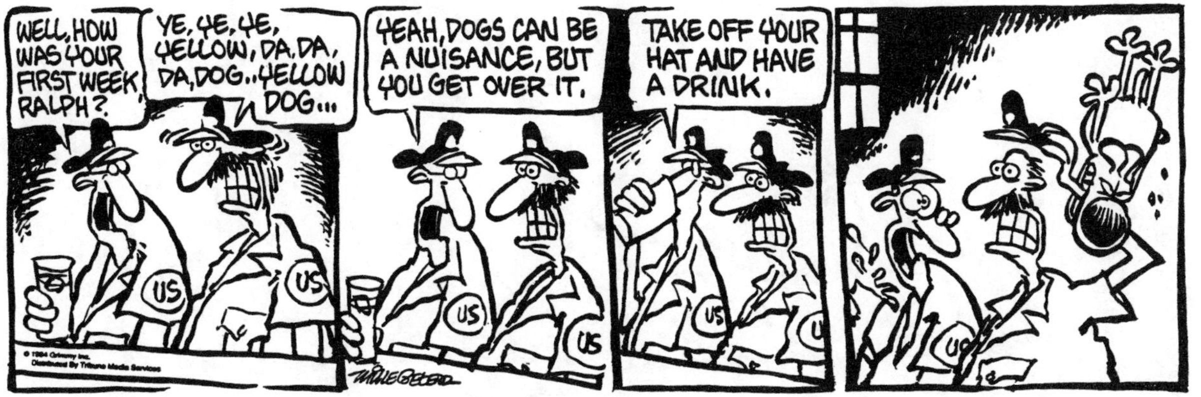
WELL, HOW WAS YOUR FIRST WEEK RALPH?
YE, YE, YE, YELLOW, DA, DA, DA, DOG.. YELLOW DOG...
YEAH, DOGS CAN BE A NUISANCE, BUT YOU GET OVER IT,
TAKE OFF YOUR HAT AND HAVE A DRINK.
US

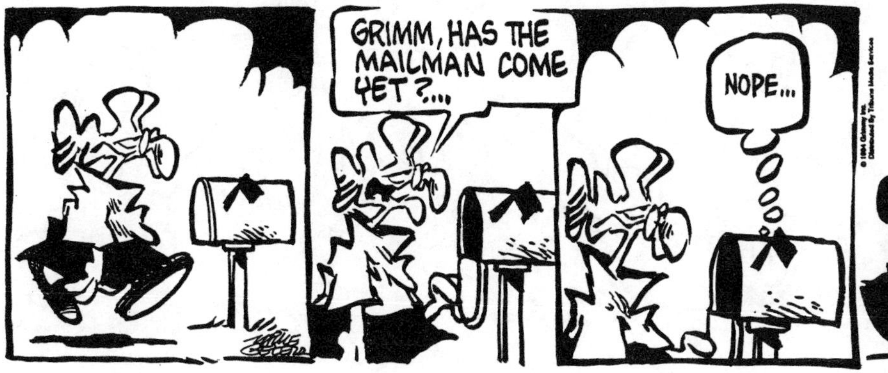
GRIMM, HAS THE MAILMAN COME YET?...
NOPE...

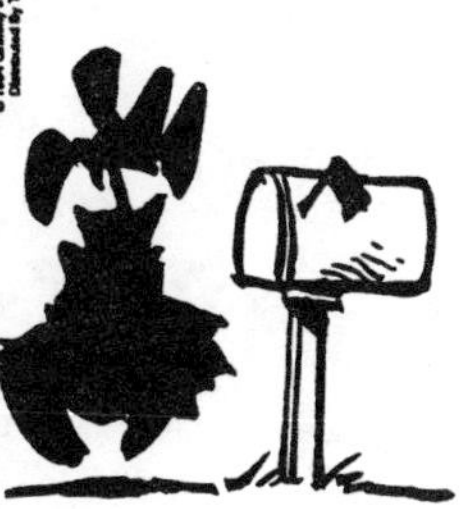

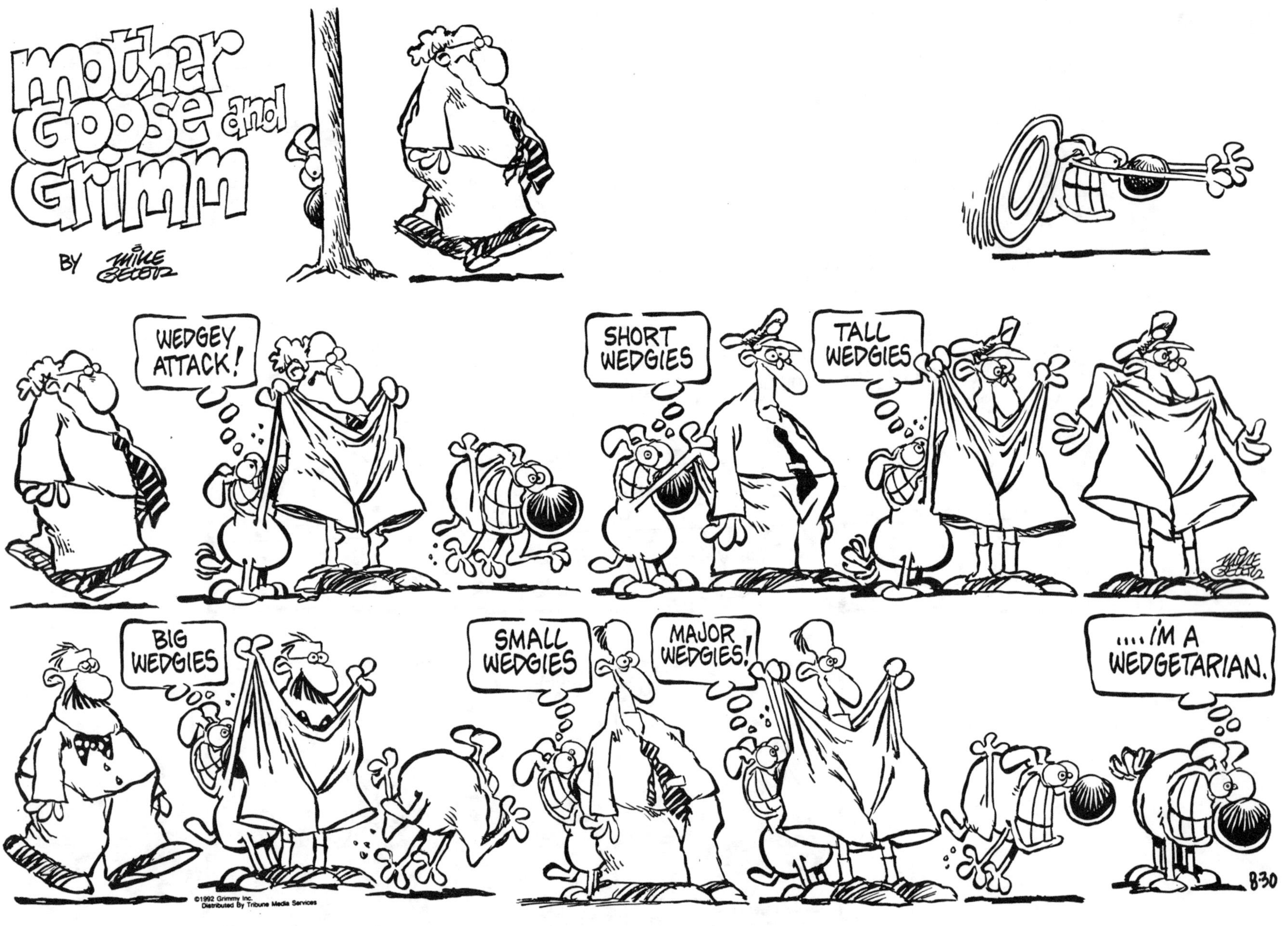
mother Goose and Grimm
BY Mike Peters
WEDGEY ATTACK!
SHORT WEDGIES
TALL WEDGIES
BIG WEDGIES
SMALL WEDGIES
MAJOR WEDGIES!
....I'M A WEDGETARIAN.
8·30
©1992 Grimmy Inc.
Distributed By Tribune Media Services

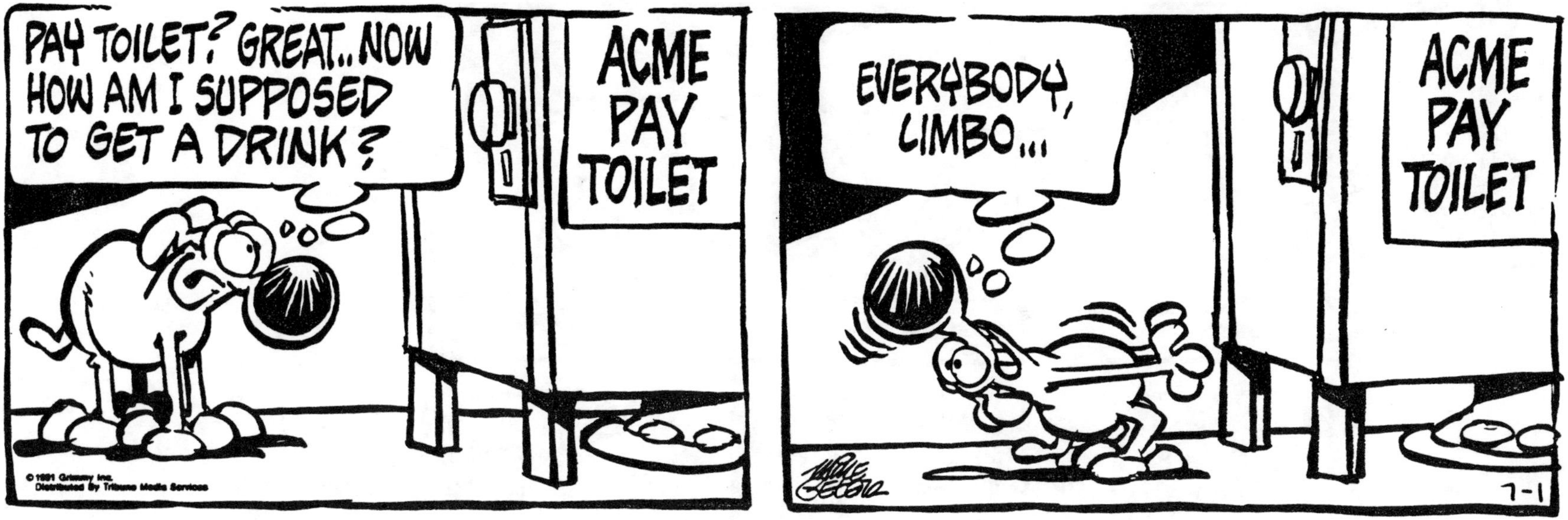
PAY TOILET? GREAT.. NOW HOW AM I SUPPOSED TO GET A DRINK?
ACME PAY TOILET
© 1991 Grimmy Inc. Distributed By Tribune Media Services
EVERYBODY, LIMBO...
ACME PAY TOILET
7-1

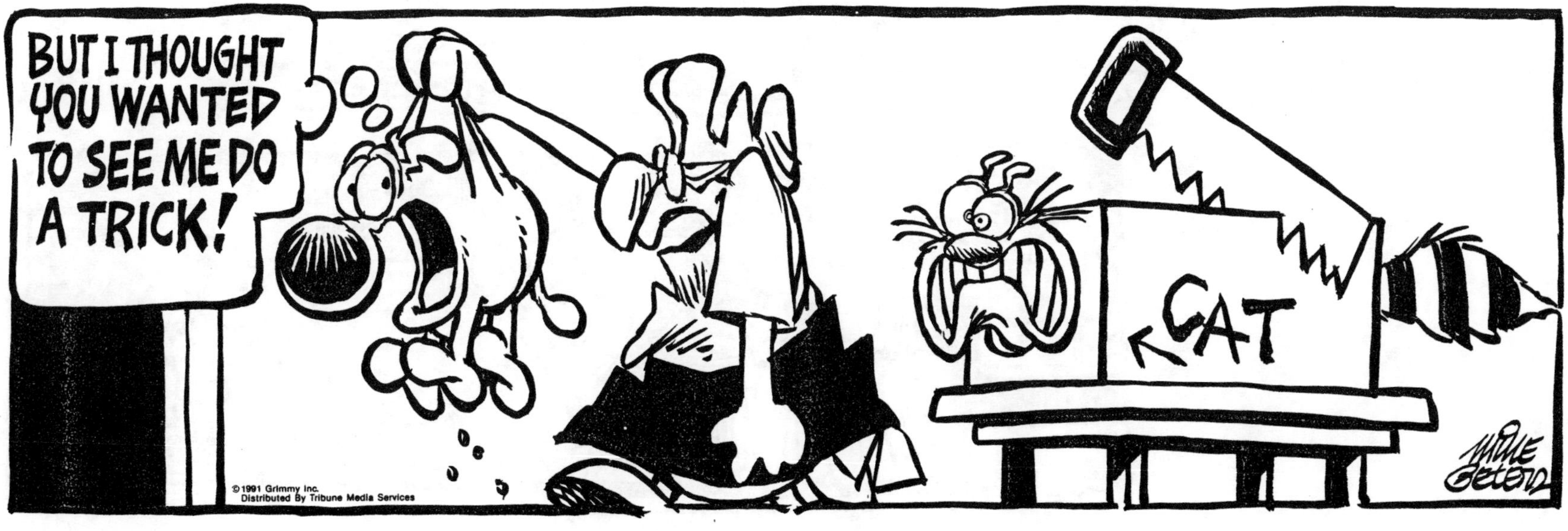
BUT I THOUGHT YOU WANTED TO SEE ME DO A TRICK!
CAT
© 1991 Grimmy Inc. Distributed By Tribune Media Services

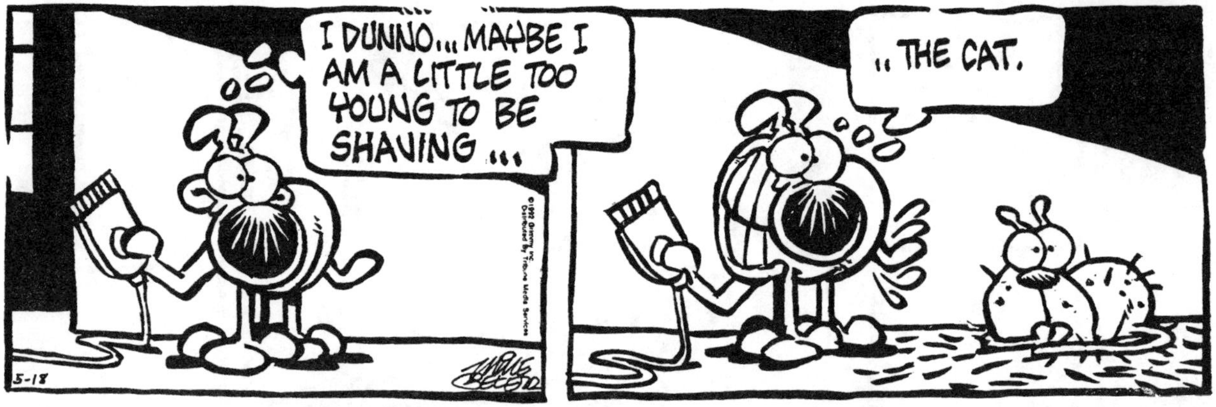
I DUNNO... MAYBE I AM A LITTLE TOO YOUNG TO BE SHAVING ...
.. THE CAT.
5-18

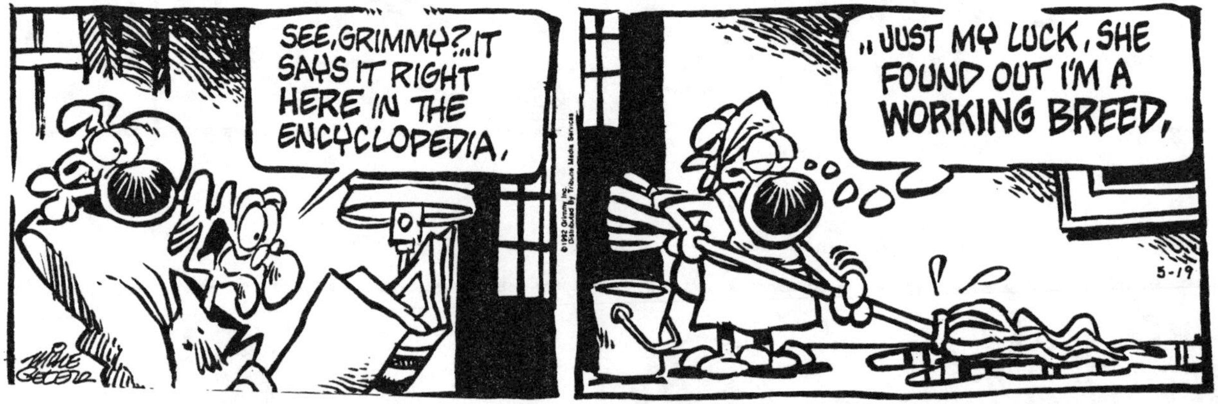
SEE, GRIMMY?...IT SAYS IT RIGHT HERE IN THE ENCYCLOPEDIA.
.. JUST MY LUCK, SHE FOUND OUT I'M A WORKING BREED.
5-19

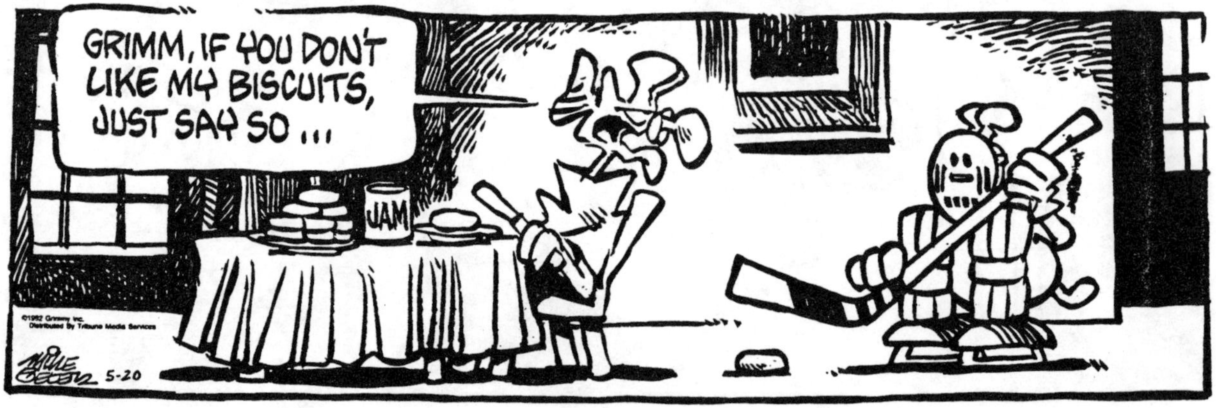
GRIMM, IF YOU DON'T LIKE MY BISCUITS, JUST SAY SO ...
JAM
©1992 Grimmy Inc.
Distributed By Tribune Media Services
5-20

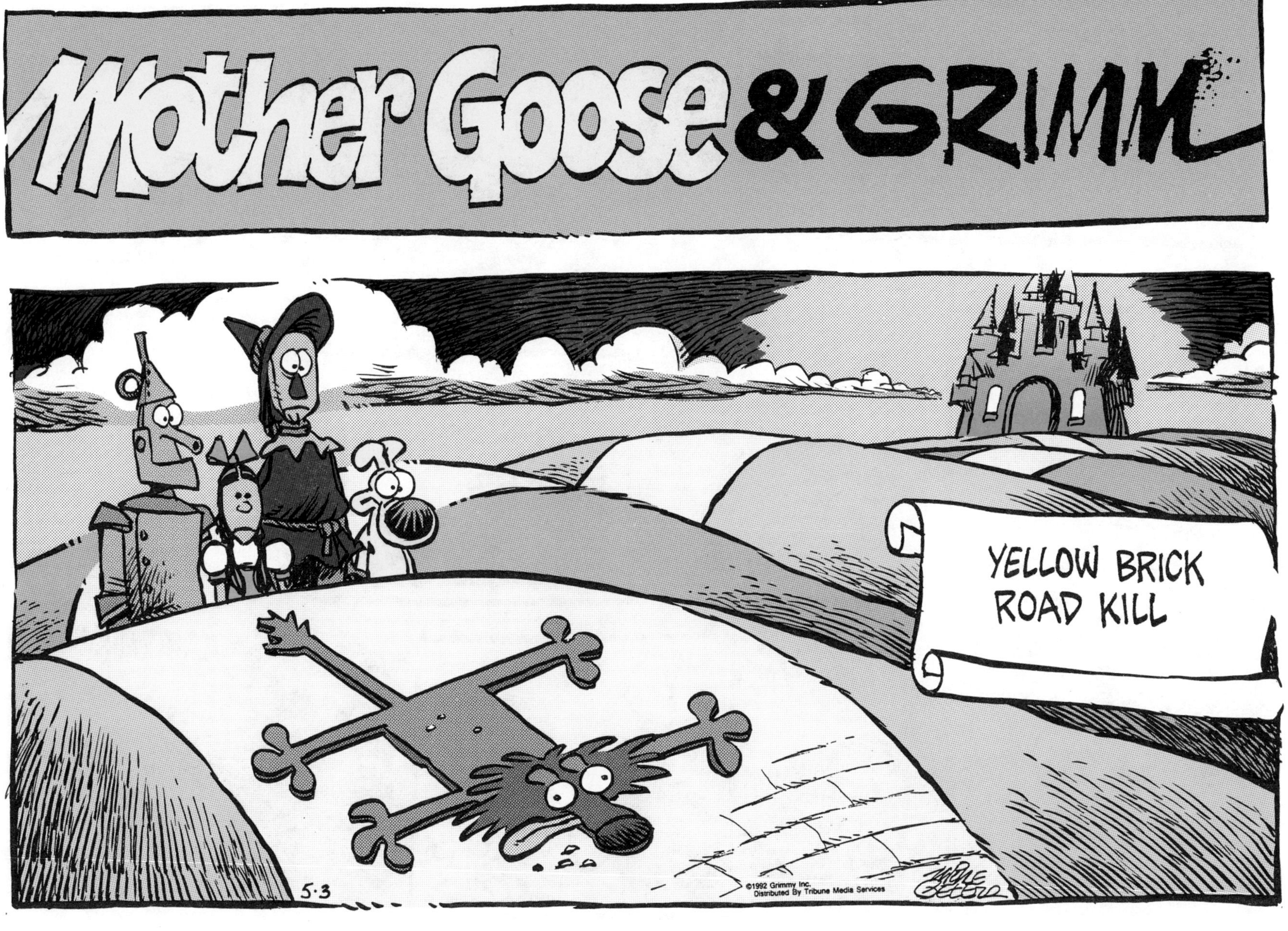
Mother Goose & GRIMM
YELLOW BRICK ROAD KILL
5·3
©1992 Grimmy Inc. Distributed By Tribune Media Services

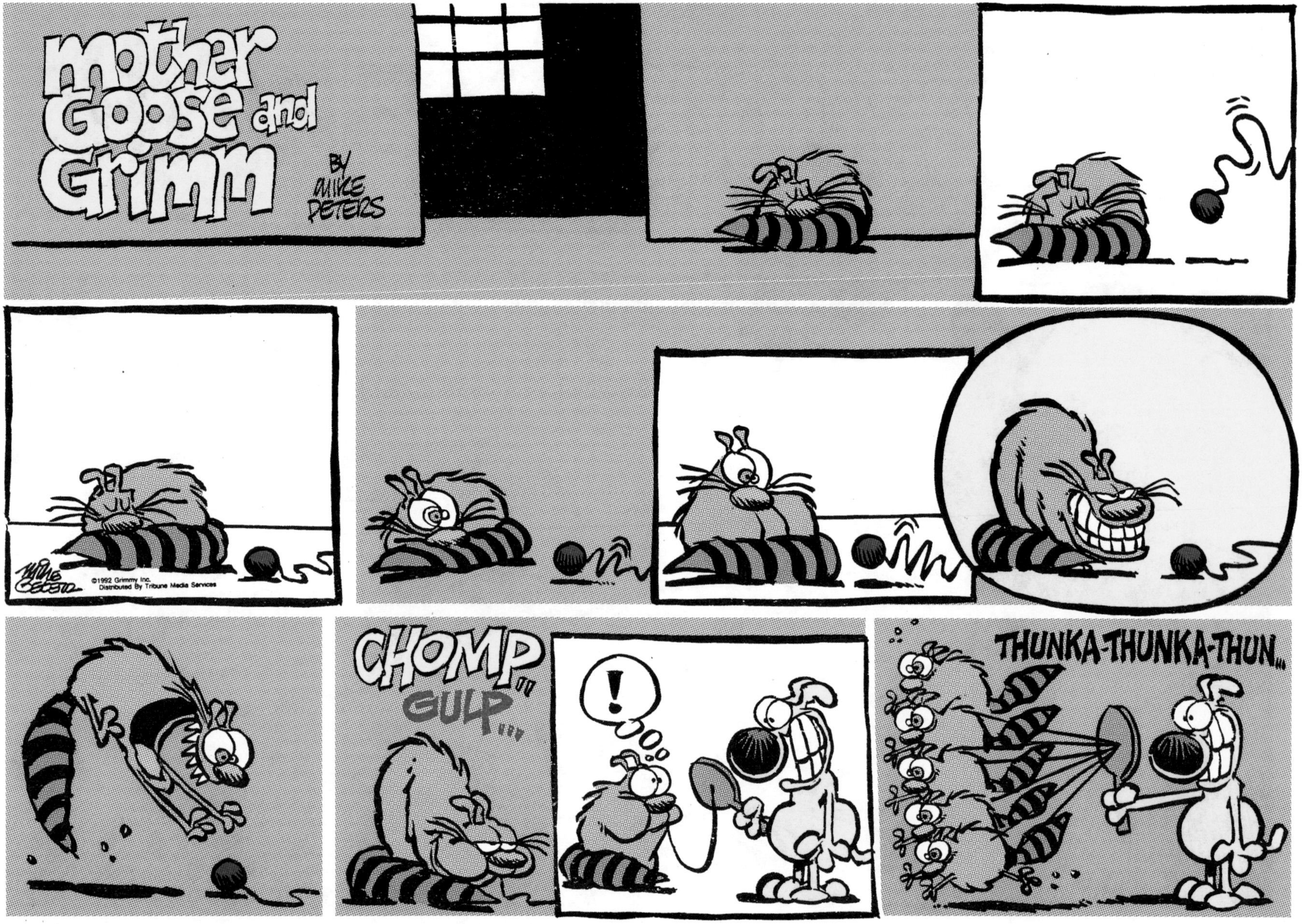
mother Goose and Grimm
BY MIKE PETERS
MIKE PETERS
©1992 Grimmy Inc.
Distributed By Tribune Media Services
CHOMP...
GULP...
!
THUNKA-THUNKA-THUN...

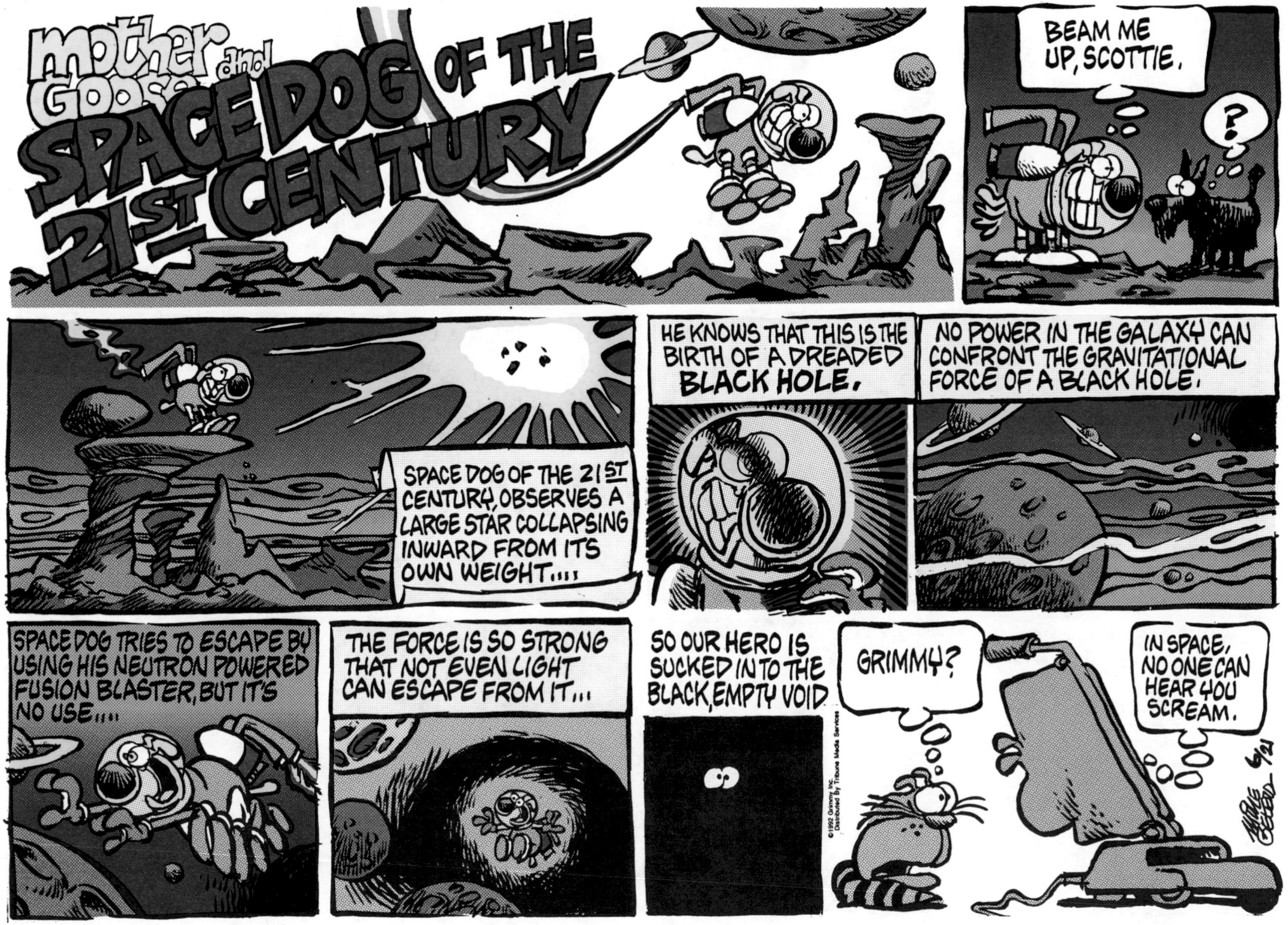
mother goose and
SPACE DOG OF THE 21ST CENTURY
BEAM ME UP, SCOTTIE.
?
SPACE DOG OF THE 21ST CENTURY, OBSERVES A LARGE STAR COLLAPSING INWARD FROM ITS OWN WEIGHT....
HE KNOWS THAT THIS IS THE BIRTH OF A DREADED BLACK HOLE.
NO POWER IN THE GALAXY CAN CONFRONT THE GRAVITATIONAL FORCE OF A BLACK HOLE.
SPACE DOG TRIES TO ESCAPE BY USING HIS NEUTRON POWERED FUSION BLASTER, BUT IT'S NO USE....
THE FORCE IS SO STRONG THAT NOT EVEN LIGHT CAN ESCAPE FROM IT...
SO OUR HERO IS SUCKED IN TO THE BLACK, EMPTY VOID
GRIMMY?
IN SPACE, NO ONE CAN HEAR YOU SCREAM.
©1992 Grimmy Inc. Distributed By Tribune Media Services

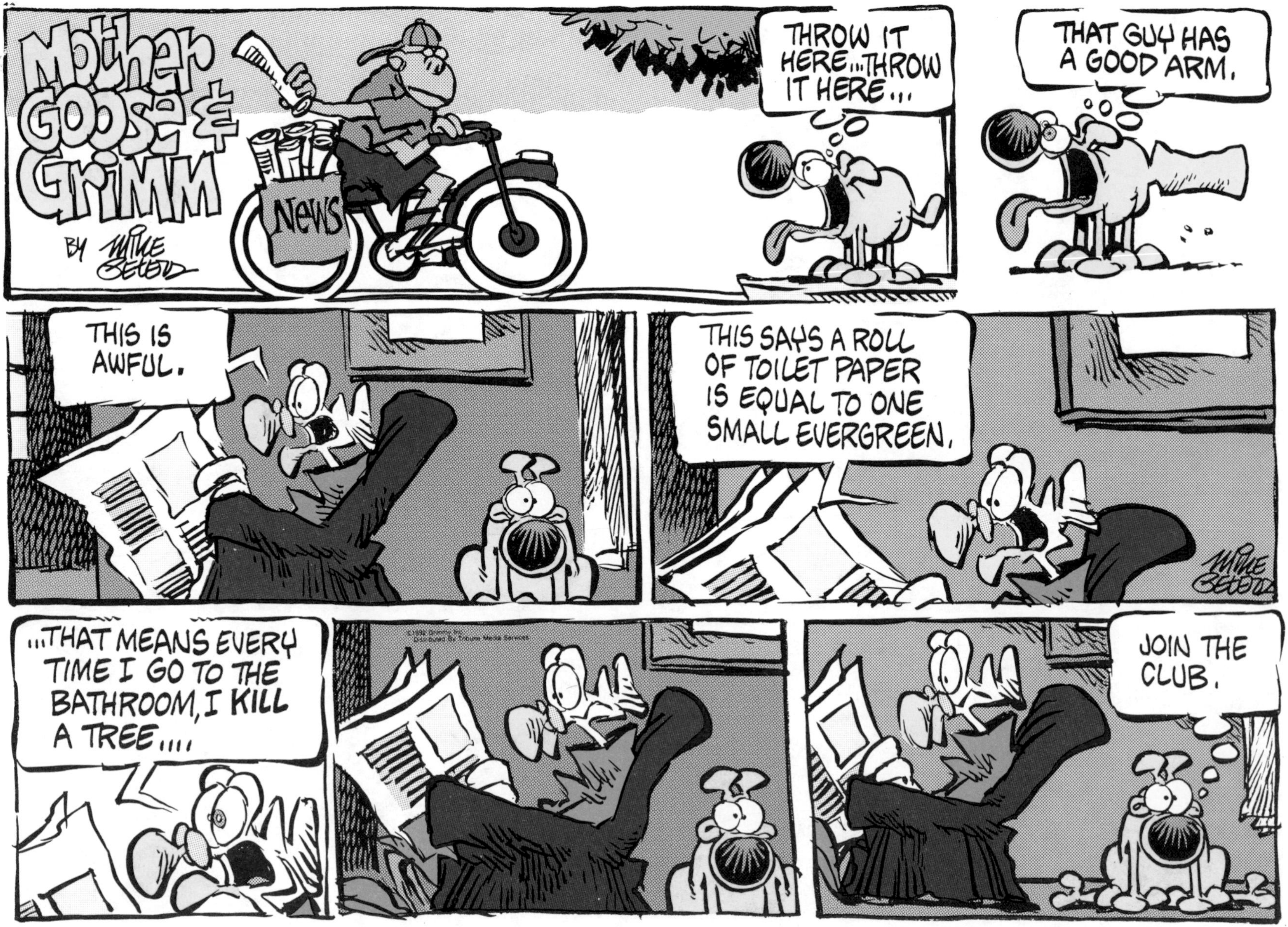
Mother Goose & Grimm
BY MIKE PETERS
NEWS
THROW IT HERE...THROW IT HERE...
THAT GUY HAS A GOOD ARM.
THIS IS AWFUL.
THIS SAYS A ROLL OF TOILET PAPER IS EQUAL TO ONE SMALL EVERGREEN.
...THAT MEANS EVERY TIME I GO TO THE BATHROOM, I **KILL** A TREE....
JOIN THE CLUB.

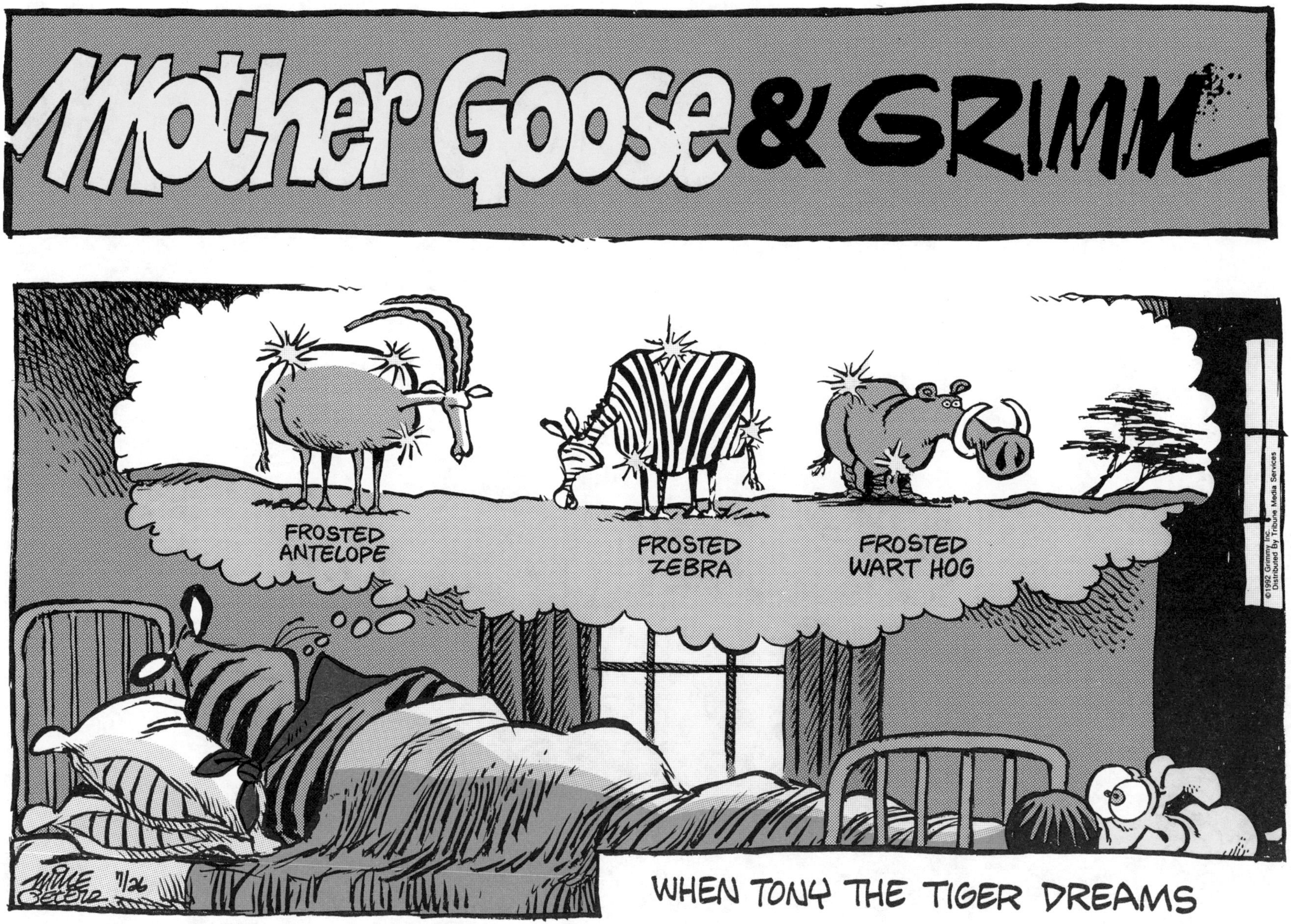
Mother Goose & GRIMM
FROSTED ANTELOPE
FROSTED ZEBRA
FROSTED WART HOG
©1992 Grimmy Inc.
Distributed By Tribune Media Services
MIKE PETERS 7/26
WHEN TONY THE TIGER DREAMS

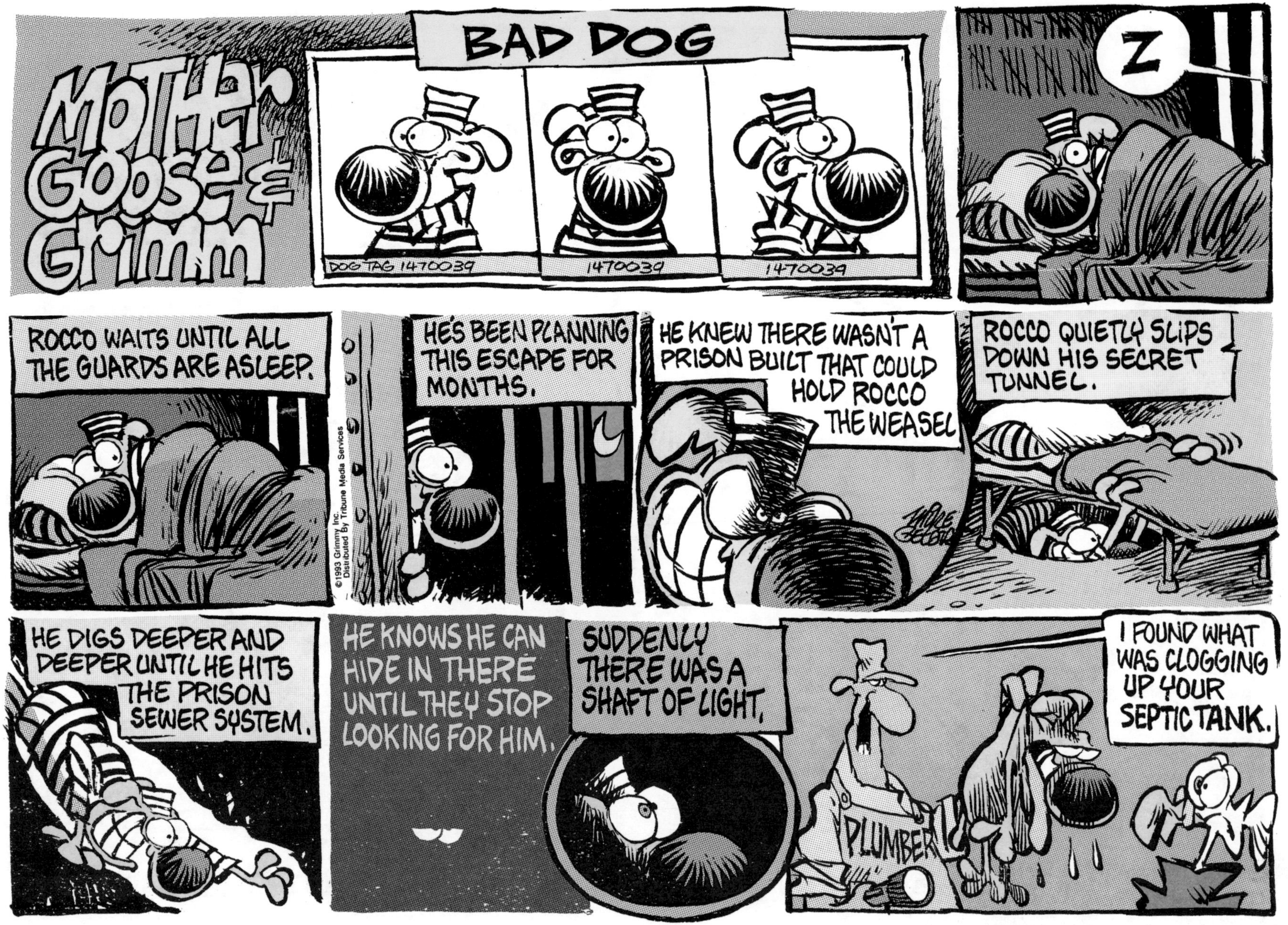
BAD DOG
Mother Goose & Grimm
DOG TAG 1470039
1470039
1470039
Z
ROCCO WAITS UNTIL ALL THE GUARDS ARE ASLEEP.
HE'S BEEN PLANNING THIS ESCAPE FOR MONTHS.
©1993 Grimmy Inc. Distributed By Tribune Media Services
HE KNEW THERE WASN'T A PRISON BUILT THAT COULD HOLD ROCCO THE WEASEL
ROCCO QUIETLY SLIPS DOWN HIS SECRET TUNNEL.
HE DIGS DEEPER AND DEEPER UNTIL HE HITS THE PRISON SEWER SYSTEM.
HE KNOWS HE CAN HIDE IN THERE UNTIL THEY STOP LOOKING FOR HIM.
SUDDENLY THERE WAS A SHAFT OF LIGHT,
I FOUND WHAT WAS CLOGGING UP YOUR SEPTIC TANK.
PLUMBER

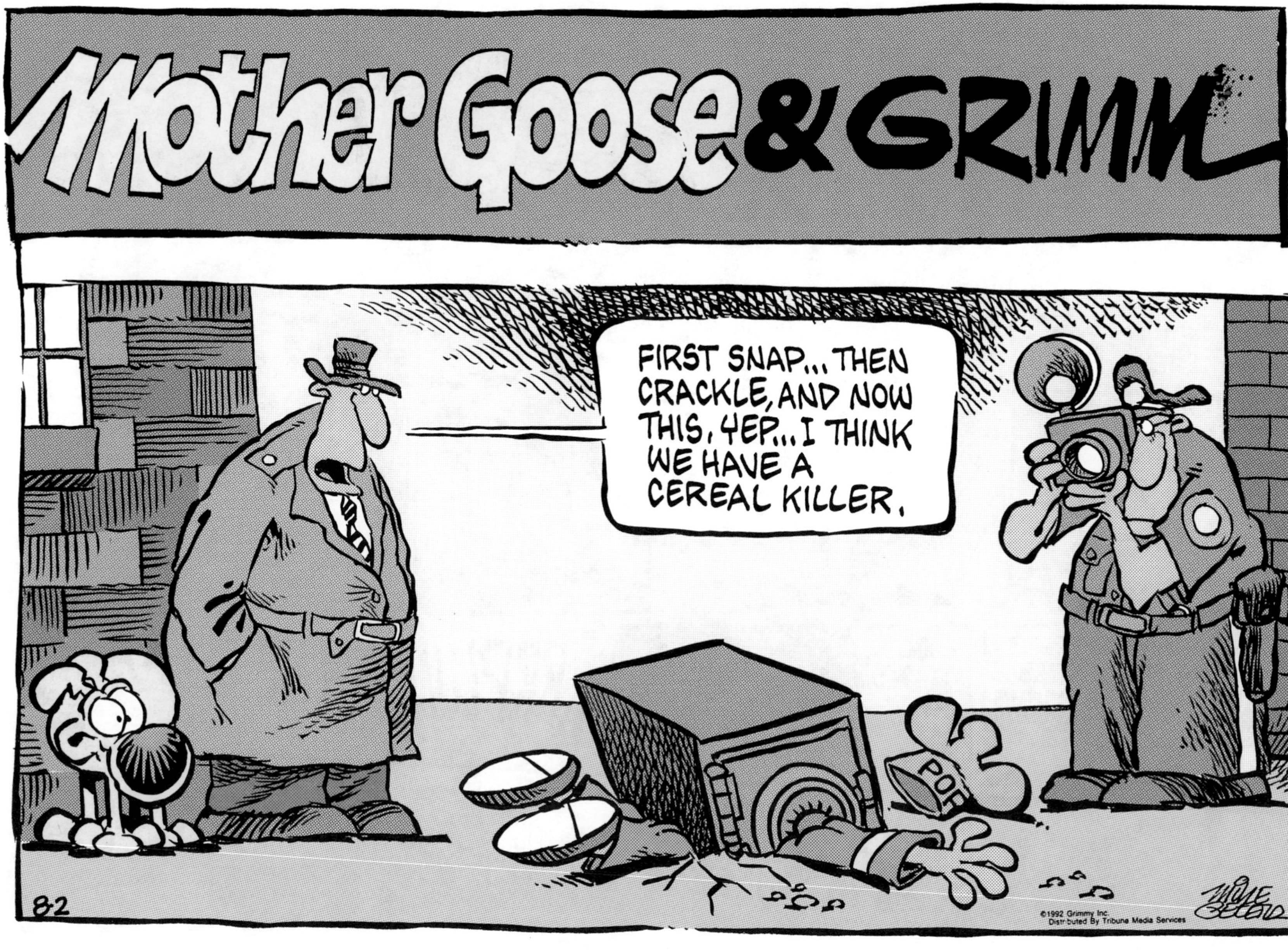
Mother Goose & GRIMM
FIRST SNAP... THEN CRACKLE, AND NOW THIS. YEP... I THINK WE HAVE A CEREAL KILLER.
POP
8-2
©1992 Grimmy Inc. Distributed By Tribune Media Services

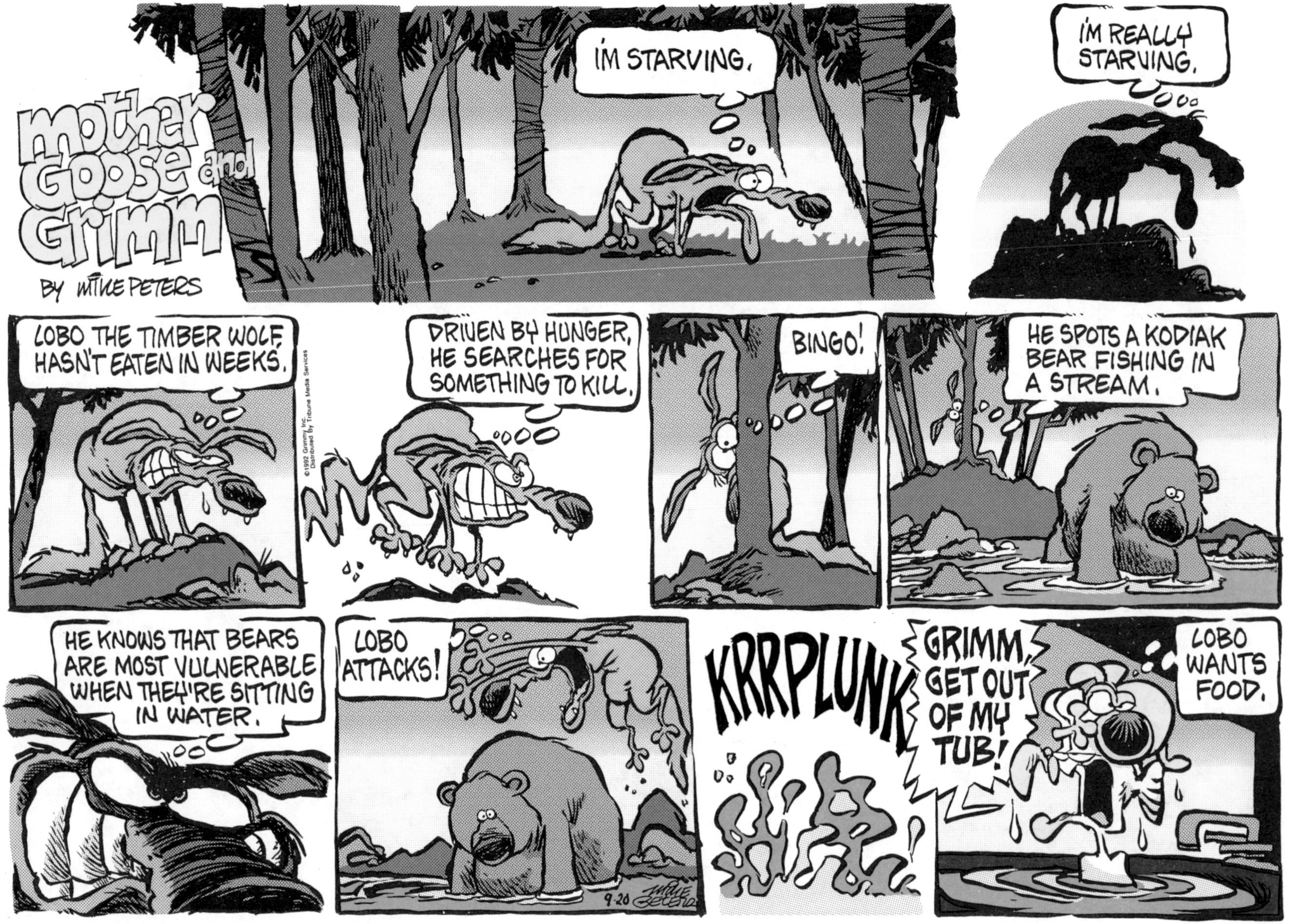
mother Goose and Grimm
BY MIKE PETERS
I'M STARVING.
I'M REALLY STARVING.
LOBO THE TIMBER WOLF, HASN'T EATEN IN WEEKS.
©1992 Grimmy Inc. Distributed By Tribune Media Services
DRIVEN BY HUNGER, HE SEARCHES FOR SOMETHING TO KILL.
BINGO!
HE SPOTS A KODIAK BEAR FISHING IN A STREAM.
HE KNOWS THAT BEARS ARE MOST VULNERABLE WHEN THEY'RE SITTING IN WATER.
LOBO ATTACKS!
9-20
KRRPLUNK
GRIMM, GET OUT OF MY TUB!
LOBO WANTS FOOD.

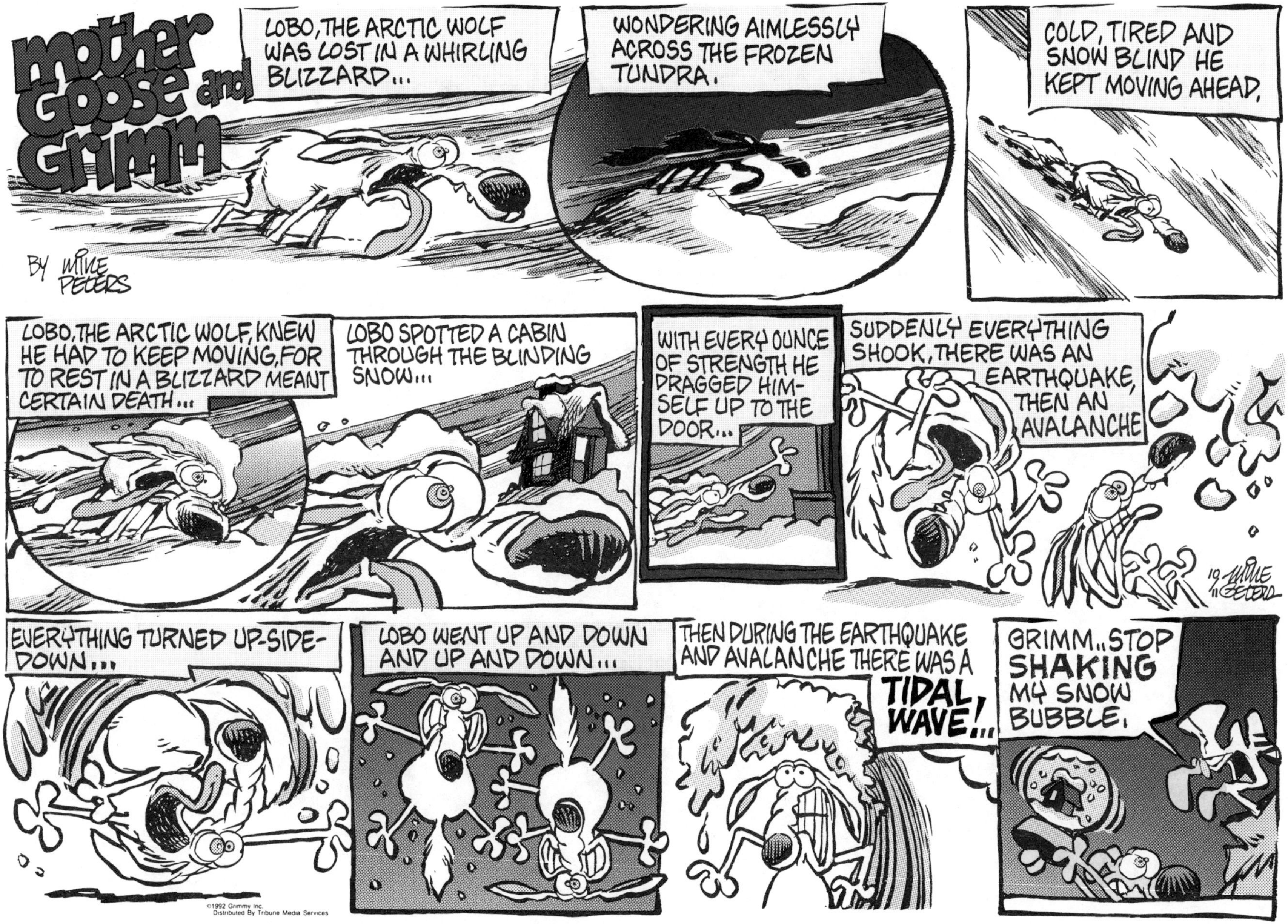
Mother Goose and Grimm
BY MIKE PETERS
LOBO, THE ARCTIC WOLF WAS LOST IN A WHIRLING BLIZZARD...
WONDERING AIMLESSLY ACROSS THE FROZEN TUNDRA.
COLD, TIRED AND SNOW BLIND HE KEPT MOVING AHEAD.
LOBO, THE ARCTIC WOLF, KNEW HE HAD TO KEEP MOVING, FOR TO REST IN A BLIZZARD MEANT CERTAIN DEATH...
LOBO SPOTTED A CABIN THROUGH THE BLINDING SNOW...
WITH EVERY OUNCE OF STRENGTH HE DRAGGED HIM-SELF UP TO THE DOOR...
SUDDENLY EVERYTHING SHOOK, THERE WAS AN EARTHQUAKE, THEN AN AVALANCHE
EVERYTHING TURNED UP-SIDE-DOWN...
LOBO WENT UP AND DOWN AND UP AND DOWN...
THEN DURING THE EARTHQUAKE AND AVALANCHE THERE WAS A TIDAL WAVE!...
GRIMM.. STOP SHAKING MY SNOW BUBBLE.
©1992 Grimmy Inc.
Distributed By Tribune Media Services

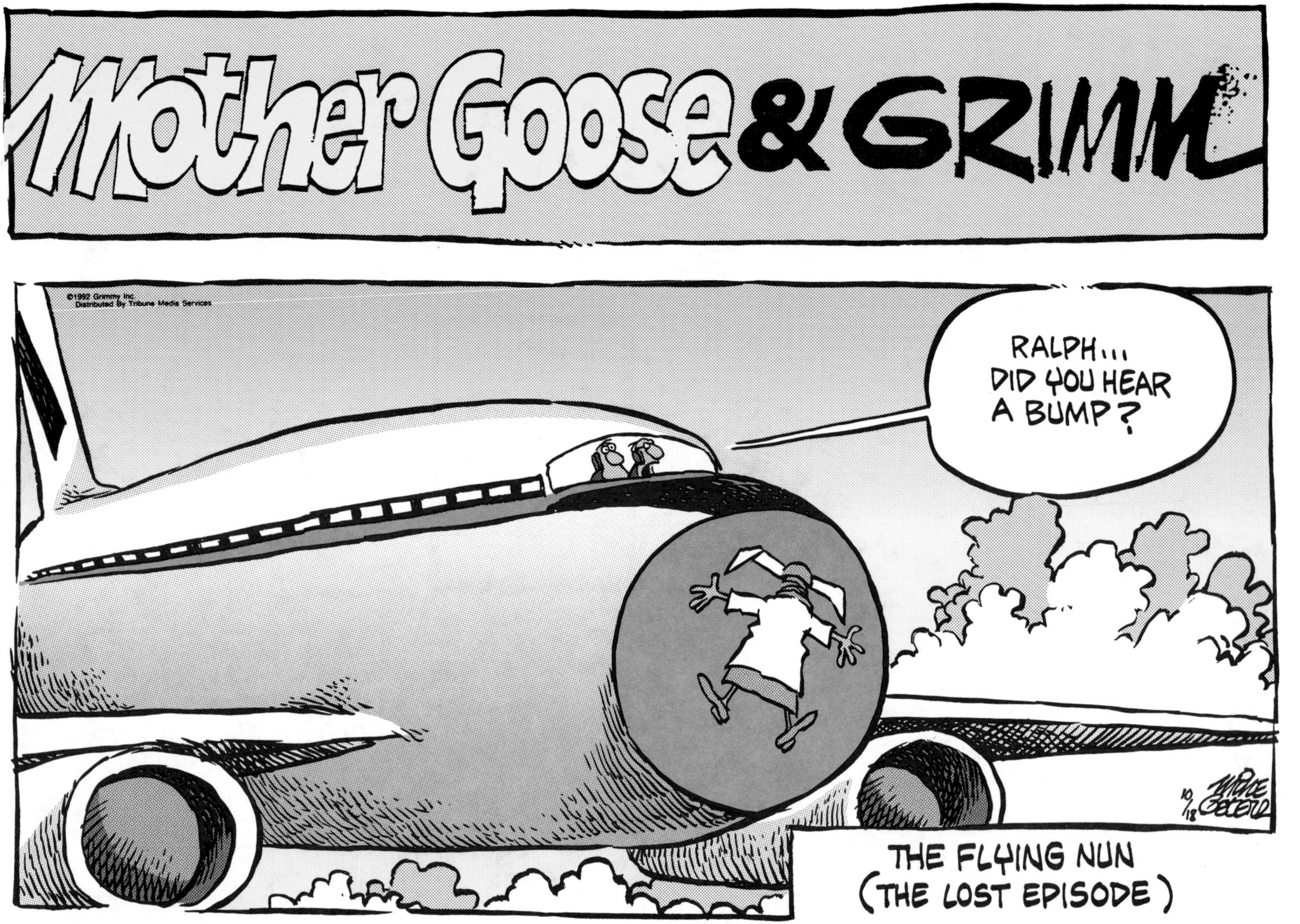
Mother Goose & GRIMM
©1992 Grimmy Inc.
Distributed By Tribune Media Services
RALPH... DID YOU HEAR A BUMP?
THE FLYING NUN (THE LOST EPISODE)

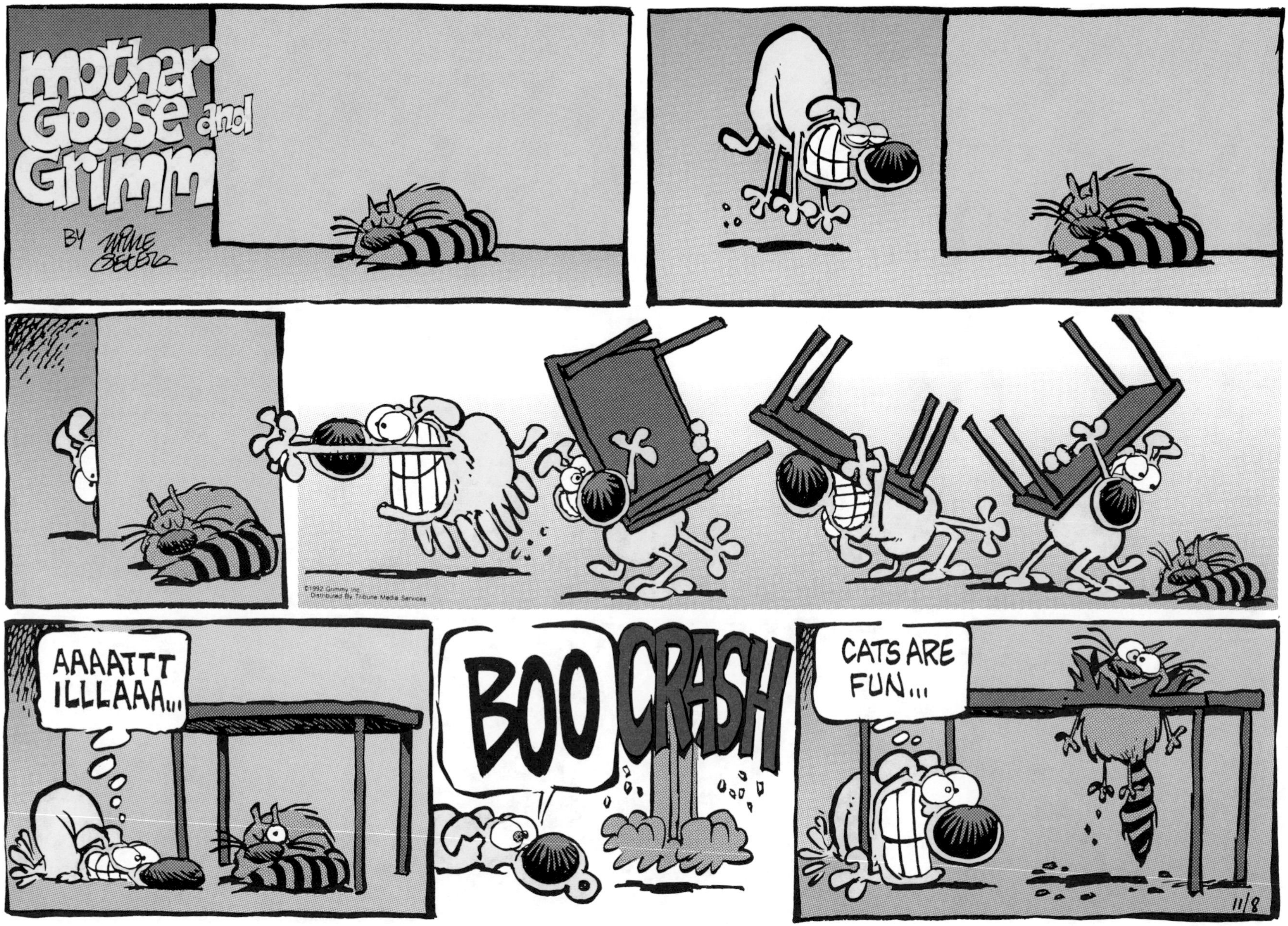
Mother Goose and Grimm
BY MIKE PETERS
©1992 Grimmy Inc.
Distributed By Tribune Media Services
AAAATTT ILLLAAA...
BOO
CRASH
CATS ARE FUN...
11/8

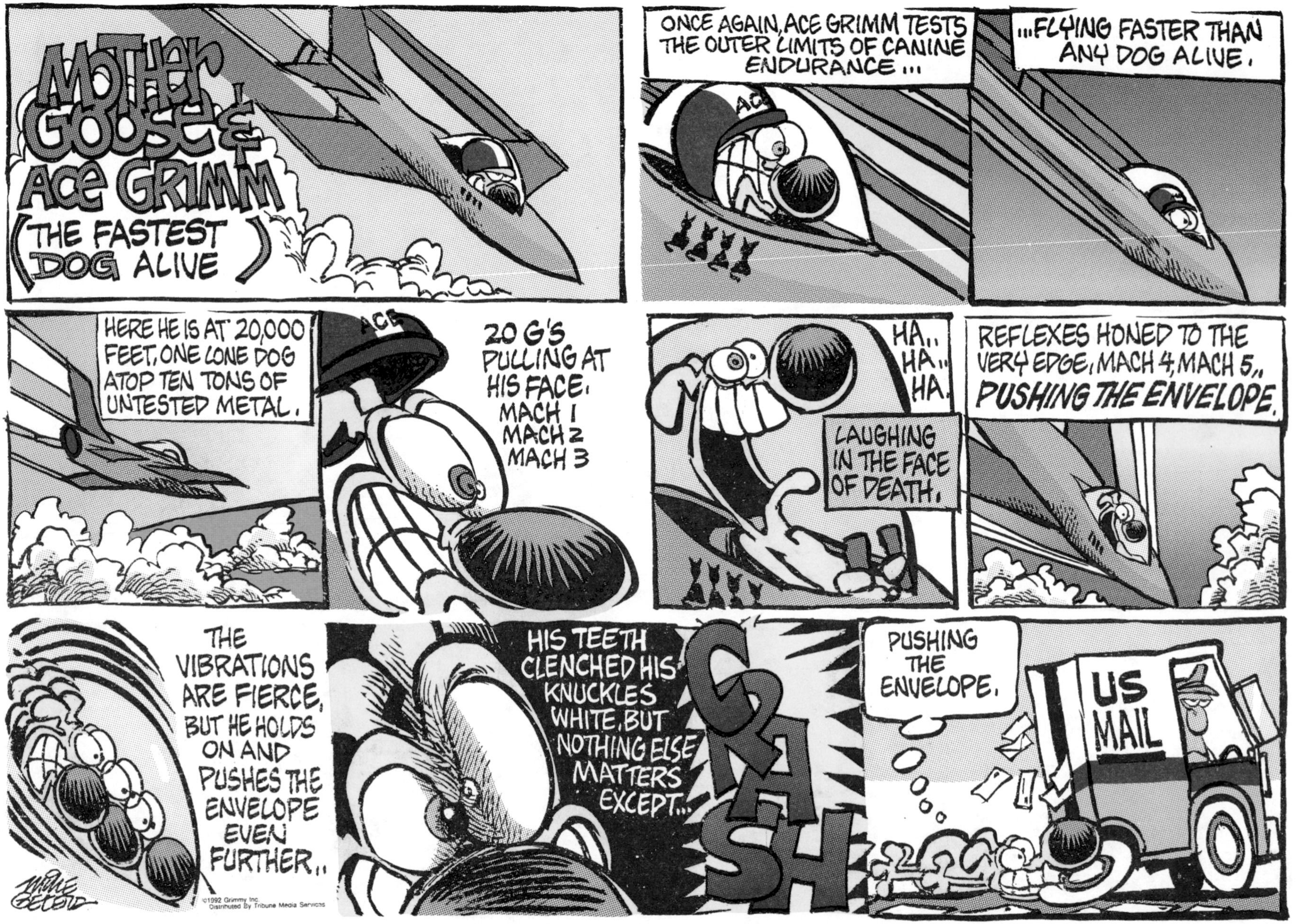

Mother Goose & Ace Grimm
(THE FASTEST DOG ALIVE)
ONCE AGAIN, ACE GRIMM TESTS THE OUTER LIMITS OF CANINE ENDURANCE...
ACE
...FLYING FASTER THAN ANY DOG ALIVE.
HERE HE IS AT 20,000 FEET, ONE LONE DOG ATOP TEN TONS OF UNTESTED METAL.
ACE
20 G'S PULLING AT HIS FACE. MACH 1 MACH 2 MACH 3
HA.. HA.. HA.
LAUGHING IN THE FACE OF DEATH.
REFLEXES HONED TO THE VERY EDGE, MACH 4, MACH 5.. PUSHING THE ENVELOPE.
THE VIBRATIONS ARE FIERCE, BUT HE HOLDS ON AND PUSHES THE ENVELOPE EVEN FURTHER..
HIS TEETH CLENCHED HIS KNUCKLES WHITE, BUT NOTHING ELSE MATTERS EXCEPT...
CRASH
PUSHING THE ENVELOPE.
US MAIL
©1992 Grimmy Inc. Distributed By Tribune Media Services

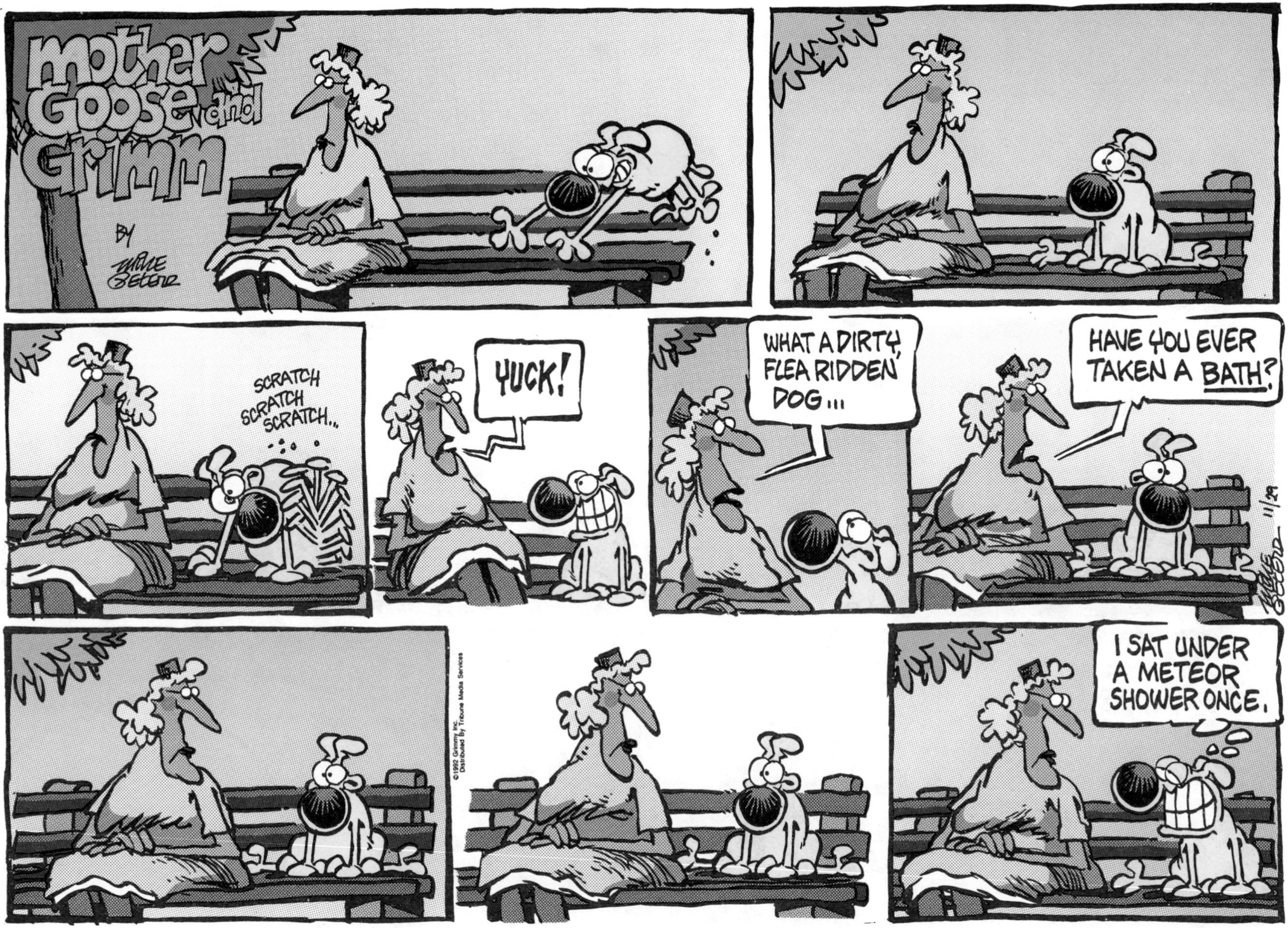
Mother Goose and Grimm
BY Mike Peters
SCRATCH SCRATCH SCRATCH...
YUCK!
WHAT A DIRTY, FLEA RIDDEN DOG...
HAVE YOU EVER TAKEN A BATH?
©1992 Grimmy Inc. Distributed By Tribune Media Services
I SAT UNDER A METEOR SHOWER ONCE.

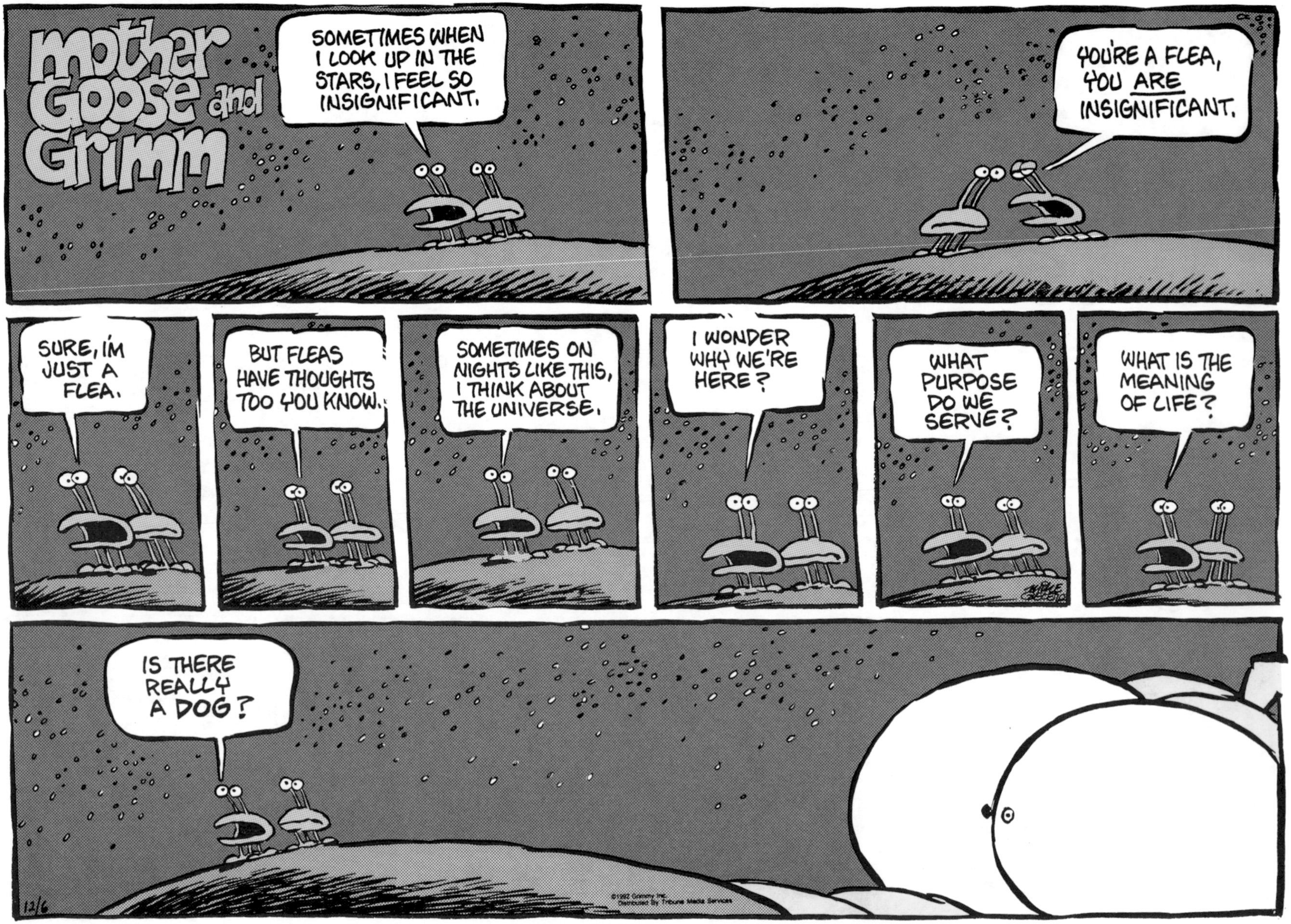
Mother Goose and Grimm
SOMETIMES WHEN I LOOK UP IN THE STARS, I FEEL SO INSIGNIFICANT.
YOU'RE A FLEA, YOU ARE INSIGNIFICANT.
SURE, I'M JUST A FLEA.
BUT FLEAS HAVE THOUGHTS TOO YOU KNOW.
SOMETIMES ON NIGHTS LIKE THIS, I THINK ABOUT THE UNIVERSE.
I WONDER WHY WE'RE HERE?
WHAT PURPOSE DO WE SERVE?
WHAT IS THE MEANING OF LIFE?
IS THERE REALLY A DOG?
12/6
©1992 Grimmy Inc.
Distributed By Tribune Media Services

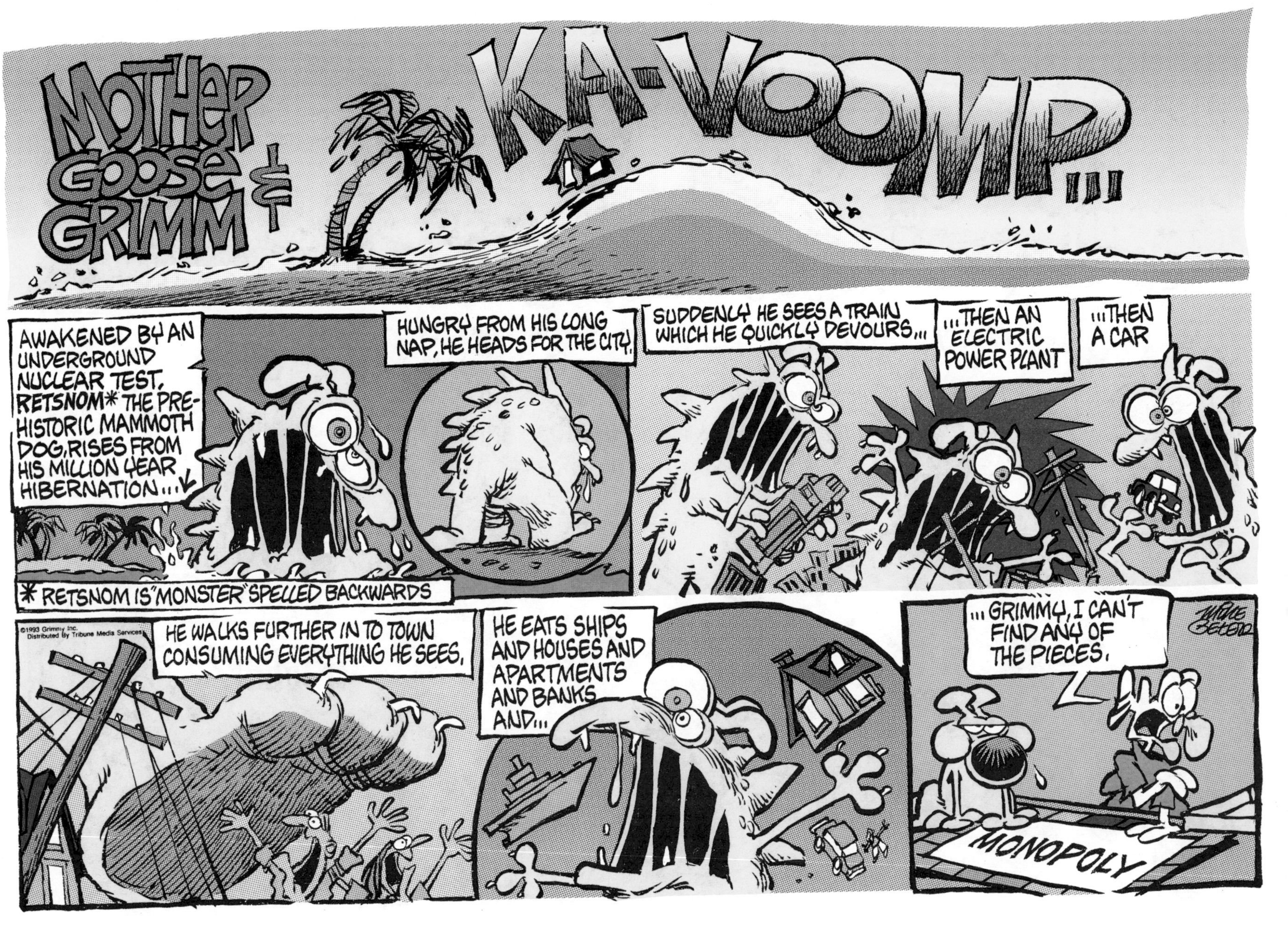
MOTHER GOOSE & GRIMM
KA-VOOMP!!!
AWAKENED BY AN UNDERGROUND NUCLEAR TEST, RETSNOM* THE PRE-HISTORIC MAMMOTH DOG, RISES FROM HIS MILLION YEAR HIBERNATION...
HUNGRY FROM HIS LONG NAP, HE HEADS FOR THE CITY.
SUDDENLY HE SEES A TRAIN WHICH HE QUICKLY DEVOURS...
...THEN AN ELECTRIC POWER PLANT
...THEN A CAR
* RETSNOM IS "MONSTER" SPELLED BACKWARDS
©1993 Grimmy Inc. Distributed By Tribune Media Services
HE WALKS FURTHER IN TO TOWN CONSUMING EVERYTHING HE SEES.
HE EATS SHIPS AND HOUSES AND APARTMENTS AND BANKS AND...
...GRIMMY, I CAN'T FIND ANY OF THE PIECES.
MONOPOLY

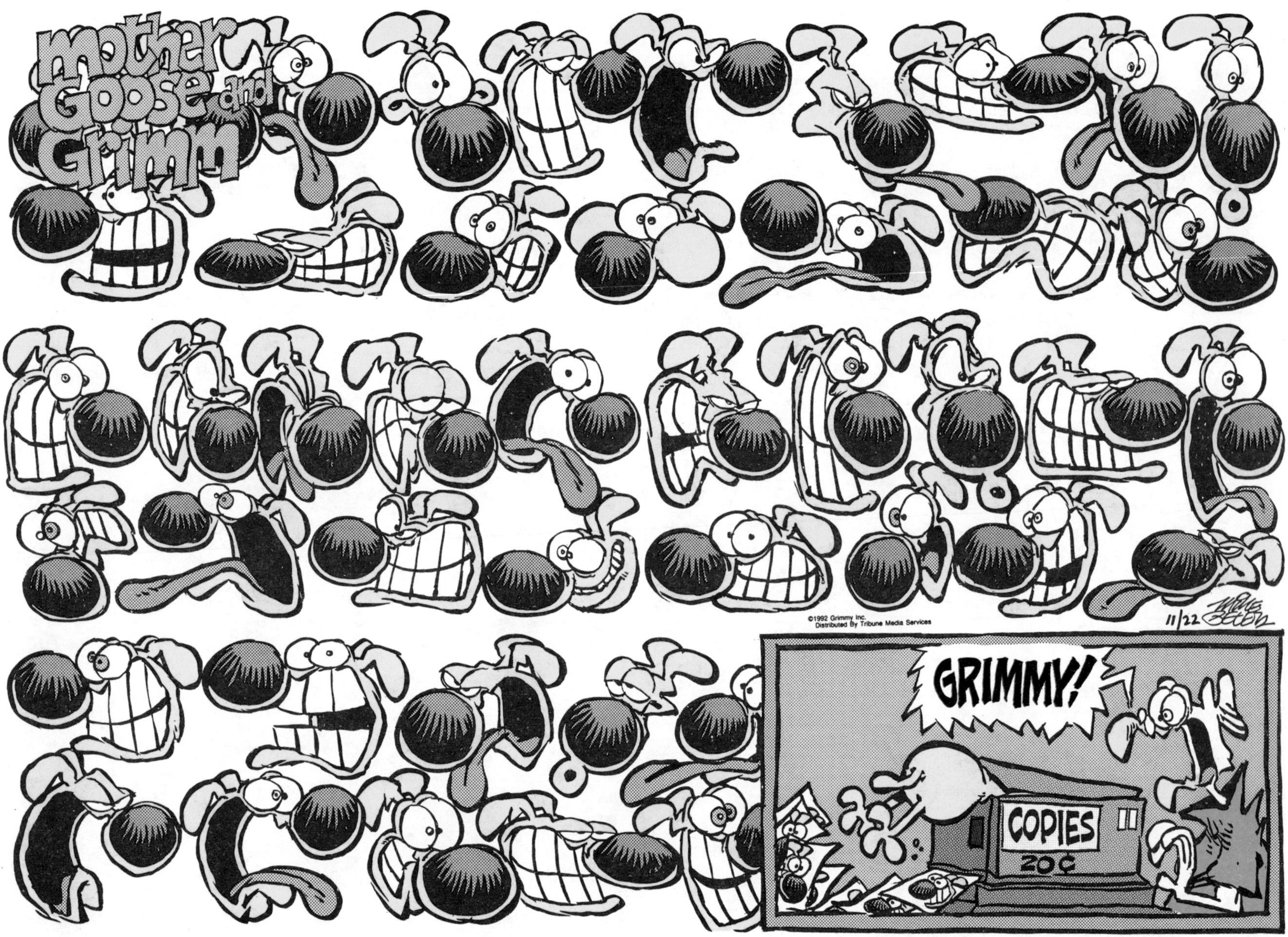
mother Goose and Grimm
11/22
GRIMMY!
COPIES
20¢

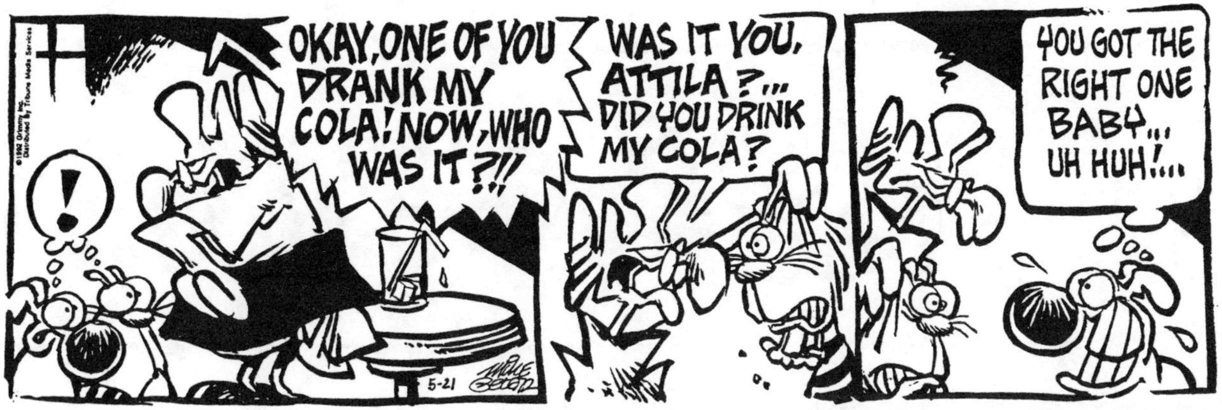

!
OKAY, ONE OF YOU DRANK MY COLA! NOW, WHO WAS IT?!!
WAS IT YOU, ATTILA?... DID YOU DRINK MY COLA?
YOU GOT THE RIGHT ONE BABY... UH HUH!...
5-21


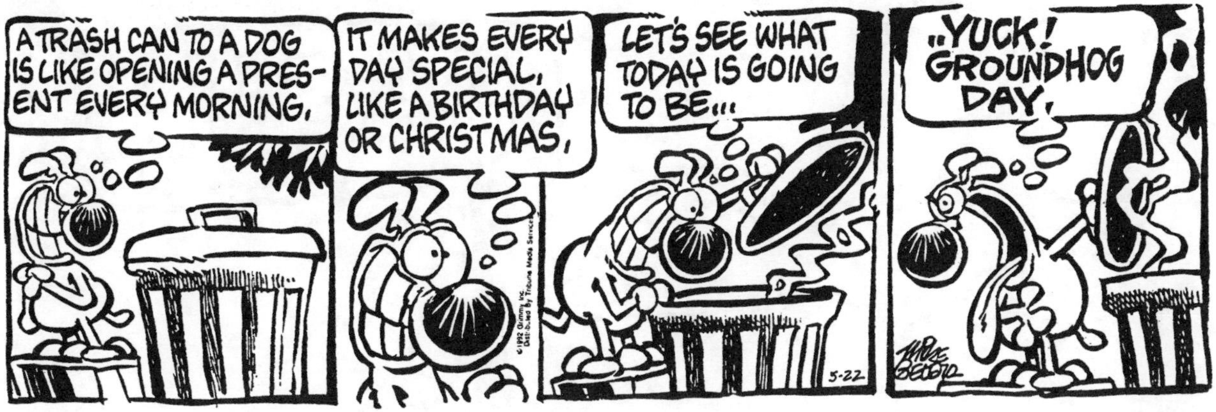

A TRASH CAN TO A DOG IS LIKE OPENING A PRESENT EVERY MORNING.
IT MAKES EVERY DAY SPECIAL, LIKE A BIRTHDAY OR CHRISTMAS.
LET'S SEE WHAT TODAY IS GOING TO BE...
..YUCK! GROUNDHOG DAY.
5-22


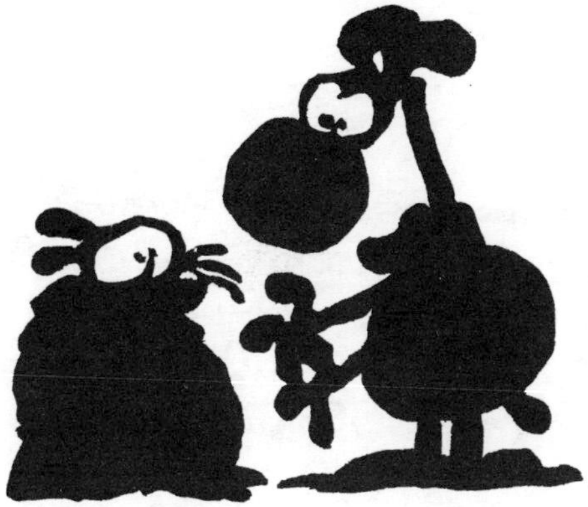

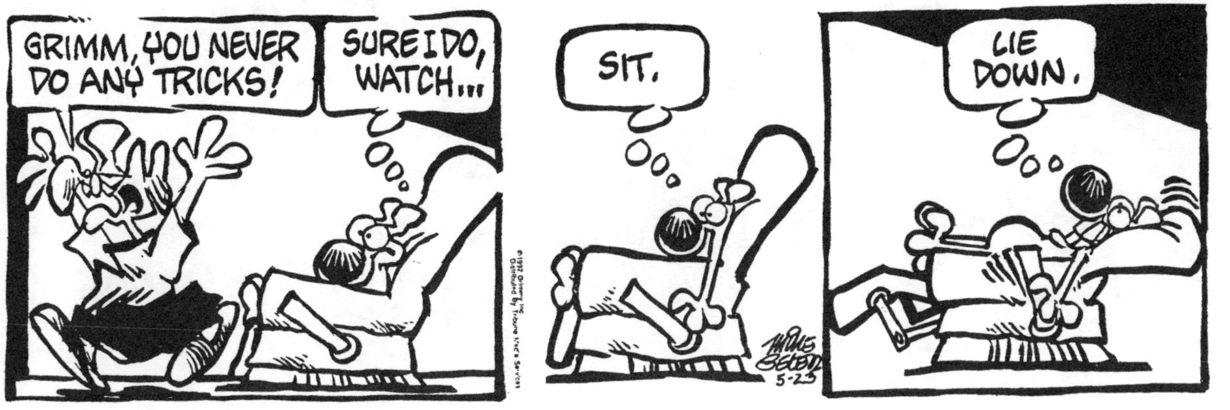

GRIMM, YOU NEVER DO ANY TRICKS!
SURE I DO, WATCH...
SIT.
LIE DOWN.
5-23

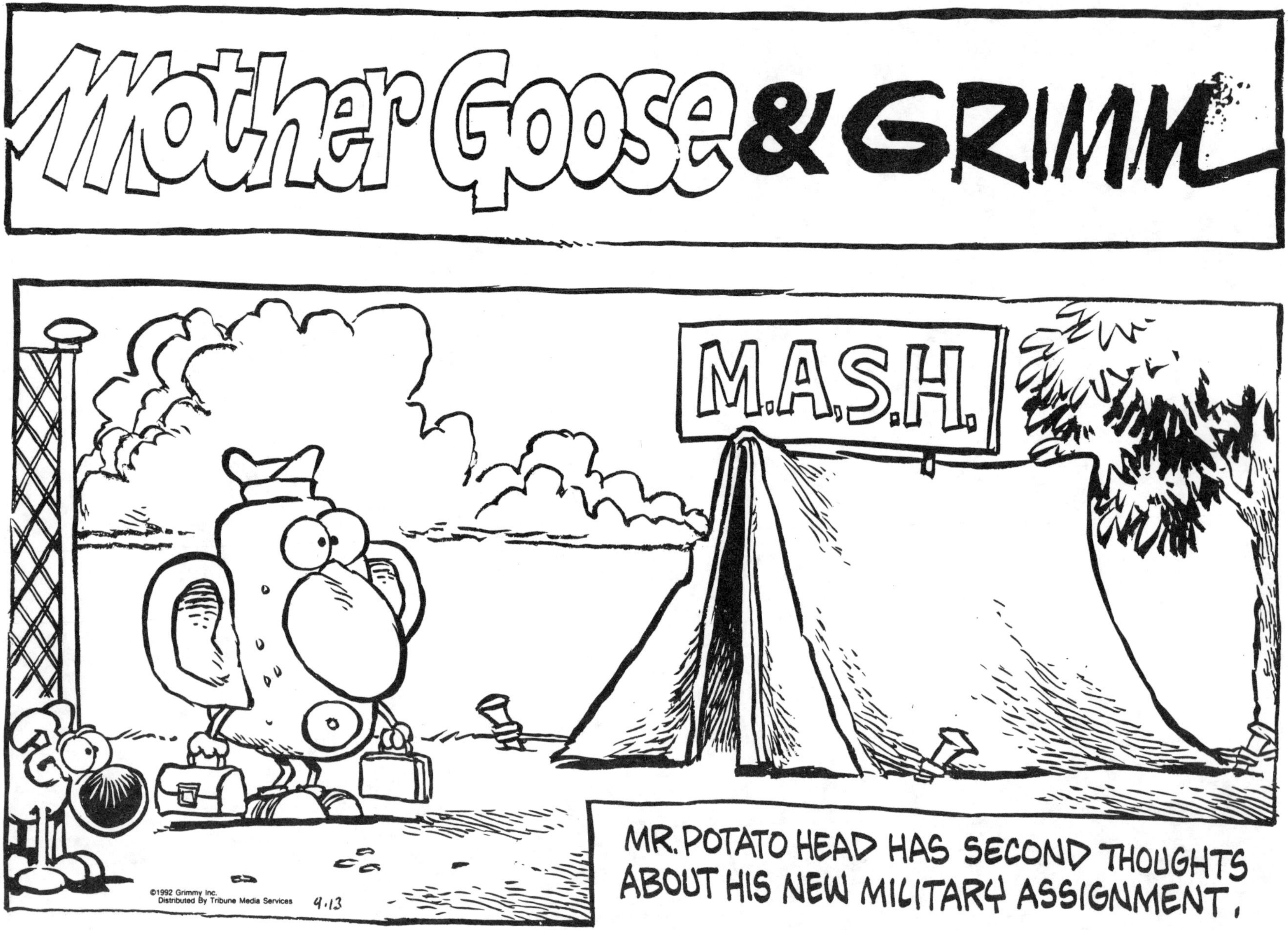

Mother Goose & GRIMM
M.A.S.H.
MR. POTATO HEAD HAS SECOND THOUGHTS ABOUT HIS NEW MILITARY ASSIGNMENT.
©1992 Grimmy Inc. Distributed By Tribune Media Services
9.13

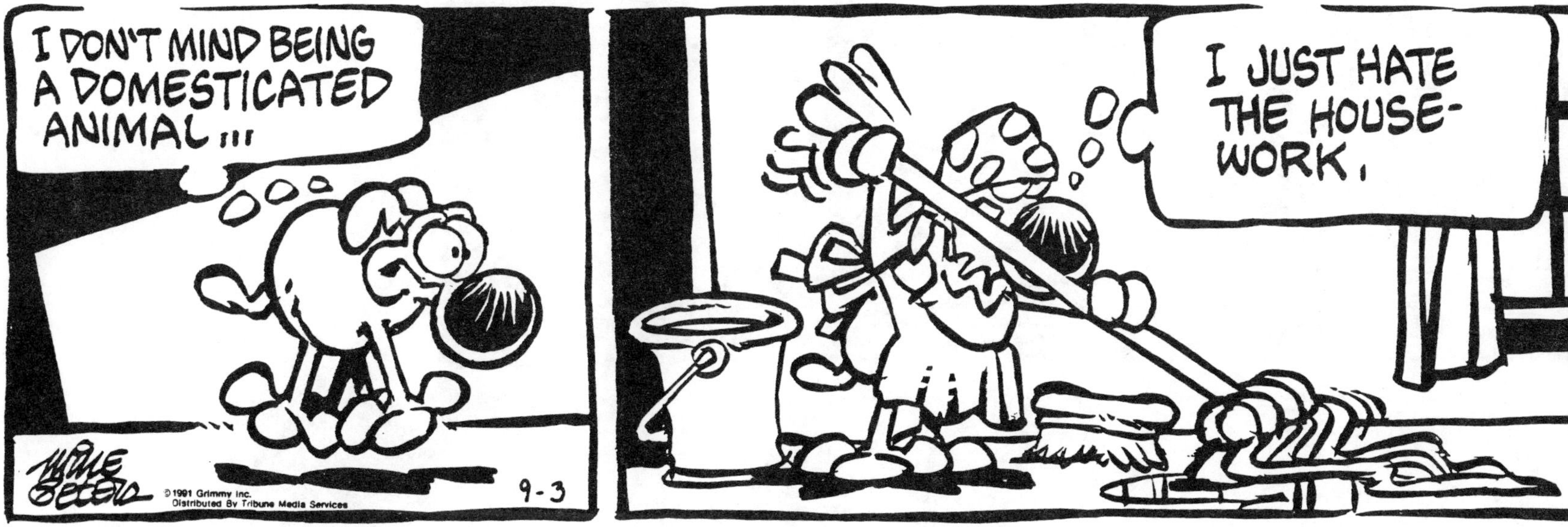

I DON'T MIND BEING A DOMESTICATED ANIMAL...
I JUST HATE THE HOUSE-WORK.
©1991 Grimmy Inc.
Distributed By Tribune Media Services
9-3


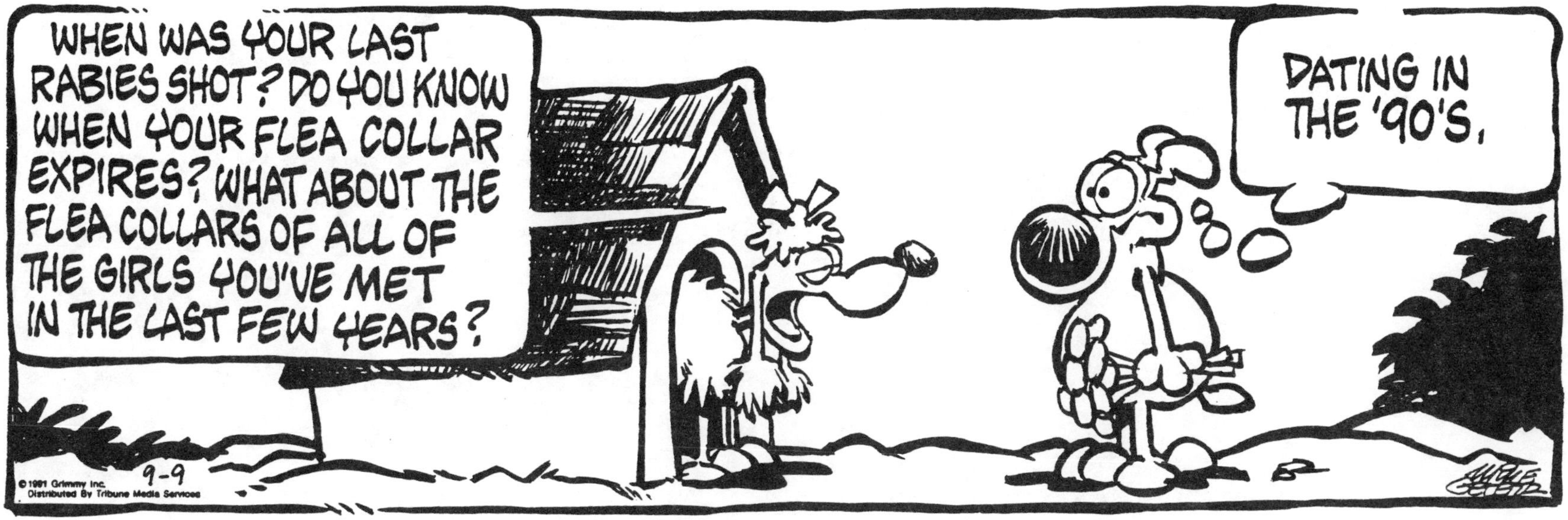

WHEN WAS YOUR LAST RABIES SHOT? DO YOU KNOW WHEN YOUR FLEA COLLAR EXPIRES? WHAT ABOUT THE FLEA COLLARS OF ALL OF THE GIRLS YOU'VE MET IN THE LAST FEW YEARS?
DATING IN THE '90'S.
©1991 Grimmy Inc.
Distributed By Tribune Media Services
9-9

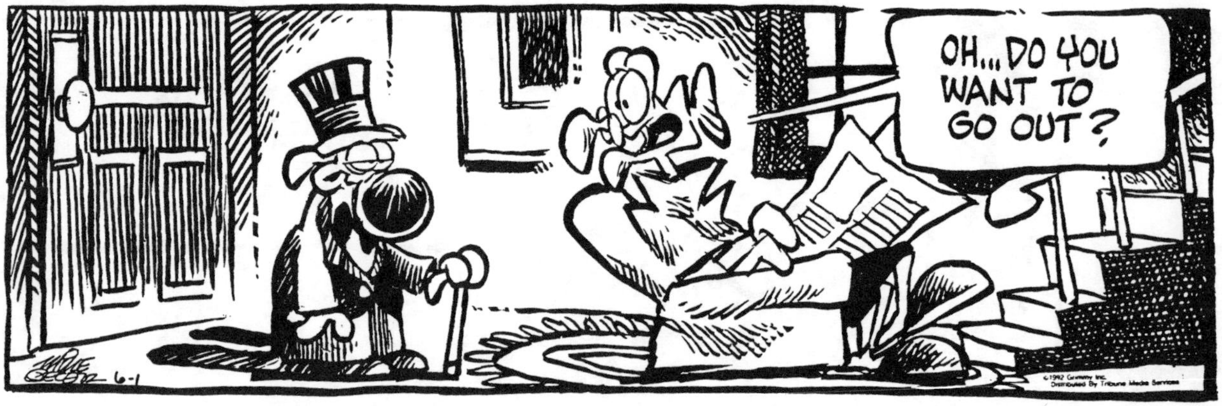
OH... DO YOU WANT TO GO OUT?
6-1
©1992 Grimmy Inc. Distributed By Tribune Media Services

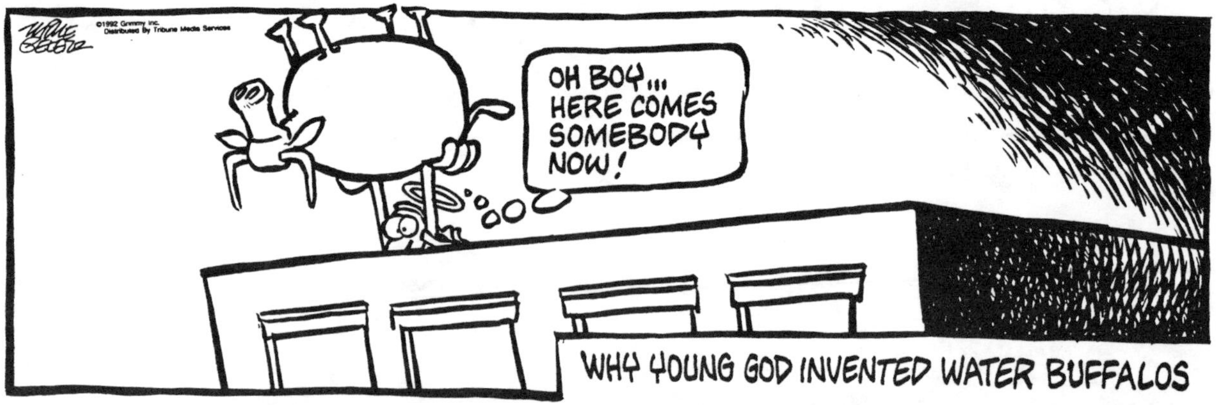
©1992 Grimmy Inc. Distributed By Tribune Media Services
OH BOY... HERE COMES SOMEBODY NOW!
WHY YOUNG GOD INVENTED WATER BUFFALOS

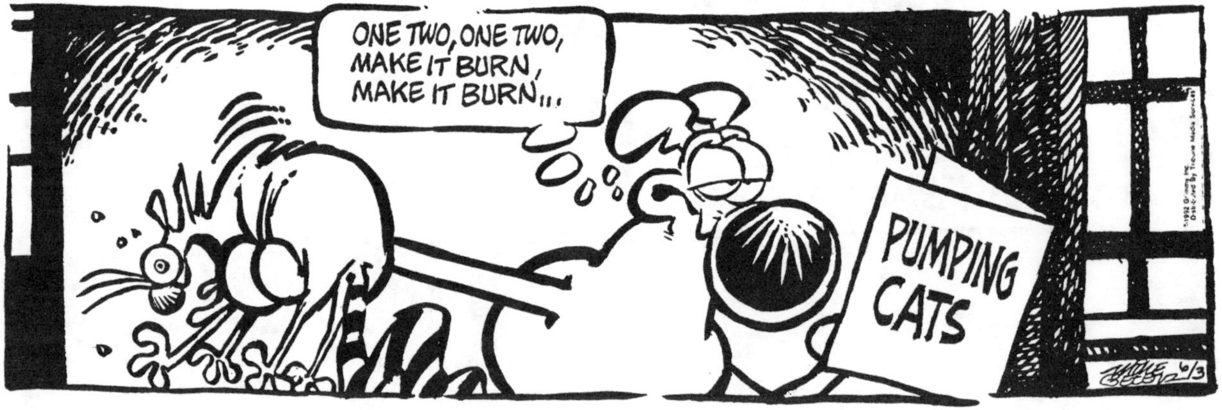
ONE TWO, ONE TWO, MAKE IT BURN, MAKE IT BURN...
PUMPING CATS
6/3

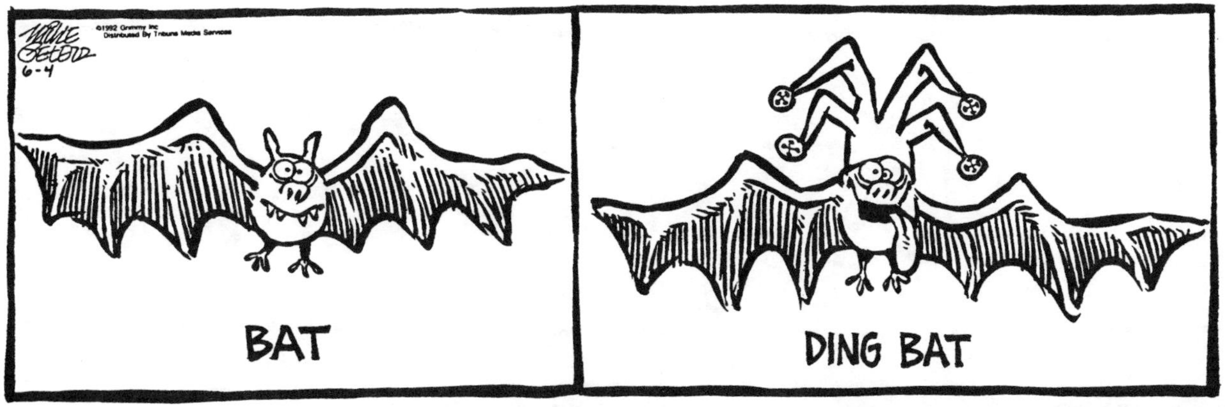
©1992 Grimmy Inc. Distributed By Tribune Media Services
6-4
BAT
DING BAT

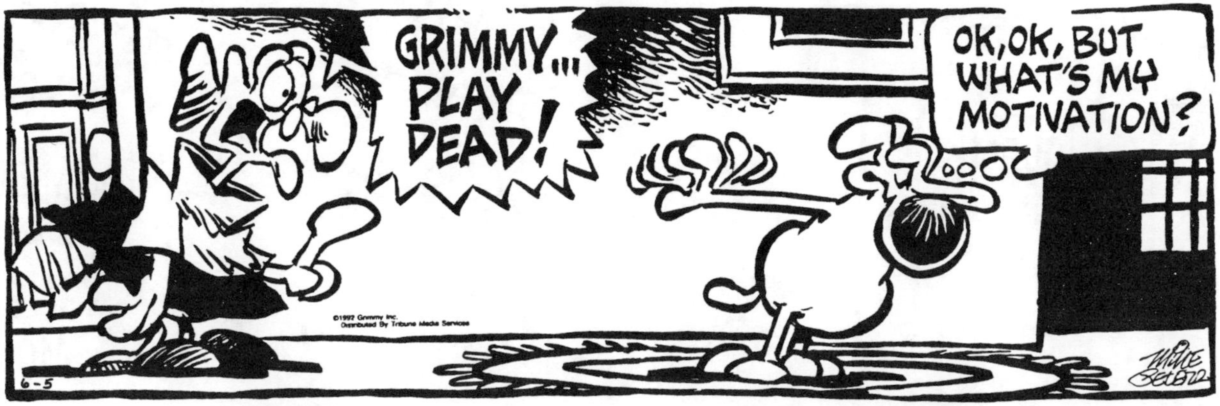
GRIMMY... PLAY DEAD!
OK, OK, BUT WHAT'S MY MOTIVATION?
©1992 Grimmy Inc. Distributed By Tribune Media Services
6-5

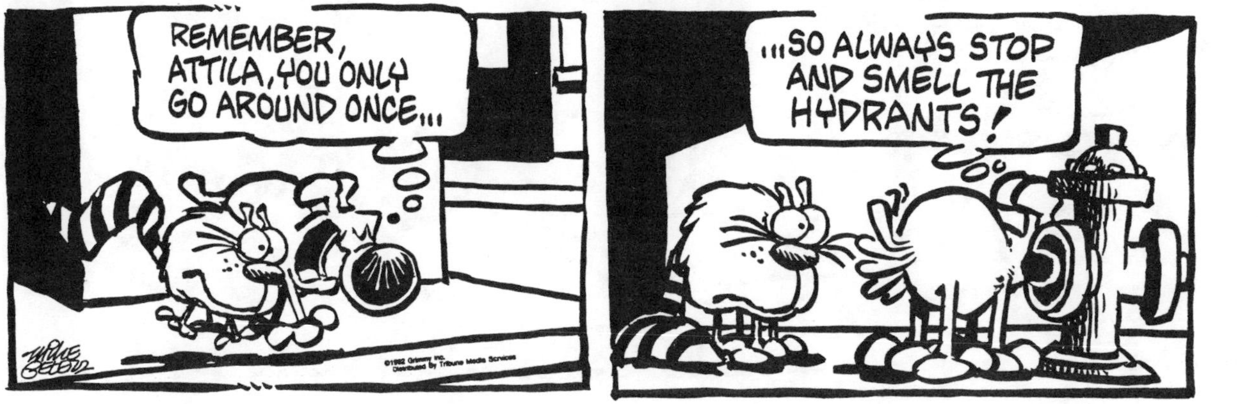
REMEMBER, ATTILA, YOU ONLY GO AROUND ONCE...
...SO ALWAYS STOP AND SMELL THE HYDRANTS!
©1992 Grimmy Inc. Distributed By Tribune Media Services

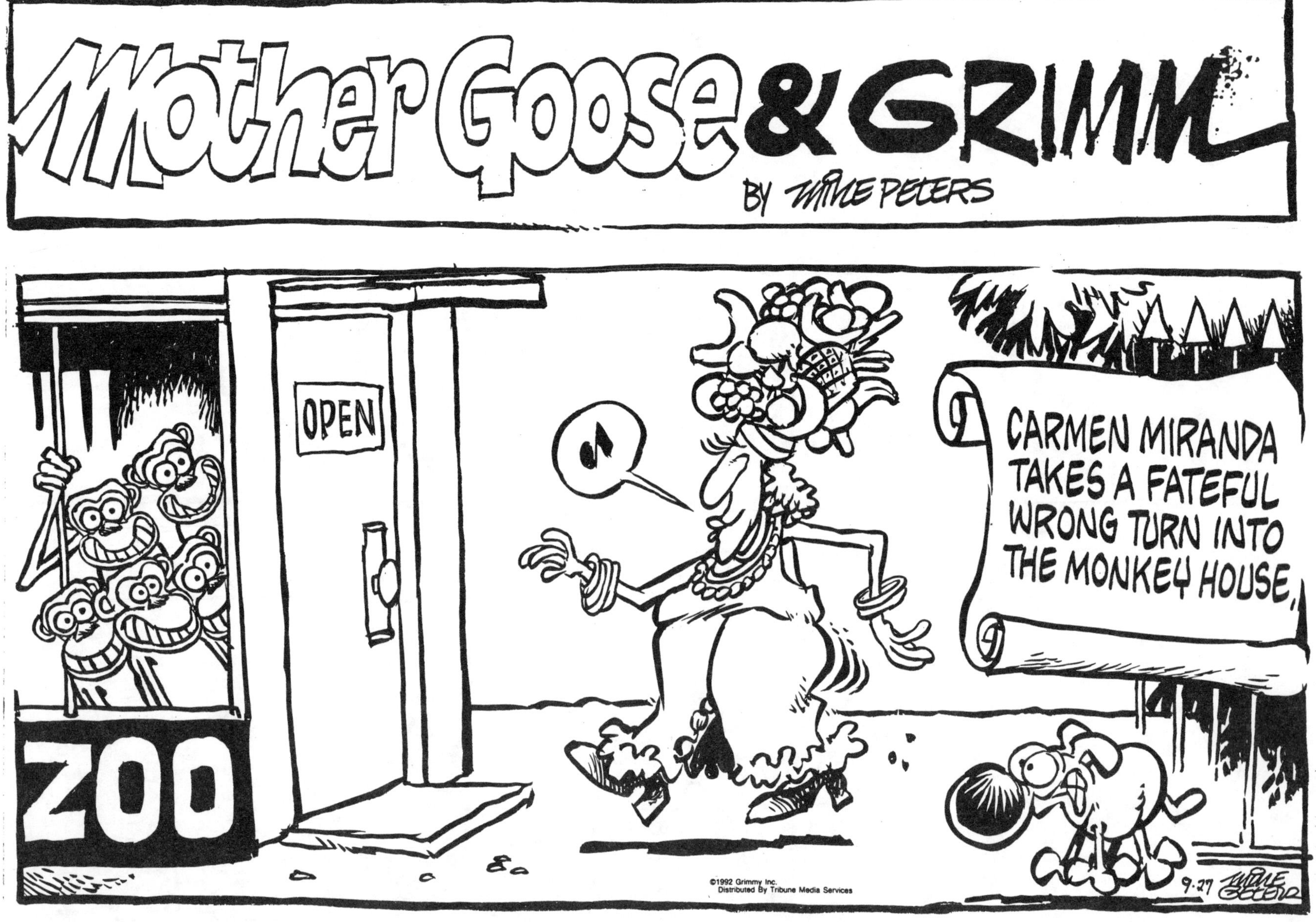
Mother Goose & GRIMM
BY MIKE PETERS
OPEN
ZOO
CARMEN MIRANDA TAKES A FATEFUL WRONG TURN INTO THE MONKEY HOUSE.
©1992 Grimmy Inc.
Distributed By Tribune Media Services
9-27

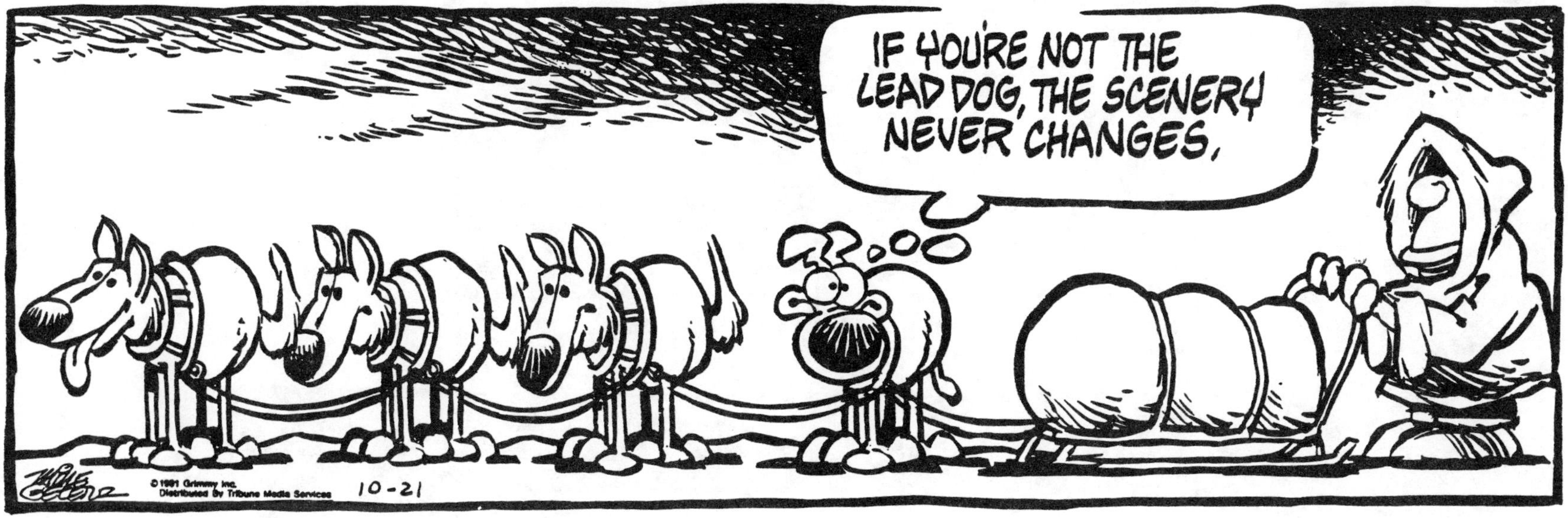
IF YOU'RE NOT THE LEAD DOG, THE SCENERY NEVER CHANGES.
© 1991 Grimmy Inc. Distributed By Tribune Media Services
10-21

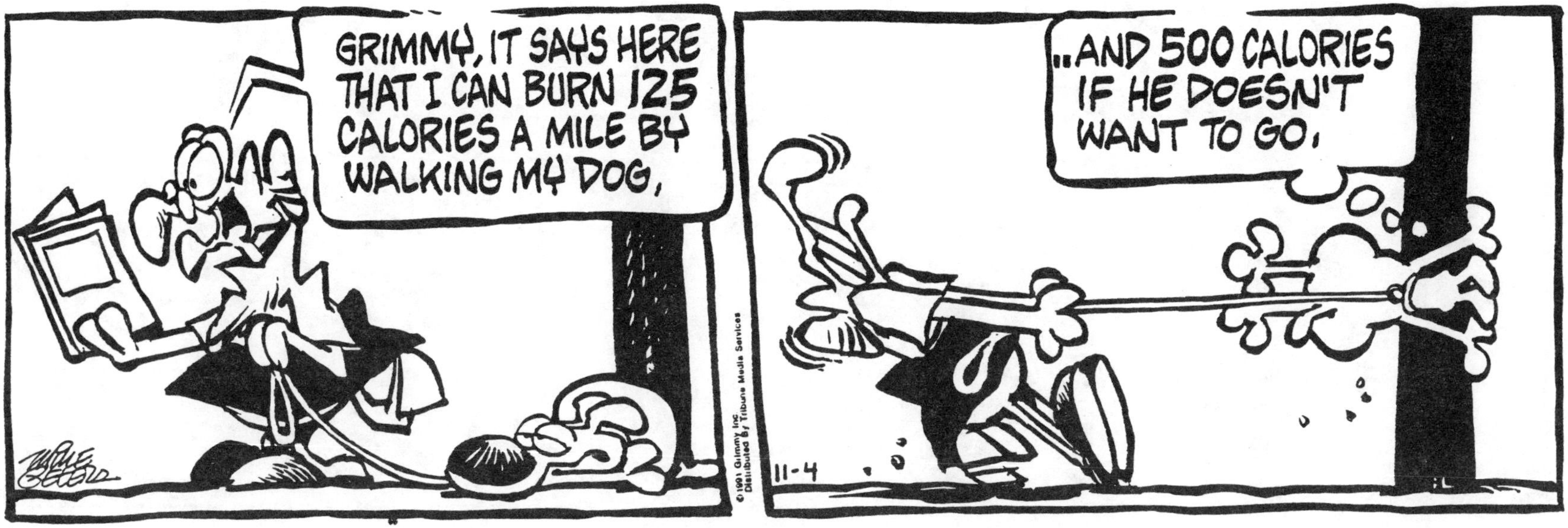
GRIMMY, IT SAYS HERE THAT I CAN BURN 125 CALORIES A MILE BY WALKING MY DOG.
..AND 500 CALORIES IF HE DOESN'T WANT TO GO.
© 1991 Grimmy Inc. Distributed By Tribune Media Services
11-4

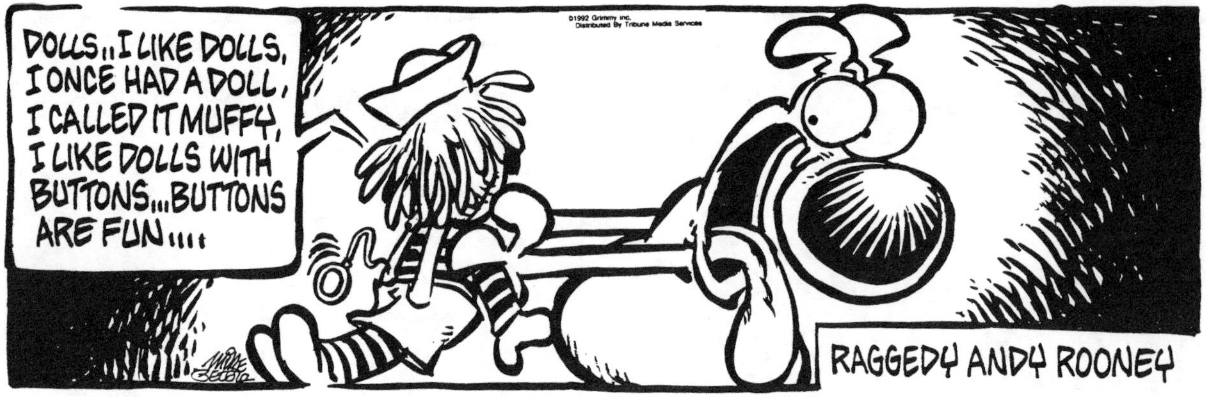

DOLLS.. I LIKE DOLLS, I ONCE HAD A DOLL, I CALLED IT MUFFY, I LIKE DOLLS WITH BUTTONS... BUTTONS ARE FUN....
©1992 Grimmy Inc. Distributed By Tribune Media Services
RAGGEDY ANDY ROONEY


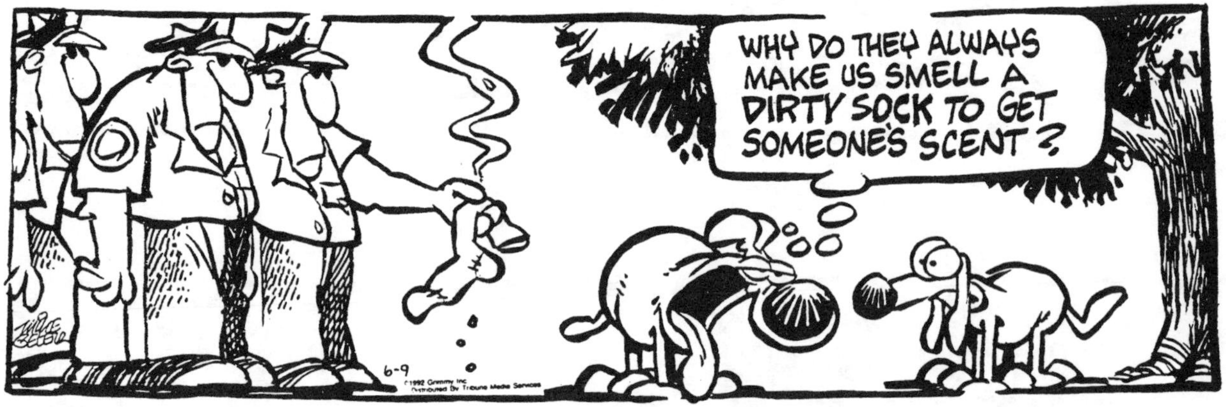

WHY DO THEY ALWAYS MAKE US SMELL A DIRTY SOCK TO GET SOMEONE'S SCENT?
6-9
©1992 Grimmy Inc. Distributed By Tribune Media Services


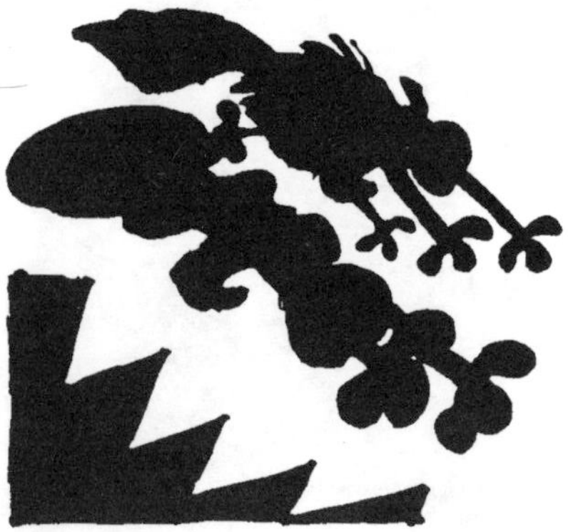

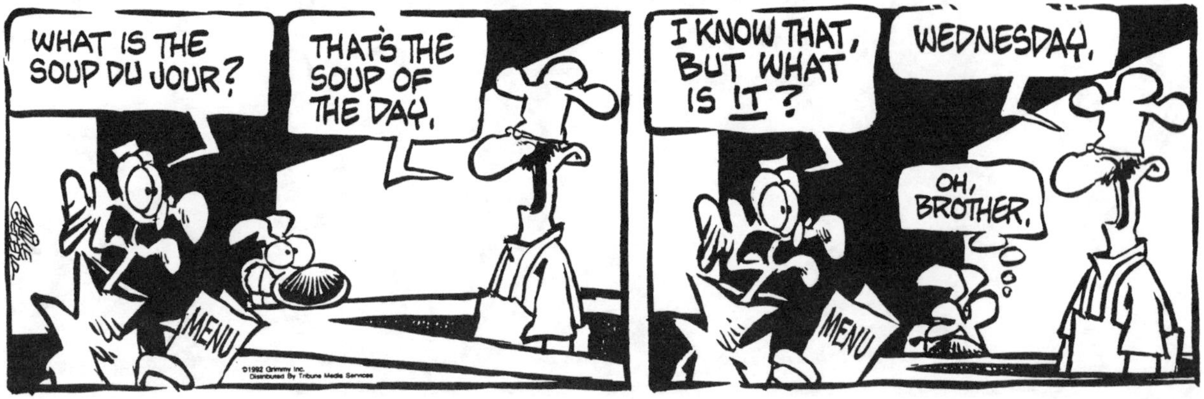

WHAT IS THE SOUP DU JOUR?
THAT'S THE SOUP OF THE DAY.
MENU
©1992 Grimmy Inc. Distributed By Tribune Media Services
I KNOW THAT, BUT WHAT IS IT?
WEDNESDAY.
OH, BROTHER.
MENU

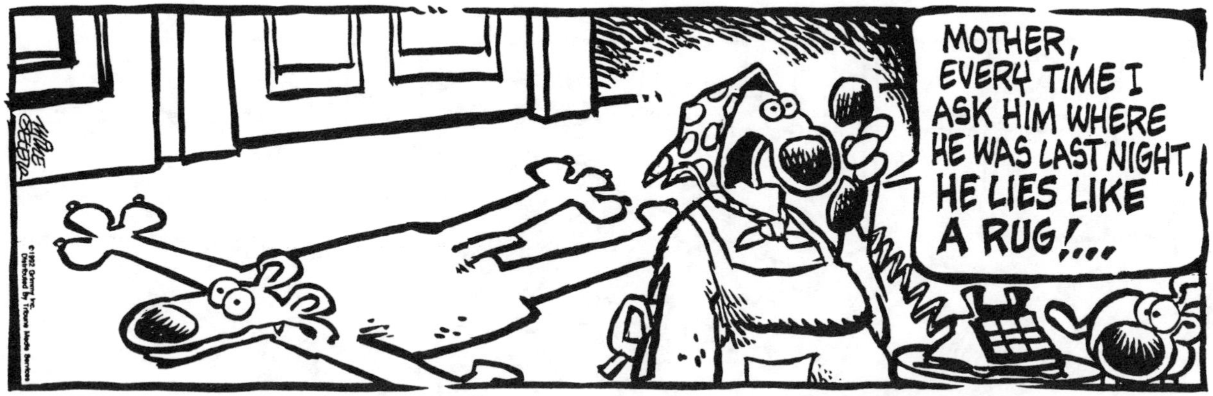
MOTHER, EVERY TIME I ASK HIM WHERE HE WAS LAST NIGHT, HE LIES LIKE A RUG!...
©1992 Grimmy Inc. Distributed By Tribune Media Services

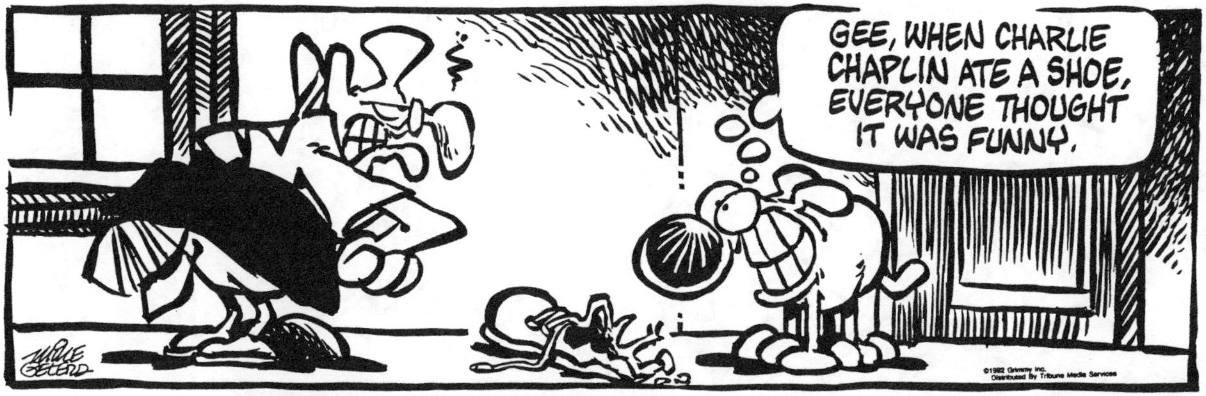
GEE, WHEN CHARLIE CHAPLIN ATE A SHOE, EVERYONE THOUGHT IT WAS FUNNY.
©1992 Grimmy Inc. Distributed By Tribune Media Services

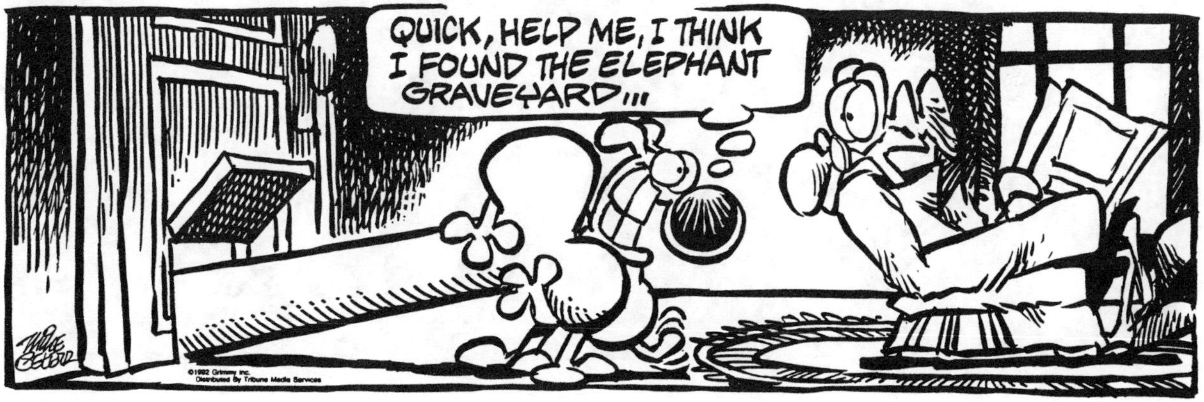
QUICK, HELP ME, I THINK I FOUND THE ELEPHANT GRAVEYARD...
©1992 Grimmy Inc. Distributed By Tribune Media Services

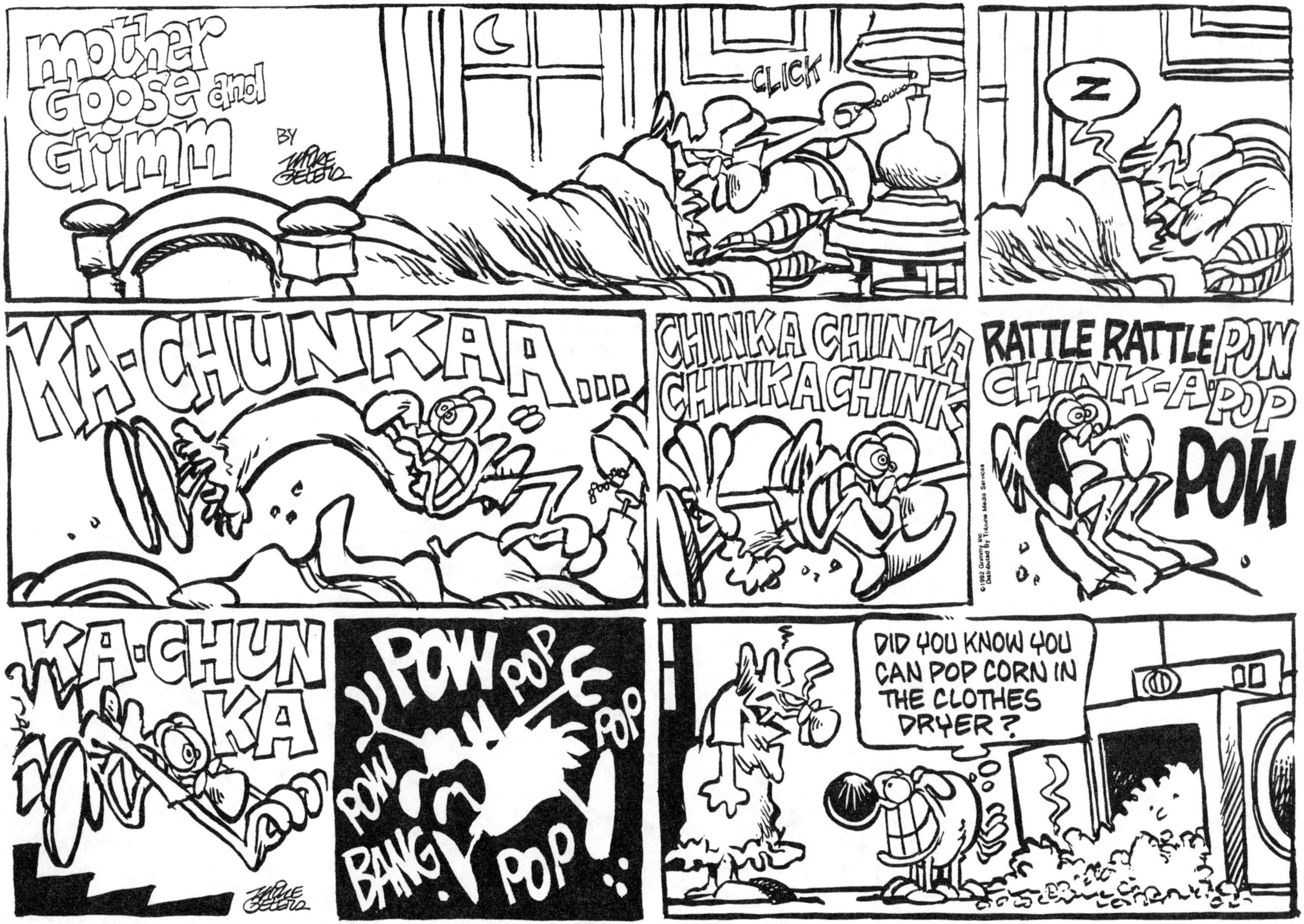
mother Goose and Grimm
BY
CLICK
Z
KA-CHUNKAA...
CHINKA CHINKA CHINKA CHINK
RATTLE RATTLE POW
CHINK-A-POP
POW
©1992 Grimmy Inc. Distributed By Tribune Media Services
KA-CHUN KA
POW POP
POP
POW
BANG
POP
DID YOU KNOW YOU CAN POP CORN IN THE CLOTHES DRYER?

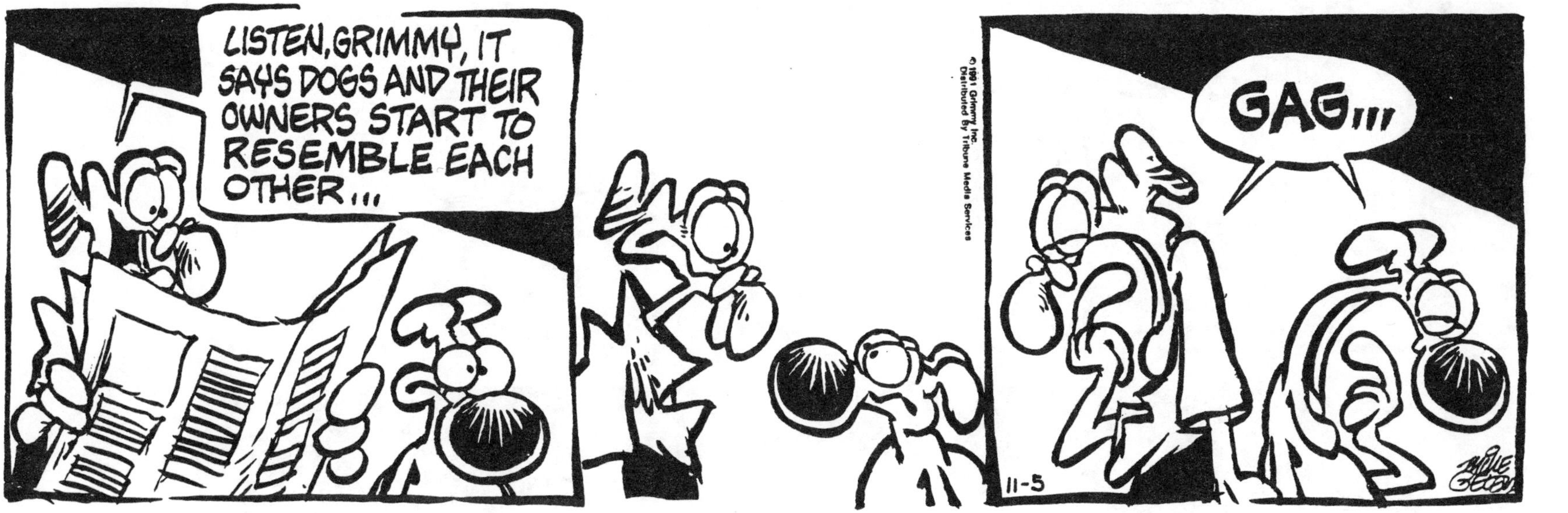
LISTEN, GRIMMY, IT SAYS DOGS AND THEIR OWNERS START TO RESEMBLE EACH OTHER...
GAG...
© 1991 Grimmy Inc. Distributed By Tribune Media Services
11-5
MIKE PETERS

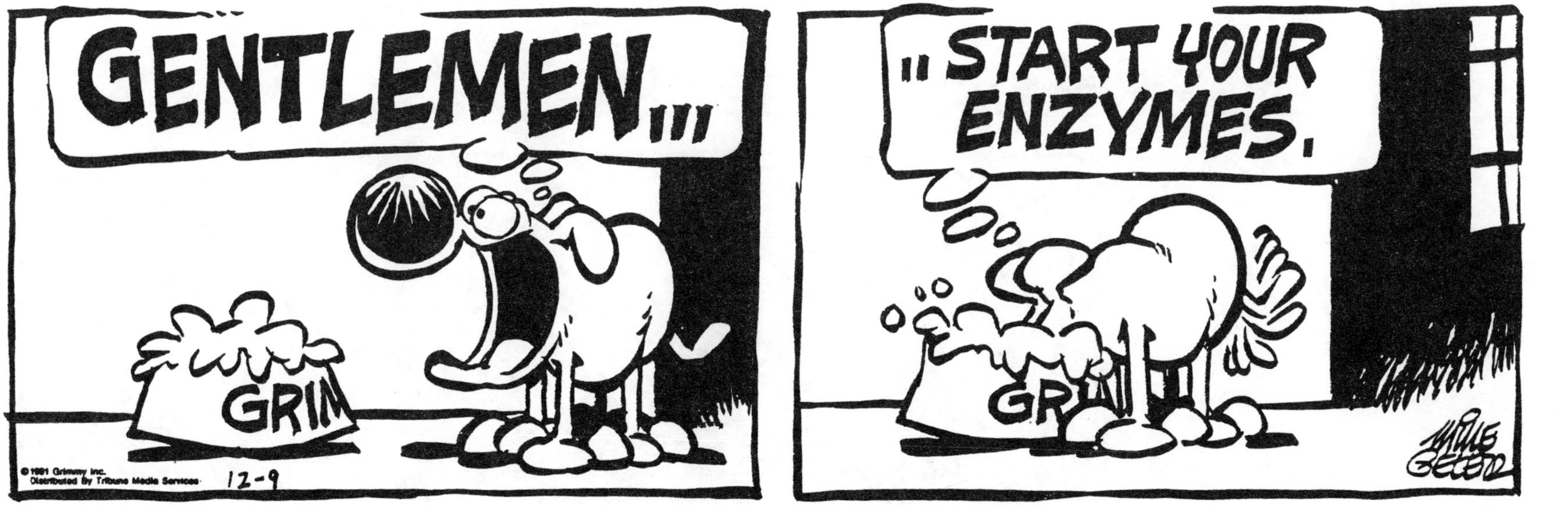
GENTLEMEN...
GRIM
.. START YOUR ENZYMES.
GR
© 1991 Grimmy Inc. Distributed By Tribune Media Services
12-9
MIKE PETERS

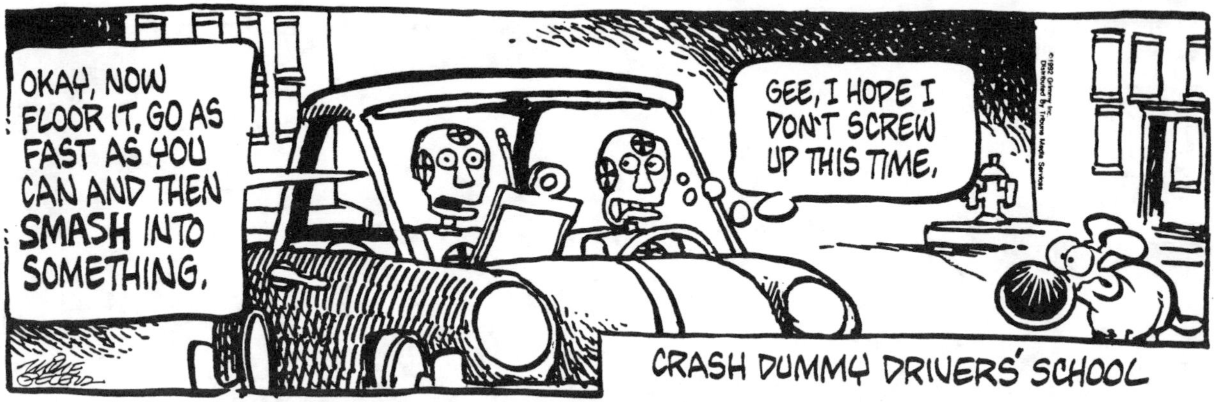
OKAY, NOW FLOOR IT, GO AS FAST AS YOU CAN AND THEN SMASH INTO SOMETHING.
GEE, I HOPE I DON'T SCREW UP THIS TIME.

CRASH DUMMY DRIVERS' SCHOOL

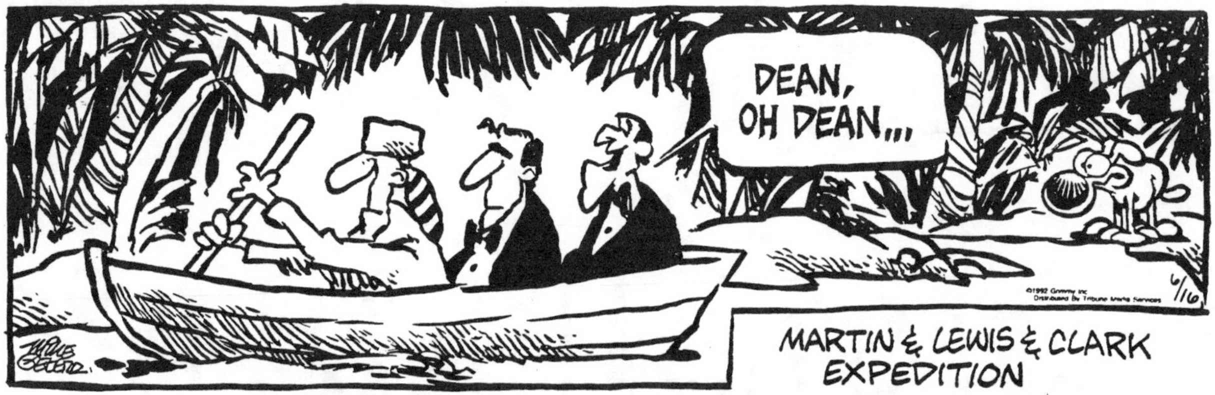
DEAN, OH DEAN...
6/16

MARTIN & LEWIS & CLARK EXPEDITION

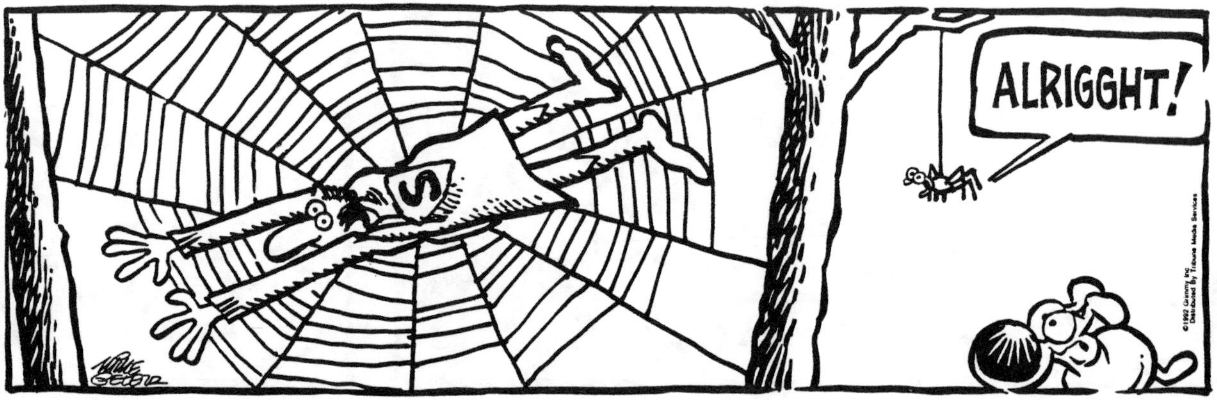
ALRIGGHT!
S

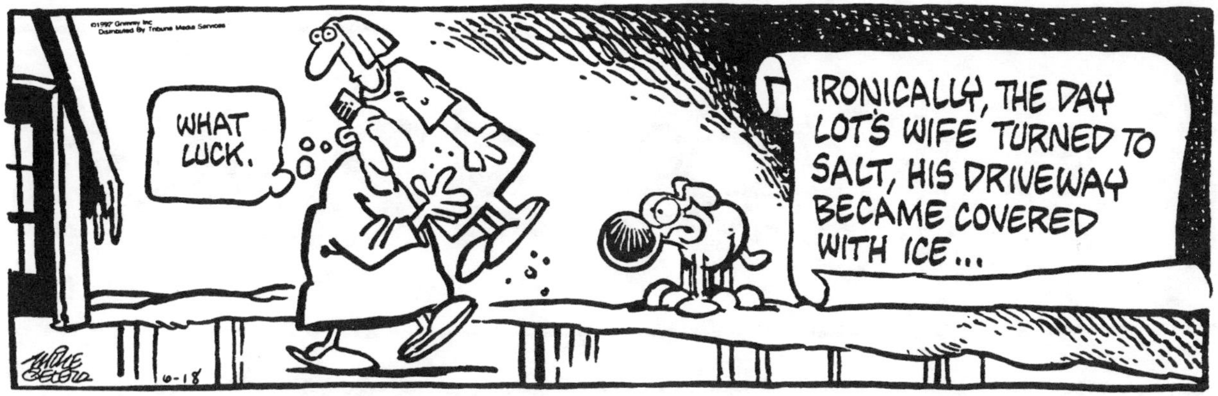
©1992 Grimmy Inc
Distributed By Tribune Media Services
WHAT LUCK.
IRONICALLY, THE DAY LOT'S WIFE TURNED TO SALT, HIS DRIVEWAY BECAME COVERED WITH ICE...
6-18

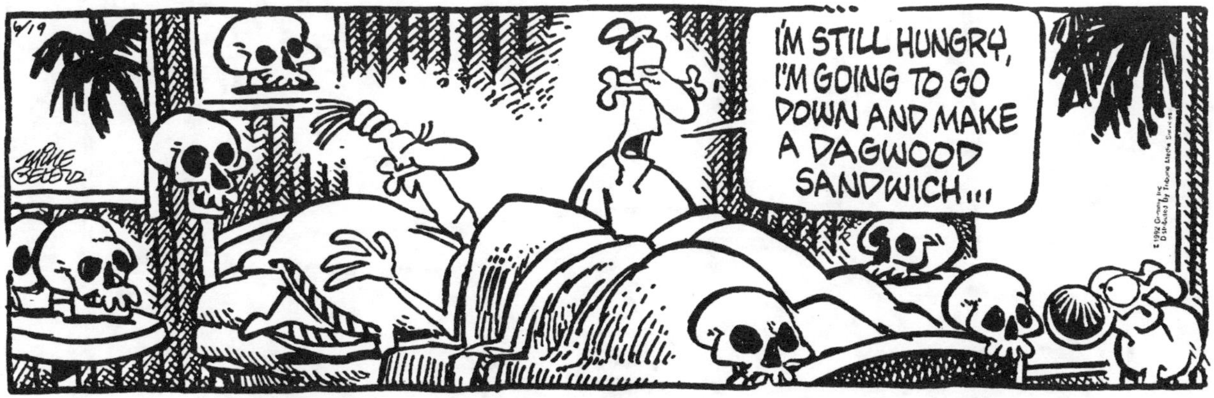
6/19
I'M STILL HUNGRY, I'M GOING TO GO DOWN AND MAKE A DAGWOOD SANDWICH...
©1992 Grimmy Inc
Distributed By Tribune Media Services

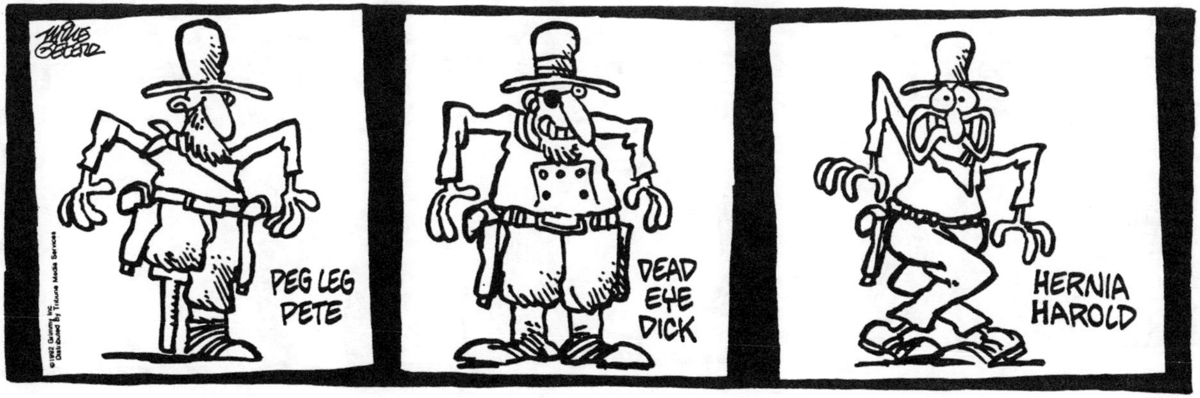
©1992 Grimmy Inc
Distributed By Tribune Media Services
PEG LEG PETE
DEAD EYE DICK
HERNIA HAROLD

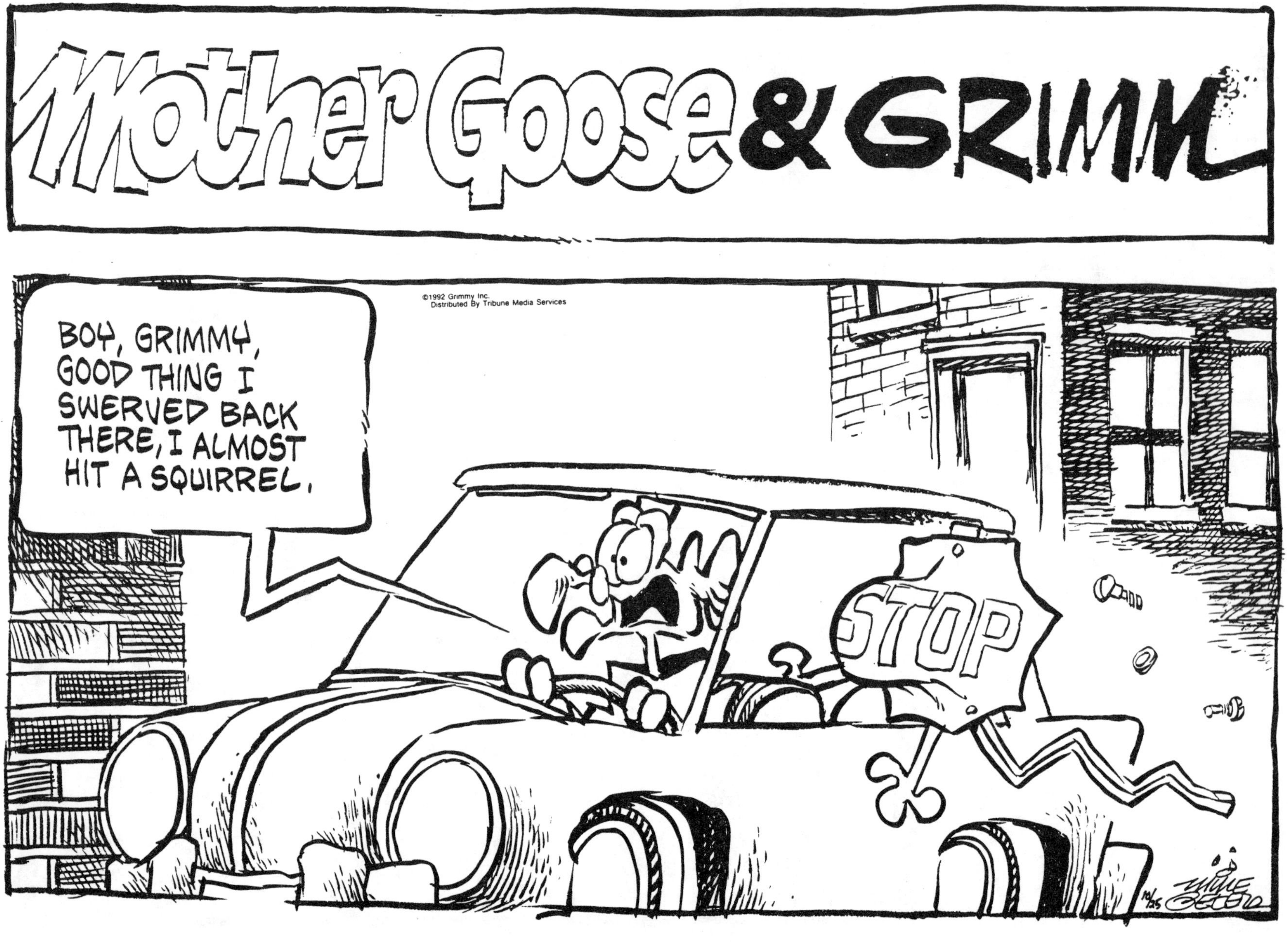

Mother Goose & GRIMM
©1992 Grimmy Inc. Distributed By Tribune Media Services
BOY, GRIMMY, GOOD THING I SWERVED BACK THERE, I ALMOST HIT A SQUIRREL.
STOP

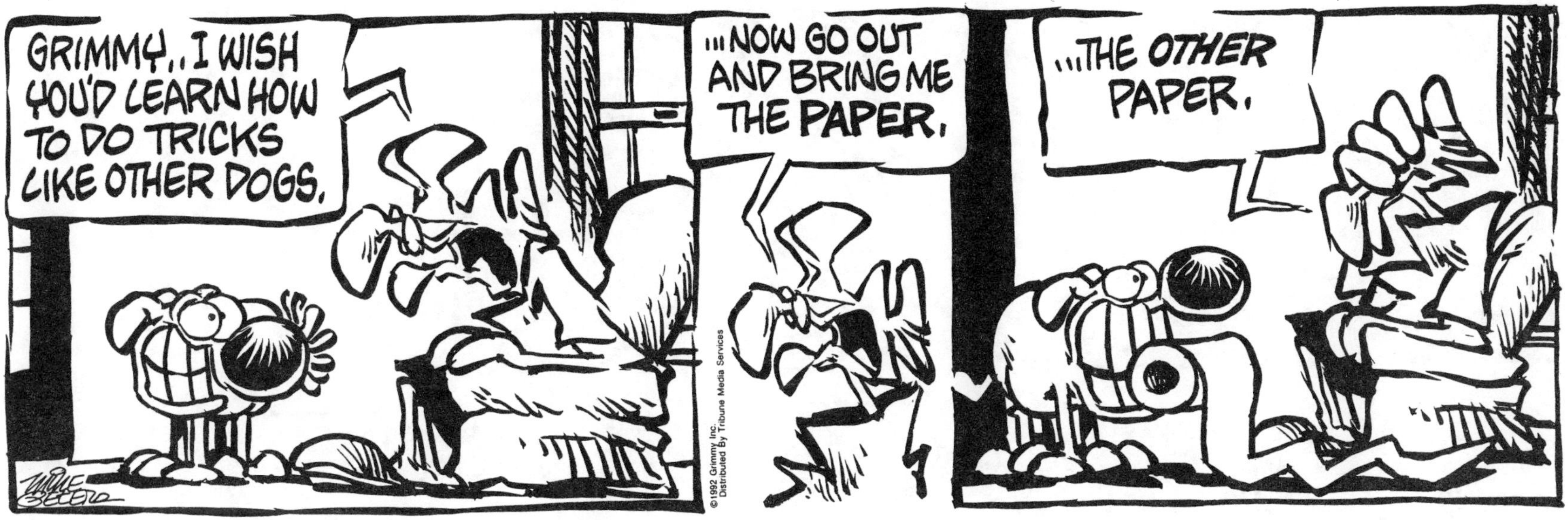
GRIMMY.. I WISH YOU'D LEARN HOW TO DO TRICKS LIKE OTHER DOGS.
...NOW GO OUT AND BRING ME THE PAPER.
...THE OTHER PAPER.
©1992 Grimmy Inc. Distributed By Tribune Media Services

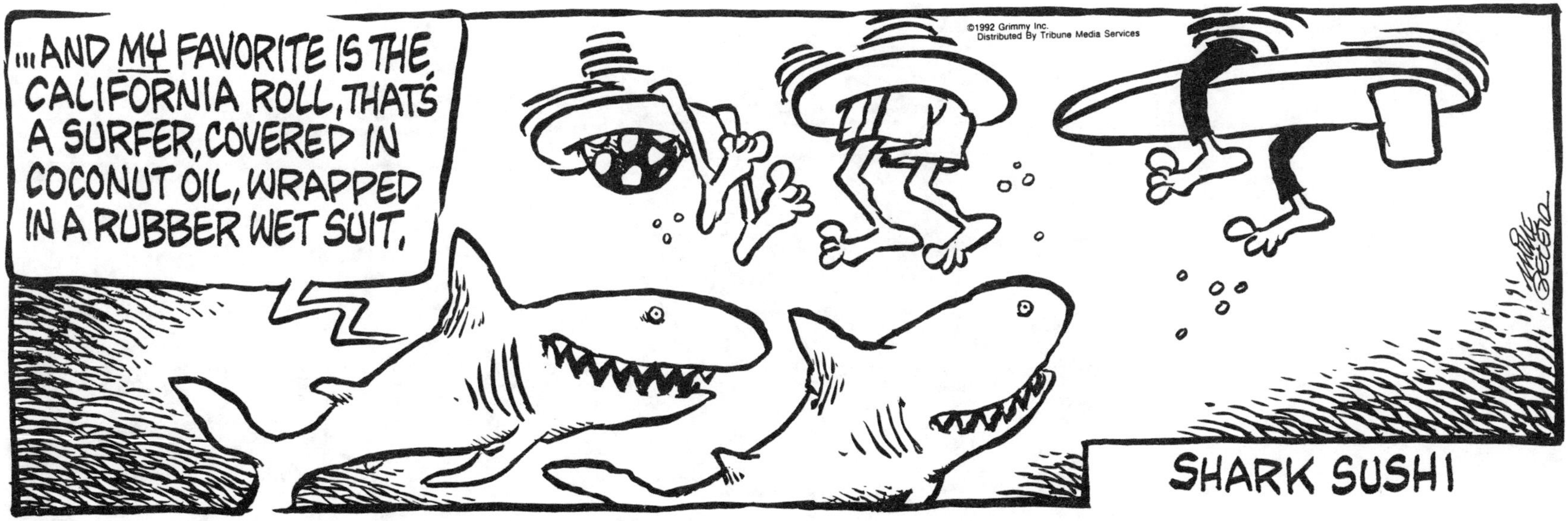
...AND MY FAVORITE IS THE CALIFORNIA ROLL, THAT'S A SURFER, COVERED IN COCONUT OIL, WRAPPED IN A RUBBER WET SUIT.
©1992 Grimmy Inc. Distributed By Tribune Media Services
SHARK SUSHI

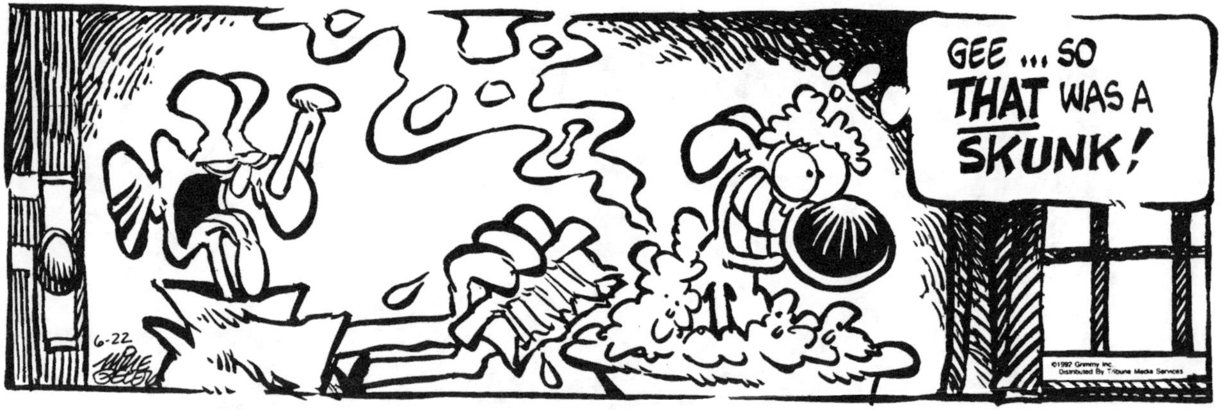
GEE ... SO THAT WAS A SKUNK!
6-22
©1992 Grimmy Inc. Distributed By Tribune Media Services

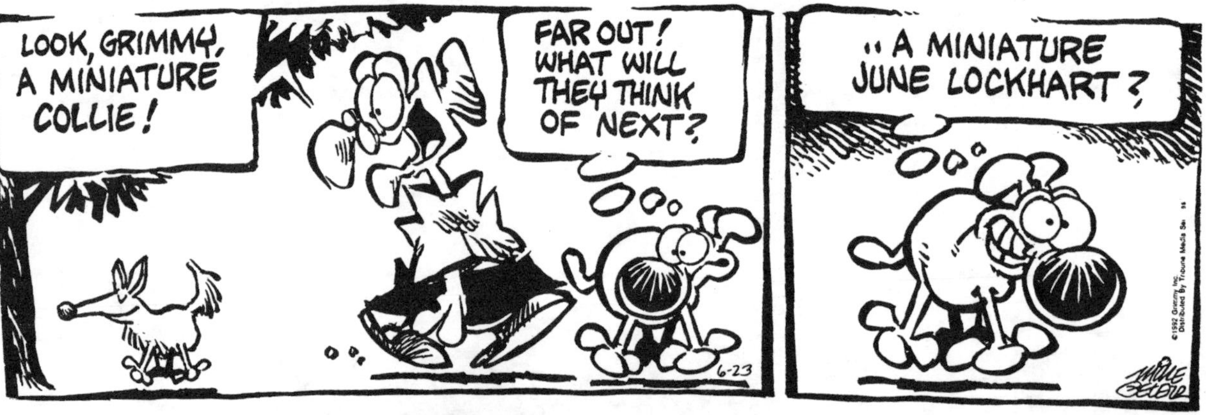
LOOK, GRIMMY, A MINIATURE COLLIE!
FAR OUT! WHAT WILL THEY THINK OF NEXT?
.. A MINIATURE JUNE LOCKHART?
6-23

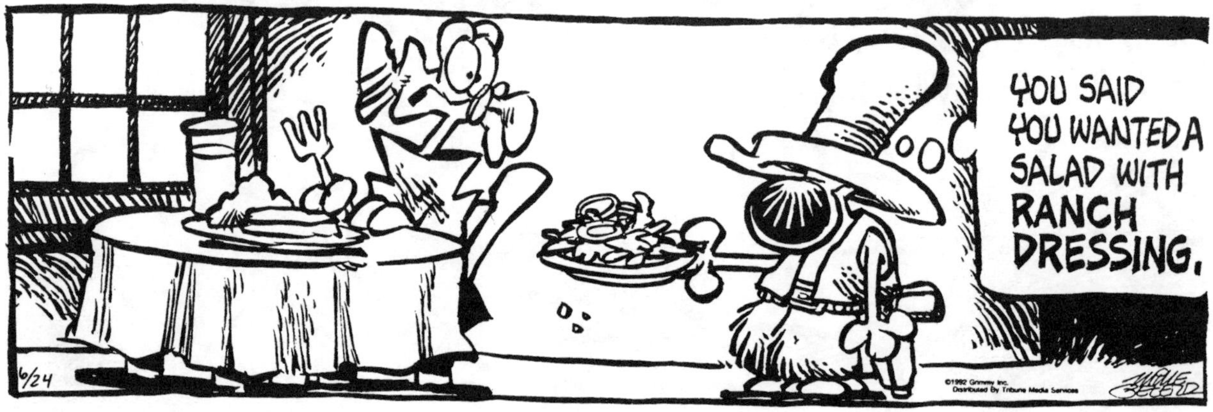
YOU SAID YOU WANTED A SALAD WITH RANCH DRESSING.
6/24
©1992 Grimmy Inc. Distributed By Tribune Media Services

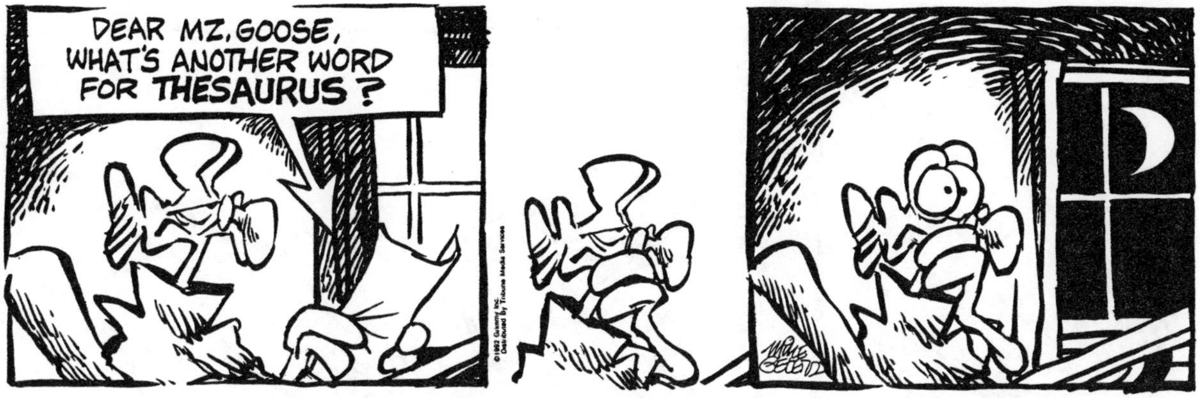
DEAR MZ. GOOSE, WHAT'S ANOTHER WORD FOR THESAURUS ?
©1992 Grimmy Inc. Distributed By Tribune Media Services

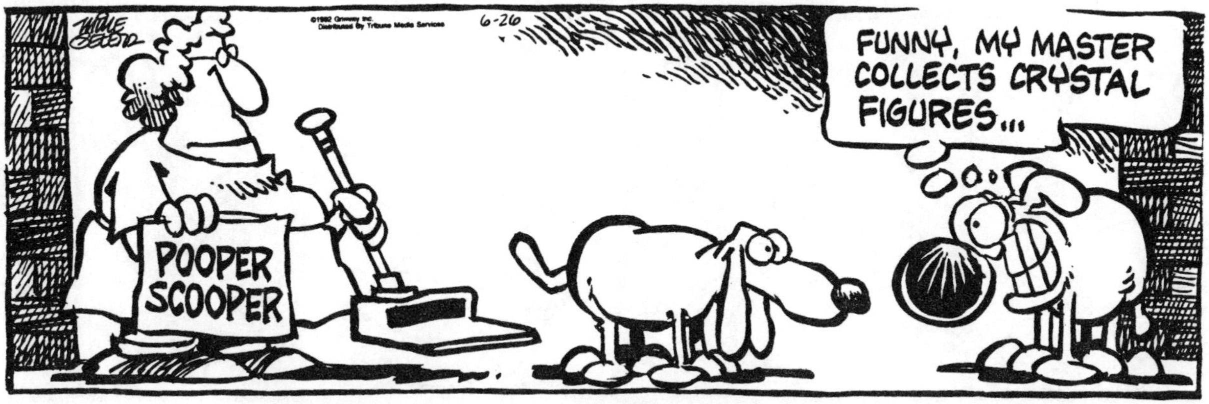
©1992 Grimmy Inc. Distributed By Tribune Media Services
6-26
FUNNY, MY MASTER COLLECTS CRYSTAL FIGURES...
POOPER SCOOPER

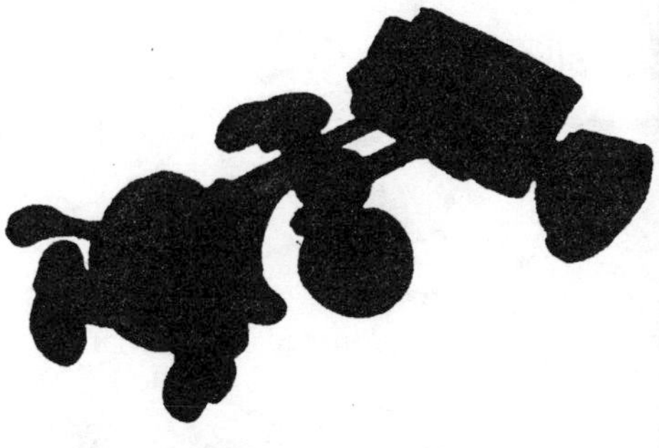

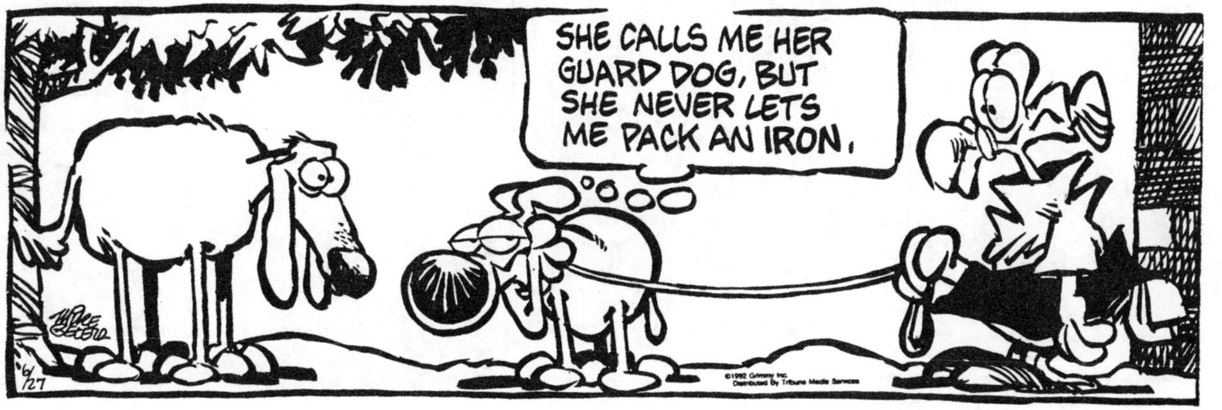
SHE CALLS ME HER GUARD DOG, BUT SHE NEVER LETS ME PACK AN IRON.
6/27
©1992 Grimmy Inc. Distributed By Tribune Media Services

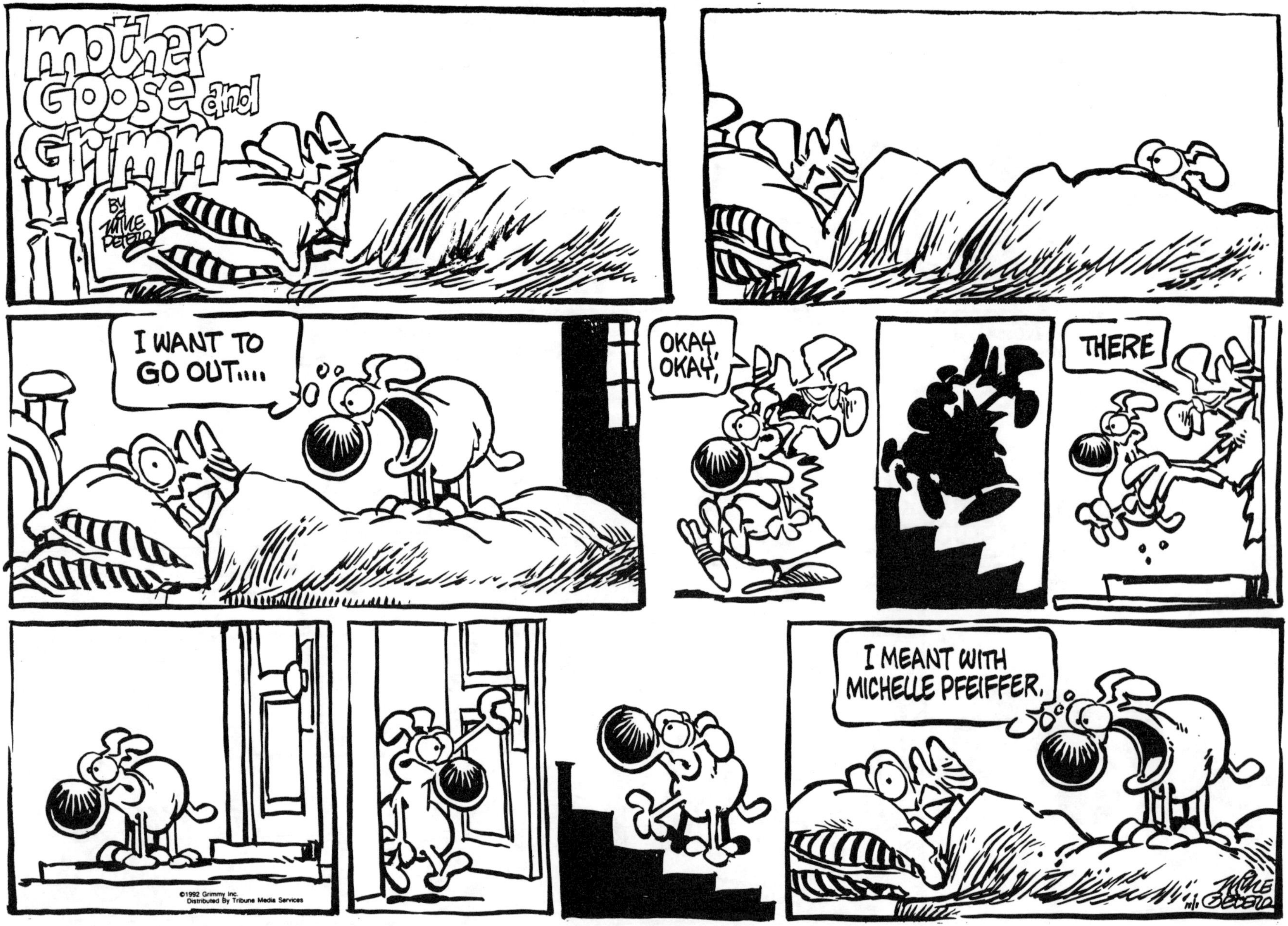
mother Goose and Grimm
BY MIKE PETERS
I WANT TO GO OUT....
OKAY, OKAY,
THERE
I MEANT WITH MICHELLE PFEIFFER.
©1992 Grimmy Inc. Distributed By Tribune Media Services
MIKE PETERS

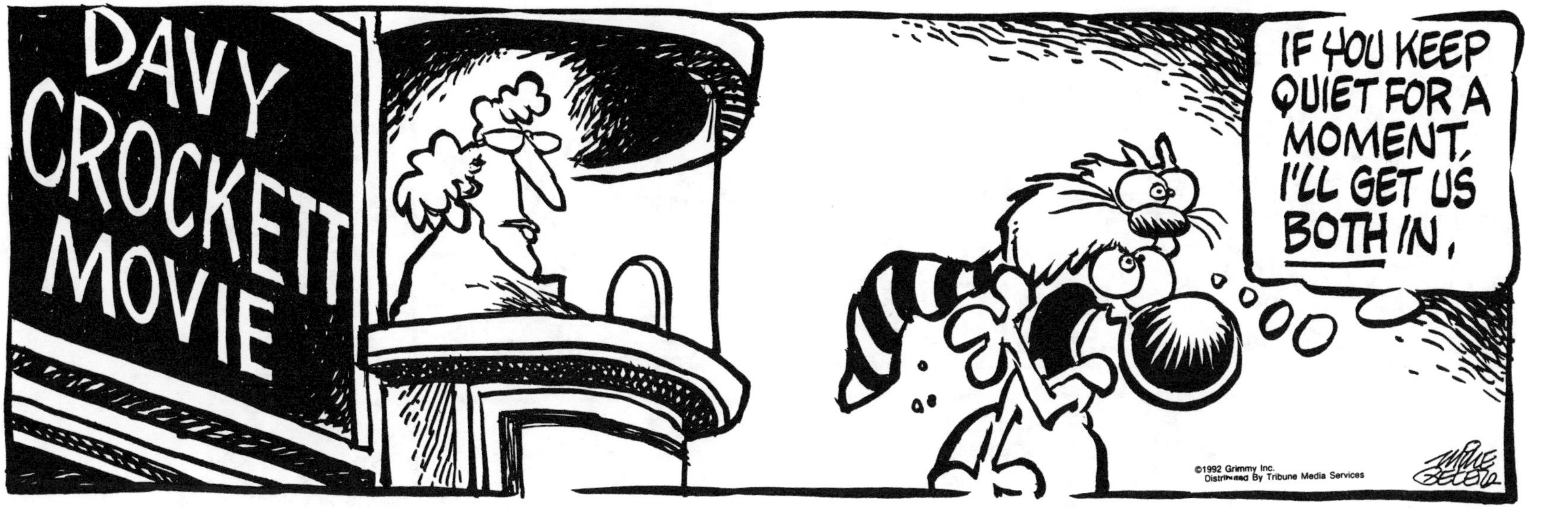
DAVY CROCKETT MOVIE
IF YOU KEEP QUIET FOR A MOMENT, I'LL GET US BOTH IN.
©1992 Grimmy Inc. Distributed By Tribune Media Services

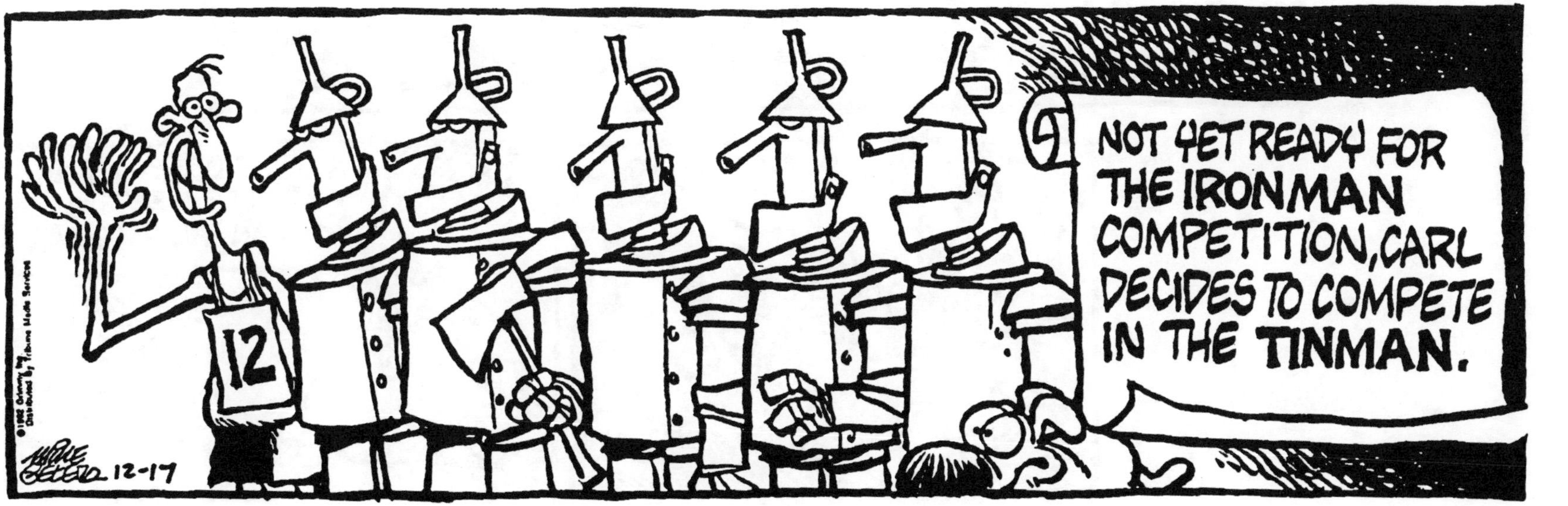
12
NOT YET READY FOR THE IRONMAN COMPETITION, CARL DECIDES TO COMPETE IN THE TINMAN.
12-17

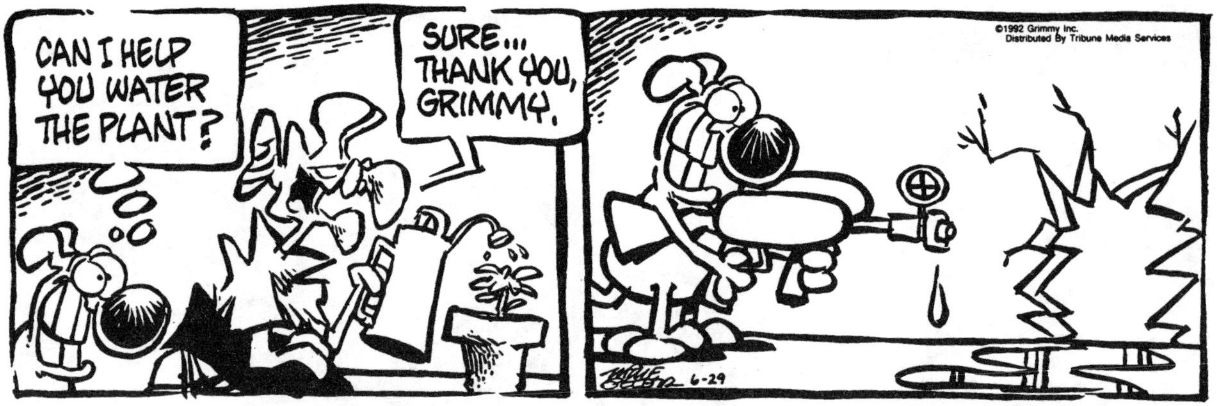
CAN I HELP YOU WATER THE PLANT?
SURE... THANK YOU, GRIMMY.
©1992 Grimmy Inc.
Distributed By Tribune Media Services
6-29

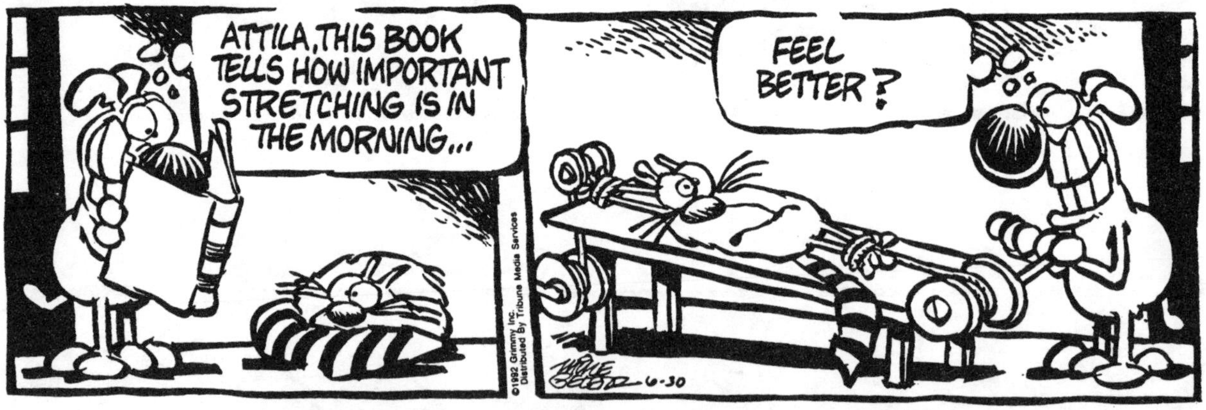
ATTILA, THIS BOOK TELLS HOW IMPORTANT STRETCHING IS IN THE MORNING...
©1992 Grimmy Inc.
Distributed By Tribune Media Services
FEEL BETTER?
6-30

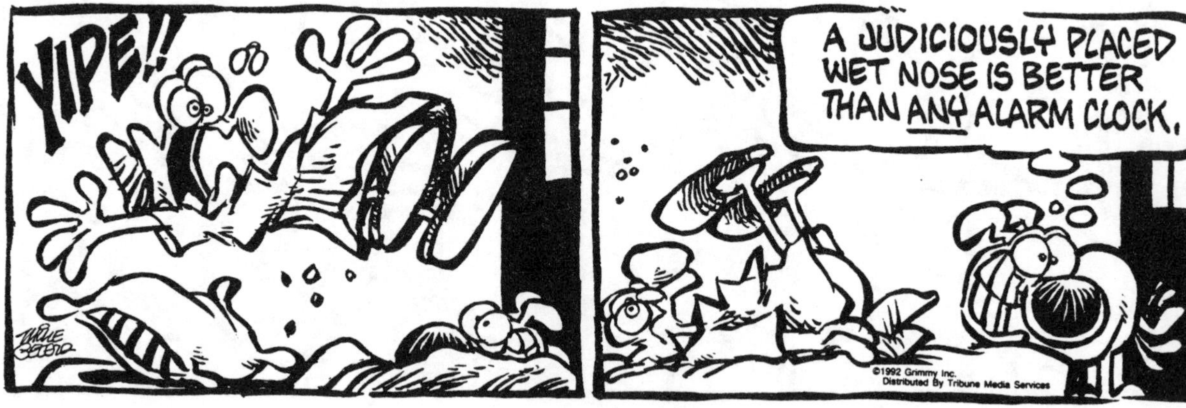
YIPE!!
A JUDICIOUSLY PLACED WET NOSE IS BETTER THAN ANY ALARM CLOCK.
©1992 Grimmy Inc.
Distributed By Tribune Media Services

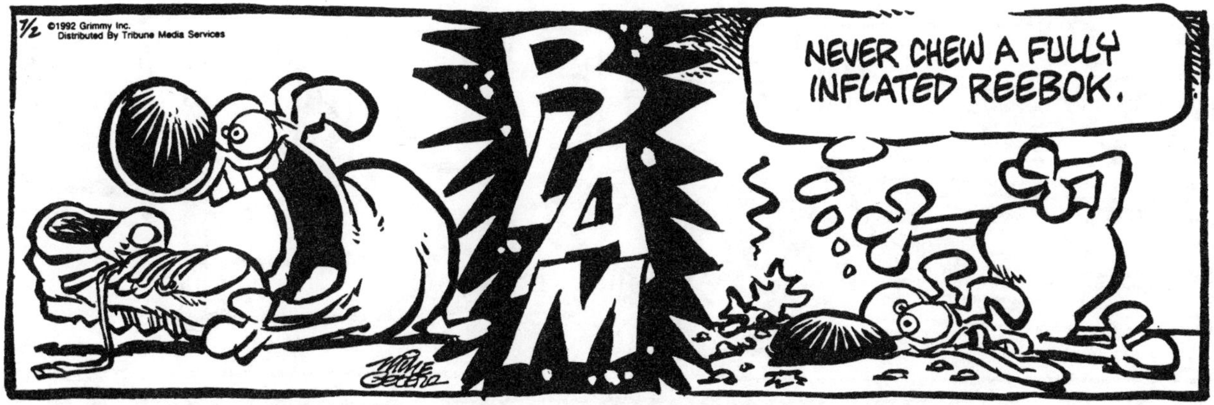
7/2 ©1992 Grimmy Inc.
Distributed By Tribune Media Services
BLAM
NEVER CHEW A FULLY INFLATED REEBOK.

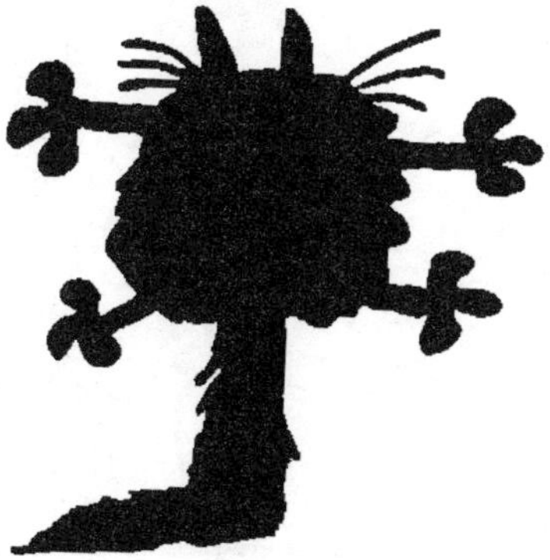

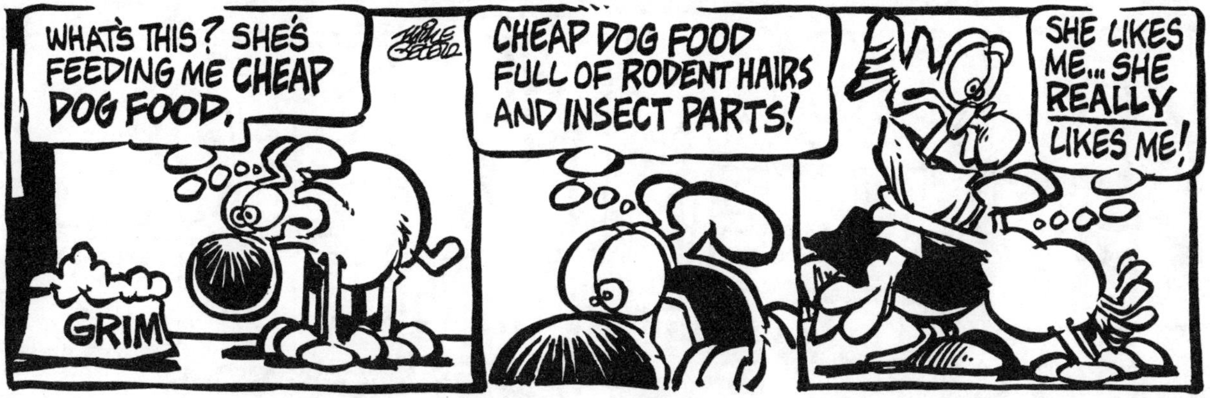
WHAT'S THIS? SHE'S FEEDING ME CHEAP DOG FOOD.
GRIM
CHEAP DOG FOOD FULL OF RODENT HAIRS AND INSECT PARTS!
SHE LIKES ME... SHE REALLY LIKES ME!

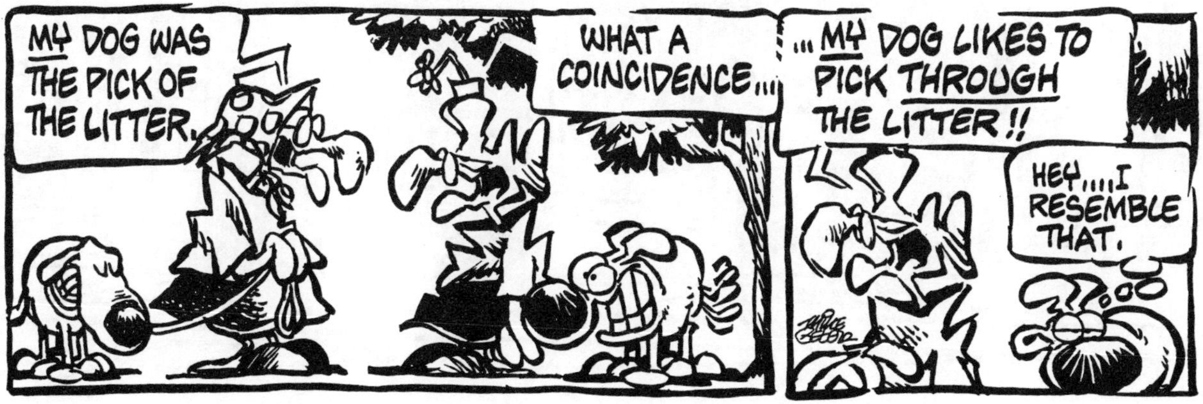
MY DOG WAS THE PICK OF THE LITTER.
WHAT A COINCIDENCE...
...MY DOG LIKES TO PICK THROUGH THE LITTER!!
HEY....I RESEMBLE THAT.

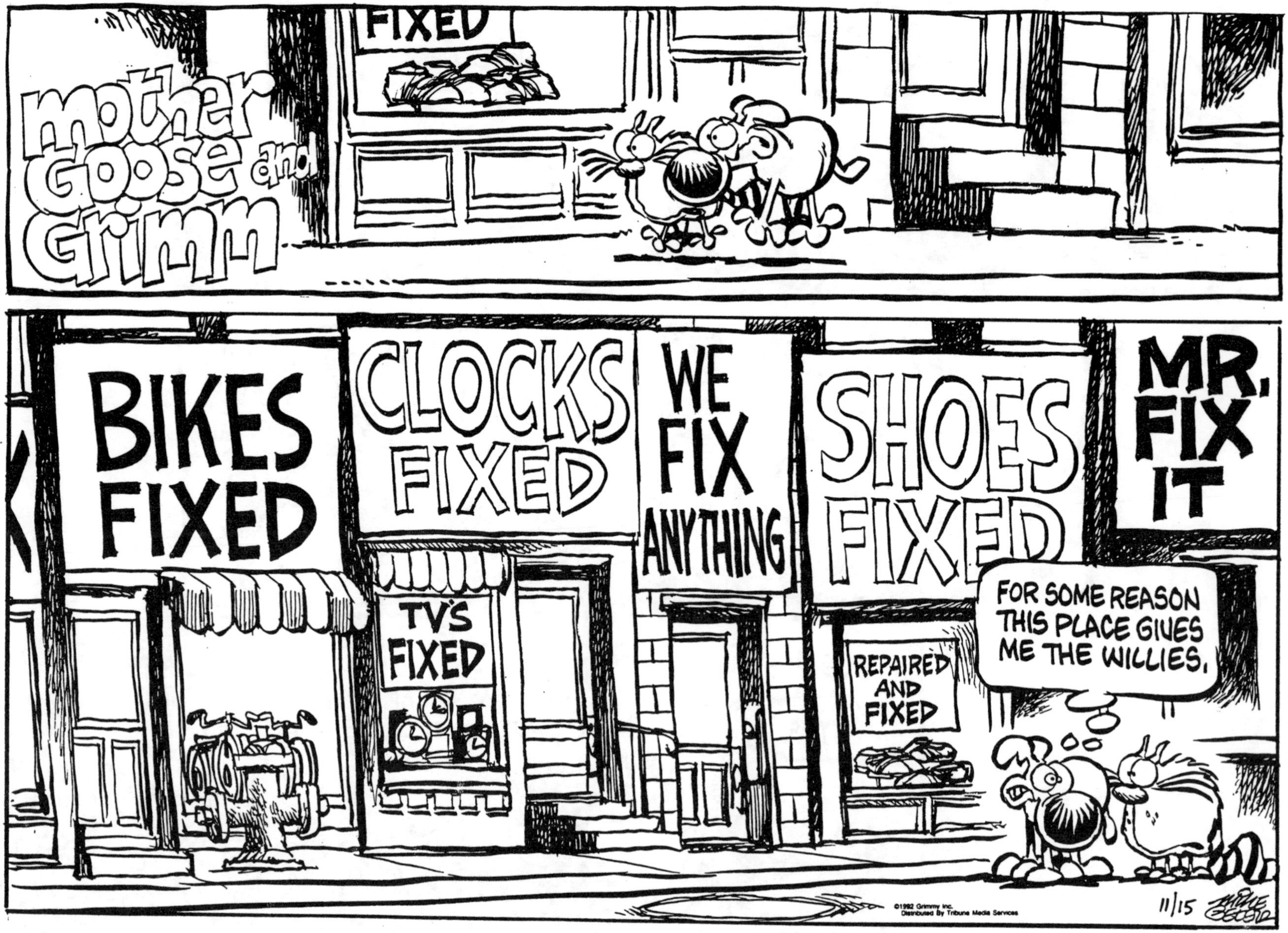
mother Goose and Grimm
FIXED
BIKES FIXED
CLOCKS FIXED
WE FIX ANYTHING
SHOES FIXED
MR. FIX IT
TV'S FIXED
REPAIRED AND FIXED
FOR SOME REASON THIS PLACE GIVES ME THE WILLIES.
©1992 Grimmy Inc. Distributed By Tribune Media Services
11/15

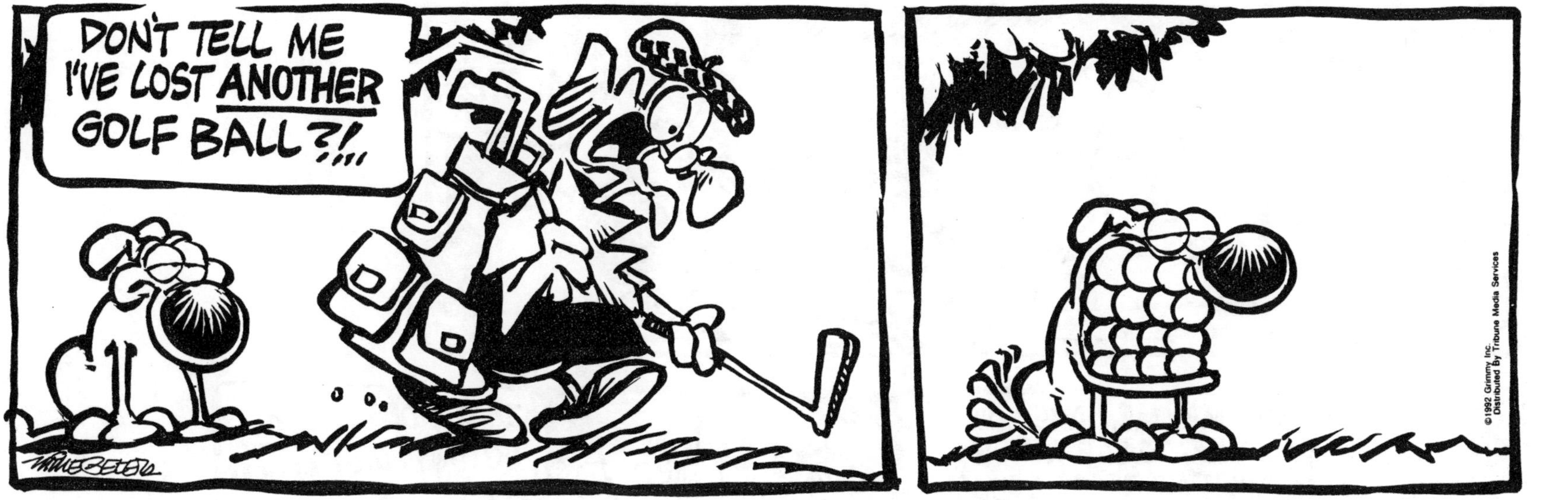
DON'T TELL ME I'VE LOST ANOTHER GOLF BALL?!...
©1992 Grimmy Inc. Distributed By Tribune Media Services

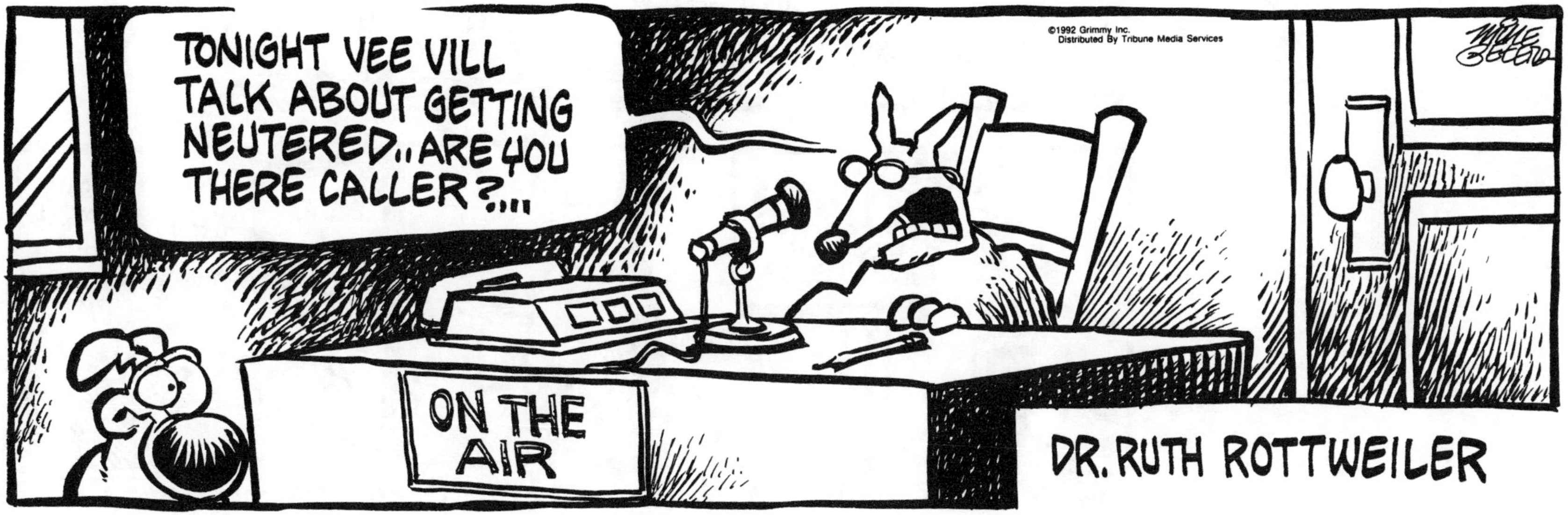
TONIGHT VEE VILL TALK ABOUT GETTING NEUTERED.. ARE YOU THERE CALLER?...
©1992 Grimmy Inc. Distributed By Tribune Media Services
ON THE AIR
DR. RUTH ROTTWEILER

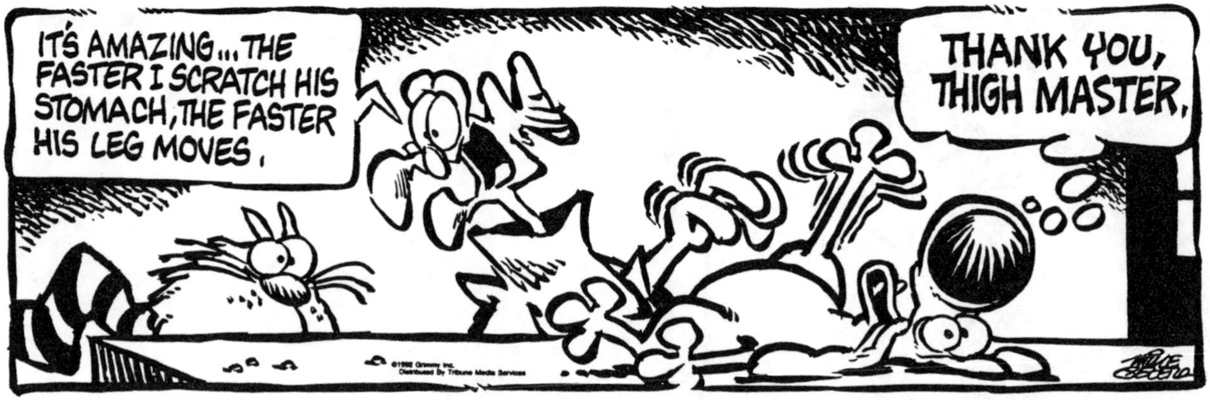
IT'S AMAZING... THE FASTER I SCRATCH HIS STOMACH, THE FASTER HIS LEG MOVES.
THANK YOU, THIGH MASTER.
©1992 Grimmy Inc. Distributed By Tribune Media Services

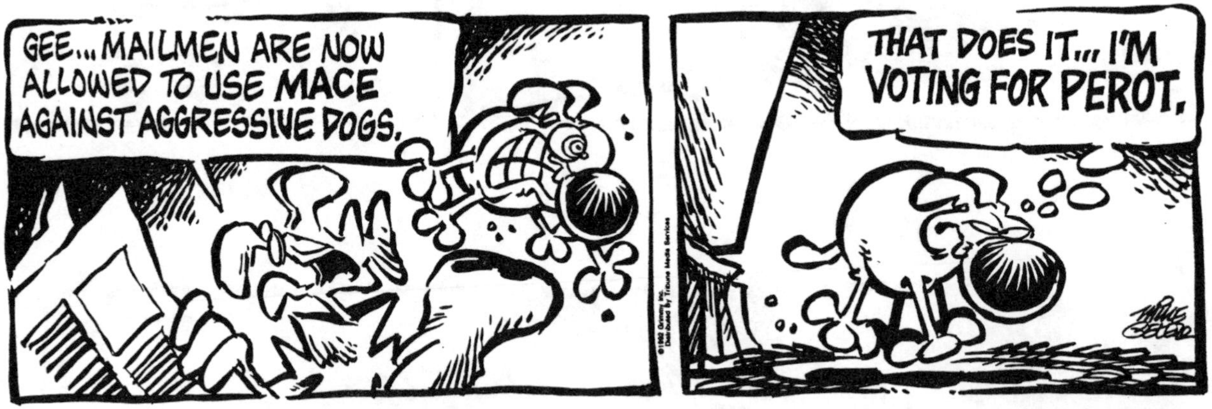
GEE... MAILMEN ARE NOW ALLOWED TO USE MACE AGAINST AGGRESSIVE DOGS.
THAT DOES IT... I'M VOTING FOR PEROT.
©1992 Grimmy Inc. Distributed By Tribune Media Services

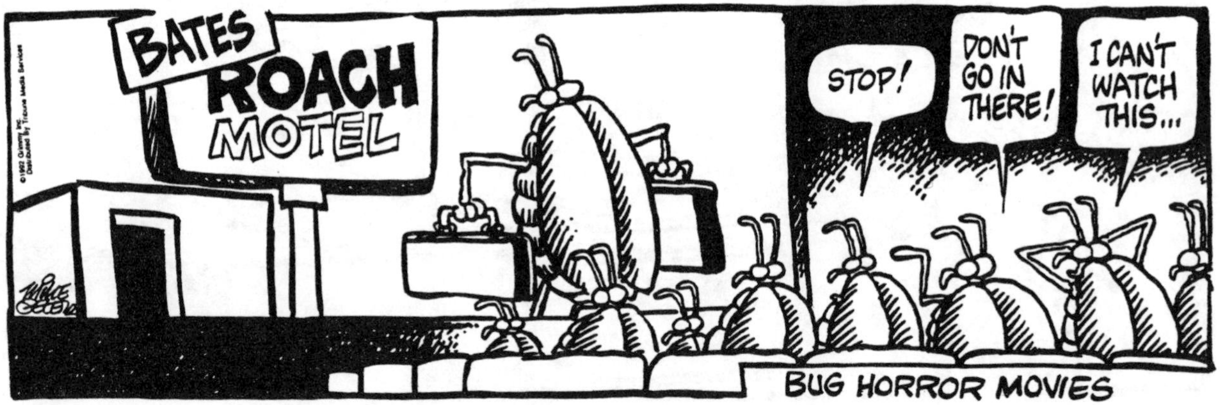
BATES
ROACH
MOTEL
STOP!
DON'T GO IN THERE!
I CAN'T WATCH THIS...
BUG HORROR MOVIES
©1992 Grimmy Inc. Distributed By Tribune Media Services

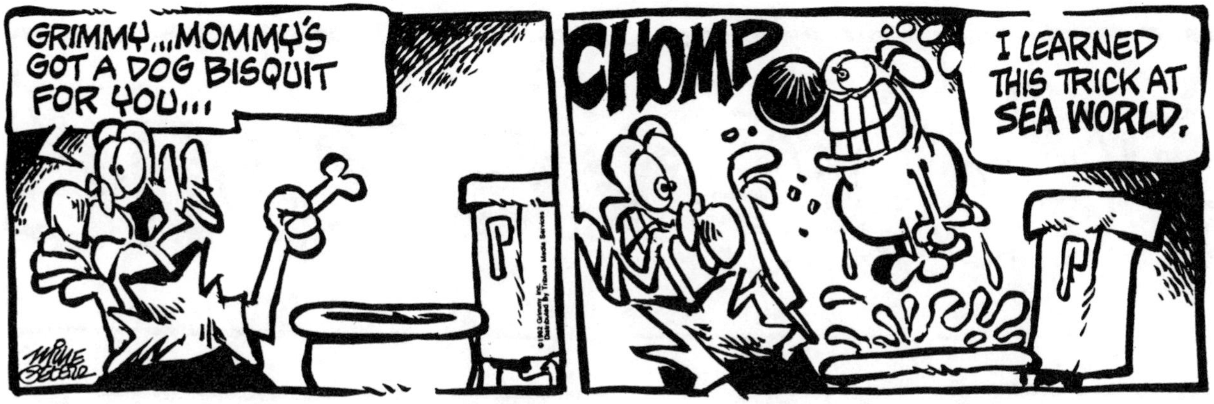
GRIMMY... MOMMY'S GOT A DOG BISQUIT FOR YOU...
CHOMP
I LEARNED THIS TRICK AT SEA WORLD.

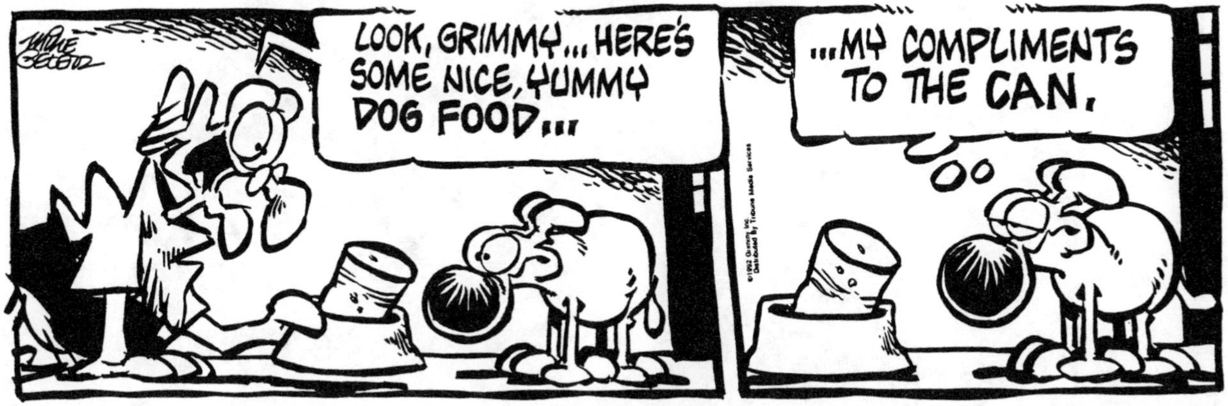
LOOK, GRIMMY... HERE'S SOME NICE, YUMMY DOG FOOD...
...MY COMPLIMENTS TO THE CAN.

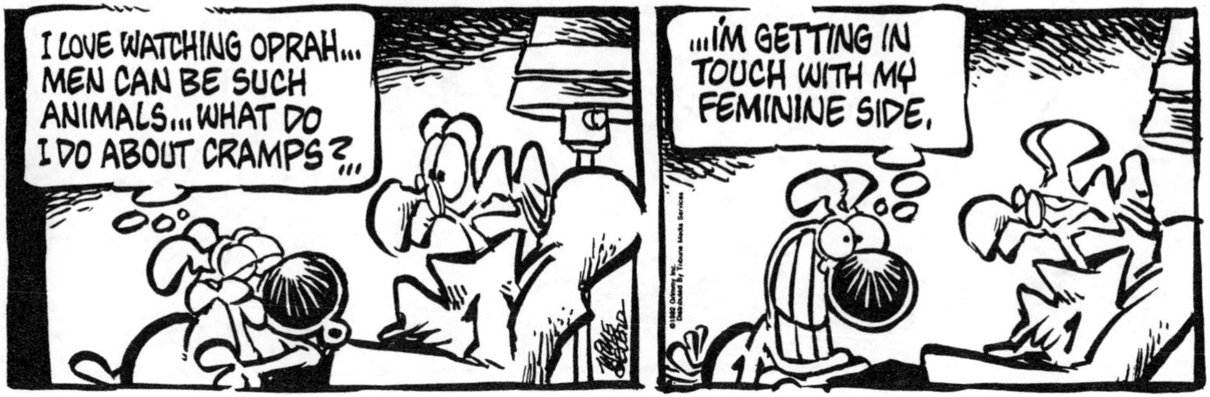
I LOVE WATCHING OPRAH... MEN CAN BE SUCH ANIMALS... WHAT DO I DO ABOUT CRAMPS?...
...I'M GETTING IN TOUCH WITH MY FEMININE SIDE.

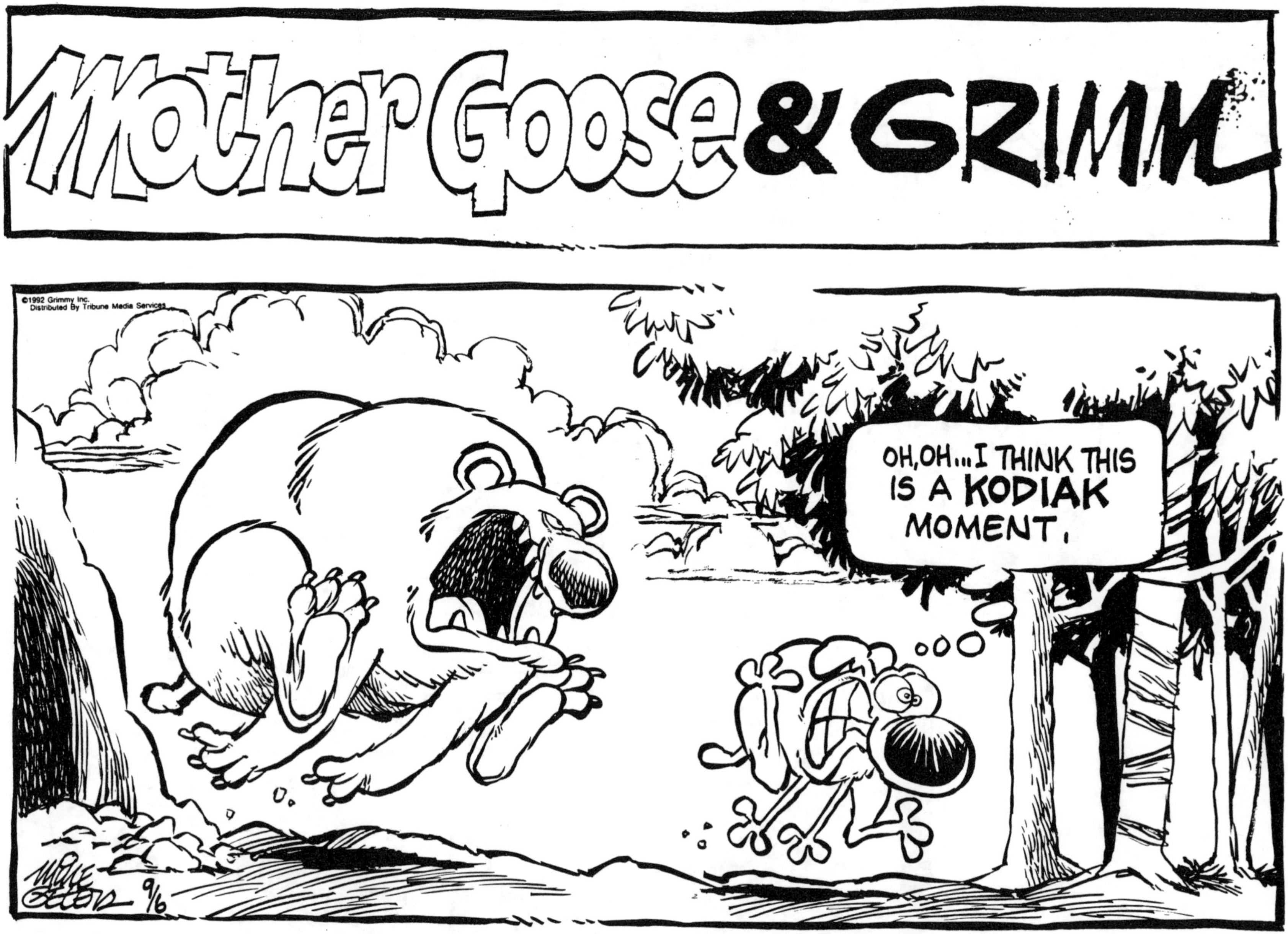
Mother Goose & GRIMM
©1992 Grimmy Inc.
Distributed By Tribune Media Services
OH, OH... I THINK THIS IS A KODIAK MOMENT.
9/6

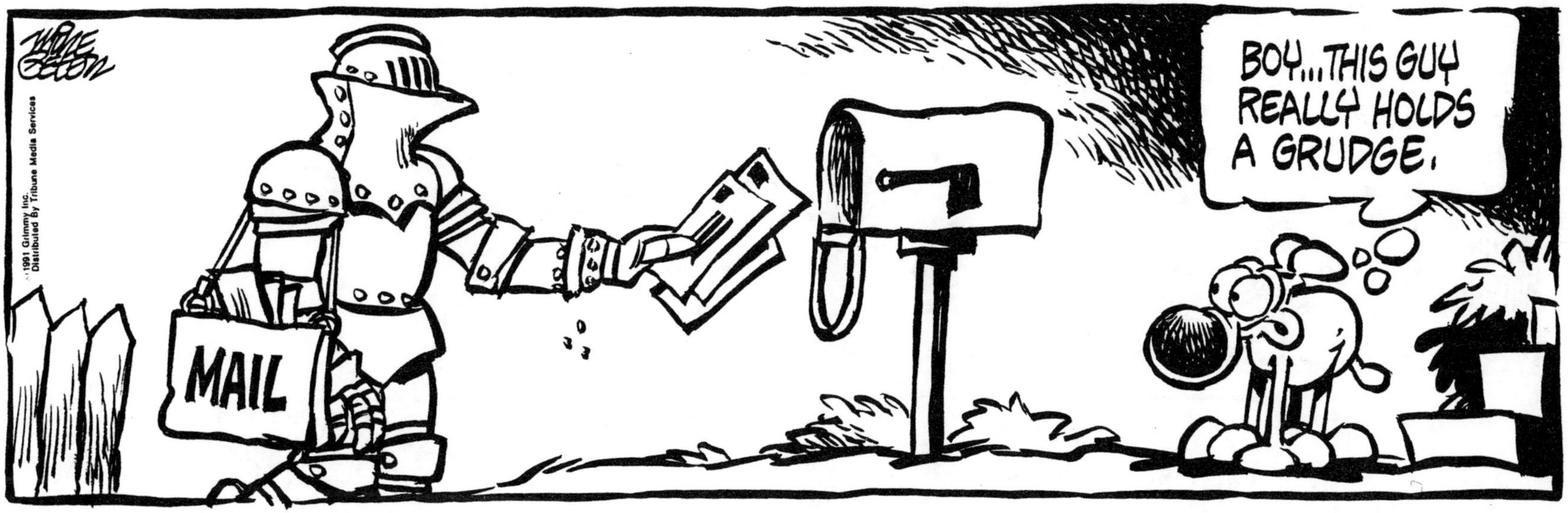

BOY...THIS GUY REALLY HOLDS A GRUDGE.
MAIL
©1991 Grimmy Inc.
Distributed By Tribune Media Services


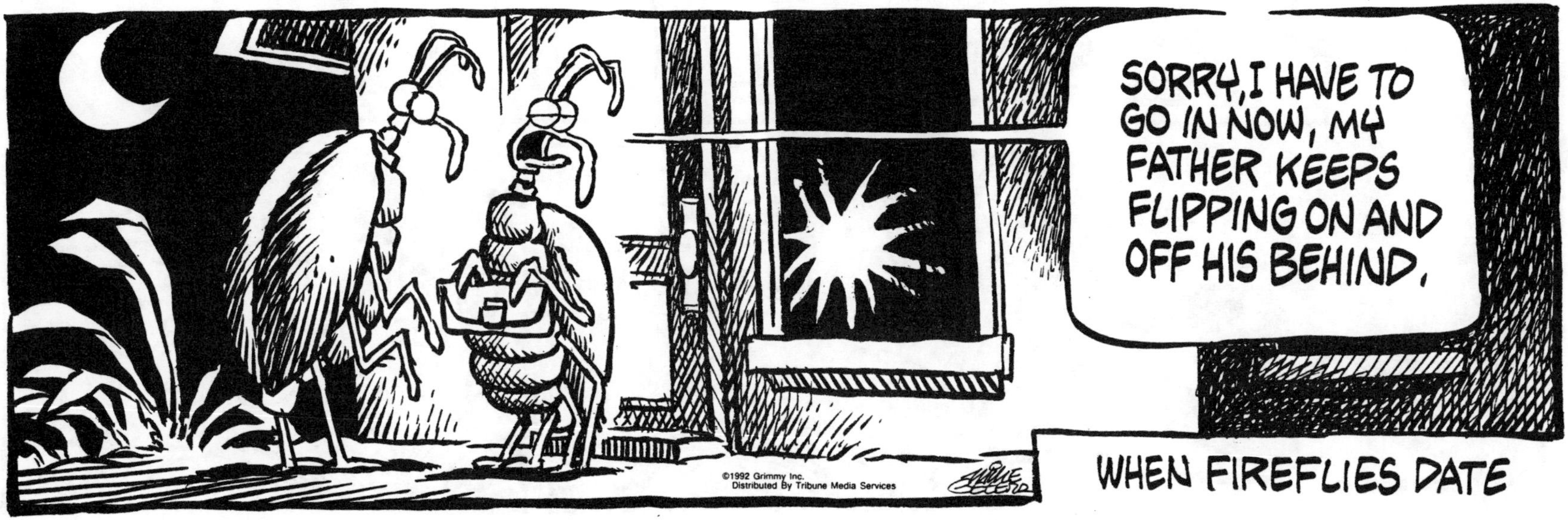

SORRY, I HAVE TO GO IN NOW, MY FATHER KEEPS FLIPPING ON AND OFF HIS BEHIND.
©1992 Grimmy Inc.
Distributed By Tribune Media Services
WHEN FIREFLIES DATE

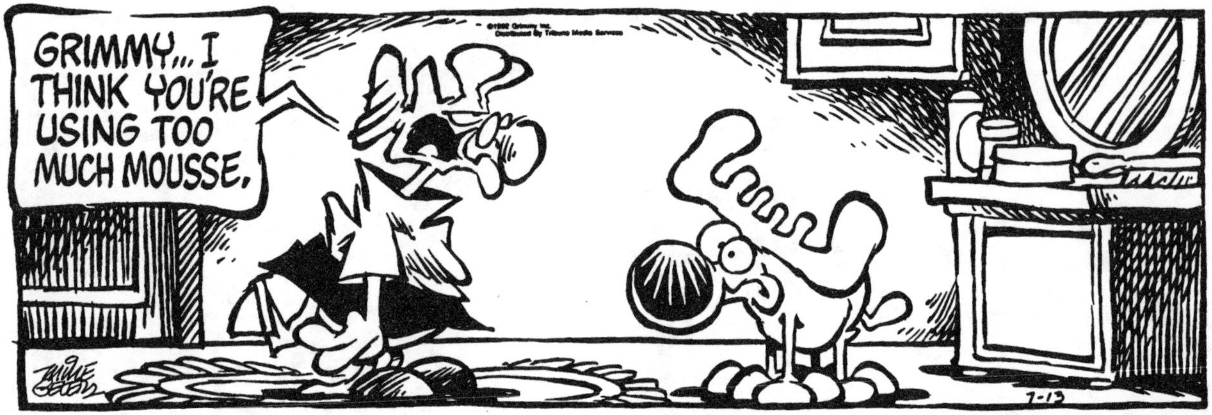
GRIMMY... I THINK YOU'RE USING TOO MUCH MOUSSE.
7-13

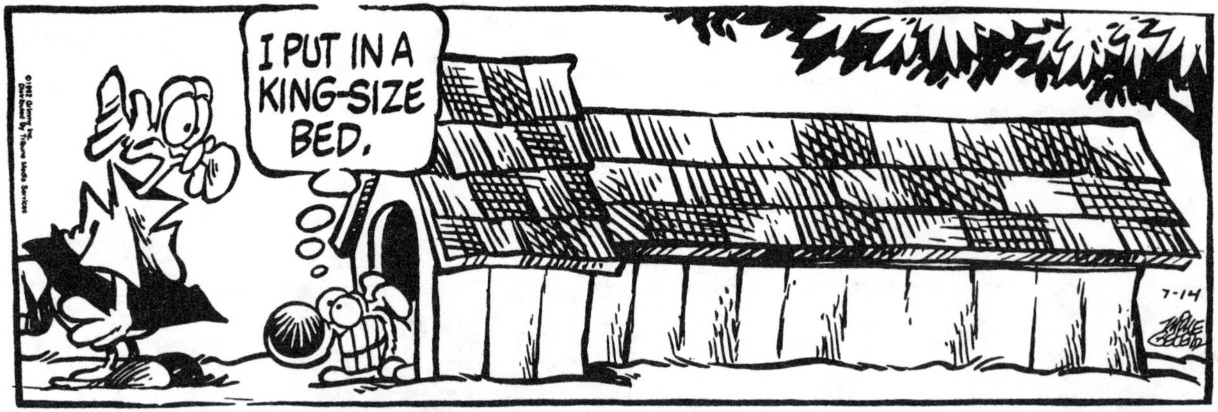
I PUT IN A KING-SIZE BED.
7-14

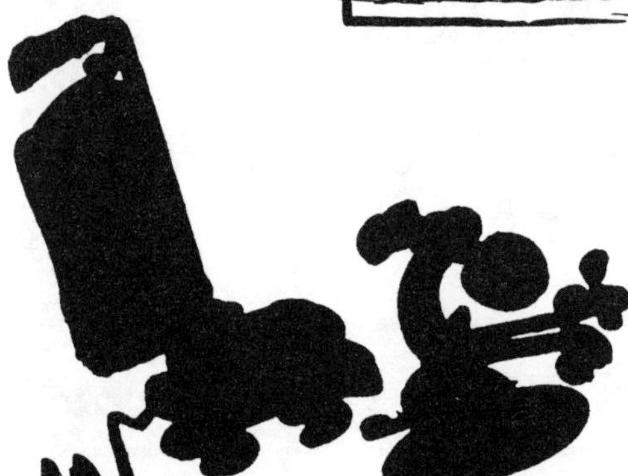

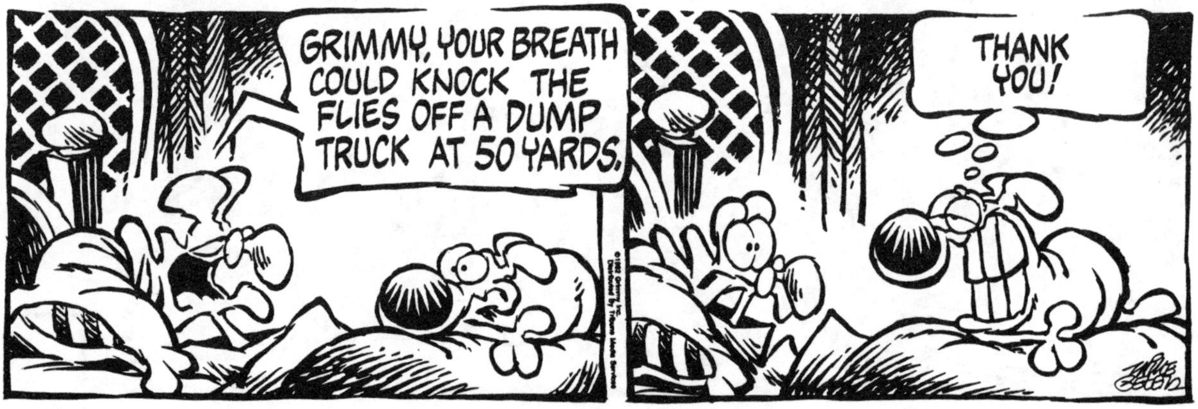
GRIMMY, YOUR BREATH COULD KNOCK THE FLIES OFF A DUMP TRUCK AT 50 YARDS.
THANK YOU!

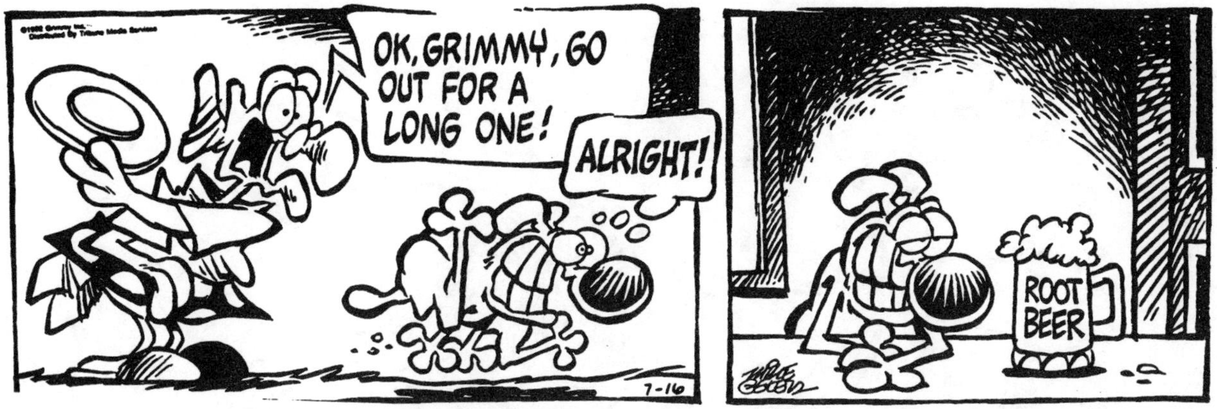
OK, GRIMMY, GO OUT FOR A LONG ONE!
ALRIGHT!
7-16
ROOT BEER

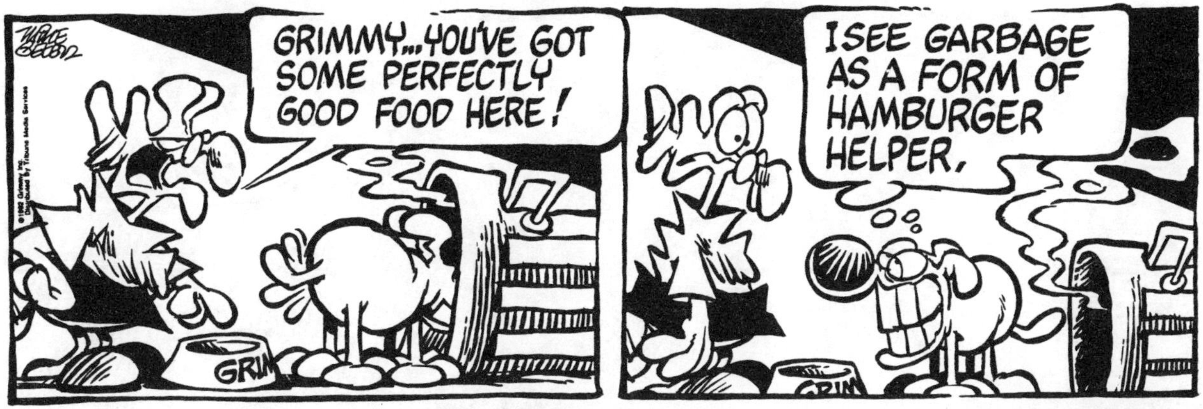
GRIMMY... YOU'VE GOT SOME PERFECTLY GOOD FOOD HERE!
GRIM
I SEE GARBAGE AS A FORM OF HAMBURGER HELPER,
GRIM

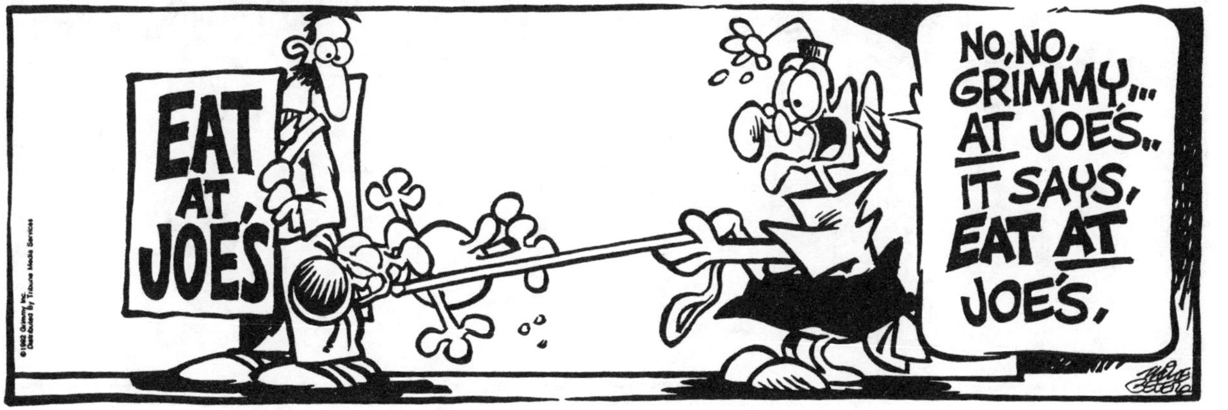
EAT AT JOE'S
NO, NO, GRIMMY... AT JOE'S.. IT SAYS, EAT AT JOE'S.

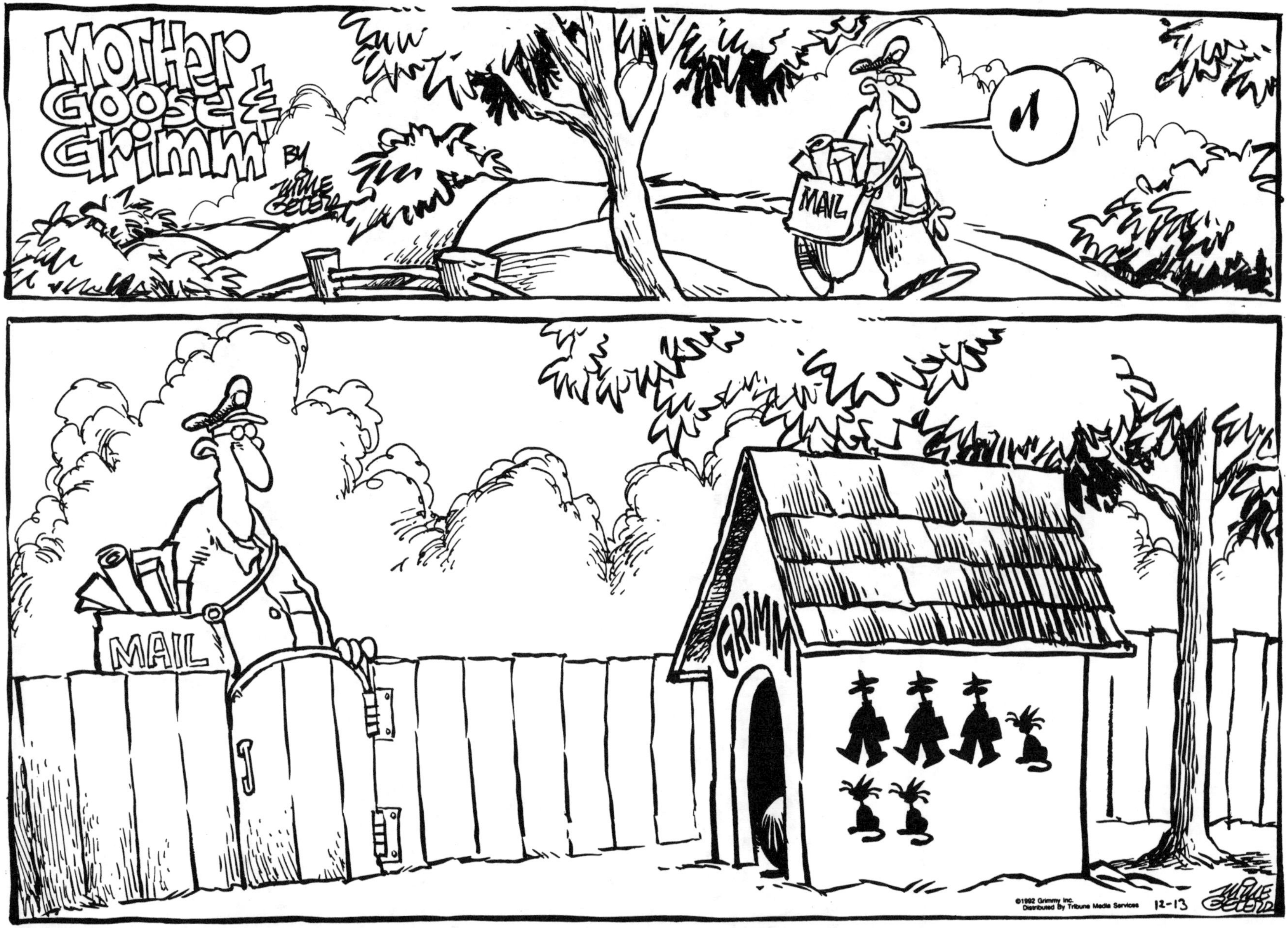

MOTHER GOOSE & GRIMM
BY MIKE PETERS
MAIL
MAIL
GRIMM
©1992 Grimmy Inc.
Distributed By Tribune Media Services
12-13

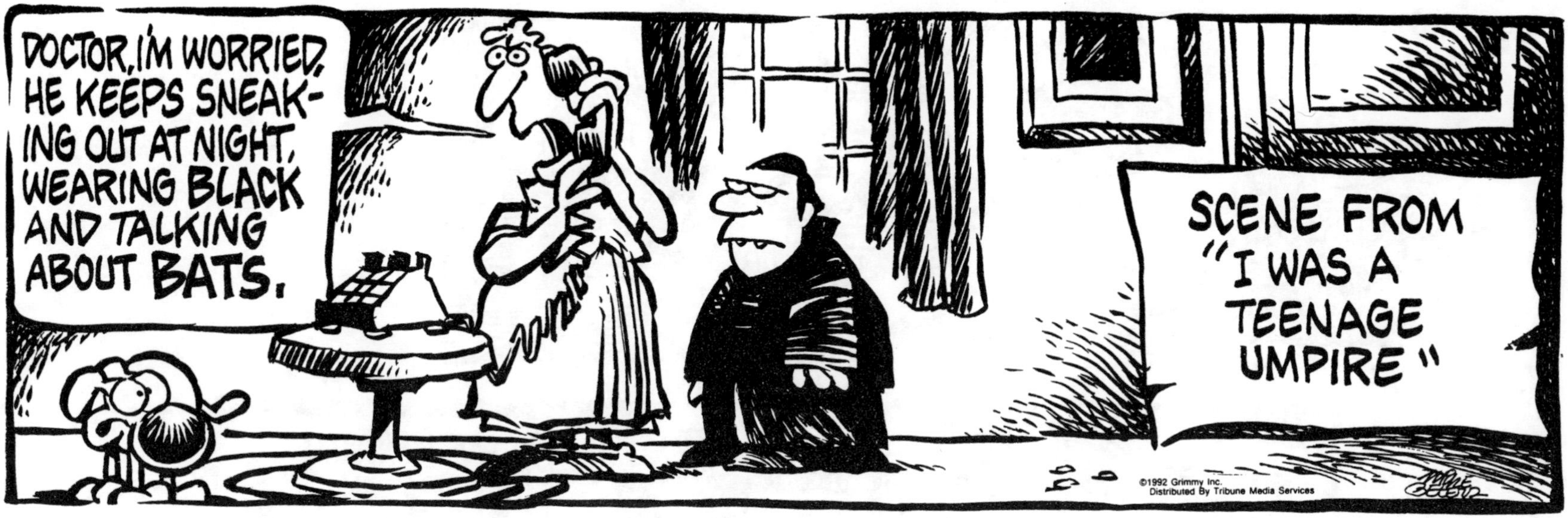
DOCTOR, I'M WORRIED. HE KEEPS SNEAKING OUT AT NIGHT, WEARING BLACK AND TALKING ABOUT BATS.
SCENE FROM "I WAS A TEENAGE UMPIRE"
©1992 Grimmy Inc.
Distributed By Tribune Media Services

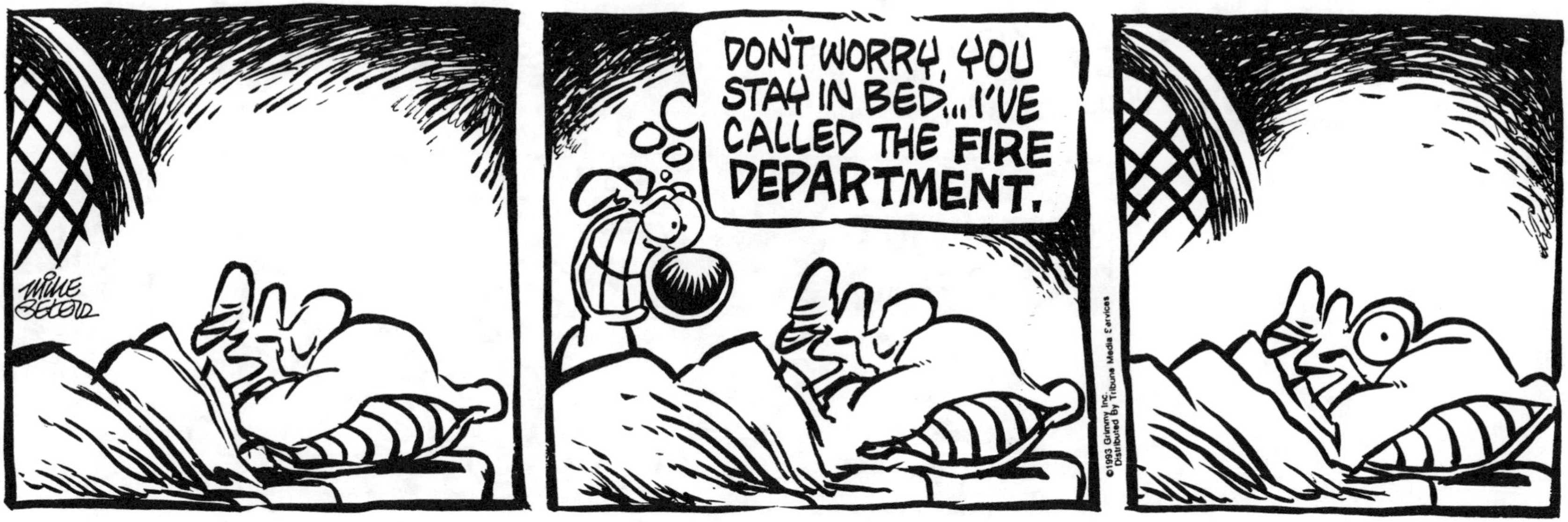
DON'T WORRY, YOU STAY IN BED... I'VE CALLED THE FIRE DEPARTMENT.
©1993 Grimmy Inc.
Distributed By Tribune Media Services

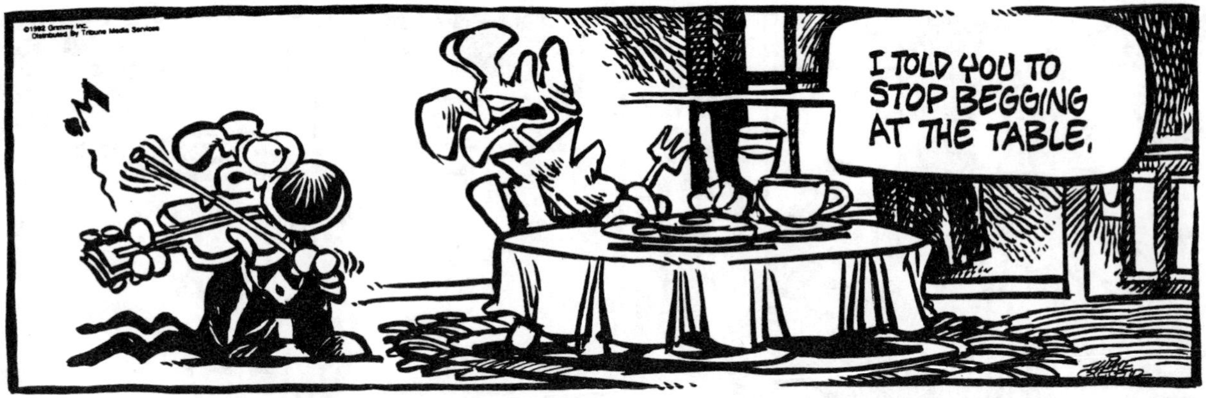
©1992 Grimmy Inc. Distributed By Tribune Media Services
I TOLD YOU TO STOP BEGGING AT THE TABLE.

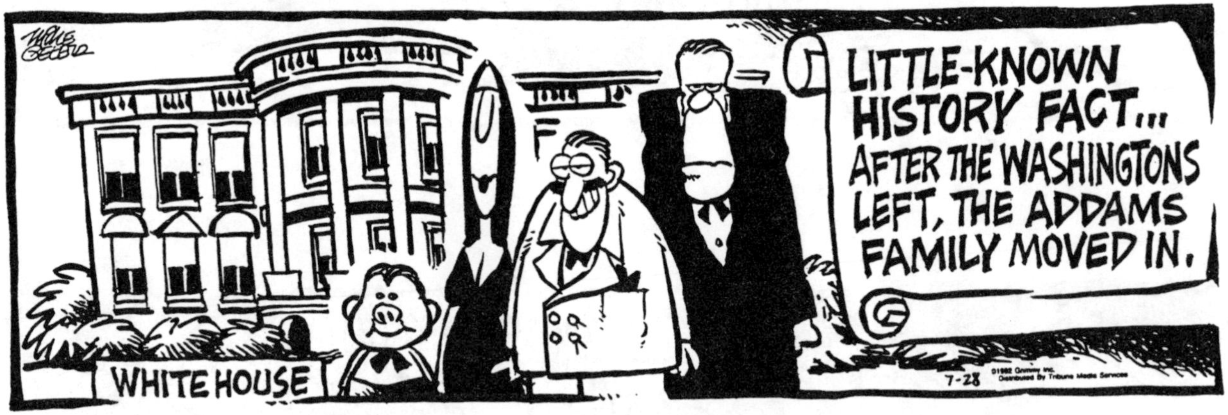
LITTLE-KNOWN HISTORY FACT... AFTER THE WASHINGTONS LEFT, THE ADDAMS FAMILY MOVED IN.
WHITE HOUSE
7-28
©1992 Grimmy Inc. Distributed By Tribune Media Services

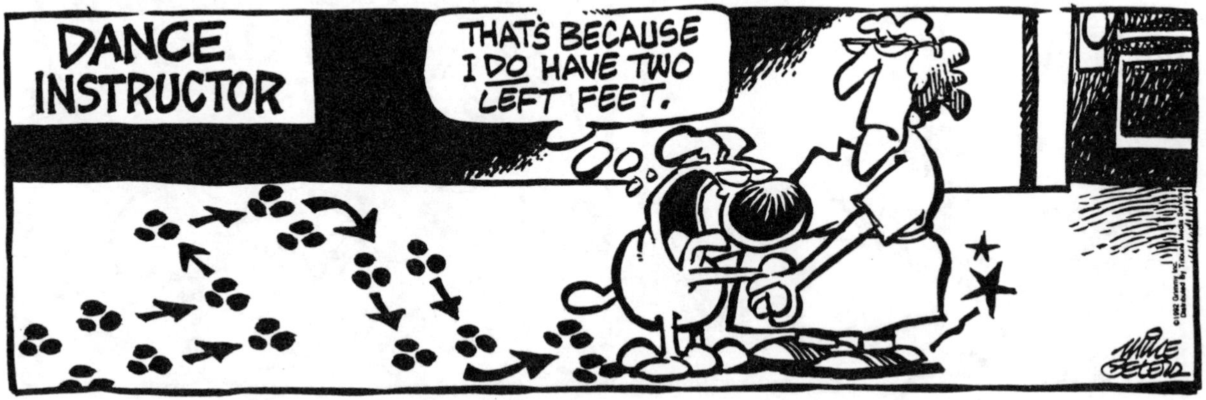
DANCE INSTRUCTOR
THAT'S BECAUSE I DO HAVE TWO LEFT FEET.

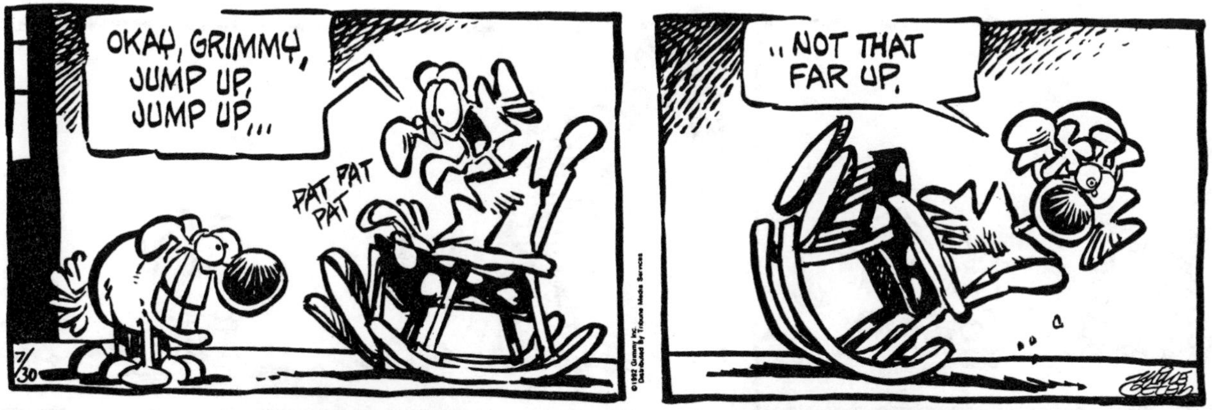
OKAY, GRIMMY, JUMP UP, JUMP UP,...
PAT PAT PAT
7/30
..NOT THAT FAR UP.

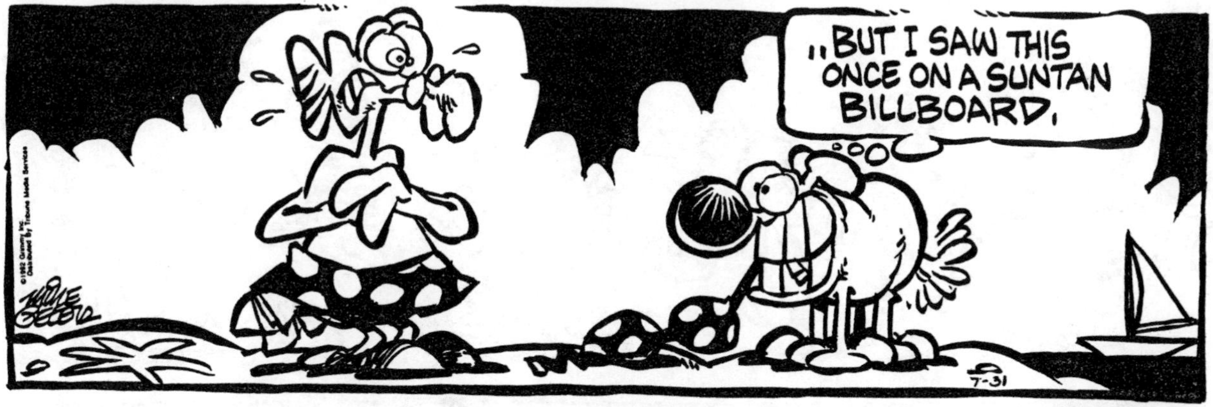
..BUT I SAW THIS ONCE ON A SUNTAN BILLBOARD.
7-31

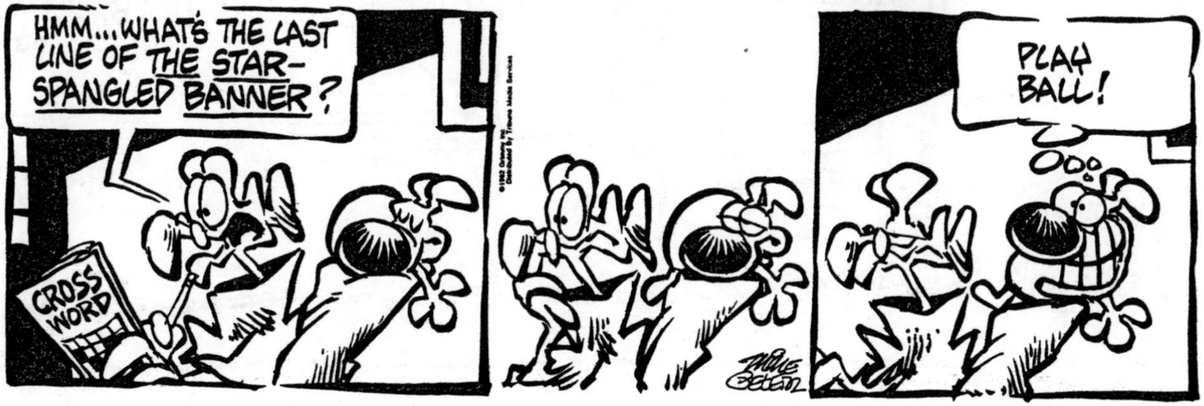
HMM...WHAT'S THE LAST LINE OF THE STAR-SPANGLED BANNER?
CROSS WORD
PLAY BALL!

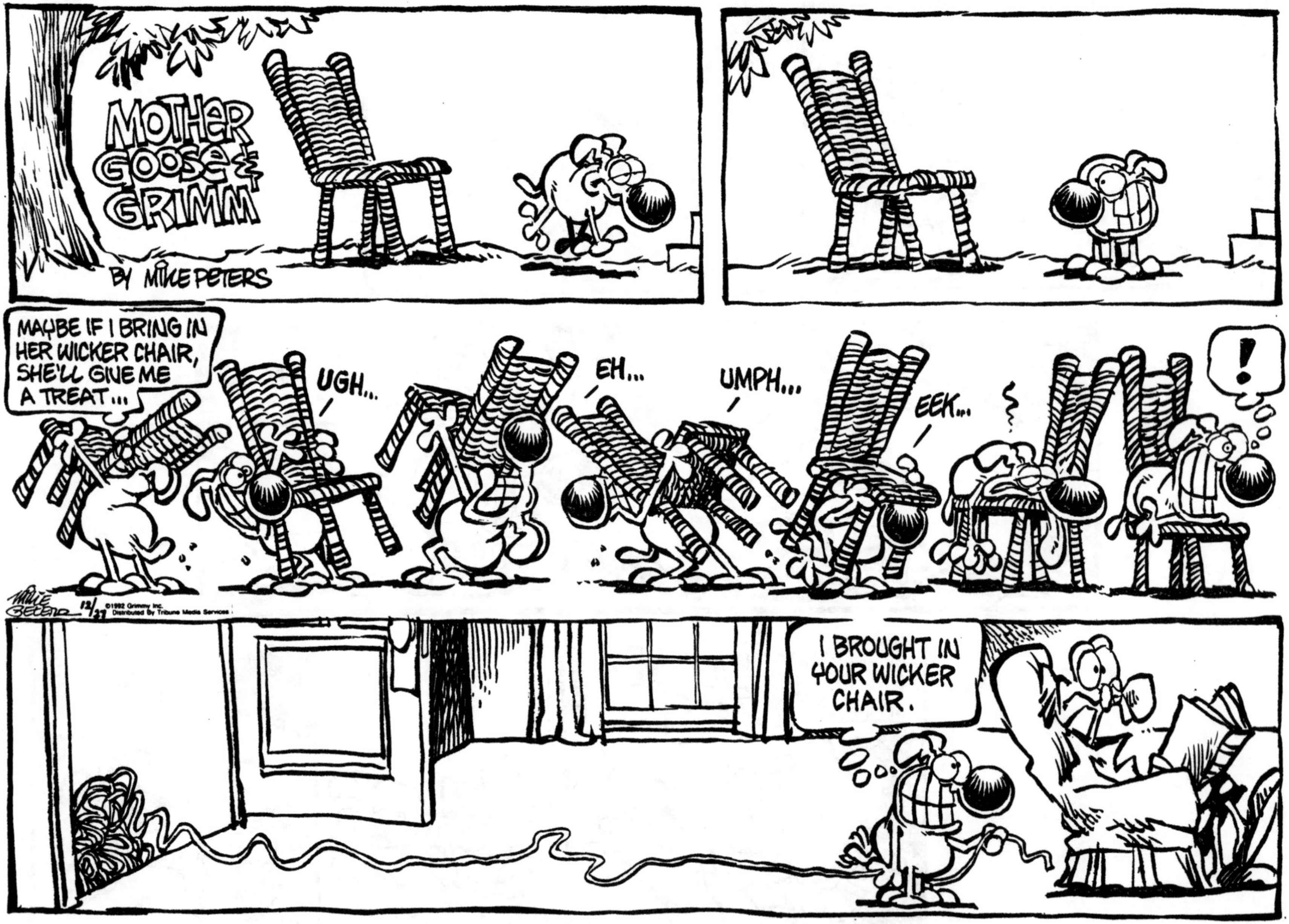
MOTHER GOOSE & GRIMM
BY MIKE PETERS
MAYBE IF I BRING IN HER WICKER CHAIR, SHE'LL GIVE ME A TREAT...
UGH...
EH...
UMPH...
EEK...
!
©1992 Grimmy Inc. Distributed By Tribune Media Services
I BROUGHT IN YOUR WICKER CHAIR.

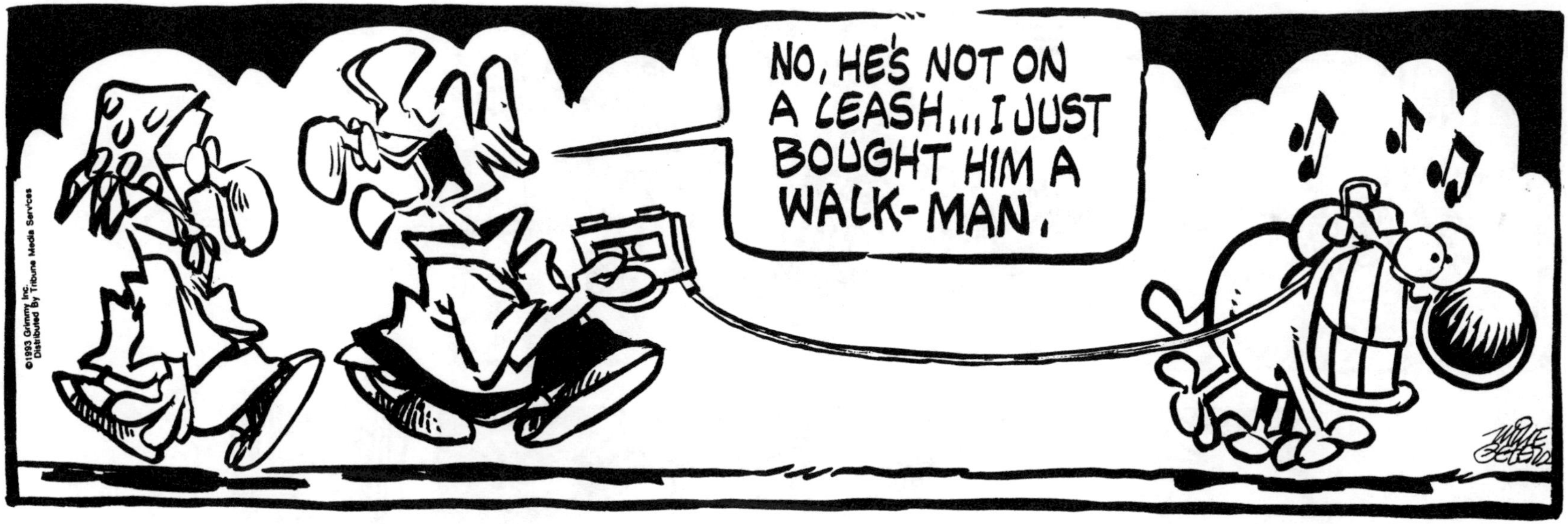
©1993 Grimmy Inc.
Distributed By Tribune Media Services
NO, HE'S NOT ON A LEASH... I JUST BOUGHT HIM A WALK-MAN.

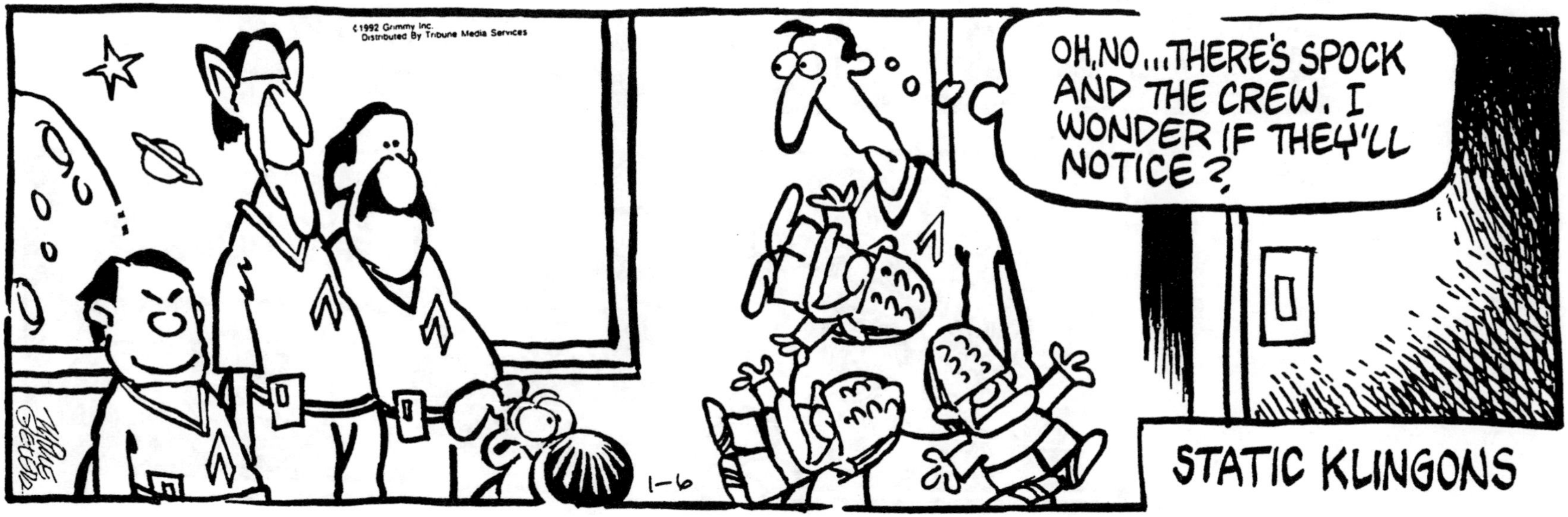
©1992 Grimmy Inc.
Distributed By Tribune Media Services
OH, NO... THERE'S SPOCK AND THE CREW. I WONDER IF THEY'LL NOTICE?
1-6
STATIC KLINGONS

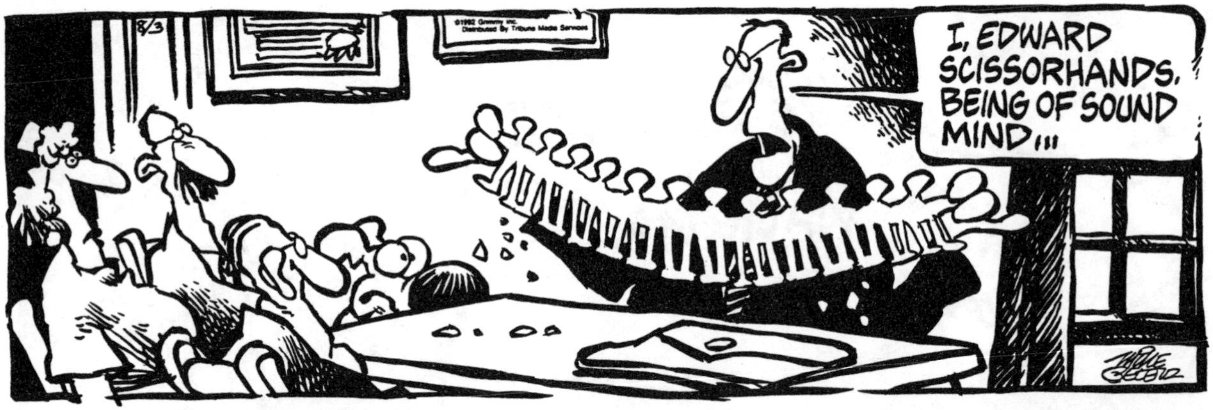
I, EDWARD SCISSORHANDS, BEING OF SOUND MIND...

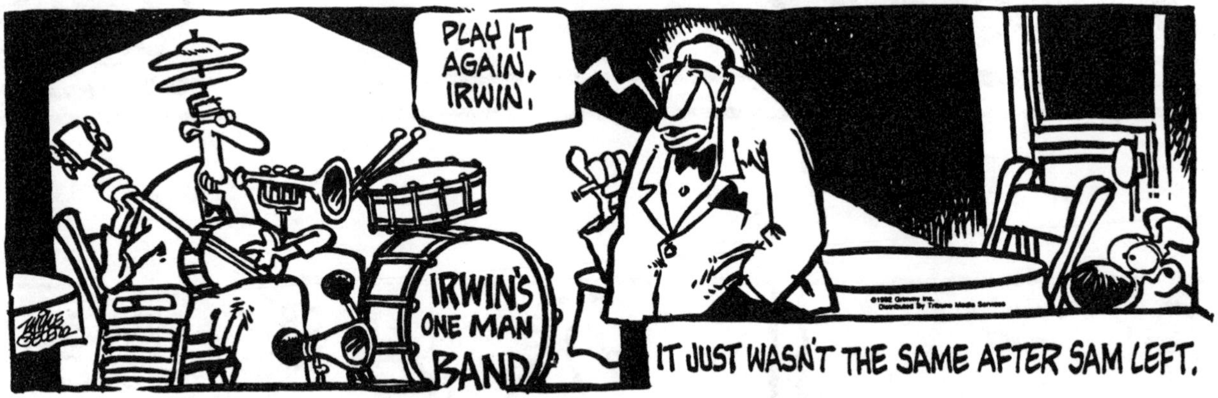
PLAY IT AGAIN, IRWIN.
IRWIN'S ONE MAN BAND
IT JUST WASN'T THE SAME AFTER SAM LEFT.

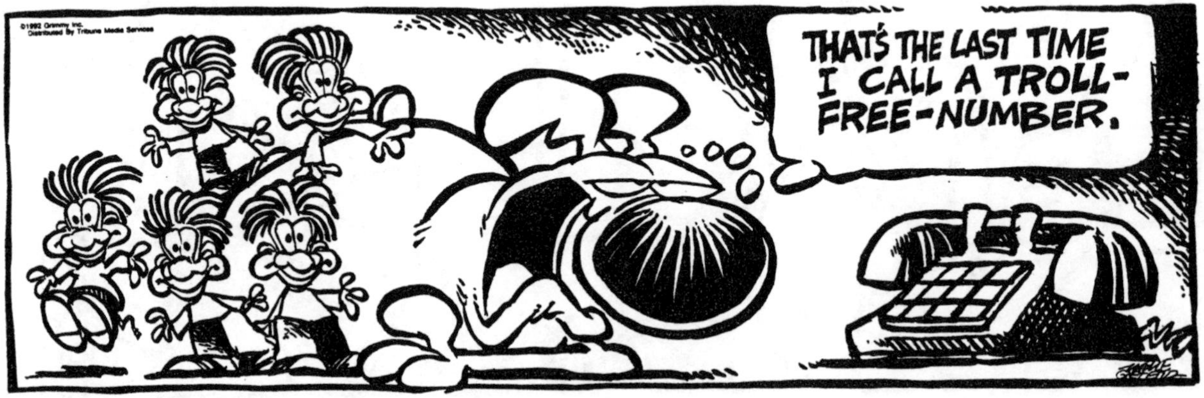
THAT'S THE LAST TIME I CALL A TROLL-FREE-NUMBER.

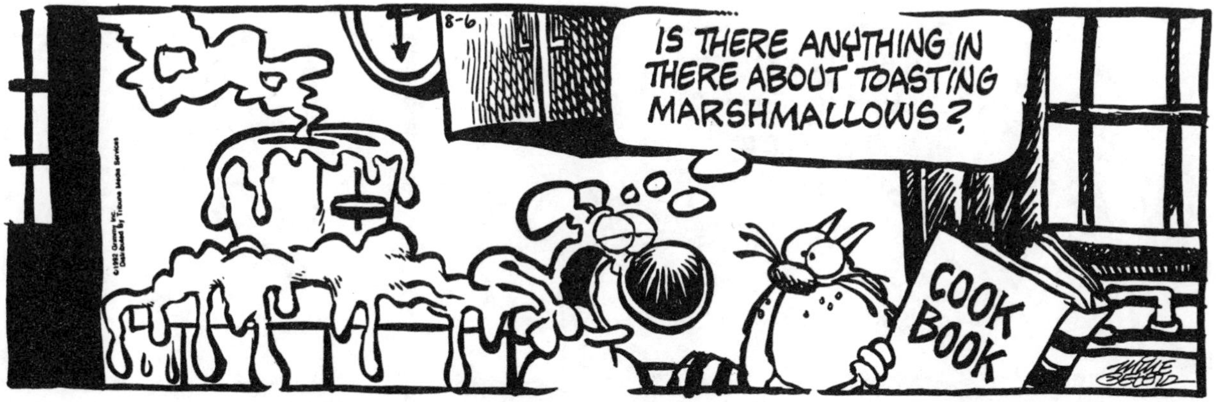
8-6
IS THERE ANYTHING IN THERE ABOUT TOASTING MARSHMALLOWS?
COOK BOOK

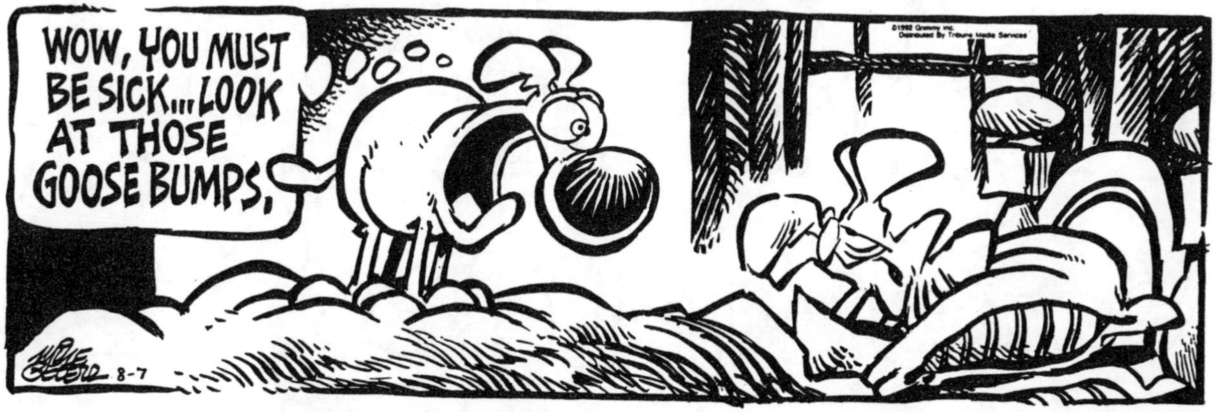
WOW, YOU MUST BE SICK... LOOK AT THOSE GOOSE BUMPS.
8-7

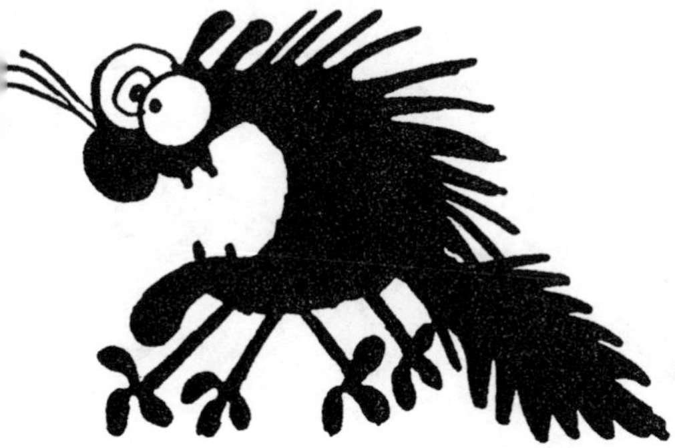

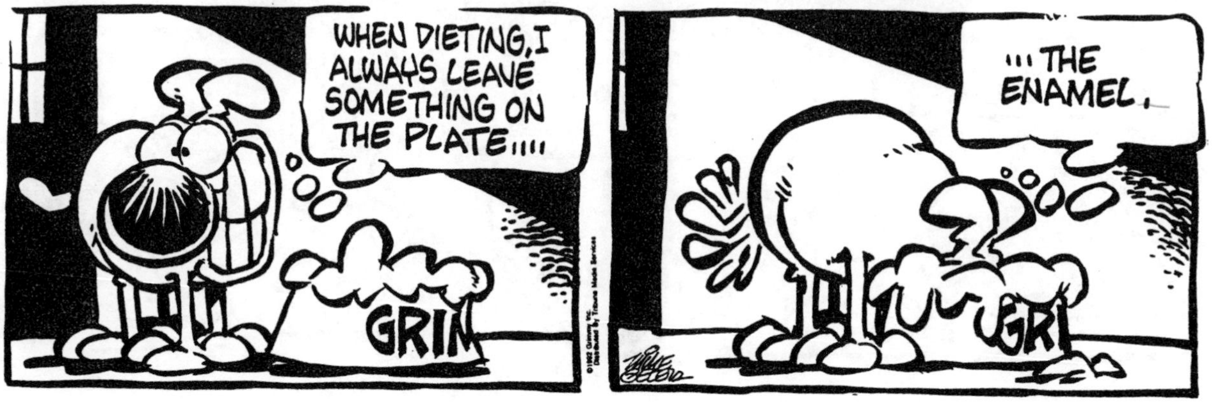
WHEN DIETING, I ALWAYS LEAVE SOMETHING ON THE PLATE....
GRIN
...THE ENAMEL.
GRI

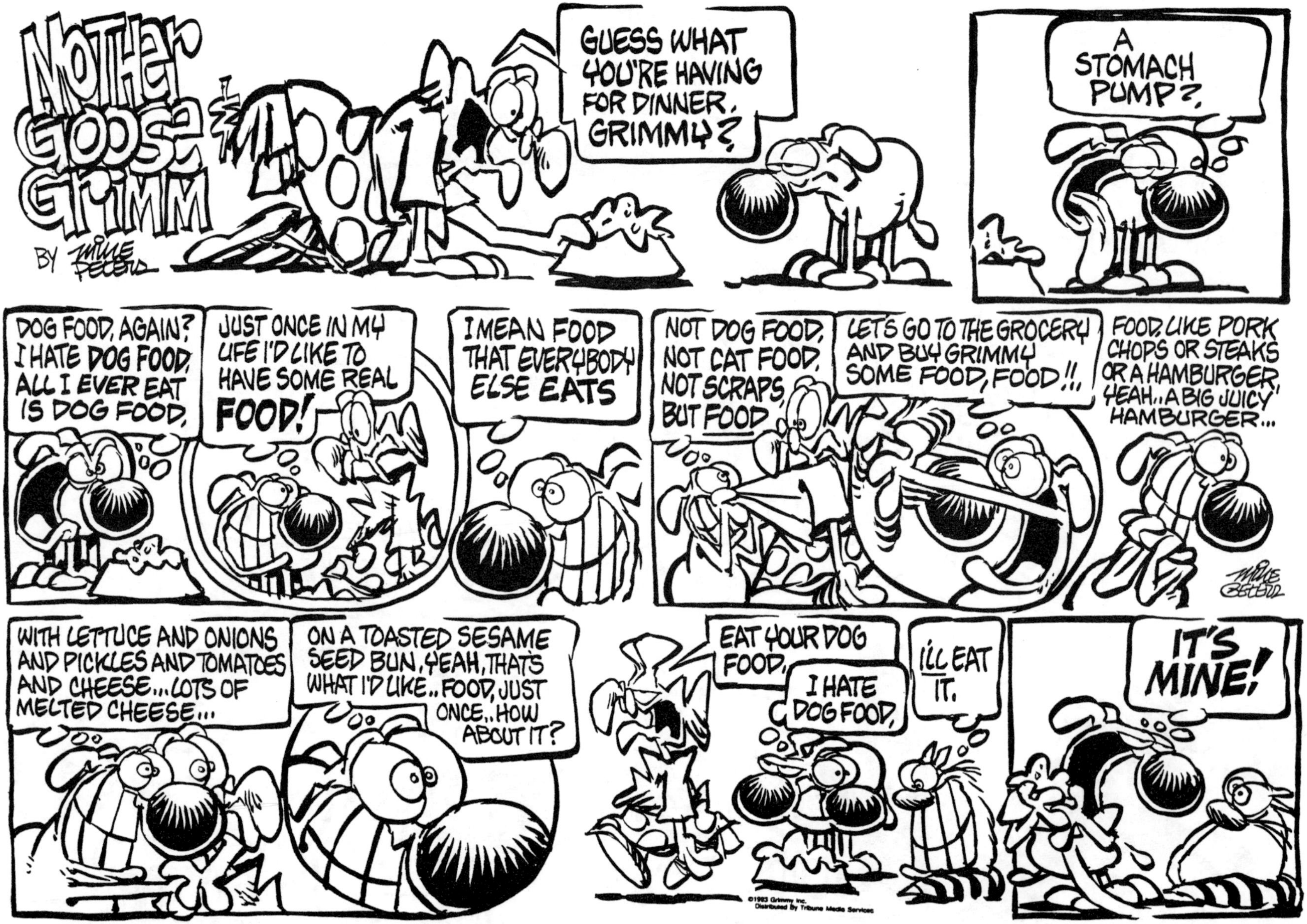
Mother Goose & Grimm
BY MIKE PETERS
GUESS WHAT YOU'RE HAVING FOR DINNER, GRIMMY?
A STOMACH PUMP?
DOG FOOD, AGAIN? I HATE DOG FOOD, ALL I EVER EAT IS DOG FOOD,
JUST ONCE IN MY LIFE I'D LIKE TO HAVE SOME REAL FOOD!
I MEAN FOOD THAT EVERYBODY ELSE EATS
NOT DOG FOOD, NOT CAT FOOD, NOT SCRAPS, BUT FOOD
LET'S GO TO THE GROCERY AND BUY GRIMMY SOME FOOD, FOOD!!,
FOOD, LIKE PORK CHOPS OR STEAKS OR A HAMBURGER, YEAH.. A BIG JUICY HAMBURGER...
WITH LETTUCE AND ONIONS AND PICKLES AND TOMATOES AND CHEESE... LOTS OF MELTED CHEESE...
ON A TOASTED SESAME SEED BUN, YEAH, THAT'S WHAT I'D LIKE.. FOOD, JUST ONCE.. HOW ABOUT IT?
EAT YOUR DOG FOOD,
I HATE DOG FOOD,
I'LL EAT IT.
IT'S MINE!
©1993 Grimmy Inc.
Distributed By Tribune Media Services

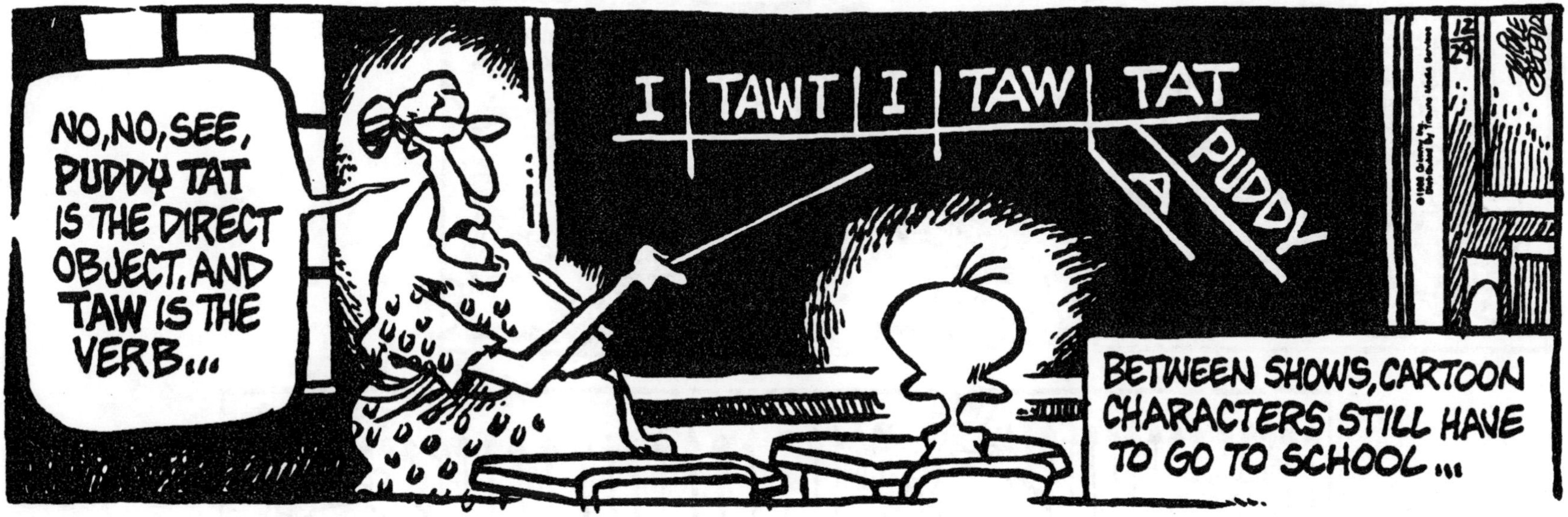
NO, NO, SEE, PUDDY TAT IS THE DIRECT OBJECT, AND TAW IS THE VERB...
I TAWT I TAW A PUDDY TAT
BETWEEN SHOWS, CARTOON CHARACTERS STILL HAVE TO GO TO SCHOOL...

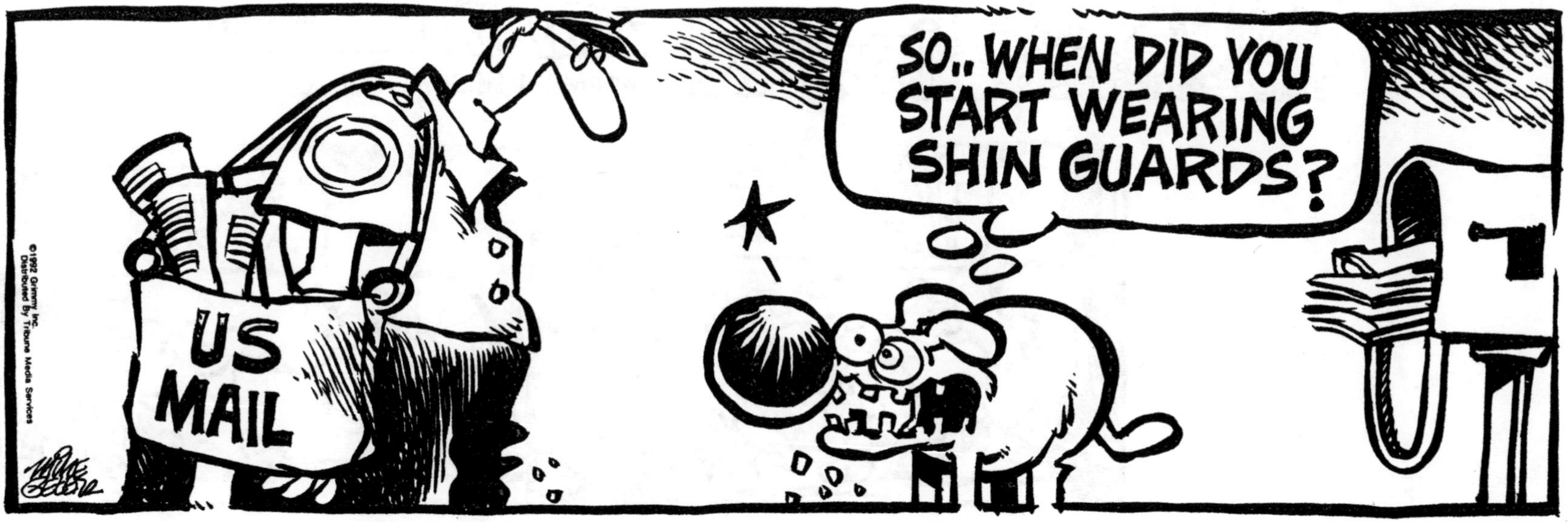
SO.. WHEN DID YOU START WEARING SHIN GUARDS?
US MAIL
©1992 Grimmy, Inc.
Distributed By Tribune Media Services

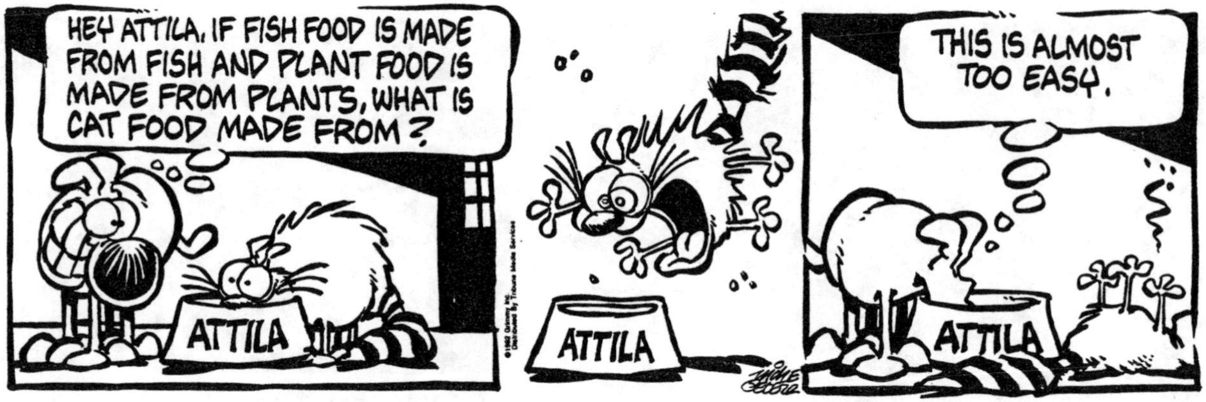
HEY ATTILA, IF FISH FOOD IS MADE FROM FISH AND PLANT FOOD IS MADE FROM PLANTS, WHAT IS CAT FOOD MADE FROM ?
ATTILA
ATTILA
THIS IS ALMOST TOO EASY.
ATTILA

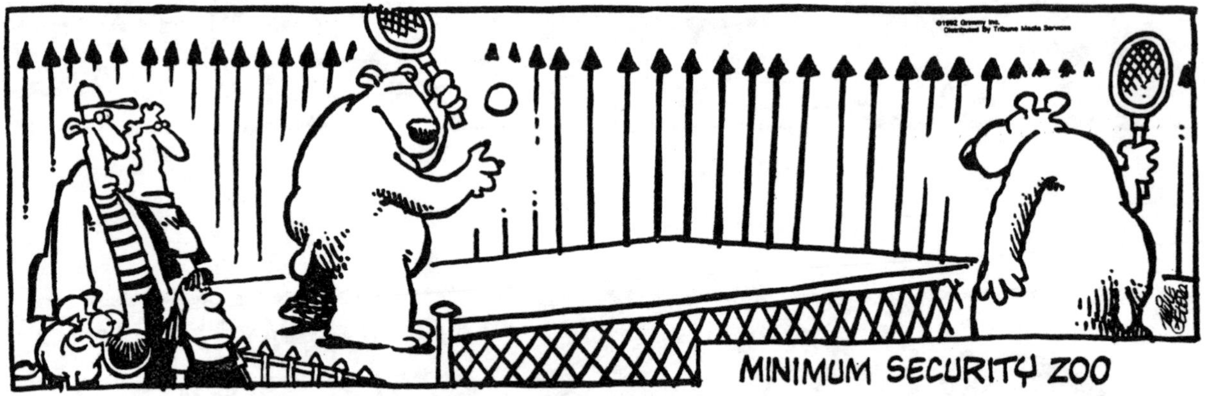
MINIMUM SECURITY ZOO

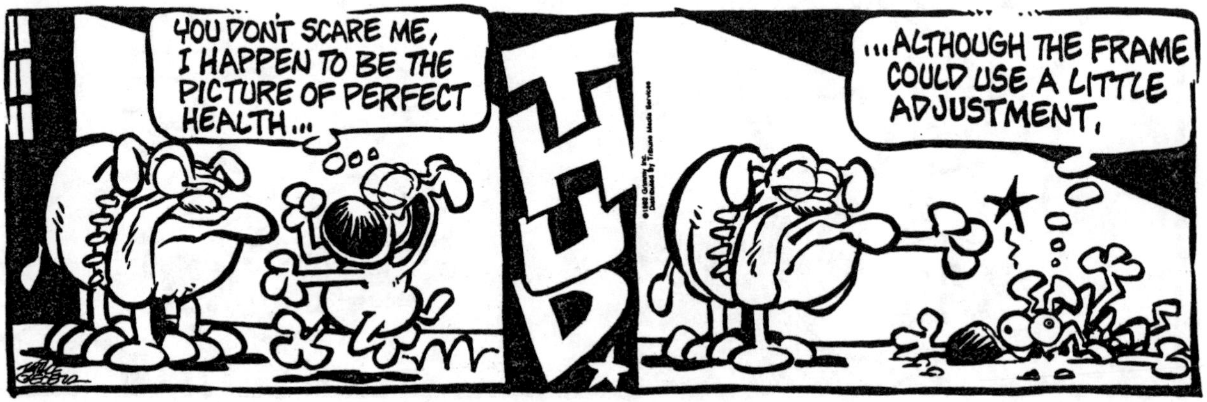
YOU DON'T SCARE ME, I HAPPEN TO BE THE PICTURE OF PERFECT HEALTH...
...ALTHOUGH THE FRAME COULD USE A LITTLE ADJUSTMENT.

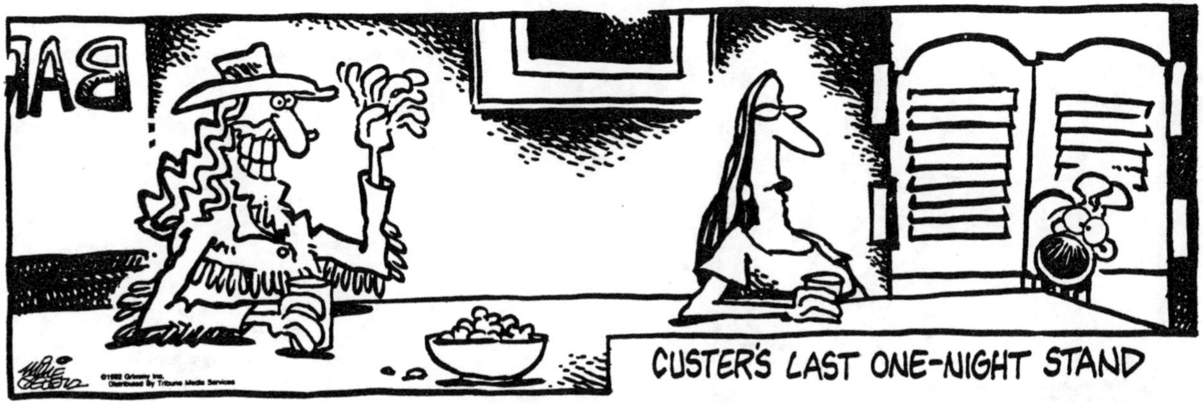
CUSTER'S LAST ONE-NIGHT STAND

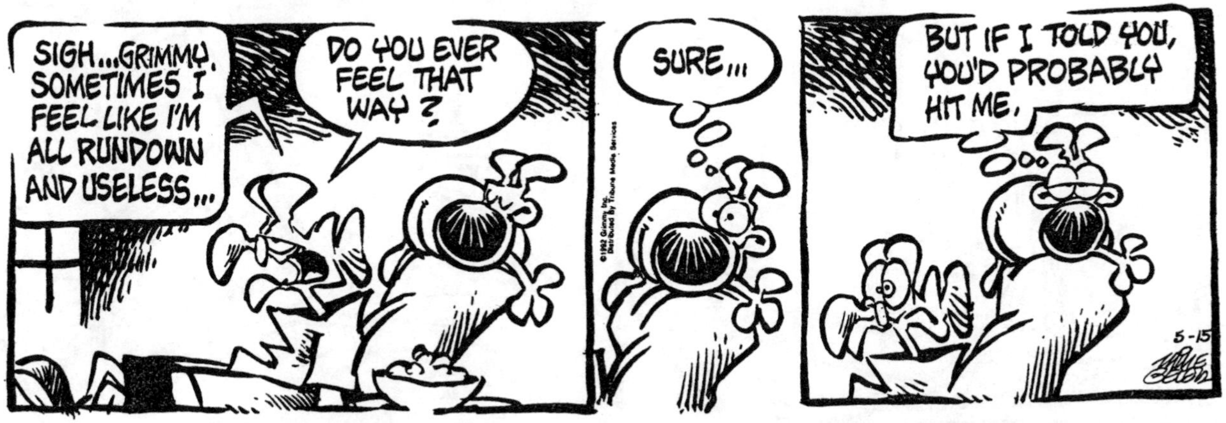
SIGH...GRIMMY, SOMETIMES I FEEL LIKE I'M ALL RUNDOWN AND USELESS...
DO YOU EVER FEEL THAT WAY ?
SURE...
BUT IF I TOLD YOU, YOU'D PROBABLY HIT ME.
5-15

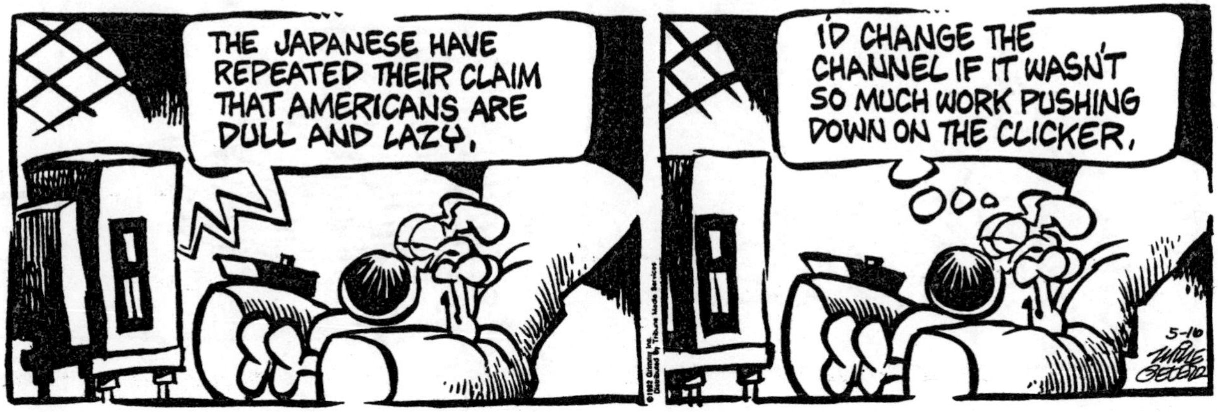
THE JAPANESE HAVE REPEATED THEIR CLAIM THAT AMERICANS ARE DULL AND LAZY.
I'D CHANGE THE CHANNEL IF IT WASN'T SO MUCH WORK PUSHING DOWN ON THE CLICKER.
5-16

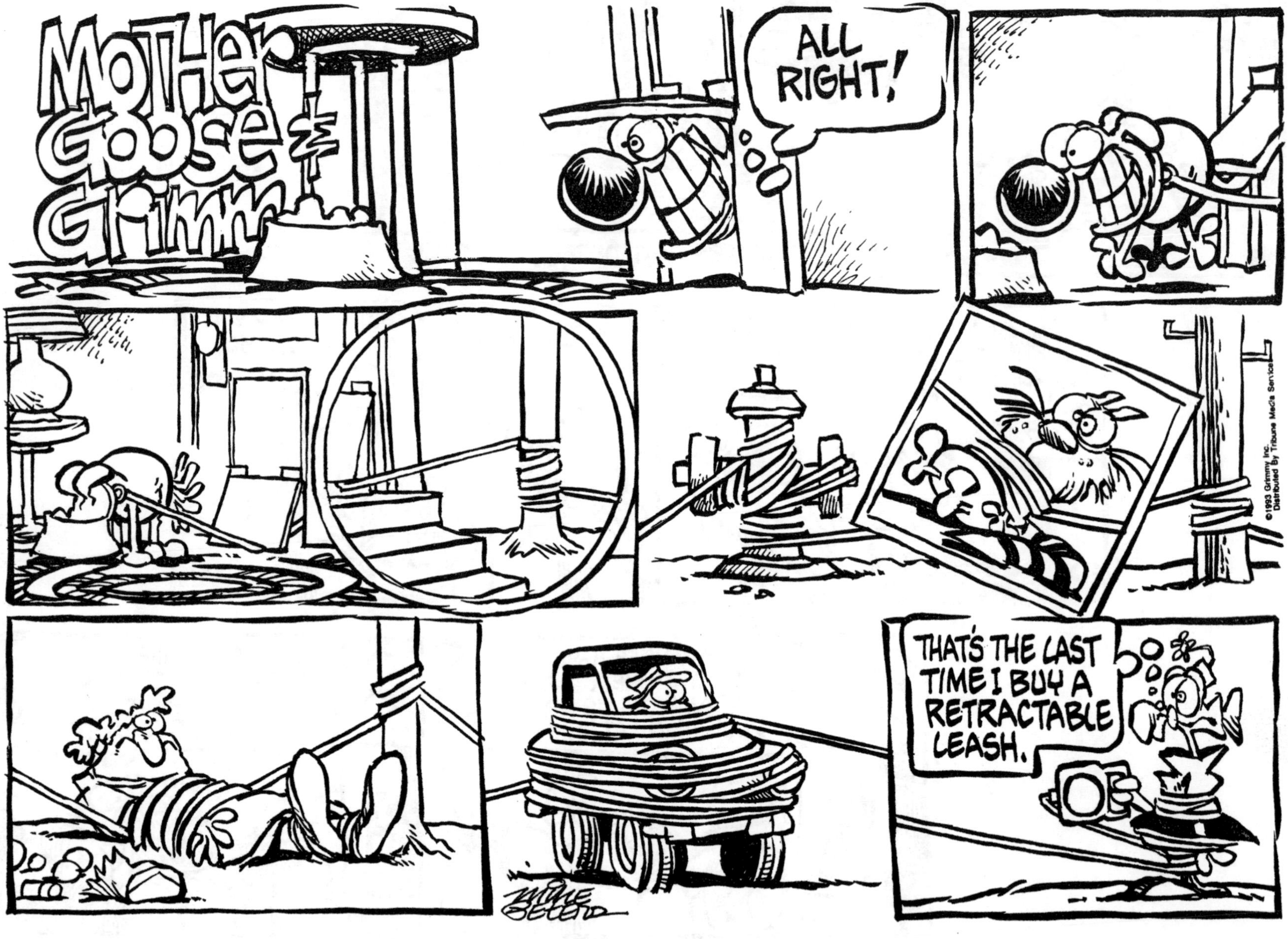
MOTHER GOOSE & GRIMM
ALL RIGHT!
THAT'S THE LAST TIME I BUY A RETRACTABLE LEASH.
©1993 Grimmy Inc. Distributed By Tribune Media Services

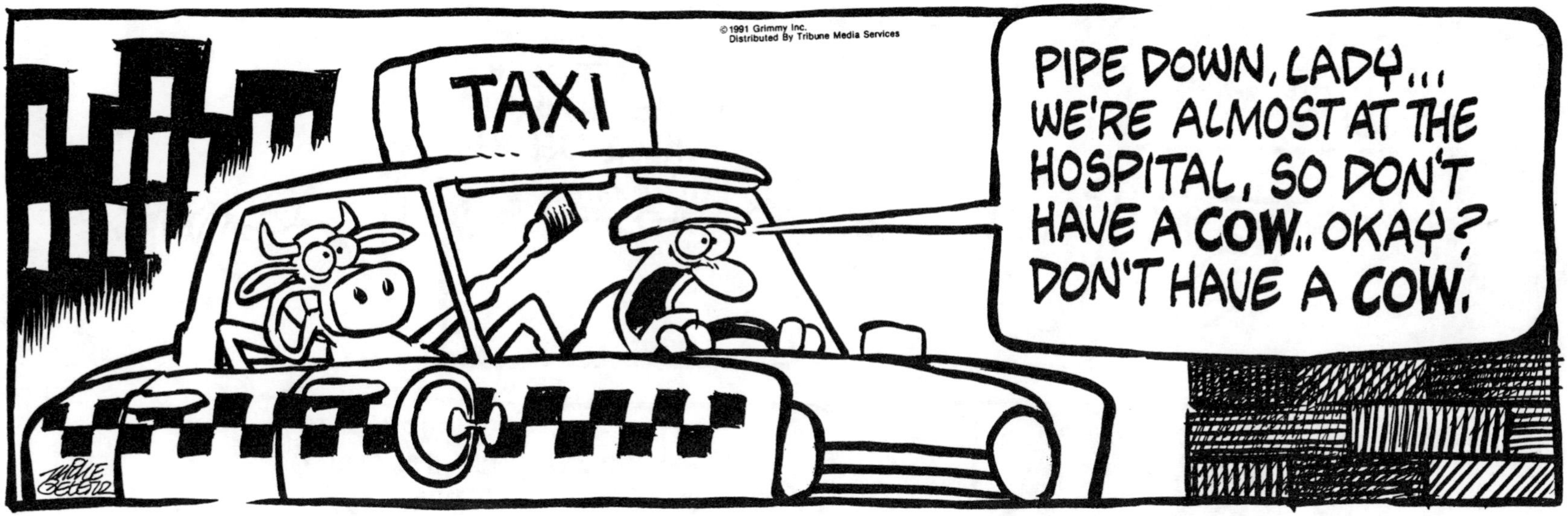
©1991 Grimmy Inc.
Distributed By Tribune Media Services
TAXI
PIPE DOWN, LADY... WE'RE ALMOST AT THE HOSPITAL, SO DON'T HAVE A COW.. OKAY? DON'T HAVE A COW.

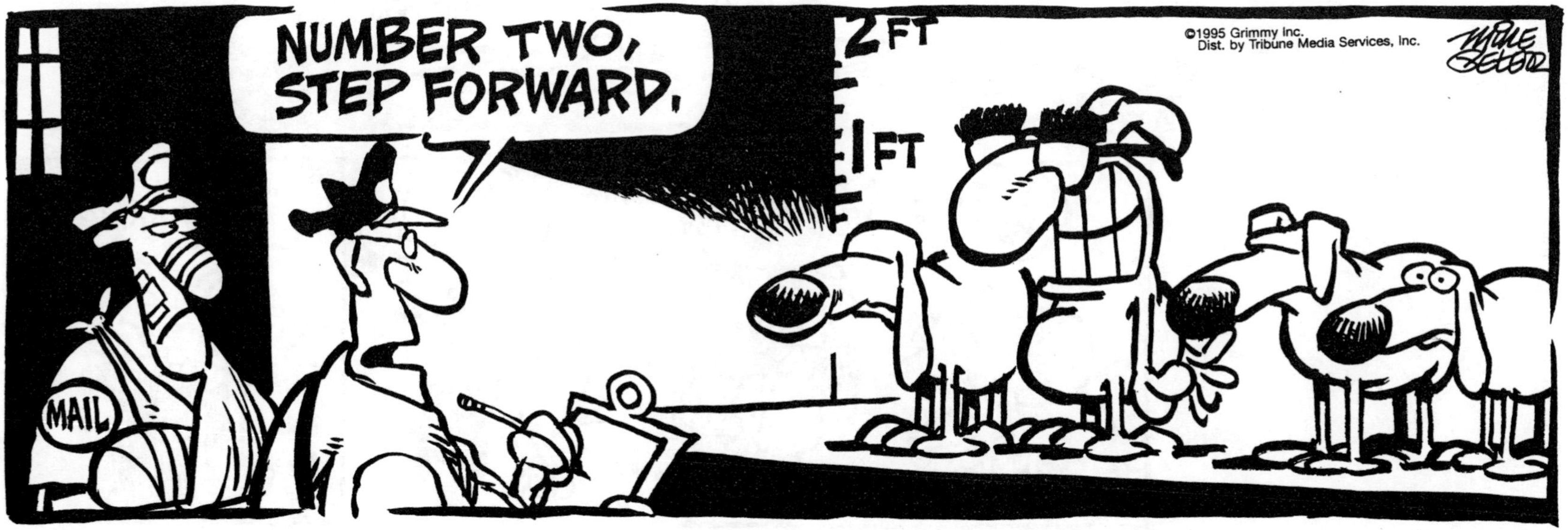
NUMBER TWO, STEP FORWARD.
2 FT
1 FT
©1995 Grimmy Inc.
Dist. by Tribune Media Services, Inc.
MAIL

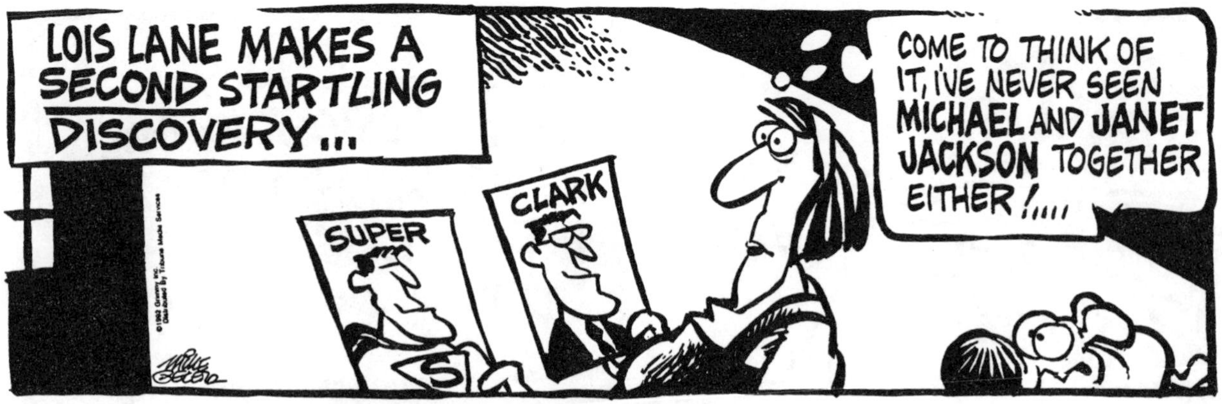
LOIS LANE MAKES A SECOND STARTLING DISCOVERY...
SUPER
CLARK
COME TO THINK OF IT, I'VE NEVER SEEN MICHAEL AND JANET JACKSON TOGETHER EITHER!....

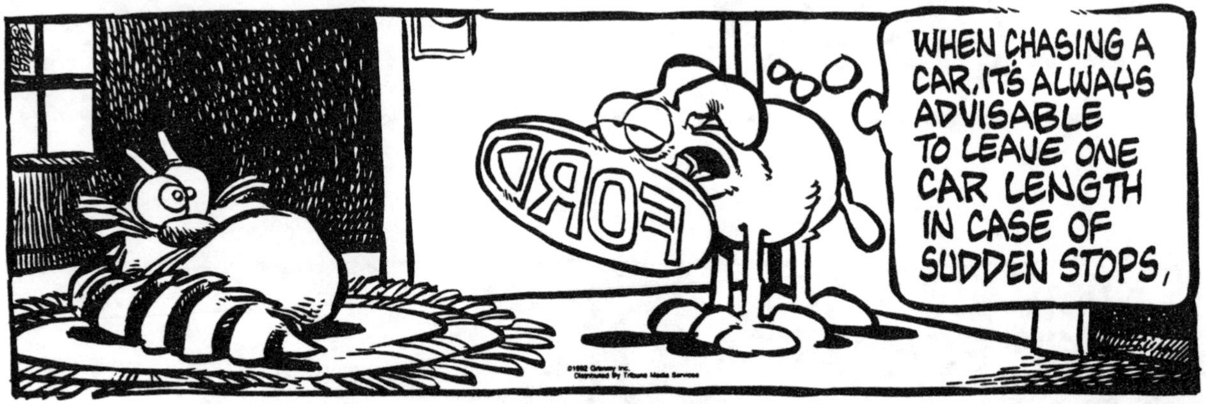
FORD
WHEN CHASING A CAR, IT'S ALWAYS ADVISABLE TO LEAVE ONE CAR LENGTH IN CASE OF SUDDEN STOPS,
©1992 Grimmy Inc.
Distributed By Tribune Media Services

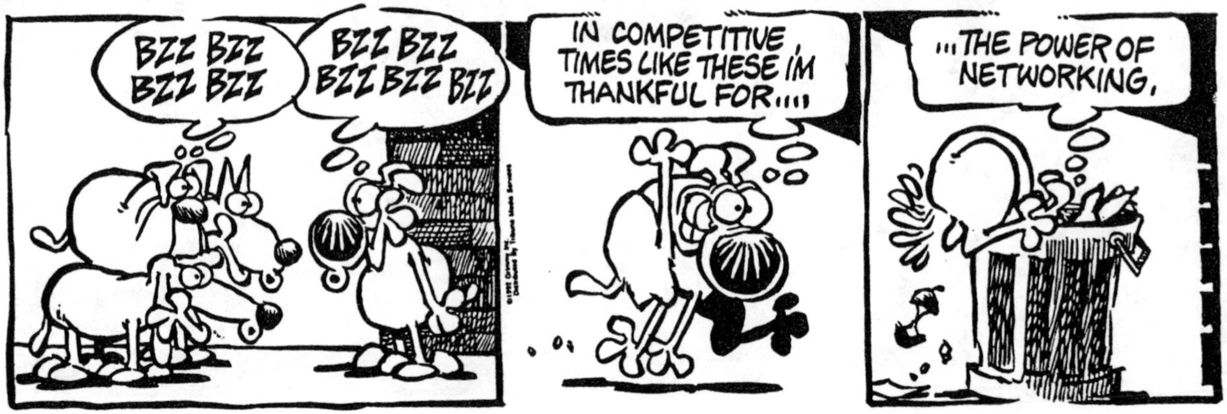
BZZ BZZ BZZ BZZ
BZZ BZZ BZZ BZZ BZZ
IN COMPETITIVE TIMES LIKE THESE I'M THANKFUL FOR....
...THE POWER OF NETWORKING,

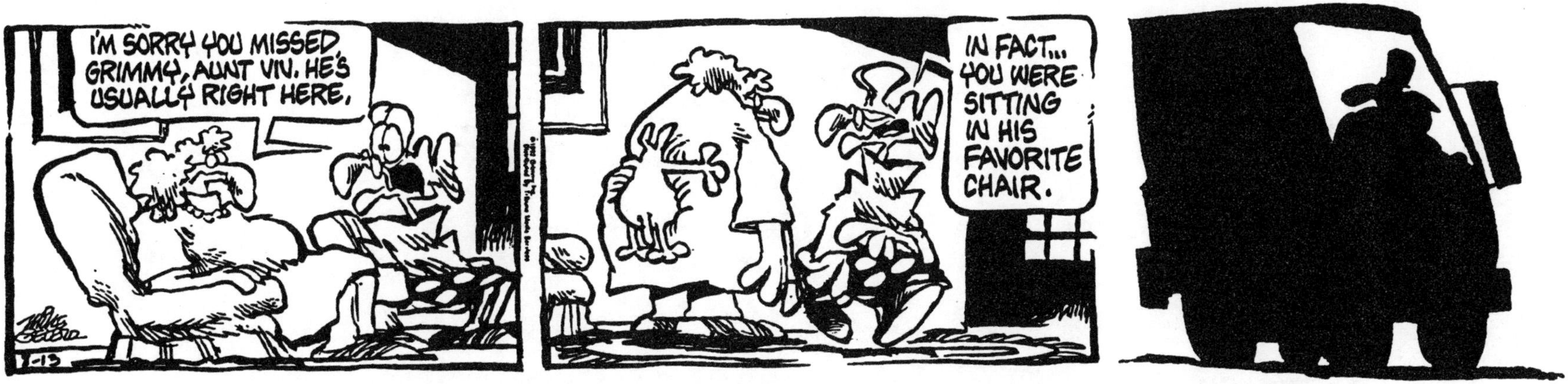
I'M SORRY YOU MISSED GRIMMY, AUNT VIV. HE'S USUALLY RIGHT HERE.
IN FACT... YOU WERE SITTING IN HIS FAVORITE CHAIR.

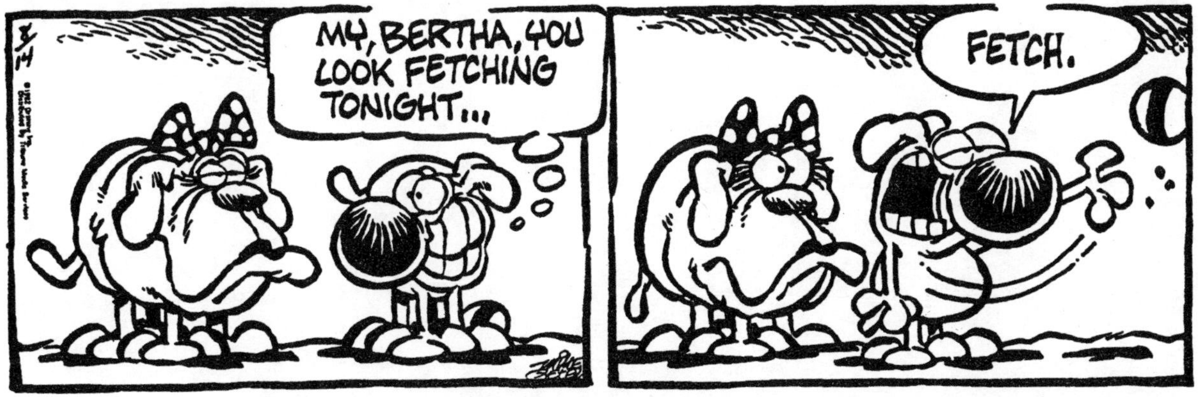
MY, BERTHA, YOU LOOK FETCHING TONIGHT...
FETCH.

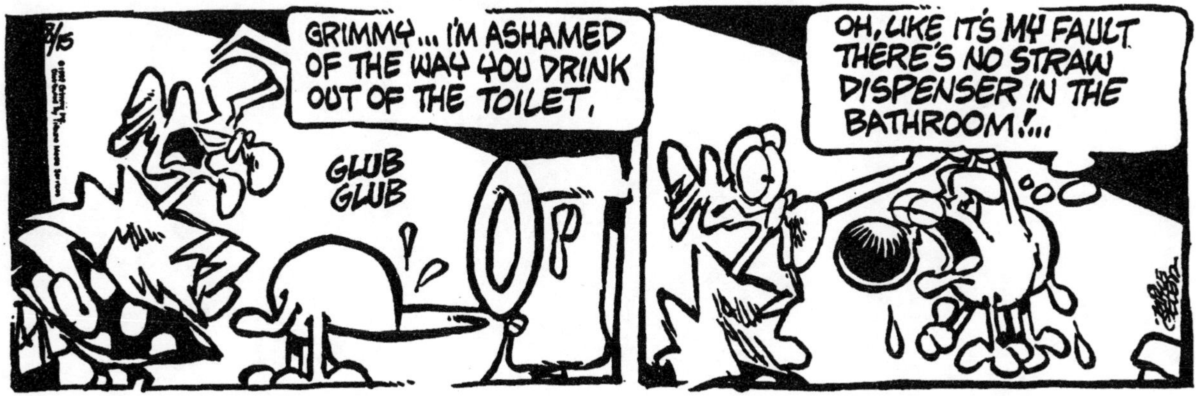
GRIMMY... I'M ASHAMED OF THE WAY YOU DRINK OUT OF THE TOILET.
GLUB GLUB
OH, LIKE IT'S MY FAULT THERE'S NO STRAW DISPENSER IN THE BATHROOM!...

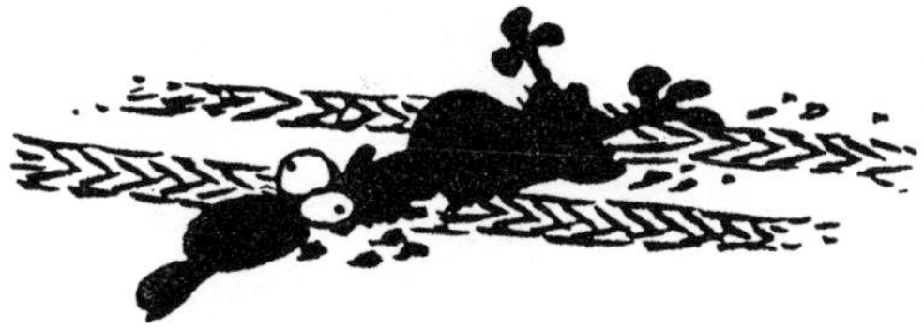

# WHERE ARE THE GOODS?

MANY OF OUR READERS ASK HOW THEY CAN BUY GRIMMY MERCHANDISE.

HERE IS A LIST OF LICENSEES IN THE UNITED STATES THAT CARRY GREAT STUFF! GIVE THEM A CALL FOR YOUR LOCAL DISTRIBUTOR.

## GRIMMY MERCHANDISE!!!

**Antioch Publishing Company**
888 Dayton St.
Yellow Springs, OH 45387

PH 513/767-7379
Calenders, Bookmarks,
Wallet Cards

**C.T.I.**
22160 North Pepper Rd.
Barrington, IL 60010

PH 800/284-5605
Balloons, Coffee Mugs

**Coastal Concepts**
1200 Avenida Chelsea
Vista, CA 92083

PH 619/598-2501
T-Shirts

**Confetti**
33 South Truman Dr.
Edison, NJ 08817

PH 800/528-4476
Plush Toys

**Gibson Greetings**
2100 Section Rd.
Cincinnati, OH 45237

PH 513/758-1819
Greeting Cards, Party
Papers, Gift Wrap etc...

**Logotel, Inc.**
9005 Red Branch Rd. Section B
Columbia, MD 21045

PH 800/237-8544
T-Shirts

**Second Nature Software**
1325 Officers' Row
Vancouver, WA 98661

PH 360/737-4170
Screen Saver Program